Happy Holidate Ever After

S.N. Moor

Contents

Hey Dad

Well, I'll be golly gosh darn. Here we are again. Different book, same story Pops. I feel confident by now you know the drill. This is your page. Your only page. Do not pass go, do not collect one hundred dollars. This is the page where your story ends. I mean, think about it this way. You can crank through the entire series in like ten minutes! Winner, winner, chicken dinner! For the SFD (Safe for Dad) version, this book wraps up the story of Everlee and her friends. After the wedding in Paris (I can't tell you who she married), they are wanting to start a family. This book follows them throughout the year, as well as years to come. Supes sweet. We get to see a new holiday for them this year- St. Patrick's day- which is super fun, and we get to find out if her and Beckett regain the title of master egg tosser at Easter. We also get to see her best friend's wedding and her brother's, which as you can expect have some funny moments. Everyone is happy and living their best life, which is why this is Happy Holidate Ever After. Now you may say to yourself, self, now she is going to write me a book I can read... and well, so the thing is... a still need more time. There are characters in this series that are begging to have their story told... so... yeah... just a wee bit longer.

This is to all the amazing women on my social media groups who have shared their love of these characters with me. Your excitement for each book fuels my desire to tell their stories and share them with you. I love the messages, discussions, and the character pictures you post. You all are truly amazing :)

Introduction

Happy Holidate Ever After is the 8th, and final, book of the series. With Everlee's IUD out, the guys have learned they have a breeding kink. This book centers around family and their life throughout the years after Christmas. It's not attached to one holiday, but covers several.

It's recommended you read Hearts and Arrows, Bunnies and Bowties, Rainbows and Unicorns, Stars and Stripes , Gobble 'til you Wobble, and Mistletoe and Holly first. If you haven't read those yet, stop here, because there are spoilers below (the title links will take you to the books).

In **Hearts and Arrows**, Everlee meets her four delicious men who give her the time of her life and the confidence she lost after dickface, Rich, destroys her. The only problem is the men make her agree to only sleep with them two times before they part ways. By the end of the arrangement, Everlee gets attached but doesn't know how the men feel, so she honors the agreement against her own desires and leaves. She's scared of getting hurt again.

Bunnies and Bowties, picks up two months later. She's been absolutely miserable, and unbeknownst to her, so have the men. Lizzy, being the amazing BFF she is, gets her back out on the scene, but she runs into her men and things are as hot as ever. She wants to talk with them about a future, but she's already committed to visiting her family for Easter. We get to meet her eccentric brother, Beckett, and her mother and father. Her mother is hellbent on a marriage and grandkids for Everlee and uses every opportunity to remind her, going as far as setting her up on a date with a lawyer. Everlee does her part but is missing her men desperately. The church her family attends is hosting a birthday party for one of their members and during the celebration Everlee comes face to face with her men (while on her date). They were all in foster care together a few towns over from Everlee growing up. Small world. As you can imagine, fireworks ensue, and Beckett picks up on all the sexual tension between them all and calls out she's in a poly relationship. Our favorite fivesome is formed and it is HOT! HOT! HOT!

Rainbows and Unicorns picks up soon after Bunnies ends. This one centers around Memorial Day and Pride Month. Sammie, a woman from the men's past enters the picture with a proposition for them that is hard to refuse. Because of personal reasons, Sammie has to go back to Texas, but offers to sell Allure back to the guys. Allure was their first successful business, a sex club, that gave them the funds to open Vixen and Bo's. Scared of how Everlee will react, they are hesitant to tell her, but when they do, she shocks them when she's excited about it. Sammie sets up a night where our fave five can visit Allure and experience Eden and Infernus (hello fave wood scene), two other areas of the club she added. While at Allure, Knox and Everlee participate in a Shibari demonstration that is... ahem... hot AF and we learn that Knox's nickname in the SEALs was Knots. In the end, they all decide to buy the business, Everlee included, so she's now an official owner of a sex club with the boys. Things continue to progress with the relationship and by the end of the book everyone says they love one another with hints of something more developing between Emmett and Jax. Lizzy is still in wedding planning mode so who knows what she'll decide about her wedding, and we also finally get to meet Betty's husband.

Stars and Stripes gives us our summertime vacation feels! Our fave five head away for a week of fun in the sun, with Beckett, Will, Lizzy and Tony, but when Beckett stupidly invites his and Everlee's mom, things get tense. She never travels alone, so why would she now? Several days later, the knock on the door shocks them all. Dearest Donna took a page out of Ev's book and travelled on her own... to the beach house... the forbidden love nest with Ev and her men. Things are awkward and their bedroom activities are put on hold, but when Everlee's life is in danger and all the men jump in to save her, the cat is out of the bag. Everlee and her mom talk, and Ev admits she's in a poly relationship. With the weight of the world off Everlee's shoulders, she can finish out the week relaxing and Donna can really meet the men. Also, in Stars and Stripes, we see Emmett and Jax's relationship start to heat up as Jax begins to explore the feelings he's been pushing down. Everlee's love and unconditional support give him the courage to explore. What does this mean for the future?

Deal with a Djinn is the fifth book in the series, however, it can be read as a standalone. Like some of our favorite shows do, Deal with a Djinn breaks from the series and our favorite characters are transported to another realm- a paranormal world, where they meet again for the first time. It's a paranormal retake on Cupid's Contract. If you've read the series, then you will likely see Easter eggs that have been planted throughout in this book. Hope you enjoy!

Gobble 'til you Wobble is the sixth book of the series. Our men decided they were ready to take their relationship to the next level and propose, but when Everlee is involved in a serious accident their plans take a detour... but not for long. Of course, hilarity ensues anytime Lizzy is around and even though she has a heart of gold, and was managing Allure for Knox and Ev, she accidentally sent a bouquet of vibrator roses to Everlee in the hospital. Because of the accident, Thanksgiving plans changed and our fivesome is no longer flying down to meet her parents. This really bums Ev out, because the guys were finally going to meet her dad in person (as her boyfriends), and because she's never missed a Thanksgiving dinner with her family. The guys decided to surprise her and bring her family to town, but made the mistake of not telling her. It's been weeks since the accident, and the guys have been scared of hurting her, so their sexy time has been put on hold, but Everlee said NO MORE! She decorated the table and undressed herself to surprise the guys when they got home from their errand (of picking up her family from the airport). Surprise is on her when her mother and brother turn the corner and find her on the table in nothing but whipped cream and pumpkin pies. The guys get some time alone with Dave and ask for Ev's hand in marriage and he gives an amazing speech and his blessing. The guys plan to ask Ev after dinner, but then Beckett surprises everyone with a proposal of his own. Our guys decide to wait until after her family leaves so it doesn't overshadow Beckett and Will. They plan a super romantic game for her around the house, taking her back through the memories and their journey from the beginning. She says yes and bow-chicka-bow-wow.

Mistletoe and Holly is the 7th book of the series. Well, it was our favorite fivesomes first Christmas together. From picking out their first Christmas tree, to the parties at Vixen and Allure, it was a sure thing Everlee was going to sit on Santa's lap and that he was going to come down her chimney. Under the guise of bridesmaid dress shopping, Lizzy is able to get Everlee to try on wedding dresses so she could help the guys succeed with their plans for a surprise wedding on none other than the Eiffel Tower. Lizzy, of course, pulled some Lizzy magic and made it a night they would never forget while almost getting them all kicked out. Jax and Emmett's relationship continues to develop while Jax learns to let down the walls around his heart as he fully steps into his awakening. For her Christmas present to the guys, Everlee removes her IUD, which sends the guys into a breeding frenzy. Lastly, while out one morning, Everlee and Knox come across a dog out in the cold, so they bring her back only to find she is pregnant. She has the six puppies at the end so there's no telling what kind of trouble the pups and Knox will get in.

EVERLEE - VALENTINE'S GALENTINE'S

ONE YEAR.

And what a wild year it's been. From stumbling over myself in front of Callum at the Valentine's cupid party, to marrying him, Jax, Knox, and Emmett on the Eiffel tower in Paris at Christmas. Lizzy and I went out this past weekend to get me a set of white wings and feathers for the upcoming Cupid party. I told the guys I'd just wear my red wings, so we didn't have to buy a new set, and Jax and Callum threaten to torch them until Knox made a big deal about it and hid them. He's told me where they are and requested I wear them around the house all day tomorrow, on Valentines, before we have to go to our respective clubs.

Tonight, they're taking me out for our Valentine's dinner, since we'll all be busy tomorrow night.

Allure is hosting a Galentine's auction, where ladies can bid on a man or woman to accompany them to an exclusive room, and they can indulge in all their desires. We've made cards that show each man or woman's specialty so they can be strategic with their bidding. Lizzy, of course, wanted to call it a Chicks and Dicks party, and when Knox and I said no, she tried to talk Jax and Callum into the name for Vixen.

Unfortunately, she had that conversation without me in the room. Seeing Jax's face would have been priceless.

Turning to look at my back in the mirror, I give the dress a slight twist so it sits properly on my hips. Lizzy was trying to talk me into getting a new dress for the dinner tonight, but I really loved the red one from my company gala last year and most of the guys didn't really get to see me in it.

Excitement bubbles in my stomach as I look over myself one last time before I meet the guys downstairs.

Shifting my ladies around, I give my shoulders a little shake and head for the stairs.

The men's voices echo up through the stairwell, and with each step I take, the more my stomach clenches. Placing my hand on the rail, so I don't trip and fall down the stairs ruining tonight before it even starts, my eyes fall on my wedding ring.

This is my life.

These are my men.

As I take my first step, the sound of my heel hitting the stairs reverberates through the stairwell, causing the men to abruptly fall silent.

By the time I get to the bottom stair, my cheeks are hurting from the constant smile I can't seem to suppress.

"Fuck me," Knox whines, shoving his fist into his mouth. It's one of my favorite things he does that gives me all the feels.

"Nope. You aren't going out in that." Jax points back up the stairs, but Emmett grabs his arm and pulls it down, holding onto it.

"Come now, Jax." Emmett's tone is soothing. "We've talked about this."

Jax bristles his shoulders, but doesn't pull his arm from Emmett's grasp.

"While I make it a point to never agree with Jax," Knox starts, "I think we should cancel dinner and just stay here. Order in some sushi. Eat it off your body." He pumps his eyebrows.

"Sorry bub. I want my steak and potato. Maybe a nice pineapple martini, some button mushrooms." Shrugging my shoulders, I toss him a playful wink. "I'll go with or without you."

Callum extends his hand towards me, and as I grab it, his warm fingers intertwine with mine before he spins me around in a circle, then pulls me into a warm embrace. "Well, you're definitely not going out without us." He slides his thigh between my legs while pressing his hand flat against my lower back, at the same time Jax slides his hand around my throat. If I was wearing panties, they'd be soaked. They know how much this little move of theirs turns me on.

"Hoo-hoo," a singsong voice chimes through the living room from the backdoor.

"God, no," Jax whines, pressing his lips to my temple.

Sliding from between Callum and Jax, I move towards the backdoor. I make it halfway until I see Lizzy walking into the room. "What are you doing here?" I laugh when I hear another groan from behind me.

"You need a babysitter. Duh."

When I look over my shoulder, the men all shrug their shoulders.

"Lizzy? What are you doing?"

She turns and goes to Luna's pen, where the puppies are jumping on the edge and yipping in excitement. "These babies need someone to watch them while you're out."

"Do they?" Jax tilts his head.

"You stop, you big love bug. If you weren't going out with Ev, you know your ass would be parked in this pen. Mr. Big and Tough is really Mr. Soft and Fluffy when it comes to these pups."

He takes in a deep breath, but doesn't deny what she says.

Luna had her puppies six weeks ago and they're getting so big and a lot rowdier. Lizzy has been over here almost every day, so the fact she volunteered herself to watch them tonight shouldn't have come as a shock to me. It's almost been a contest to see who spends more time with them- Jax or Lizzy.

"You better stop!" Lizzy laughs, stepping into the play part of their pen. Knox ordered this type of pen where the walls snap together so we can make it as large or small as we want. They've taken over most of the living room. Jax and Knox, of course, had to make it the equivalent of a five-star hotel.

If you ask Jax, Knox was the one going over the top since he's the one responsible for putting up the pen. However, Emmett has a video of Jax leaning against the doorframe, coffee mug in one hand, feet crossed at the ankles, while he directs Knox with his free hand. Knox, aka Jax, thought it best to build a small pen within the larger one so the pups could have a sleeping and eating area away from where they run around.

"Be free, my little babies!" Lizzy shouts, opening the door of their sleeping pen into their playpen where she's sitting. The puppies push through the door and maul her with all the corociousness that six golden retriever pups can manage. "Ow!" she screams. "Blue bit my finger!"

"You're my boy blue!" Jax taunts.

"Boo, boo," Lizzy calls. "Blue bit my finger and it's still hurting," she says in an English accent.

Knox and I burst into laughter while the others stare at us with furrowed brows.

"Are you serious?" Knox yells, then says with an English accent. "Charlie bit my finger… and it's still hurting."

"Nothing?" Lizzy and I ask at the same time.

A minute later, Knox has the video up on his phone, and everyone, except Lizzy, gathers around him to watch it. She's currently flat on her back, being attacked with licks and nibbles.

The others barely have a smile on their face when the video finishes.

"Whatever," Knox defends. "It's funny."

"Are we safe to leave her here with them?" Jax nods towards Lizzy.

"All good, daddy Jax," Lizzy answers for the group.

"Never call me daddy."

Lizzy sits up, so we can't see her face, but I'd bet the club she just whispered daddy. She climbs out of the pen, cradling Lulu in her arms. She's the purple ribbon pup and the only one that has a name because Lizzy has claimed her. Lizzy is counting down the rest of the weeks until she can take her home, and Jax is counting down the weeks to stop getting daily Lizzy visits.

He talks a big game, but on more than one occasion he's asked about Lizzy when she shows up later than normal. He makes up some excuse, but we all know he gets a little worried.

"You all stay out as late as you want. I'll take care of these babies and let Luna out."

"They were just fed some soft food about an hour ago," Jax starts. "Also, make sure their water bowl stays full and don't let green near it unsupervised. He likes to climb in and sit."

"Thank you, da- Jax."

"Let's go, daddy," Emmett says, tugging him to the door, chuckling.

Jax cuts his eyes at Emmett but doesn't say anything.

Callum climbs in the front passenger seat beside Brady, who's driving tonight, while Knox climbs in the back row. Emmett is behind me, holding the back of my dress up while I walk down the stairs, when Jax steps back into the house.

"Also, blue likes to bite the edge of the water bowl, so be careful because he'll also flip it. And we have three plastic water bottles on the counter. Make sure you check the lids are screwed on tight before you give them to the pups. They like to push them around and play with them."

"Got it!" Lizzy shouts before laughing into a scream. The tell-tell sign she's being nibbled by several pups.

"Let's go, daddy. They'll be fine," Emmett calls over his shoulder.

"E," Jax responds with a low growl, making us both stop and turn around.

My stomach tightens at the feral look in his eyes.

"Let's go bros and lady!" Knox yells, sticking his head out of the backdoor. "I offered to stay here and have a fuck fest, but nooo. Ev has to have her steak and potatoes with martinis and mushrooms and shit, so now I'm hungry."

Jax rolls his eyes, so we climb into the car.

"Let's go eat," I say, grabbing Emmett and Jax's legs.

EVERLEE - ROOM FULL OF MIRRORS

AFTER DINNER, I SUGGEST we go ice skating, but the men shake their heads with a mischievous look in their eyes.

"Boys..." The word drags out with a slight quiver in my voice.

"We have other plans, love," Callum says, sliding his hand down my back and slipping his pinky under the edge of my dress.

"What are these plans you speak of?"

"That would be for us to know and for you to find out?"

The constant smiling is taking a toll on my cheeks, as a dull ache settles in my muscles. "Brady, you'll tell me, won't you?"

His eyes meet mine in the mirror and even though I can't see the smile on his face, I can see it in his eyes. The kind of smile which says I'm completely delusional if I think I'm getting any information from him.

"So, Lizzy showing up wasn't an accident?"

"Unfortunately, no," Jax grumbles.

Emmett smacks Jax on the shoulder. "You're the one who said-"

"E!"

Emmett laughs.

"What did he say?" My brows perk on my face as I glance back and forth between Emmett and Jax.

"Nothing," Jax fires back.

"I don't believe you."

"He said," Emmett starts, then pauses, clearly enjoying Jax's reaction.

"That Lizzy is the only one he'd trust with the puppies while we're out."

My mouth falls open in shock as I suck in a whistling, loud, deep breath. "No," I whisper.

"Yep." Emmett is holding his stomach from laughter as lasers are shooting across the car at him from Jax.

Snapping my head back to Jax, I climb onto his lap and wrap my arms around his neck. "You said that about Lizzy?"

"Stop. Both of you are reading too much into this."

"I still think you're trying to pretend you don't like her when really you do," Knox enters the conversation.

"I still think it was a mistake being nice to you at Ms. Mary's all those years ago. I've often thought if we were complete assholes to you, you probably wouldn't be a thorn in my side today."

"See, when you say things like that, it's proof you really love me." Knox squeezes Jax's shoulder with a friendly shake.

"We're here," Callum calls.

Excited, I look outside and see the familiar brick exterior of Allure. My heart flutters with excitement.

"What are we doing here?"

"We rented a room for the night."

"How? I manage the reservations. I didn't see anyone's name on it."

"Luna Begood," Jax says, sliding his hand up my leg under the slit in the dress. The tip of his finger brushes against my pussy before he stops and pulls his hand back out.

"Lu-na." My words stutter as realization washes over me, causing my stomach to tighten with excitement. I remember seeing that name now because it reminded me of our Luna, but I never put two and two together. "Luna Begood." Laughter bursts from me.

Brady pulls to a stop by the owner's entrance, so we climb out. Callum's voice becomes a mumbled whisper in the air, saying something about the morning, but I don't pay attention. My mind is focused on trying to remember which room I had Luna marked down for on the reservation. Part of me wants to remember, while the other part of me doesn't, so I'm surprised.

Emmett slips his hand around my hips and squeezes. "We're putting a baby in you tonight."

Since taking my IUD out at Christmas and giving it to the guys, they have been absolutely feral. They've all been passing around baby books and what to expect at all the different stages of pre-pregnancy, pregnancy, and post-pregnancy. Emmett and Knox put a calendar on the backdoor of the pantry to track my menstrual cycle, even though it's still spotty as everything fires back up again. We all knew it could take a few months for my body to get back to normal, but it's the one time they take red as a sign to go, go, go!

"Or we'll keep trying, over and over again," Jax whispers, slipping his hand down the back of my dress like Callum does, and stopping when he breaches just past the edge of the fabric. Enough to tease, but nothing else.

Knox swipes his badge, and we walk into the dark hallway. Bass pulses loud and deep, reverberating through the walls and across my chest. It's a slow, steady beat that has this way of making you want to dance like a snake and rub your hands on yourself in a slow, seductive way.

We enter the main room on the right side, down from the demo rooms. It looks like a good night. After New Years, we added a small stage in the middle of the main room for demos. There is a three-hundred-and-sixty-degree unobstructed view of the stage. It's decorated this week with red velvet and satin, with a few hearts sprinkled in for the holiday. Around the stage are small tables with seating, and high-back cushion chairs sprinkled within.

Glancing at my watch, it's almost ten, which means a show is about to start. Madame Dubois has taken over as manager for all the shows and entertainment for the club, which is nice. She was always doing it before to help us out while we learned the ropes. *Wink. Wink.* But it really seems to be a natural fit, and it takes another thing off our plate. Plus, she got a title and more money because of it, so win-win.

She rotates shows at various times throughout the week, ensuring that if you miss one, you can always catch it at a different time on another day. Sometimes, they're interactive with the audience and other times, it's just someone on stage.

The floor is packed, leading me to believe that a couple has volunteered and been chosen to have sex. Sounds a little strange, but it's like a real life porno and one of our more popular shows.

"Do you want to join them?" Callum's breath dances across my skin and down my spine, causing goosebumps to spread over my body. He presses his chest against my back and flattens his hands on the front of my hips as he pulls me against him. His hard length presses at my lower back, causing me to gasp.

"Do you want to kick them off the stage?" My lips gently graze the corner of his when I turn my head to look at him.

"Maybe next time. We have another surprise for you." He plants a quick peck on my nose, then pushes me along, never breaking his hold on me. He walks, and his cock brushes against my ass with each step we take. His groans as he gets harder and harder, makes me wetter and wetter.

Knox runs up ahead to room 6(9) and punches in the assigned code for Luna Begood. Each time someone reserves a room, the computer generates an access code the member can enter when they're ready, without checking in.

He pushes the door open and I can't wait to see what we have in store. When reserving the room, the reservee can customize it to their liking and preferences. Even save those selections for future reservations to expedite the process.

When we turn the corner, my heart leaps out of my chest.

They have large standing mirrors setup in an octagon formation, with a small opening on the front side, wide enough so we can walk into the center. All the mirrors are on stands with wheels, so we can move them around with ease and close the gap, sealing us in.

In the middle of the octagon is a bed and a sex swing suspended from the ceiling with a thick strap for me to sit on with cuffs for my wrists and ankles. We have several variations of sex swings, from actual swings, to larger swinging platforms, to ropes, and lastly, this. While I love Shibari on the ground and having Knox tie me up, I'm not as much a fan of the suspension. The ropes cut into my skin a little too much, but I really love being fucked in the air, so this swing is the perfect compromise.

I almost squeal out and clap my hands, but I try to keep my cool. But seriously! A sex swing in a room of mirrors.

D.R.E.A.M!

Jax closes the door behind us, and the automatic lock engages. The grind of the gears sends my heart into a battle with my ribcage as it beats harder and faster.

Jax slides his right hand around my hips and uses his left to sweep the hair away from my neck as he plants heated kisses under my jaw. My knees buckle for a second, so I grab onto his hand.

The low chuckle that rumbles from his chest shoots straight to my core, nearly melting me into a pile of flesh goo.

When my eyes focus, they fall on Emmett, Callum, and Knox, in their black pants, and white button-up untucked with the top few buttons unbuttoned as they take their cuff links off.

Fuck me.

And just behind them, in the mirror, is me, with a very primal looking Jax, staring back at me.

At us.

His hand slides up to my throat as he watches me watch him. His cock is pressing hard against my back and it's taking everything in me right now not to lose what little control I have and turn around and rip his clothes off.

But that's not the game we're playing.

They want me submissive tonight and damn, do I want to be dominated.

Even though Jax is not clamping his hand around my throat, I still forget to breathe. I'd say I let out the breath I didn't know I was holding, but Lizzy's not here and that would also imply that I took in a breath.

No. My dumbass blows out a breath and does nothing. Just stares googly eyed at a bunch of cocks... a flock of cocks, and doesn't breathe.

Jax's hand releases from my neck and slowly pushes the straps of my dress off my shoulders as he plants kisses on my neck again. Between the men's eyes watching me and Jax's lips brushing against all my sensitive parts, I'm about to combust.

As soon as the dress falls past my breasts, my nipples shoot out, more erect than a plank on the side of a pirate ship. If they had little mouths, they'd be rejoicing their freedom from the confines of my dress.

My teeth scrape across my bottom lip as I watch the men slip out of their pants. Knox and Emmett leave theirs puddled on the floor where they fall, but Callum bends down, folds them quickly and lays them on the corner of the bed.

As my dress falls down my body, Jax brushes his lips down my spine, getting lower and lower. Goosebumps erupt across my skin again, and my stomach tightens and my pussy pulses.

"Jax."

"Shh, mama. Don't speak."

A zing shoots through my body to my heart. He just called me mama and I swear to all the baby gods out there… That has to be a kink or something. I want to ask him to say it again, but I also don't want to open my mouth because I want to be their good girl tonight.

Jax kisses each of my ass cheeks and blows a warm breath that makes its way to my clit. It takes everything in me not to rotate my hips to bring his mouth closer. His hand slides down my leg to my ankle, where he grabs it and helps me step out of my dress. Once both feet are out, he tosses it out of the way and the other men stalk over to me, looking like the sex gods they are as Jax stands back up.

Emmett brushes his hand over my stomach. "Mama."

A lump forms in my throat and I swallow… hard.

Emmett sinks to his knees in front of me and a tingle shoots through my body with heady anticipation. His beard brushes against my leg as he inhales a deep breath. The old me would have cringed, but the new me. The *me* these men helped create is confident. They love me so much that it makes it easy for me to love myself. Their love and appreciation for every part of me, scars and all, is like a wall defending against the doubt.

"Hey, mama…" Emmett looks up at me, hands wrapped around the back of my knees.

"Hey," I whisper, a giddiness taking over me. "I wasn't sure if I wanted flowers for Valentine's, but I'm sure your tu-lips will change my mind."

Emmett looks down, trying to hide his laugh, then looks back up. "I was going to ask if you wanted Jax and I to take you."

A smile stretches along my lips, and I nod emphatically. "Very much."

"We'll take care of you on the bed then, after Callum and Knox take you on the swing."

Butterflies dance in my stomach. The swing.

When I step towards it, Emmett stops me. "Where do you think you're going?"

"The swing."

"Not yet, love. We have the entire night here, and we're going to take our time with you."

Last time they said this, we fucked for several hours. It wasn't constant the entire time, but there was some sort of stimulation from someone. It was sensual, hot, romantic... and exhausting. My ass, both literally and figuratively, was worn out the next day.

Emmett plants himself between my legs, raising up on his knees for a second and swipes his tongue along my pussy, letting the tip of his tongue flick my clit.

A low hum of appreciation vibrates from my chest.

Emmett licks again, pulsing his tongue inside of me. I hate having orgasms standing up because it's like a battle for my body. Orgasms make my legs weak, which I'm using to stand on so it's like they fight against it because they don't want to fail at their job and make me crumble to the floor, so they hold out for as long as they can, keeping my orgasm away until BAM! And damn if it isn't one of those deep, rock your bones kind of orgasms because your legs have teamed up with the tongue or dick between your legs to edge the fuck out of you, only making it more intense.

My eyes glance across the room and I find Callum standing with his cock in his hand, slowly stroking it while he stares at me. Fire spreads through my body like a wildfire in a dry forest.

Knox is in the swing, spinning in a circle, looking up at the hooks and strings that's holding it to the ceiling like he's trying to figure out if it can hold his weight. He should know. He made us reinforce and get the large hooks and straps so it can hold up to one thousand pounds.

Something brushes along the outside of my leg and when I look down, Jax has moved from the back to the front, where he's crouched beside Emmett, still dressed, but shirt untucked and partially unbuttoned. He looks like a sexy mafia king right now with the white shirt contrasting his tan skin, dark hair and five o'clock shadow.

Jax grabs Emmett's jaw and turns him so they're face to face. Jax glances up at me and my pussy throbs with what I know is coming next, and the fact Jax looked at me to make sure I'm watching makes me even hotter. He tosses me a quick wink, then turns at takes Emmett's lips with his. Watching their lips meld together, their tongues slide into each other's mouth, their fingers gripping in one another's hair like they can't get enough of one another...

H.O.T. Hot!

Jax hums and almost like they're talking to one another through their minds, they both turn at the same time and press their tongues to my pussy which is now dripping. Their tongues lick up my arousal while still brushing against one another, both of them eating me out while Callum and Knox watch.

Jax pulls away and stands, moving behind me, and lifts me onto Emmett's shoulders so he can bury his face between my legs. My head falls back against Jax, who slides his hand up around my neck and squeezes for just a second, and our eyes lock in the mirror. He's asking for permission without saying the words, so I give a slight nod.

A puff of air escapes as excitement zings through me and my orgasm pushes closer to the edge.

Jax's mouth latches onto the side of my neck opposite his hand and bites. A moan escapes as the pain quickly turns to pleasure and my hips buck uncontrollably on Emmett's face. Jax sucks hard enough on my skin to leave a mark, but I love it. Let him mark me. I will happily wear his badges around so everyone knows who I belong with.

Sliding my hand to wrap around the back of his neck, I hold him to me- wanting him, needing him, to suck hard. To completely claim me.

"Oh God. Emmett..." I pant out, rocking my hips faster and faster.

Emmett's hands clamp hard around my thighs, holding me still at the same time Jax releases my neck with a little pop.

"Look at me," Jax commands with a deep growl.

My eyes snap to his in the mirror, and he looks completely feral. It feels like a rock just dropped from my throat to my stomach, pushing my orgasm along that much faster.

A smirk curls on the corner of his lips as he slides his hand around my throat, still not squeezing yet. He's waiting... watching.

Emmett presses two fingers inside of me and the pressure with his mouth causes me to cry out. He finds that magical spot inside of me and my head falls back and my hips thrust faster, feeding the beast inside.

"Don't move," Jax demands, but I don't listen.

My body is in control right now.

"Don't move." This time his words are slow and deep, followed by his hand clamping around my throat.

Our eyes lock on one another in the mirror, and tears trickle down my face. It's so intense. Emmett's tongue, Jax's hand around my throat, watching me.

My lungs burn with the lack of oxygen as my orgasm slams into me. Jax releases and it's like the huge gulp of air I suck in is oxygen for the raging orgasm inside of me. Emmett doesn't stop and I cry out. The loudest wail I've ever made as this orgasm washes over me like a tsunami.

When I try to move my legs off Emmett's shoulders, he grabs them and holds me to his face while I come around his tongue.

"Fuck me," Knox whimpers, hanging from the strings in the swing no longer moving.

"Yes, please."

Emmett releases my legs so I can stand and I feel like a newborn deer, legs like noodles and all shaky.

I hold my hand out and Callum stalks over and swoops me up into his arms, his bright blue eyes drinking me up.

"My turn."

CALLUM - PATIENCE

SHE'S STARING AT ME with those eyes. Fuck. Those eyes. The eyes that have had me from the first time I saw her looking up at me with those red wings a year ago.

"Did you come on Emmett's tongue like a good girl?"

"Yes," she squeaks out in that all-too-innocent voice she does that makes me wild.

Before I sit her down, I give her leg a gentle squeeze, then slowly lower her to the floor, so she rubs along my body. My cock seeps with arousal as it aches to be inside of her tight, wet pussy, but I have to pace myself.

Her perfectly round, tight ass bounces as she walks towards the swing and I swear I could watch her all night.

With a soft command, I urge her to climb onto the swing, the gentle sway of the ropes beckoning her.

Knox holds the main strap steady so she can climb on without losing her balance. While he loops the wrist cuffs around her hands, I work on sliding the bottom cuffs around her ankles. The balance of the swing spreads her legs wide for us, inviting us all to have a look at our wife's pretty pink pussy.

The slight sway of the swing and the lights reflecting off the mirrors cause her arousal to glisten like fresh fallen snow as it drips out of her.

A hand squeezes my shoulder, and when I look, Jax is standing beside me with a smile on his face and Emmett right behind him.

"Let's put a baby in her tonight," Jax says, reaching behind him to grab Emmett's hand.

My heart flutters in my chest with happiness. My brothers, our wife. Jax has come so far out of his shell. The walls were built years ago, and I knew this boy, this man, was still inside of him trying to get out. I never thought I'd see the day where he'd just let himself be... happy, unguarded.

To simply want something.

Before Ms. Mary, we grew up in a world where dreams were for the weak. Instead of instilling hope and purpose, they played on repeat, tormenting our minds. It gave me purpose, but not Jax. Not until Everlee.

"Let's."

It's only been a couple of months since we got married and she took her IUD out, so the chances are still slim, but they're getting better every day.

Stepping forward, I run my hands delicately along her ankle, to the inside of her knee, and pause at the inside of her thigh.

"Cal," she pants, eyes flicking between me and the guys behind me, eager to feel my cock inside of her.

"Yes?" One of my favorite things is to tease her. The way she looks so needy and wanting of my touch. A zing of excitement shoots down my spine to my cock, causing it to twitch.

"Cal." Her tone drops with her chin.

A chuckle escapes, so I close the distance between us until the head of my length is barely touching her hot, wet center. She feels so good, but I resist the urge to press inside of her.

Not yet.

"You're an ass." She tries to swing her hips, but the swing gives her nothing to push off of so she doesn't move.

"I know, love." My fingers glide along the contours of her hips, tracing a path up her abdomen, until I remove them, watching her writhe with desire.

"Knoxxy baby," she growls out with a restrained tantrum, tilting her head back.

His eyes brighten, and a smile spreads across his face. "Yes, Evey baby."

"Please put your cock in me."

A low rumble echoes from his chest and his eyes dart up to meet mine, but I shake my head. He's torn between wanting to satisfy and fuck our girl, but also enjoying the show.

"Now Everlee. You aren't being a good girl."

The glare I get when her head snaps back in my direction stops my heart for a second before laughter bursts from me.

"Not funny Callum."

"I'm quite enjoying this. Boys?"

They all nod and mumble their equal enjoyment and she frowns and tries to shake her arms and legs free, but they're not going anywhere.

God, I love this woman.

Knox runs his hands over her shoulders, then wraps them around each of her breasts, squeezing, before he pinches each of her nipples between his thumb and forefinger. Her back arches and her pussy brushes along my cock.

"Knox," I growl with frustration.

That was a mistake.

Everlee locks onto that and arches her back again, brushing her pussy along my cock. I don't move it. I know I should. I know I shouldn't give her the satisfaction, but the look of pleasure and excitement in her eyes like she's getting away with something. It's intoxicating.

"Do you want my cock?"

"No!" she spits out, eyes set in defiance, but lips panting for more.

Stepping forward another half step, my cock presses hard against her entrance but doesn't go in.

Her lips part, but she doesn't speak.

"Are you sure?"

She nods, eyes narrowed into thin slits.

Smiling, I wrap my hand around the base of my cock and swipe it along her entrance and watch as the bead of my arousal mixes with hers. My chest tightens, and a pulse stretches down my length as I fight the urge to fuck her.

"Now?" My resolve is waning as fast as water washes sand away.

She turns her head to the side.

My hands grip around her hips, and I jerk her onto my cock. That first thrust in shoots a tingling sensation up my neck to my scalp. Her head snaps back in my direction with a delicious fucking smile spread across her lips that makes me feral for her.

With ease, I push her away and jerk her back onto my shaft, the sounds of our bodies colliding, making a soft thwap.

Her voice echoes through the air, a passionate combination of anger and desire as she cries out, "Callum!"

My thrusts speed up and the chains on the top of the swing clang, rattling through the room. She looks up, watching me, then her eyes flick behind me and she smiles. I look in the mirror behind her and find her watching my ass.

"I could... eat... off your... ass," she says.

Smiling at her, I slow to a stop and press my cock deep inside of her and rub on her clit.

"Callum!"

"You're saying my name an awful lot, baby."

"Because you're teasing me and I don't like it."

"You don't like it?" I tilt my head to the side and look at her pussy wrapped around me with her come leaking out of her. “Seems like you’re lying to me, or maybe yourself.” I pinch her clit between my fingers and she cries out, but her walls clamp tightly around me.

“Cal-” Her words are cut off as I pull my dick out of her and drop to my knees.

“Let’s see.” Taking three of my fingers, I swirl them around her entrance, then plunge them inside and curl them before I slowly ease them out. “You’re soaked.”

“Ca-”

I press them back inside and suck her clit into my mouth before running my tongue over her entrance, licking up her arousal. After a minute, I pull back and look at her. Her neck is strained trying to watch me.

“I’m sorry. Were you saying something?”

“You-”

I jump to my feet and shove my cock inside of her, unleashing all of my need.

“Oh... my... God!” she yells out.

“Are you going to be a good girl and come all over me?”

“Yes! Yes sir!” she screams when I rub circles over her clit. “Yes!”

Her walls pulse around me, and I know she’s getting close. When I pinch her clit, she screams out and her pussy clamps around my shaft.

“Callum!”

“That’s my good girl.” Grabbing her hips, I thrust hard and fast until I spill inside of her.

Tears are streaming down the side of her face into her hairline, but the look in her eyes is pure fire and love.

“Now me,” Knox says.

EVERLEE - GOING FOR A RIDE

THE MUSCLES IN MY body are still humming when Callum pulls out and Knox stalks around to the front. He looks down at me and smiles his delicious, devious smile.

"We're going to fill you with so much come tonight you're going to be dripping with it for the next week." He laughs. "But you won't know if it's from tonight because we're going to fuck you tomorrow too, and the day after, and the day after." His hands slide up my body and grip around my breasts before his thumbs rub over my nipples like he's playing a video game. "Do you know why?"

Completely enamored by his beauty, I shake my head, unable to form words.

"Because you're ovulating." His words come out in a whisper as his hands slide down to the inside of my hips. "These little almond-shaped kiwis are screaming for us."

"Oh. Is that what they're doing?"

He brings his hand to his ear. "Jax. Emmett. Do you hear that?"

"You? Dumbass. How can I miss the grating sound?" Jax retorts.

"Ha, ha, brother. No. That's the sound of her ovaries crying out for my come. It's saying feed me... feed me. Nom, nom, nom."

"I literally can't with you," Jax chuckles, before pulling Emmett's hand to his lips.

Knox lines his cock up at my entrance as his teeth scrape over his bottom lip. He looks so incredibly sexy when he does that. When they all do that. It does something inside of me that makes me hot.

"Want to go for a ride, mama?" Knox asks with a mischievous gleam in his eye.

My left eye squeezes closed as I study him, trying to figure out what exactly he meant. "I don't know."

He laughs. "I think you'll enjoy it. Though I'm not one hundred percent it will work."

"I trust you."

A smile brightens his face as he leans over and plants a kiss on my lips. Just when I think he's done, he sucks my bottom lip into his mouth and gives it a little nibble, then lets out a moan.

He stands up and his eyes rake over my body and he pauses at my pussy.

"Knox..." I drag out the word hanging in the air.

"Evey baby?" With a gentle push, he slides inside me, savoring the feel of our connection.

My eyes close, soaking in this bliss. I expect him to pull out, but he doesn't, so I open my eyes and see him reaching up for the ropes on either side of him.

"Knox... what are you doing?"

"We're going for a ride."

"A ride-"

With his cock still pressed deep inside of me, he walks the swing backwards.

"Knox. I don't know if this is the best idea," Jax calls from behind him.

Emmett offers encouraging words, trying to calm Jax.

"If you hurt her with your wild antics, Knox..."

Before Jax can finish, Knox gives one more step and then pulls himself up on the ropes enough so his feet are off the ground and we go swinging back towards the men. When we get to the maximum height of the arc on the other side, Knox thrusts his cock inside of me, sending us to the other side.

Knox's forearms and biceps and triceps, and every other cep is bulging in his arms right now as he holds on to the swing. His core is engaged and looking so tight and ripply, while his hair flutters in the wind.

For a second- a millisecond- I forget we're having sex.

We swing up and he pulls his cock out a little as we ride the arc back towards the boys. Just before we reach the top, he pushes his cock in and gives an extra thrust, propelling us back across to the other side.

He does this a few more times, then leans over and grinds his hips into me as the swing slows to a stop. He's panting, and I'm sure it's because his upper body is on fire from holding his weight up the entire time, but he still has a smile spread across his face.

"Yeah, that wasn't as fun as I imagined," he remarks.

"You don't say," Jax chimes in as he and Emmett walk over to the bed. "We'll be waiting over here for you when he's done playing."

"Don't look at them. It's me and you time right now." He presses two fingers under my jaw and pulls my face back to him.

"Did you just rizz me?"

"It's what all the cool kids do."

Jax mumbles something, but a second later, all I see is Emmett rolling on top of him and pinning his arms to the bed.

My stomach tightens watching them.

"Mannnn, it's like a two for one dick special over there. I can't compete with that," Knox whines.

"I love your dick. I love your dick in my pussy, in my mouth, in my ass..." I smile up at him. "Between my breasts. I don't let anyone else fuck my breasts but you."

"I'd fuck them now, but I want to come inside of you."

"Then do it. Don't worry about them. Just you and me." The fact I can't run my hands up his body is driving me wild.

He winks, then glides his hands up my leg and presses inside of me.

JAX - TWO FOR ONE DICK SPECIAL

HE THINKS HE CAN just climb on top of me and press my arms to the bed like he owns me? If I wasn't so turned on right now, I'd fuck him until he remembers his place, but I can't because his cock is rubbing against mine and I've lost all control over my body.

The wet slaps and moans of Knox fucking Ev behind Emmett echo around the room, which only makes my cock leak with desire. Emmett closes the distance between us and his hard length rubs along mine as his nipple ring touches my chest.

"I had them put our little surprise for Ev under the pillow," he whispers with his cheek barely touching mine.

Slowly turning my head, we look at each other, and I kiss him. Deep. My tongue slips into his mouth as he grinds his cock on me. Nerves and excitement bubble under my skin at the thought of Emmett, Ev, and me together.

I love her, and I love this man.

Tonight was supposed to celebrate our one-year anniversary of finding one another, but it's so much more than that. It's also marks the beginning of a journey I didn't know I was on. The one where I've found more happiness in the world than I knew existed. The journey that let me tear down walls and find myself.

It's so funny to think back to just a year ago and see how much has changed. Literally, our entire lives, my entire life, has changed. I'm finally accepting the man I kept hidden for so long, we're married, we have seven furry hellions running around the house, we're trying to have kids, and I voluntarily called Lizzy over.

And I couldn't be happier.

The entire house wants kids running around and I do too, which I never thought about before. I was always scared. I lived my life in fear, which I think is funny because had you asked me a year ago, I would have laughed at you, but I've slowly come to realize that was all I was living in. Fear of relationships. Fear of commitment. Fear of letting myself be happy. And fear of being true to myself and my desires. I'd built my world on a bed of sand and was terrified of anything that would or could wash it away. But Ev... she slowly replaced each piece of sand with something stronger.

Rock solid.

I don't live in fear anymore, but simply love.

Pushing the heel of my foot into the mattress, I flip us over and mount Emmett. He stares up at me, lips parted. Unable to control myself, I grab his thick, pierced cock and run my hands up his steel shaft, the balls from his Jacob's ladder rippling under my touch. He sucks in a breath and my eyes lock on his.

"Do you like this?"

He shrugs with a glint in his eye. "It's ok."

I can't help the involuntary twitch in my lips with the happiness I feel. He loves to get under my skin, to push me, and I love it.

Eyes narrowing, I lean forward a little. "Just ok?" I rub my thumb over the tip of his cock and press with a gentle firmness, smoothing out the arousal that's pooling there, betraying his lie.

"Ehh." He shrugs again, panting. His eyes flick over my shoulder for a second and before I can turn or react, a body presses up against my back and I feel the petite hand of Everlee sliding around my hips and around the base of my cock.

"Are you teasing our man?" she whispers with her breasts pressed firmly against me, as her warm breath shoots down my neck.

"He-" The firm grasp of her hand, coupled with the clamp of her teeth on my neck, robs me of words.

When I turn, I see her looking in the mirror, watching us. Watching me.

She can see everything. How excited and turned on I am.

"I can't wait to feel both of you inside of me tonight. I don't want to wait another second."

"We have a little gift for you..."

"All I need and want is right here."

Looping my arm around my back, I hook my hand around her waist and scoop her to the front of me. She lets out a squeal, and she scrambles, landing on Emmett's chest.

"What was that for?" she chuffs.

"I wanted you here."

Her eyes fall down my body to our cocks sitting right at her entrance and her teeth scrape over her bottom lip as she eyes them hungrily.

"Come here," I growl out, wrapping my hand around the back of her head and pulling her lips towards mine.

The muscles in her body relax as our kiss deepens. Our tongues pulse and swirl in one another's mouth as the kiss becomes more erotic and hotter, like lava rumbling inside of a volcano ready to explode.

Her hips start grinding, brushing against the tips of our cocks. When she can't take anymore, she pulls away from my kiss and wraps her hands around our shafts, stroking them up in one motion and presses the tips together. Her eyes focus on the bead of pre-cum that's oozing out of each of us, lips parted, and chest rising and falling rapidly.

"E," she says softly, gliding her hands back down our shafts.

"Yep," he says, reaching behind him.

Laying on top of the pillow is a tube of lube. He grabs it and hands it to her, as if he was reading her mind.

She flips the lid open, squirts some in her hand and rubs them together before stroking down our cocks again.

My breath stutters as I inhale, savoring the feeling of Emmett and Everlee around my cock.

"Do you like that?" Her tone is low and sultry.

"You know I do."

"How much?" She bites her bottom lip, eyes never leaving our dicks in her hand as she strokes them at the perfect speed. Fast enough to drive us wild with lust, but slow enough to keep our orgasm away.

"I think you know."

"I want to hear it." Her hand slides off Emmett's, which falls against her pussy, as her hands snakes down my shaft to grip my balls.

My breath stutters again, and my eyes narrow on hers.

"Say it." Her grip tightens on my balls.

"Everlee," I warn.

Her pupils flash, and that's when I see it. She wants to play rough. She wants me to take control and fuck her. Fuck them.

"Say it, Jax."

"No." My eyes set on hers and I can see the vein in her neck throbbing, pulsing. "Be a good little girl and sit on Emmett's cock."

Her eyes narrow, but she doesn't move.

"Now."

Still nothing and I can feel her excitement radiating off of her in waves.

My hand clamps around her throat, and I pull so her face is an inch from mine. In a deep and low growl, I warn, "Climb on his cock, or I will make you, princess."

When she doesn't move, I release her throat and push her backwards so her back is on Emmett's chest and her legs are spread open around me and her pretty little pussy is on display.

"Are you dripping for us?" Pressing two fingers inside of her, I scoop out a mixture of come and arousal, then rub it all over the outside of her pussy and around her clit. Her back arches as her head presses into Emmett's chest, but I use my other hand to push her back down.

Wrapping my hand around Emmett's cock, I line it up at her pussy. "You wouldn't climb on his cock like a good girl. Instead, you want to be a little brat, so I'm going to fuck you with Emmett's cock."

With him lined up, I grab onto the tops of her thighs and pull her onto him at the same time I thrust my hips against them. My cock rides up his and brushes over the outside of her pussy. She cries out and Emmett moans.

Fuck me.

That's a deadly sound.

I push her back until his tip is just inside of her entrance and then I pull her forward again, and ride my cock up his shaft and across her clit.

She lets out a mangled plea, but I try to focus on anything but her noises. When I look up, it doesn't help, because I find myself staring back at me in the mirror fucking two people and a tingle shoots down my spine.

My eyes snap back to hers. "Do you like that?"

"Yes," she pants out.

I lean over her and press my cock between her slit and rock back and forth. The base of Emmett's cock and his balls rub against mine, nearly sending me over the edge.

"Jax," Emmett warns and my eyes fall on his, dark as the night, pupils completely blown. He swallows, then continues, "If you're wanting us to *both* fuck her, then I'm going to need you to stop fucking *with* her and actually *fuck* her." His hands slide over her breast and pinch her nipples, causing her to buck.

"Fine," I huff, disappointed in my lack of control with them. They have a grip on my heart and my cock.

Glaring playfully at Emmett, I slide my shaft down, grab the lube and rub my fingers along Emmett's hard length, and slip them inside of her. I make sure to run my fingers over each of his piercings before I split my fingers and run them back down. Suddenly, I have an urge to try to jack him off while he's inside of her. As if sensing what I want to do, his head pops up to look at me. For good measure, I run my fingers up his shaft again and when I drag them out, I apply an extra pressure around his cock until he's cussing my name.

"What? I was just stretching her."

"Shut the fuck up."

Ev laughs, causing E to moan.

"What's wrong?" I playfully taunt.

I don't wait for an answer as I reposition myself. Ev slides back until the tip of Emmett's cock is just outside of her entrance. Running my hand up our cocks, I press the head of our dicks together and slowly slide them inside of her.

This is always my favorite… watching her pretty pink pussy stretch around us, swallowing us.

Pushing in slowly, inch by inch, I get about halfway in before I pull out just to the tip, then press in again. This time I push in deeper and it takes about two more times before we're fully inside of her.

"I love to watch your pussy take our cocks," I mumble as I slowly slide mine out, gliding it across Emmett's piercings. "And I love the feel of Emmett's ffff…" I blow out a breath when I push back in. "Cock."

"Fuck us, Jax." Her voice squeaks out as she runs her hands up her body and covers Emmett's hands, which are still gripping her breasts. "Make me come around you."

Her right hand slides down to her pussy and starts working over her clit and her hips buck, causing our shafts to rub against one another.

"Fill me with your come."

Teeth clamped onto my bottom lip, I lean over and take her mouth with mine, then move to the side and take Emmett's.

Everlee's panting in my ear and I feel her knuckles brush against my lower abs as she works her clit, watching us.

Chuckling, I turn my head to look at her. "You better not make yourself come with our cocks in you. You come when we let you."

"Jax." She pouts, and her finger slows, but doesn't stop moving.

"Everlee," I warn, then lift Emmett's hand and suck her nipple into my mouth, biting down hard enough to make her scream out, but not hard enough to bring blood. "Do not come, or I will punish you."

Her pussy pulses with excitement.

God, I love this woman.

Her hands fall from her clit, and she rolls her eyes hard, then turns her head. Full of sass, she says, "Then you should do your job then. And stop kissing Emmett. You know how that turns me on."

"Yeah, Jax. Stop kissing me," Emmett chimes.

"Both of you are brats."

"But you love us," Emmett retorts. The devilish look in his eyes makes my heart flutter.

Pressing my hands to the bed, I work my hips, thrusting inside of her over and over again until I know she's on the edge of losing herself. Her screams and pants are becoming louder and more animalistic as she fights with herself. The brat or the good girl. Who do we get tonight?

"Jax," she cries out. The one word laced with so many emotions, but the undertone of it all is a plead. She's begging for me to allow her to release. Her pussy is pulsing almost as fast as my heart, and I can feel her holding her breath.

"You don't hold your breath. I take it from you and I give it."

My fingers clamp around her neck, and I squeeze. "Emmett, pinch her nipples and don't let them go until she's coming around our cocks and sucking in the air I allow her to breathe in."

"Oh, fuck," he mumbles, pinching her nipples.

She bucks on our cocks as I continue to rock into them, moving with ease, sliding back and forth over Emmett's enormous cock.

"Do you want to come for me?" I ask, staring into her beautiful eyes.

Her fist pops into the air and nods up and down, signing the word for yes.

My grip tightens, cutting off all the circulation, and I fuck her. Them.

"Goddamn." Emmett's voice quivers.

Everlee's hand latches on to mine and I watch her intently, looking for any sign I'm going too far, but she hasn't given the sign yet.

Her eyes close for a second and panic prickles under my skin, then her eyes burst open and her pussy clamps so hard around me she rips my orgasm out and milks my cock. I explode inside of her with such force that it feels like I'm being ripped in two. Like a firehose that is out of control.

"Oh shit. Fuck. Damn. Oh!" My hands fall from her throat at the same time Emmett's release her nipples. My body is still fucking her hard through the orgasms, confused about what it should be doing. I was close, but not that close.

A second later, a fresh warmness melts over my length as Emmett releases. Everlee is still crying out.

"I've got strawberries!" Knox walks into the mirrored section of the room, holding up a silver platter.

"Fuckin' strawberries." I laugh, then collapse onto Everlee and Emmett.

I hadn't even noticed he or Callum had left.

"He's coming." Knox smiles. "Not like you, wow. But he's coming. Getting the champagne."

I stare at him for a second and don't say anything. My brain is still a jumbled mess, trying to figure out where that orgasm came from. It's like my brain was in a field frolicking along thinking it had all the time in the world and then all the sudden... BAM!

"Did you break him? I teed up a perfectly good 'Shut the fuck up' moment and nothing. Not a single word."

"I don't know," Ev shrugs.

Sandwiched in between Emmett and me, she reaches her hand toward Knox. "Feed me."

"Gladly." Knox walks over and holds a strawberry by the greenery over her lips and lowers it.

Without hesitation, I grab the strawberry with my mouth and take a huge bite. Chunks of chocolate fall over her chin and cheek as she lets out a loud groan.

"Ass! That was mine."

"What's yours is mine, love."

EVERLEE - GETTING READY FOR THE BAR CRAWL

IT'S ALMOST ST. PATRICK'S Day and Beckett and Will texted about a week ago and said they wanted to fly up to visit us and the pups since it's been a while. I told them we'd see them at the end of the month when we go down for Easter, but they insisted. Seemed a little odd, but I didn't want to push it because I was missing my brother and I know he wanted to get his hands on the puppies. He and Will already said they want two, which is exciting, because I don't think my heart could take giving them to strangers and I don't think the guys would let me keep all of them. I mean Knox would be on my side, and shockingly enough, maybe Jax, even though he pretends like they annoy him. Between Lulu going to Lizzy and two others going to Will and Beckett, that leaves three for us, plus Luna, which I think is perfectly fine.

"How does my hair look?" Knox asks, bouncing down the stairs into the kitchen and sliding his fingers through his wet locks.

"Will you stop?" With a laugh, I playfully hold his face in my hands.

"I haven't seen my boos since Christmas and I want to look my best for them."

"Your boos?" With a tilt of my head, I shoot him a mischievous smirk.

"Don't be jealous. You're the only McKinley for me." He grabs my hips and pulls me towards him into a hug.

"Good thing, buddy."

The doorbell rings, and Knox lets out a squeal and a little hop, then takes off in a run towards the door.

Jax, Emmett, and Callum walk into the kitchen and take a seat at the bar.

"What? You didn't want to run to the door also?" Jax asks with a smirk.

"He's very excited. He's been talking about them all week." I grab a bottle of water out of the fridge, then lean against the counter.

A shrill jumbled greeting bounces through the halls into the kitchen. When the guys walk in a minute later, Beckett is carrying Knox, who is hanging on him like a koala wraps around a tree.

"I think he missed you." I chuckle, giving Will a hug first, then Beckett, once he's free of Knox.

"How was your flight?" Callum asks.

"Good. Easy." He steps between Jax and Emmett and wraps an arm around each of their necks. "Now, where are these little bundles of love?" Becks asks. The question was more filler than anything because there's no way anyone could miss the pups. They're squeaking, whimpering, barking and nearly climbing out of their pen.

"Over there." I point, walking beside Callum. He wraps me in his arms and gives me a quick kiss on the forehead.

Beckett cries out and scurries across the room.

"Are you ok getting two puppies?" Jax asks Will, standing from his seat to walk with Will over to the pen.

"I don't really feel like I have an option." He laughs. "These puppies have dominated our conversations for weeks."

"Same."

"Oh stop. You big oof." Emmett grabs Jax's arm and shakes. "You're with these pups more than anyone in this house."

Jax shoves Emmett off with a playful smile, then grabs his arm and brings him back in for a quick kiss on the head.

Beckett looks like a giant gorilla climbing into a small box. He finds a seat against the wall and Knox opens their little door and they burst through, trampling over themselves to meet their new friend.

"Oh my heart. Will," he cries, sticking out his bottom lip.

"I see Becks, I see."

Emmett pats Will on the back. "Good luck, brother."

"Only two, Beck. That's what we agreed to."

"That's all we're giving up," I second.

"Lulu is the one in purple and has already been claimed by Lizzy."

"Well, she's not here."

"Who's not here?" Lizzy calls out, sticking her head into the room.

Jax jumps in mock horror. "She's like a little gremlin that one can summon by speaking her name."

"Jaxie poo. I've missed you, too."

"I don't see how. It's only been a day since you've seen me."

"Well, my other favorite men were coming to town, so I may have stalked their flight to see when it landed, did some quick math and then voila!" She throws her hip to the side and her hands in the air.

"That doesn't sound like you," Jax grumbles, arms pinned to his side as Lizzy squeezes him in a tight hug.

She gives me a quick hug and kiss on the cheek before walking over to the pen. "Where's my Lulu?" Lizzy coos, climbing in and sitting by Beckett. "Hello, love." She leans her head on his shoulder.

"Hey yourself." He kisses her temple and hands her Lulu, who is fighting to make her way over to Lizzy.

"There's my little girl." Lizzy looks up at us. "I've got her room all ready."

"Room?" Jax scoffs.

"Yes, for when she's older. For now, I bought her a pen similar to this one, a nice bed her and I can cuddle in when we're not on the couch watching our favorite movies. I also got her nice ceramic dog bowls and Tony said he will build me one of those fancy doggie food dispensers. Her harness and leash will be in tomorrow." She squeals with excitement, scaring Lulu. "I'm sorry, baby." She plants a gentle kiss on her head, then cradles her under her chin.

"Will..." Beckett whines, "I can't choose. Help me." He reaches out for Will, who is standing with his arms crossed beside Emmett.

"Babe."

"It's hard."

"That's what Everlee said," Will grabs his stomach and laughs.

Beckett's eyes get huge and the entire room freezes. Even the dogs stop moving and barking. "Wilhelm Cavish. That... that... no...you..."

Knox bursts out laughing and claps Will on the back. "My man."

Blushing, Will tries to smooth things over. "I wouldn't dare pick because I'll take no blame when they pee and poop in the house or eat your shoes or something else. Because when they do, you're going to blame me and say it's the dog I picked. Even if it's the dog you picked. So if I don't pick, then there is no way it can be my fault. I know your game, buddy."

Beckett scrunches his nose and claps his fingers in the air like a mother trying to shush their child. "That's a lot to unpack, sir."

"Ooh kinky." Knox and Lizzy say in unison, then look at each other and laugh, then mumble something about the 'sir'.

"Seriously?" Jax asks. "There's two of them."

The room erupts in laughter again.

"Someone call him McKinkley." I chuckle.

"Not even close, sis. You take the cake on the McKink status."

Nodding my head to the side, I shrug. My heart feels so happy. This is what I needed. It's been three months since I removed my IUD, and while I knew it was going to take time, I'm still not pregnant. I keep telling myself I don't need to rush things, but I can't wait to start a family. There's no way it can't be me if there's a problem, because the chances of four of them having issues with their sperm... highly unlikely.

I'm trying not to put too much stress on myself because I know that doesn't help. I went to school with a girl who tried for years to get pregnant and couldn't, so she adopted... and by the time all the paperwork went through and the baby was born, she found out she was pregnant... with twins. She went from no kids to three kids under six months, nearly overnight. I mean she's happy and documents her story all over socials, but it was almost like her body was like oh you aren't stressed anymore, here you go.

Lizzy's been good. I was nervous she was going to ask if I was pregnant all the time. She asked a few times at first, but hasn't recently, which I'm thankful for. She trusts I will tell her when I am, but constantly telling her I'm not would be hard.

I caught Jax rummaging through my trash last week, looking at the discarded pregnancy tests. I didn't say anything, but quietly backed away. He hasn't mentioned it, so neither have I. Something tells me he wants a baby more than he wants to admit out loud, same thing with the puppies. Jax has come a long way in letting down his walls and giving us a peek behind the curtain, but in some ways, he's still so guarded in fear of letting us know he *wants* something.

"So, what are we doing today?" Will asks, climbing into the pen with Lizzy and Beckett.

"They're having a bar crawl downtown, then parade tomorrow."

Beckett screams out. "Yellow just peed on me."

"Aww, he likes you, babe."

Beckett throws his head back in the air and lets out a fake cry.

"Oh, don't pretend you don't like being peed on, big boy," Lizzy says, patting him on the shoulder.

"It was one time," he defends, then looks at Will. "I'm kidding. I know some of my proclivities may lead you to believe I was, in fact, serious, but judging by the look on your face, I felt I had to clarify."

"I'm not yucking anyone's yum... just..." Will shakes his head.

"Who knows, you could like it," Lizzy coos, then holds up Lulu and starts speaking in a baby voice. "Couldn't he? Yes he could."

"So..." Jax draws out the word. "Do you boys have any plans?"

"Not'a one."

"Then I vote we go do the whole St. Patty's bar crawl. They've shut off McClintock Road and brought in vendors and bouncy houses for kids."

"Define kids," Beckett asks, sitting yellow back down and laughing when he tries to jump back in his lap.

"If it's maturity level, I'm sure you and Knox will be just fine," Jax jabs, stepping up behind me and crossing his arms over my chest and gripping the opposite hip.

Without missing a beat, both Beckett and Knox pump their fists into the air.

"I may meet you all down there. I have to run a few errands for wedding things first, so it depends on how long that lasts."

"Take your time. No stone left unturned when it comes to your wedding," Jax chimes.

"Aww, boo. You can pretend that you don't like me, but I know the truth." She plants a quick kiss on Lulu's head and sets her back down. "I must go. I just wanted to stop by for a second and say hi to my besties."

"I've gotten most of the responses for your bridal shower," I say, grabbing her hand and helping her over the pen.

"My dear sweet Emmett, letting us have the entire top floor of Bo's." She walks across the room and wraps her arms around him.

"Anything for you, love."

"Put a baby in our girl." She pats his chest.

"We're trying."

"Gross!" Beckett shouts. "I know you all have kinky sex and I can joke about it, but not you. You aren't allowed to talk about it." He shakes his shoulders like he just got a chill down his spine.

"Anyway…" I try to step away from Jax, but his arms clamp down harder around me, so I turn my body to watch a flitting Lizzy bouncing around the room like a butterfly trapped in a cage.

Lizzy gives hugs to everyone and when she gets to me, she pins me in a Lizzy and Jax sandwich and he just stands there. She gives me a quick peck on the forehead and hustles towards the backdoor. "Too-da-loo, lovebirds."

"Bring Tony, if you come today. It's been a while since I've seen him," Beckett shouts as he climbs out of the pen.

Lizzy tosses her hand over her shoulder and closes the door.

"Whew." Jax sighs and lets me go.

"Were you using me as a shield?" I turn around, laughing.

His brow peaks on his forehead, but he doesn't say anything.

Knox claps, then hops up and down. "Let's get this party train started." He pumps his fist in the air. "Woo woo."

"Chugga chugga," Beckett says.

"No. Just no." Will laughs.

"I knew I liked you." Jax claps his hand on Will's shoulder. "Hey Knox, toss me some leashes. I'll take the little hellions out before we leave."

"I'll help," Will offers.

JAX - HONEY

THE CROWDS ARE CRAZY out here today. A bunch of drunk people dressed head to toe in green, with oversized hats and glasses with green and white striped leggings and socks.

Knox's head is bouncing back and forth through the crowd as he makes his way over to us with an arm full of beers in leprechaun shoes with clear legs attached.

Idiot.

A smile pulls across my lips as I watch him get closer and closer.

It's hard not to be jealous of him sometimes. With the shit he's seen and experienced, he just has a positive attitude and outlook on life. It's like nothing ever bothers him and he's never worried about anything.

Things are going to work out. That's what he always says and they do for him. He's just a lucky son of a bitch.

My eyes dart over to Ev, who has her arms looped between Beckett and Will's, and she's looking up at her brother with the biggest smile spread across her face. She's so happy he's here. Every time he's here. There's this connection they seem to have that's almost like that twin vibe you hear about, but obviously they aren't twins.

This is good for her. Having him here.

Even though she hasn't talked about it much, I know the fact she's not pregnant yet worries her. Maybe not at first because she knew it was going to take some time, but after Valentine's, I know she was hopeful.

Last week we were running low on toilet paper, so I stuck into her bathroom because I know she likes to keep a few rolls hidden and I found several tests in her trash. I couldn't stop myself. I knew I shouldn't do it, but I picked up a few and looked at them. Negative.

I was bummed and Knox found me a little while later and somehow got me to talk. It's like this gift he has that just gets me to open up. It's also why he was our go to interrogator in the SEALs. His ability to extract information was unheard of.

He told me it would all work out and that it's just not our time yet and things happen for a reason. And I believe that. I do. But for so long, I didn't want kids and now that I do… it's like I don't want to wait.

"Here we are!" Knox announces, offloading beers to everyone.

He was just going to look and see what they had, so I don't know what changed.

"Dudes and my lady." He tosses his shoulder up and winks at Ev. "It was chaos, so I got us all the beer special so we didn't have to go back and wait in that crazy line."

"It's green," I mumble, looking at it.

"Oh, stop crabby patty."

"Just making a statement," I say, lifting it to my lips.

"So, where are these jumpy houses?" Beckett asks, taking another sip of his drink.

"You can't be serious," Ev chuckles.

"Of course I'm not…" His words fall off at the end and he cuts his eyes at Knox like a kid who just walked into a candy store, but has been told he can't get anything.

"How are your parents?" I point to the sidewalk along the edge of the road under an awning. The bustling street makes me feel like a boulder in the middle of a stream.

I know Ev was excited to come down here, and Knox too, but damn it. I hate it. All the people and noise and... just everything. Callum, too. I know he's cringing because it's not an easily controllable environment. Emmett just goes along for the ride, so he's a horrible tie breaker.

"They're good. Excited to see everyone in a couple of weeks. Mom's been talking about the egg toss. You know." He points his finger at me. "The fact she's so eager to see Ev and I lose is a little concerning."

Knox throws his arm around Beckett's neck. "Well, if you need any pointers for this year, let me know."

Beckett pushes him off. "Give me a break. You got lucky."

"Dude, you totally botched the throw to Ev."

"Did I?" His brow quirks. "Perhaps I threw the game to test out a little theory."

"You didn't." Her words are low and her tone is shocked.

That evil genius.

He shrugs. "I'll never admit to anything."

I can't help but smile. He's a dumbass like Knox, but a good man.

We stand on the sidewalk trying to figure out where we're going to go next and end up finishing our beer. Not contributing anything to the conversation, simply because I don't care, I offer to go wait in line to get us more drinks. Hopefully, by the time I get back, they'll have decided on food or games and please God, not dancing. There's some sort of clogging stomping sound echoing between some buildings and I feel like it's a siren call to Ev and Knox and then my ass will get dragged into the middle of it because where she goes, I go. But damn it. I don't want to have any part of that.

"Hey! Watch it, buddy." My arms prickle when I recognize that voice filtering over the crowd. Lizzy.

"You watch it." A man responds with a deep voice and a tone I don't like.

Gaze flickering across the heads of people around me, I spot her- them, near the front of the line. She's turned back in line, waiting patiently, but some drunk asshole in a green shirt with the sleeves ripped off is pressing his chest against her shoulder. She's trying her best to ignore him, but he's an idiot who was never taught manners.

"Will you please back up?" She turns to him and gives him all the sass she can muster.

"How about you go?"

Her brows furrow in confusion. "Maybe you should pass on the beer. My two-year-old niece could come up with a better retort than that."

The man steps forward again and pulls his fist up.

Damn it.

Well, if I beat some guy's face in today, that would make this whole thing a lot more fun.

I step out of line and push through the crowd with ease. They feel like weeds in my path. Plentiful in numbers, but easy to pluck out of the way.

My hand wraps around the man's wrist, who is still holding his arm over his head, stepping at Lizzy, trying to scare her. This man is easily twice her size, but surprisingly, she doesn't flinch. She has some balls on her, that's for sure.

"Hey honey," I say from behind the man.

Her eyes look up to meet mine and I can see the stress melt from her shoulders. Most wouldn't be able to see it, but I can. I know her. Like a splinter that has worked its way into your finger and no matter how hard you try to remove it, you just can't quite get to it.

"Hey." She smiles and lets out a breath.

"Is everything ok?"

The man, a little slow on the uptake, speaks with fury. "If you don't let me go, then I'll..." his words fall off when he turns around and is eye to nipple with me. I shouldn't feel the amount of joy I do when I watch all the emotions flitter across the man's face, landing on terror.

"Sorry. What were you saying?"

"Man. You need to get this bitch checked."

My hand slides up his arm to his hand and I grab his fingers and bend them backwards until he is on his tiptoes, screaming.

"Fuck! Man!"

"You don't call her a bitch. Or any woman, for that matter. You don't push up on a woman or try to intimidate them with your size. It doesn't make you a stronger man, but a weaker one. And you sure as shit don't hit or threaten to hit. Because when that happens, I have to step in and I don't enjoy stepping in, because sometimes I lose control with jackasses and I was really trying to have a good day here without losing control." I press down on his fingers until he's standing higher on his toes and screaming out again.

"Is there a problem over here?" A uniformed police officer walks up to us.

"I don't have a problem. Do you have a problem?" I ask the dickhead.

"No. No. No. No problem."

"See officer. No problem. I was just reminding this man of his manners." I release his hand and pat him on the back, at the same time he holds his hand and tries to rub the ache out of it.

The officer doesn't move, but watches us, then looks at Lizzy and nods his head.

"Can I buy you a drink?" I offer to the officer.

"I'm on duty."

"I'm sure they have water or something else. It's probably going to be a long day out here." My eyes fall back on numb nuts who's still soothing his hand. Poor guy won't be able to jack off with it tonight without thinking of me.

"No, thank you. Just try to make it easier on us and stay out of trouble."

"I have no intentions of causing a problem, officer." I have every intention of ending one, though, should the need arise. But I don't think he needs to hear that.

"Next," the bartender calls out.

I usher Lizzy forward. She props her arms on the little ledge, stands on her tiptoes and orders. The officer takes a few steps away, but is still watching us, rather, douchecanoe.

She orders her drink and I get several more beers and order a water for my new friend.

On the way over to the group, she looks up at me for a second but doesn't speak. Gratitude and happiness cross her face, but the last is a mischievous little grin and before she opens her mouth, I know I'm about to regret stepping in and saving her. "Thanks for earlier."

There's a long pause and I don't speak because I know she's not done, so I wait. I wait for the other shoe to kick me in my balls, because it's Lizzy.

"Honey." She throws her head back, laughing.

There it is.

"I knew you liked me. I mean, I didn't think you loved me, but hey, I'm game if Ev is." She laughs again.

Ev's face pulls into a smile as she watches us walk up, wondering what is going on. *Me too, Ev. Me, too.*

"Looks like you may have to share boo boo," Lizzy says, giving Ev a hug.

"Oh lord. What happened?"

"Jax called me honey."

"Shut the front door." Beckett's mouth drops. "Why? How? Deets!" Beckett grabs her arm, spinning her around.

How is it I attract a gaggle of chatty Knoxs? It's like the longer they're around him he just embeds... him, his personality, into them and they replicate. Like a virus or something.

"Nothing too exciting. I was just minding my business, and he was so excited to see me. Walked right up and said hey honey. Completely took me by surprise."

"I bet it did. If that's what happened." Ev smiles, popping her brow on her forehead, not buying the story.

"Well, I may have left out some key pieces of information."

"You don't say," Callum chimes in, taking a beer from me.

"A man may have been a little drunk and got a little close to me and I told him to back up. He may have snapped at me, so I snapped back and then he may have tried to scare me. And then maybe, just maybe, this handsome devil walked over."

She pats me on the chest, and all I can do is chuckle.

"You should have seen it. The other guy nearly shit his pants when he turned around. He's too drunk to stop running his mouth, but I thought he was going to piss himself. Classic."

"Where's Tony?" Ev asks.

Lizzy's face drops. "Oh shit! I was supposed to get him a drink, then go back." She laughs again. "One of your men calls me honey and I forget where I am, what day it is, and who I'm engaged to. No wonder why you spend most of your time on your back in bed, or upright, or in swings, or on rope, or-"

"Fuck Lizzy!" Ev slaps at her, the cutest hint of pink tinging her cheeks when she looks at me.

I toss her a quick wink, and a new wave of pink crawls up her chest.

"I need to go find Tony."

"No need," Tony says, walking up to the group. "When you didn't come back, I figured you left me for Ev. Even after we're married, I'll still be waiting for the day." He laughs.

"I don't know. Maybe Jax now. He called me honey."

Tony looks at me and I can't help but roll my eyes and shake my head.

"Well, as long as it's not Knox. He's too chipper." Tony laughs and steps out of reach of Knox's swing.

"Man. Not cool. I thought we were bros." Knox puckers out his bottom lip and crosses his arms.

"I'm kidding." He turns to me. "Thank you, Jax, for stepping in and saving Lizzy. I don't know what she did, but I'd have to assume she ran her mouth a little too much to the wrong person."

"Hey!" She slaps his chest, and the crowd laughs.

"It's such a cute little mouth, though." Tony grabs her under the chin and pulls her in, kissing her.

"Thank you, daddy," she whispers, when he pushes her away. She takes a sip of beer and says, "He could have called me honey on his own though, unable to hide his pent-up feelings for me any longer."

"He could have." Tony loops his arm around her waist and pulls her to him. "But if that's the case, I would be forced to fight for you, because I'm not losing you and... he would probably kill me. Man's a beast." He kisses the tip of her nose and if hearts could pulse out of her eyes, they would. They are completely smitten with each other. It's almost nauseating to look at, but then I think about Ev and Emmett and while I'll be damned if hearts ever pulse from my eyes, it would be close.

My eyes fall to Ev, who is just beaming with happiness as she watches her best friend and all feels right with the world.

"Now what?" Knox claps.

"We have tonight and then head out super early tomorrow morning, so do with us what you want." Beckett laughs. "Within reason. I know how you kinky fuckers like to play."

"Fire daddy Becks!" Knox teases running his hand down Becketts arm before jumping on his back for only a second. "We have the gang all here. I say we go clogging or river dancing or whatever they are doing on those boards at the end of the street. It's like the beat of their feet is calling to me." He throws his arms out like a zombie and starts walking away.

"Idiot," I sigh.

The crowd laughs, and for some reason, we all naturally follow him.

It's what we do. We follow Knox.

EMMETT - SHOWER TIME

THE NIGHT CLINGS TO me like smoke in wet hair. After the festival downtown, we somehow got wrangled into going out to a club where we stayed for way longer than we should have, but Everlee was happy. It's also been a while since we've all been able to go out, especially when her brother is in town. In the past, someone's had to work, but with the shifts we're making to step away from the day-to-day operations of the businesses, it's really opened up our calendars.

I step into the shower, letting the rainfall hit me in the face and run down my chest. It's been a long day, and after some lady was playing around with some guy she was flirting with and dumped her entire drink on me... A shiver runs down my spine just thinking about it.

A little drop here or there, I get. I don't like it, but I get it. No. This was an entire drink. And to make it worse, it was a sweet fruity drink, so it's super sticky. A few times, I had to stop Knox from licking me. Like a freaking deer to a salt lick. Only he's not a deer and I'm not salty. Well, emotionally maybe.

Closing my eyes, I run my hands over my face and listen to the soft whoosh of the water falling to the floor and the slight gurgle of the drain drinking all the sugar water down.

Hands slide around my waist, startling me, before they run over my semi-hard cock, bringing it fully erect.

They're larger than Everlee's, and my stomach tightens.

"What are you doing?" I lean back into Jax's chest.

"Helping you get clean."

A low, appreciative hum rumbles in my chest as his hand continues to slide up and down my cock. His steel-hard shaft pressed against my ass makes my stomach tighten with anticipation.

This year has been a complete whirlwind of emotions for us. When Everlee walked into our lives, she was a like a tornado, a wrecking ball. Never in a million years did I think that ball of light would take our family and flip it on its head.

Our life is so perfect and getting better every day and I look forward to what this year is going to bring.

Jax interrupts my thoughts when he swipes his finger over my arousal at the tip of my cock and then sucks it into his mouth. He walks around slowly and drops to his knees in front of me, and my eyes pulse with darkness at the edges from excitement.

"Goddamn. I don't know if I will ever get used to this," I say, running my fingers through his dark, wet hair.

"Hmm?" He runs his tongue up the underside of my cock and my knees get weak. Just the anticipation of his lips around me is about to make me blow my load in his face.

"I said..." Jax's tongue swirls around my tip and I whimper. "I don't know... if I will... ever get... uuuuuu..." He sucks the head of my cock into his warm, wet mouth, making me sound like a broken record. "Fuck me," I sigh out in frustration.

"I plan to. Now, what were you saying?" His eyes look up at me while his hand strokes along my length in firm tugs.

"You're an ass. You know that?"

"So I've heard. Now keep talking."

Blowing out a breath from my nose, I try to rush the words out again. "I don't know if I will ever get used to seeing you on your knnneeeeeee-" Jax sucks me all the way in, robbing me of my words. This fucker is toying with me and he knows it. "Knees. Knees. Knees." I just hit the back of his throat. "Fuck you. I'm done talking."

Jax lets out a muffled laugh with my cock in his mouth. He's never sounded so sinister.

My hands latch to the side of his head as I press my cock into his mouth, taking control. Jax is always in control. Well, most of the time. Not tonight. He can take over when he's fucking me later, but right now. Right now, I'm taking over, because I need this release like I need oxygen.

Jax seems to sense the shift, because he adjusts on his knees like a catcher in baseball so he can take me better.

"I'm going to come so far down your throat."

Jax lets out a hum of approval around my cock, the vibration nearly making me come. Fuck! Maybe I need to tell him about the menstrual tracking calendar Knox has, so it prevents me from coming in six point nine seconds. I laugh at myself. Since Everlee, her and Lizzy's sixty-nine jokes have creeped into our lives. Thermostats, tips on bills, random every day sayings and thoughts. God, I love that woman.

Jax's hand wraps around the base of my cock, his sign that he wants control for a minute, so I give it to him. He runs his tongue up and down my length, then against my balls, before running it back to the tip. His mouth guides me in slowly, like he's testing his limits.

Oh, shitake mushrooms. He's trying to take me down his throat. My hand presses against the cool wet tile so I can prop myself up as my head falls back. This is something he's been doing, trying to see how far he can take me, and I don't know why I find it so addicting... and hot. So, so, so hot.

Tears prickle at the edges of my eyes as I lean forward and watch him take me in further, inch by inch. I'm not a small guy by any means, so the fact he has most of my cock in his mouth... A tingle shoots down my spine and my balls start to tighten. Nope. Nope. Do not blow yet.

Pinching my eyes shut, I take in a few deep breaths. He slides me out of his mouth slowly and every muscle in my body clenches tight.

"Jax," I whisper out.

He looks up at me with a mischievous smirk spread across his face.

"Jax," I warn now. "You're teasing me and it's late. I don't have the same tolerance as Ev. I'm in a fuck around and find out kind of mood right now."

Jax presses his hand on his knee as he chuckles. "You threatening me?" His eyes sparkle with happiness.

"I'm just giving you a fair warning."

"You going to fuck my throat?" His voice drops low and his eyes darken.

Letting my teeth scrape over my bottom lip, I watch him without speaking. He wants me to fuck his face. This has all been a game to him to see how much control I have.

He runs his tongue over his bottom lip as he watches me.

"Jax," I nearly pant out as my resolve fades.

"E," he says in a way that only he can that makes me feel like I have fireworks erupting inside of me.

My hands clamp around his head, and I growl out. He places his hand on my thigh, but doesn't push away. "I love you," I whisper out before pressing my cock into his mouth so he can't answer back.

His eyes snap to mine and then go wild as he sucks my shaft.

Damn, that felt good. I've been wanting to tell him for a while, but this has all been new and I didn't want to scare him away or make this awkward, but I don't care anymore. My heart was aching with the need to tell him.

I lose control and press in hard and fast, but he doesn't move. "Your mouth feels so good." Ass muscles clench with each thrust until my balls tighten again and need consumes me.

"Jax."

It's one word.

A warning.

His hands wrap around the back of my legs as he pulls me towards him.

A second later, I'm shooting so hard down the back of his throat I raise on my toes and a moan bursts from my lips.

As soon as he sucks the last drop from me, he stands and wraps his hand around the back of my head and drives me back against the shower wall with his lips on mine. His hard length presses between us, rubbing against my cock and abs. His tongue moves in with a fever and speed like his life depends on kissing me.

"I love you?" He pops off our kiss and asks, anger searing the words, before he presses his lips to mine. He pulls off the kiss again, torn between wanting to kiss me and get whatever he needs to off his chest. "You say you love me, then shove your cock in my mouth."

Before I can respond, he kisses me again, so I press my hands to his chest, pushing him away.

"Well-" I start, but he cuts me off.

"You don't fucking talk anymore," he snaps. "You had your chance and now you're done. Turn around," he commands, grabbing my arms and spinning me so my chest and palms are flat against the cool tile.

"Jax."

"Not a fucking word."

He grabs the lube off the shelf and pops the cap before pressing his fingers inside of me to prep me. His movements are fast, not rough, but also not gentle.

He lets a low grumble, but doesn't speak.

Maybe I shouldn't have said anything?

"J-"

"I said not a fucking word. If you don't shut your mouth, I'm going to fill it with *my* cock so you can't speak."

Is that what this is about?

He grabs the lube again, and if I had to guess, he's prepping himself. He tosses the lube down to the floor, not even bothering to fully cap the lid before he presses his tip at my entrance.

His hand slides up my back to between my shoulder blades and he pushes me slowly, so my hips bend just enough. His length glides in. The further he inches in, the more heat I feel on my back from his chest, drawing closer to me until his cheek is beside mine.

His unspoken words linger in the air, making my heart beat wildly in my chest. I want to speak, to tell him to just say whatever he wants, but I don't. Instead, I listen to his puffs of breath as he slides his cock out of me, then pushes back in again. The sigh between his teeth that I know means he's fighting with himself to take me hard. He's trying to enjoy the feeling, but also wants to take. To take me. To take this feeling.

He's moving in slow, steady movements, pressing all the way inside until he's hitting all those delicious spots that make my eyes pulse with stars.

"Emmett." He thrusts a few more times. "Don't you fucking ever-" His thrusts are becoming quicker, more staccatoed. "Tell me you love me." His hands press on the wall on either side of my head and his voice is becoming thready as he nears completion. "And then stick your god damned cock in my mouth again."

"Sor-"

His hand grabs my head and turns it. "I said not a fucking word. My cock is buried in your ass, and I'm not taking it out, but you will suck my fingers." He presses the two fingers he didn't use earlier into my mouth. "Suck."

My cock springs back to life under the feel of his length sliding in and out of me, his dark and commanding words, and his fingers in my mouth. It's like the trifecta.

Wrapping my hand around his, I work his fingers like I work his cock and feel him twitch in my ass as his breath stutters. The thrill that I get knowing the effect I have on him... it's electrifying.

His forehead presses to my shoulder while he tries to steady his breathing.

He rips his fingers from my mouth, plants them on my waist, and unleashes. The thwaps from his hips slapping against my ass fill the air, and I know he's close. I clamp down and he screams out as he unloads inside of me, blurting with it a string of cuss words.

"You ass," he says, after he stops thrusting. He pulls out and spins me around, pressing his chest against mine as the cold tile bites at my heated skin. His eyes flicker back and forth between mine. "I love *you*, E." His voice cracks and he leans in slowly, taking my lips with his. When he pulls away, he presses his forehead against mine. "I have for a long time and was just too scared to know what it meant. I'm sorry I denied us *this*... for so long."

"It was worth the wait." I kiss his chin and nod my head up before sucking his bottom lip in my mouth.

Our kiss is deep, slow, passionate.

This man.

EVERLEE - ALARM COCK

MY STOMACH CLENCHES AND my hips grind as my eyes fight the sleep away. Blinking a few times, I try to focus, but the room is too dark. However, I'm greeted by something else.

"Good morning," a voice whispers.

Knox.

Looking down my body and between my legs, Knox has his chin perched on my thigh.

Struggling to stay awake, I search the room for any clue about the time, but the closed curtains block any signs of light.

"What time is it, Knox?"

"I don't know.

"Is it even morning?"

"Well, it's in the AM." He chuckles. "I just got home from dropping your brother and Will at the airport a little bit ago. Took a shower and found you in here looking so sweet, so I wanted a taste."

That would put it somewhere around six in the morning.

"Speaking of..." He dips his head back down and swipes his tongue across my clit.

Moaning out his name, I slide my fingers into his hair and grip, letting my eyes close while I let myself indulge.

His tongue presses in at the same time he lifts my legs and ass off the bed.

"Knox."

"I got you, baby girl." He gives a quick lick up, then pulls back. "You taste like heaven and I'm putting a baby in you today."

My stomach tightens. It's taken longer than I hoped, but I guess it's to be expected. I just need to trust that things happen for a reason, so when we're meant to have kids, it will happen. And until then, we can explore all the many ways to try.

Knox's mouth latches onto my clit as he sucks and licks, pushing my orgasm closer and closer. There's a slight shuffle on the bed and a second later, he's pressing something at my opening.

"Knox?"

When I hear a click and the once familiar hum, I know it's the green monster. It's been several months since I've used him. And while part of me misses the idea of our connection, the men have more than satisfied me in every way possible.

As if hearing my thoughts, Knox answers, "I charged him up for you. Poor guy was dead." He pushes him in, watching as my pussy stretches and swallows him inside. There's something that makes me so hot having him watch it disappear inside of me. The green monster moves, hitting on all of my spots.

Knox lowers me back to the bed and rubs his tongue over my clit.

"Knox," I pant out.

My head presses into the back of the bed while my back arches towards the ceiling as he pulses the green monster in and out. Knox plants kisses up my stomach, along my ribcage, then takes my left breast into his mouth. He nibbles on my nipple causing a tingle shoots straight to my core.

"I can't wait to press my cock so deep inside of you, then load you full of my come," he growls out against my chest as he moves to the other nipple.

"I don't know what you're waiting for." Running my fingers through his hair, I grip and lift his head. "Seriously." I set my eyes on his and dip my chin.

A mischievous smile tugs at his lips. "Well, then. What me lady wants, me lady shall get," he says with an accent.

He always knows how to make me laugh, but with the green monster working me closer to my orgasm, it sounds like a strangled cat. "Me lady?" I pant out, fists grabbing the sheet.

"We have the shamrock shake at Vixen tonight, so I'm working on me Irish." He pulls the green monster out and tosses it across the room. "I can't have your pussy pulsing around anything else but my cock, lil' lass."

"This is going to be an all-day thing, isn't it?"

"You have no idea."

"You're Kn-Knox!" He punches his cock into me, sending my ass up the bed and causing my eyes to pulse for a second. The green monster is big, but damn it. Knox fills me completely.

"What were you saying?" He lowers his head, his lips inches from mine.

"You're Kn-Knox!" I scream out again as he pulls out and punches back in again.

"I love when you yell my name out." He slides his hands under my back and rolls us, so I'm on top of him. "And this is my favorite position because I love to watch you ride me."

"You just like to watch my boobs bounce."

"That too." He winks. "Now, ride me."

"Are you a four-leaf clover?" I quirk my eyebrow at him. "Because you're getting lucky." I'm laughing and shaking my head before I can even finish. Why? Why did I give in to his quirks?

"Yes!" He pumps this fist in the air and shoots off the bed, pressing his chest against mine. "I fucking love you."

I can't stop laughing as Knox plants kisses all over my neck, lips, jaws, and chest. He leans back and thrusts wildly while his finger plays with my clit.

"Knox," I whimper, grinding onto his cock and against his finger.

"You're so wet. You're dripping down my cock."

My body feels electric right now as jolts shoot through me, from my toes to my fingers.

Knox's hand wraps around the back of my head before his lips crash to mine and his tongue pushes in.

No! I try to push him away. "Kn-"

He doesn't let me. The way his hips move, like an ocean wave, is sending my orgasm closer and closer to the edge, but I can't fucking concentrate because all I can think about is that he's kissing me with minty breath and I have funky troll breath.

"Knox." I push him away hard enough to get his name out.

"What?" he pants.

"I can't kiss you."

"You just were," he says, hips not slowing down.

"You know why."

"So worried." He leans back in, but I turn my head so he kisses my cheek. Without missing a beat, he bites my neck and sucks. Hard. He's trying to leave a mark.

I love it. My nipples get harder, if that's possible, and my core tightens.

He bites and sucks one more time, letting my moans guide him, before he pulls out and flips me over so I'm on my hands and knees. He presses in and I feel him deep inside of my belly, the ache that turns from pain to pleasure each time he pushes in.

My head hangs low to the bed as I let him pound into me. He's so deep, it's like he's trying to shoot his come straight into my ovaries.

His hand slides around to my clit, circling and pinching.

"We're going to come together," he pants, chest pressed to my back. "I've heard that if you come when I do, your orgasm pushes my little baby makers along."

"That's a rumor."

"I don't care. I want to put a baby in you."

"Put a baby in me, Knox."

With that, he pushes in deep and I see stars. "Damn."

His finger moves with precision, coaxing my orgasm out of me like he's in a race.

"Knox. I'm about to..." I can't even say the word because my body loses control.

He stops moving his finger, grabs both of my hips and unleashes. His angle changes and he's hitting a new spot, and that's it. It's all I need.

"Come for me, baby," he commands.

My orgasm tears through me, and a second later, Knox screams out.

"Milk my cock, baby."

"Damn." His words send needy little pulses through my body.

His thrusts slow, but his cock still pulses inside of me.

"Hold on," he warns a second before his arms grip my thighs and he's lifting my ass into the air.

Nearly being turned on my head, I scream out as I scramble to avoid face planting on the bed. "What are you doing?"

"Making sure none of it comes out."

"What in the fuck is going on in here?" Jax asks from the door.

When I try to turn to find him, my arms give out and I face plant.

"I'm putting a baby in her."

Jax stalks across the room at the same time Emmett and Callum walk through the door, laughing.

"Will you put her down? You're going to break her neck."

"No, I'm not," Knox defends, swatting at Jax with one hand while Jax tries to remove his grip from my thighs.

"Knox. I'm going to count to three."

"Lies."

"I'm not lying. Put her down or I will make you."

"You never get to three. That's the lie. You always say I'm going to count to three, but you never do. You always act at two. It's like you never learned to count past two." Knox lets me go just as Jax raises his hand.

"Were you boys up, or did we wake you?" I ask.

"Cal and I were up. I fixed breakfast for Will and Becks before they left." Emmett smiles and looks at Jax. Something has changed between them. There's a... calmness, maybe? It hasn't been there before. Whatever it is, it makes me happy.

Callum sits on the corner of the bed, tucking his ankle under his knee. "Having a good morning, love?"

"It's getting better," I say, rolling onto my back. Even though Jax is watching Knox to make sure he doesn't lift my ass in the air again, Knox still manages to rest my legs on his, so they're raised slightly.

"*I-rish* you were all here earlier..." Knox pauses for comedic effect.

"Fuck me. It's St. Patrick's day." Jax lets out a heavy sigh.

"Oh stop. You know you want to get lucky," Knox continues with a huge grin spread across this face, giving me a wink.

Jax slow blinks like he's trying not to lose his shit and all I can do is smile and reach out for him. I'm the luckiest woman in the world to call these men mine.

He brings my hand to his mouth and brushes a kiss across my knuckles.

Emmett crawls onto the bed and curls in beside me. He smells like Jax. Nestling my nose against his neck, I give him a quick kiss on his throat, breathing in their combined scents, then let my body relax.

"I'm going to check on the pups and then I'll be back," Jax says.

"I'll be back," Knox mocks in a low voice.

Jax cuts his eyes, but doesn't say anything.

“I already did. I’ve let them out and fed them,” Callum says, sliding out of his shoes and unbuckling his pants.

A yawn sneaks up on me, and I cry out in frustration. “No. No yawn. I’m not tired.”

The men laugh. “You’re exhausted. I can see it in your eyes.” Callum nods at me.

“But.”

“No, buts. We’ll give you a proper Irish morning at a more reasonable hour,” Callum asserts, leaving no room for discussion.

“I love yous.” Letting my head fall to my pillow, I pull the comforter up to my chin.

“We love you too,” Jax chuckles as he walks across the room.

Sleep pulls hard at me. I want to stay up and please them and be pleased by them, but it’s like the sandman is dumping truckloads of sand on my eyelids, burying me.

Knox’s arm wraps around my chest, pulling me towards him so my back is touching his chest.

Seconds later, I’m floating.

Damn it.

I forgot to pee.

Darkness.

EVERLEE - MORNINGS

WHEN I GET DOWNSTAIRS after my morning shower a few hours later, Callum is sitting in his usual place with his coffee in hand, while Jax is sitting in the dog pen letting the puppies climb all over him. Emmett is standing between the stove and the island with his white apron on, spatula in hand, with a smile spread across his face.

"Morning love," Callum says first, sitting his pen down from his latest crossword.

"Morning to you." I give him a quick kiss, then walk over to Jax and climb into the pen. When the puppies see me, they all jump from Jax's legs and arms and climb over each other to get to me.

"Traitors," Jax mumbles, straightening his legs and crossing them at the ankles.

After I give each of the pups a rub behind the ears, I walk over to Jax, straddle his legs, then sink onto this lap. "Good morning."

His hands glide up my back, followed by several wet noses and needle-like claws.

"Scram." He swipes his arm slowly, moving the pups off his legs with a tone that's more playful than irritated as he wraps one arm around me, using the other to block.

Jax reaches beside him and grabs an empty plastic bottle and tosses it to the other end of the pen. All the pups except orange run after it. Orange does a determined waddle walk, ignores my leg and Jax's arm and climbs up them and rests between us.

"I guess orange isn't having any of your games this morning."

Jax lifts him a little, so he stretches his little potbelly out across Jax's chest. "You just want some cuddles away from all your brothers and sisters, don't you?" Orange stretches his paws out and I swear my heart bursts.

Giving Jax a quick kiss on his lips, I stand and walk over to the island where Emmett is watching us.

"Good morning." He sits his spatula down, wraps his arms around me and spins before lifting me to sit on the counter beside the stove. He slides between my legs and gives me a kiss before flipping the omelet in the pan.

"Dare I ask where Knox is?" Jax asks, climbing out of the pen with a gleam in his eyes.

"He said he'll be down in a minute and asked if you, specifically," I nod at Jax, "can get him his tea."

"Fat chance." He looks down and smiles. "Hey girl."

Even though I can't see her, I know Luna has her head resting on his leg. It's their thing. Every morning, she walks over and boops Jax. Only Jax. It's the weirdest thing.

"Do you know where I found her this morning?"

Emmett's hand gliding up and down my leg pulls my attention for a second.

"My bed," Jax continues, when no one speaks.

"Well, why weren't you in it?" Callum teases and Jax just cuts his eyes.

Happiness bubbles in my chest as I glance over at Emmett, who is all smiles.

"Lady and gentlemen," Knox announces from the stairs.

"Oh, brother." Jax rolls his eyes and turns his body away from the stairs.

"This is Knox's second favorite holiday. Well, so he says every year, but then he says every other holiday is his second favorite, so I really don't know." Emmett plates the omelet and slides it across the counter before stepping in between my legs again.

Knox walks down wearing his tiny, tight black boxers that's more a version of men's lingerie than anything else, and the oversized green sequin hat and matching oversized bowtie he bought yesterday. He tried to get one for all of us, but Jax firmly put his foot down. So it ended up being Beckett and Knox and they, of course, had to get pictures in the photo booth of them together.

The fridge is littered with strips of photos. Some of Beckett and Will, some of Beckett and Knox, Lizzy and me, the men and me, and then lastly all of us. Getting nine people in that tiny booth was a challenge and our faces fill each box. The last picture is my favorite, I think. Both Beckett and Knox, at the last second, decided to turn and stick their tongues in Jax's ear and his face... the camera captured it perfectly. His eyes are huge, his mouth is open and his brows set.

What the photo doesn't capture is the chaos that ensued afterward as they bolted from the booth. Jax chased them for a while then eventually gave up, but something tells me it's not over.

Knox skips down the last few steps, then opens his arms wide. "What do you think?"

"Take it off," Jax crows.

"Kinky. I like your style," Knox retorts.

"Not what I meant."

Knox looks at me and smiles. "Are you from Ireland? Because my hearts been Dublin."

"That doesn't even make sense," Jax bites back.

"Do you want an omelet, Greenie?"

"I'd love one, thank you. Six eggs, sausage, and cheese."

"Ooh, that sounds good." I lick my lips.

"I was already making that for you, well, two eggs instead of six." Emmett winks, then plants a kiss on my forehead and beats a few eggs in the bowl before pouring them into the pan.

"Yo, bro." Knox walks over and stands beside Jax, looking him up and down with large sweeps of his head.

"What do you want? It's too early for this shit."

"You aren't wearing green. It's like you're giving me permission to pinch you, you kinky fucker."

"Touch me and you lose your fingers."

"Thank you, daddy," Knox fires back before darting out of Jax's swing and taking the seat at the end of the bar.

"I was hoping you weren't going to do..." Jax's hand waves up and down. "This."

"Oh stop. I didn't have time to put out my decorations this year because we've been so busy with the clubs." He exaggeratedly nods his head in my direction, almost causing his hat to tumble off. "Speaking of, we have that interview tomorrow." He points at me.

"Oh, right." The thought of having someone to manage Allure soon fills me with excitement.

Part of our new year's plans, not resolution, as Knox was so adamant about, is to take a step back from the clubs. Still own them, but find others who can manage the daily activities. As we focus on growing our family, it's impossible to think we can do that while running two hugely successful clubs that require so much time and attention late into the evening.

Jax and Callum have already promoted Low and have been slowly stepping away over the last month, spending more time at Allure with Knox and me, and Emmett has been working with his head chef, Colby, to promote him to a new general manager position. Emmett says he wants to step back, but he also loves Bo's, so I'll believe it when I see it.

Knox claps his hands. "Who's ready for today?"

Laughing, I grab the plate from Emmett and walk over to the bar opposite of Knox. "What did you have in mind?"

"Don't encourage him." Jax tilts his head to the side and tosses me a sly look that immediately brings a grin to my face. He can pretend to hate that Luna is here or pretend that he can't stand Knox, or Lizzy for that matter, but the truth is, he loves them. He loves them all.

"Well, I figured we would go downtown to the parade for a little before we have to head to the clubs tonight." As Knox smiles, his eyes crinkle at the corners, radiating joy.

"What else? That seems too... simple." Emmett slides a green omelet over to him.

Knox's hand covers his lips as he pretends to cry over the omelet. "You know me so well."

"I had to go buy green food coloring just for you."

"Beautiful. Masterpiece." He takes a large bite and rolls his eyes, savoring the flavor, then kisses his fingers. "Fluffy, and just the right amount of sausage and cheese."

Knox kisses the tips of his fingers and Emmett lets out a mangled chuckle.

An hour later, Callum, Emmett and I are downstairs, dressed in some combination of twill pants, jeans, and green shirts. Jax is wearing mint-green twill pants that hug his legs like a snakeskin on a snake and a white button-down shirt with sleeves rolled up, highlighting all the tattoos on his arms. When Emmett and I see him walk down, we have to grab onto one another for support as our knees buckle at the same time.

"Who says we have to go downtown today?" I ask, watching him take a seat in the last bar chair, arm slung across the back with one leg straight, while the other foot props on the rung of the chair. Forcing myself to swallow, I glance at Emmett who's having to roll his tongue back in his mouth.

"Will you two stop?" Jax asks with a casual grin on his lips.

"Will *you* stop? I don't know if we should go out with you in public like that." Emmett pumps his eyebrows as he slides his arm around me and pulls me tight.

"Here he, here he," Knox announces, walking down the stairs, back straight, still wearing his oversized green sequin hat and bowtie. At least this time he's wearing jeans, which is fortunate, but equally a shame. He's sporting a bright green short sleeve button up with green and gold shamrocks all over it.

"I don't think that's how it goes," Jax says, standing up.

"How what goes?" Knox's eyes fall on me, looking me up and down.

"It's hear ye, hear-"

Knox cuts Jax off. "Damnnnn girl." He grabs my hand and spins me around. "Did you sit on a four-leaf clover because your backside is looking oh so fortunate!"

"Christ!" Jax throws his hands up in the air.

Callum laughs, patting Jax on the back. "Shall we head out?"

Knox hurries behind the counter and grabs something. "But of course!" he announces, thrusting a bejeweled green scepter into the air.

"Do you think we can leave him there?" Jax whispers as we walk out of the room.

"Stop. He's cute." I push him on the shoulder and as my hand is falling back to my side, he reaches behind me and grabs it, interlacing his fingers in mine and pulls be forward.

"Have you thought about what will happen when you get pregnant?"

His question catches me off guard and a knot forms in my throat. What is he talking about?

"You will have a baby-baby and a grown-baby to deal with."

Chuckling, my fingers grip his hand tighter. "That's why I'm lucky and got three of you to watch him while I watch the baby-baby."

"Ha. No. I call dibs on the baby-baby. I will even buy one of those bras with the boobs on them and hook it to bottles to nurse the baby, if that's what it takes," Jax says, climbing into the car.

"Did I hear a boob bra for nursing?" Knox asks, poking his head forward. "Count me in." He grabs his chest.

"Your dumbass would put the boob bra on, then strain your neck to drink out of the nipples," Jax chuckles.

A sly smile spreads across his face. "You know me so well."

CALLUM - ROAD TRIP

WE'RE TEN HOURS INTO a thirteen-hour drive to Everlee's parent's house. The first several hours started out fun, with chatting and singing. Knox brought a baby name book, so that killed another two hours as we discussed names we liked and didn't like. Unfortunately for Knox, Knox Jr. was overruled, as were Abel, Axel, Lattimer and Wolf.

"How much longer until the next stop?" Everlee asks peaking over the back seat. "Pups are getting a little eager to run around."

We got one large cage they could all stay in because trying to get them individual cages would have taken up too much space. As it is, they have the entire back of the suburban and all of our luggage is in one of those contraptions on top of the car.

"I'm trying to get through Charlotte, then figured we could stop for a quick bite to eat and let them run around."

"Oh, we should stop and see if Michael's in. Pop in and say hello," Knox says, leaning between the front seats.

"Already messaged him. He's somewhere in South America on a job," Jax says.

"So why couldn't we use his plane then?" Knox huffs, sitting back down. He looks at me on his left, then Ev on his right. "Don't get me wrong. I love the bonding we're doing... but a plane would have been a lot better."

"He needed it to get down there. We could try to get it on the way home and just leave the rental down there," Jax's fingers thrum lightly on the steering wheel at the background music.

"I will call him now," Knox chimes.

"Already got a voicemail in to him."

"Well, look at you... Mr. Get-Shit-Done."

"I was in a car with you singing Mariah Carey and Celine Dion for three hours straight. I've also put in several offers to just buy a plane," Jax says in all seriousness.

"You tease." Knox bats his hand, then grips Ev's leg and lays his head on her shoulder.

Jax's eyes meet mine in the rearview, and I can't help but chuckle.

"I wish we lived closer," Ev mumbles, more to herself than anyone in particular.

Part of me wonders if these feelings will get stronger once she's pregnant, or after we have kids. I know her family is really important to her and every time her parents or brother visit, she lights up. I don't think her brother wants to move because he has a good thing at the firehouse and her parents have a great community with their church, plus no one ever retires and moves north. They always move south, so...

Part of me has always wanted to live on the beach and after our trip last summer, that feeling only grew, but we have the clubs and the restaurant. The clubs we could manage from afar, but I don't know if Emmett would leave Bo's. That is his love, even though he has talked about stepping away from it some so he could focus on our family.

Who knows?

"What time do you think we'll be there? I'm going to check-in online to get the code. Lizzy volunteered to swing by the grocery store for us and load up the house," Emmett says, swiping up on his phone.

"So, does it matter what time we get there if she's getting there first?" I ask, cutting my eyes to Ev, who clearly thought the same thing I did.

Emmett laughs. "I guess that did sound weird. Lots of things going through my head, plus I wasn't paying attention. I'm checking in now to get the code for Lizzy. She just wants to know when we're going to be there."

"Tell her midnight," Jax chimes, laughing and switching lanes.

"You stop," Everlee chuckles, resting her head on the side of the window.

"She's just asking because it's been two days since she's seen Lulu," Jax retorts.

"You made us rent a suburban so we could bring six puppies and a dog with us," Knox says, sitting up.

"I wasn't going to leave them there with a sitter, I, nor the pups, have ever met."

"Can't wait until you're a daddy," Knox adds, "To kids. Since you're already my daddy."

Everlee laughs and I toss a glance at Knox, who pumps his eyebrows so happy with himself.

"Lizzy said she'll have pizzas in the oven for us for dinner," Emmett continues.

"Didn't know you and Lizzy were besties," Ev says.

"Jealous?" Emmett taunts, looking over his shoulder at her.

"Not at all. I'm good at sharing."

"Touché."

Four hours later, we're parking beside a small beige car at our rental. It's a gray two-story house tucked back on the property with a long driveway surrounded by fields and woods. There's a large wraparound front porch on the house and two tall oak trees that stand on either side of the house with a rope swing attached to one. It's a cute house, about ten minutes from Ev's parent's house. We tried to get the same place we had last year, but it wasn't big enough for all of us and the pups, plus Jax insisted we have a fenced-in yard so they could run. The pictures for this one also showed a creek nearby that would be fun to play in during the summer.

As soon as Jax cuts the engine off, we all fall out of the car and reach towards the sky, stretching. After the last stop, the time seemed to drag on forever. Even Knox was quiet, which is saying a lot.

The front door bursts open and Lizzy runs outside with her arms waving in the air, screaming in celebration. On-lookers would assume she is a crazy woman, but we just know this to be normal Lizzy.

Everlee laughs and holds her arms out only for Lizzy to run right by her to the trunk of the car.

"Never would I have thought this day would come," Everlee teases, jogging to the back and wrapping her arms around Lizzy from behind.

"Hey love!" Lizzy tilts her head into Everlee. "Where's my little boogie boo?"

As soon as the trunk opens and Lulu sees Lizzy, she starts with this little yelp whine.

Luna hops out of the trunk and walks a few steps, then stretches her paws out. "Careful," Jax warns. "Let's get the cage on the ground first. Last thing I need is for them to run out of the cage and topple out of the car."

Lizzy claps, but doesn't say anything, just backing out of the way as Knox and Jax lift the cage out of the trunk and place it on the ground.

Jax opens the door and all the puppies work their way out, squeezing through the door two at a time and hop through the tall grass. At first they don't know what to do because it's so tall and they've never felt it before. A few of them just freeze and pee, turning their little heads towards the sun while blue says screw it all and just hops all over the place attacking the tall grass like the blades have attacked him.

Lizzy picks up Lulu and gives her kisses all over her head and tucks her against her chest. "Pizzas are in the oven staying warm. Your mom said to call when you get in, and your brother said he'll be by in a little while. They're finishing up a call and will probably be by around nine to give you enough time to settle in."

"That angel," Knox says, running around with his arms open wide while the puppies chase him.

When he was talking to Ev on the phone earlier, he promised he wouldn't stay for long. He just wanted to see the pups for a second and introduce his firehouse to the guys.

"Does Becks know which ones he's going to keep?" Lizzy asks, putting Lulu down so she can go run in the field.

"I think blue and yellow," Ev answers, then laughs when she looks back out at the field.

Knox has now fallen on the grass and all the puppies are climbing all over him, licking and nibbling him.

"Should we go inside and let the pups in the backyard?" I ask, watching Jax and Emmett get the hardshell carrier down.

"Yea, probably a good idea. There was a note on the counter that said not to leave animals out overnight because of coyotes in the area," Lizzy calls over her shoulder as she picks up Lulu.

"Leave these little angels out?" Knox holds up green and sings the song from that kid's lion movie.

"Can we leave Knox out? He'd probably scare them away?" Jax chuckles, walking the luggage inside with Emmett.

"Har har." Knox pushes to stand. "Come on puppies."

None of them listen.

"It's their first taste of freedom, not on a leash." I laugh, watching Knox, trying to get them to follow him. He's crawling across the ground, barking like a dog. It's good to see him like this. He's been more at ease over the last several months. Things are in a good spot with his dad.

They talk regularly and he's been over for dinner twice. Almost like everything that was darkening his doorstep is slowly being put behind him.

Jax and Emmett walk back outside and pause on the front porch, watching Knox act like a fool. Jax hops down the three stairs and pats his leg, and Luna trots over to stand beside him. He rubs her head, then whistles out. All the puppy's heads stick up, including Knox's, and they all race towards Jax.

"That is just wrong!" Knox whines, standing up and brushing his hands over his pants.

"Not you. You've been a bad boy!" Jax points at Knox.

"Kinky, daddy." Knox runs his finger down his chest, laughing, and the rest of us walk towards Jax and pick up a puppy or two to get them inside.

"Thanks for doing all this," I say to Lizzy, following her in.

"Please. It wasn't much. Anything for my family. Plus, I plan on being repaid with Emmett's superb cooking sometime soon. Maybe this week when I pick up my Lulu girl."

"Yea. I think that works. Maybe Thursday. I think we're going back Tuesday and this drive was a little longer than we expected with all the stops for the pups. Although they are trying to get Michael's plane again."

Lizzy pumps her eyebrows and nudges my arm with her elbow.

"Stop," Everlee laughs.

"I'd ask for a ride back, too, but I know how you kinky fuckers are." She gives Ev a hug. "Well, I must be going. Just wanted to see my girl and make sure you all got in ok. Tony and I are having dinner with my dad tonight, so wish us luck."

"Luck," Everlee says, walking her out.

Jax and Knox are setting up the dog pen in the living room, so I pull the pizzas out of the oven and grab some plates out of the cabinets. It only takes two tries before I find them.

It's a beautiful house. You can tell it's been around for a while, even though they've remodeled at some point. Inside is open and spacious, with light gray walls carried throughout the entire house. It's a little odd setup, because once you walk in, the stairs are right in front of you with a sitting room on a raised platform to the left and to the right is the kitchen and behind that, one level below, is an oversized living room that leads to the backyard. It feels like when they remodeled, they also added onto the house and shifted the rooms around a bit, but didn't level it out. Lots of single steps up and down.

Even though someone painted the ceiling white, remnants of old cabinet outlines are etched into the house like it's saying "don't forget about me." It's a small C-shaped kitchen with a low countertop that curves around with enough seating for eight.

"Oh, good." Everlee sighs, walking into the kitchen and wrapping her arms around me. "I'm starving."

"I've got something that can fill you up."

She gasps and tries to pull out of our hug, but I clamp my arms tighter around her.

"I expect that from Knox, not you."

"I heard my name," he says, walking into the kitchen.

I give her a quick kiss on the head and open my arms, but she gives me a quick squeeze first.

"Are the pups all set up?" Emmett asks, hopping down the stairs.

"Yep. Daddy Jax is being super protective and moving everything away from the cage."

Jax must have heard him from the living room because he yells a threat to Knox about calling him daddy Jax.

"Do you want to eat outside? I saw there's a screened-in porch," Everlee asks, opening all the lids of pizza until she finds the pepperoni.

She's so basic and I love it. Pepperoni for our girl and that's it. Knox is ham and pineapple. Jax, Emmett, and I are pretty much anything. Put all the meats and veggies on it. The more the better.

"Do *you* want to eat outside?" I ask, grabbing a few slices of my own.

She nods and starts walking that way.

The screened-in porch is large, with several couches and coffee tables. Beyond it is a backyard with a slight slope that feeds into the woods on the other side of the fence. Off in the distance, beyond the insect's nightly serenade, is the hushed trickles of the nearby creek.

The back of the fence has a little gate and there is a path that has been carved out in the woods over time that weaves through the trees. Maybe tomorrow we can go exploring a little before we head over to Ev's parent's house.

The weight of the evening slowly creeps over us, blanketing us when Ev's phone rings from inside.

She looks over her shoulder, but doesn't move. I can see the sleep weighing on her eyelids.

"It's probably my mom. I will call her when we go inside."

A second later, Knox's phone dings. He looks at it, then smiles. "Beckett can't come over tonight. They got another call."

"Oh thank the Gods," Jax moans. "I wanted to see him, but it's so peaceful out here that it made me exhausted."

"Same," everyone else agrees at the same time.

EVERLEE - HAPPINESS

Every time I come home, I'm reminded about how much I miss it. The temperature and the general feeling of comfort. It just feels... peaceful.

And humid.

Last night, after Beckett said he wasn't coming over, we all found the nearest bedroom and crashed. There are only four, so I slipped out of my clothes and crawled into Callum's bed. Seeing him in all his glory always turns me on, so I thought I would make a little something happen and got as far as putting my hand around his cock before I fell asleep.

The next morning, when I get downstairs after my shower, Callum and Emmett are sitting on the back porch watching Knox and Jax play with the puppies in the backyard. Luna joins in the fun, periodically running and leaping on Knox, who then chases her around.

"This is the life, isn't it?" I lean down to give them each a kiss.

"We were just saying the same thing." Emmett sweeps his arm around me and pulls me onto his lap. "I made some breakfast for you. It's in the oven staying warm."

"I'll get it for you. I need to take our plates in." Callum pushes up from the seat and grabs the four plates on the side tables.

"So you all ate out here?"

"Yes. It felt great this morning. Jax and Knox went for a run, so they needed to cool down. We were going to wait for you, but when you didn't get up at your normal time, we thought we would let you sleep in."

"Thanks. I need it."

"Evey baby!" Knox yells, running over to the porch to look at me through the screen. "How was your morning?"

"I just got up... well, a little bit ago. I took a shower first."

He smells the air around me and smiles. "Yes, much better."

I roll my eyes, laughing at him.

"What time are we headed to your parents?"

"Whenever, but I figured sometime after lunch. With us having dinner there, I didn't want to subject you all to hours of my parents."

"I love your parents." Knox smiles.

"I know you do."

When Callum walks out a second later with my plate of pancakes, Knox turns and walks back over to Jax, jumping on his back.

This just feels right... being here. Part of me wishes we could move here, but I can't ask the guys that. Their life is back home and my life is with them.

Mom calls just before noon and invites us over for lunch. She used the whole, 'I got too much food at the grocery store' excuse, and the 'I'm just so excited to see you, it's been so long' excuses. We grab all the pups and get them into their crate in the car, grab their leashes, bowls, food, and travel pen, then climb in ourselves. Pulling out of the driveway, it dawns on me we should have just invited them over to our place, but I wasn't thinking.

When we pull up to my parent's house, they walk onto the front porch and wait for us. When they hear all the pups in the back, mom lets out a squeal and nearly leaps off the front porch and runs over to the car with her hands clasped across her mouth.

"I didn't know you were bringing them too."

"We couldn't leave them at the house."

"Oh my goodness, look how precious! Beckett has been talking about them so much, and showing me pictures, but I didn't realize *how* cute they were."

"Let's get them in the house and then you can play with them."

She tilts her chin down and whispers, "Are they going to make a mess?"

"We'll walk them outside for a minute to see if they go potty before we bring them in. Callum and Emmett can set up the temporary play pen."

"Ok good." She bats the air, gives one more squeal, then walks back up to the porch saying something to dad.

By the time we get inside, Emmett is in the kitchen with mom, and Callum and dad are sitting at the table talking about who knows what.

"Hopefully, your brother will be up soon."

"Becks is here?"

"Yep." Mom gives a weird nod, then goes back to talking with Emmett about some recipe she's recently discovered.

A smile creeps along my face, and when my eyes fall on Knox, he pumps his eyebrows. I can read that boy like an open book, and he can read me just the same. We slowly back out of the kitchen and walk upstairs.

Tiptoeing down the hall, we get to Beck's room and listen for a second. His deep breathing filters through the door, so we slowly turn the handle, step in, and close the door.

Knox and I stare at each other for a second, unsure what to do. We both knew we wanted to play some sort of prank on him, or maybe wake him up, but now that we're in his room, we're at a loss. Maybe should have paused in the hall to come up with a plan.

After a second, Knox holds his finger up and smiles before he walks towards the bed. He signals for me to take a video, so I slip my phone out of my back pocket and start recording. Knox climbs into bed and wraps his arm around Beckett and whispers into his ear. Beckett mumbles incoherently and rolls over, making Knox the little spoon, then Knox screams and scrambles out of the bed.

Beckett wakes up, startled, and Knox clenches his ass cheeks.

"What the fuck, dude?" Knox yells. "That was my ass."

Shock robs me of breath or mobility. I'm frozen in my place, watching everything unfold.

"What were you doing in my bed?" Beckett pushes to sit up, glancing at me, then pulls his sheets up his chest to his chin.

"I was just coming to surprise you."

"Well, that fuckin' backfired, didn't it?" Beckett runs his hands through his hair.

"What's going on in here?" Callum asks walking in.

"Nothing!" Knox shouts.

Callum looks at me and I still can't speak. The emotions and thoughts pulsing though my body are contradicting one another, forcing me to stay in place.

Jax walks in a second later. "What did you do, Knox?"

"Me? Why is it always my fault? How do you know it wasn't Ev or Beckett?"

"Because Ev can do nothing wrong and Beckett was sleeping."

My muscles relax. "Thanks boo."

"That's bullshit," Knox mumbles.

I turn the camera off and tuck my phone back in my pocket.

"Hey Beckett." Jax waves and Beckett waves back. "I'm going back downstairs so you all can sort this shit out."

"I'm coming with you." Callum nods with a light chuckle.

Mom's voice echoes up the stairwell, asking Jax if everything's ok then makes some joke, blaming me and my shenanigans.

"What are y'all even doing?" Beckett asks.

"Why are you here and not at Will's place?"

He looks at me, then glances at Knox before he looks back at me.

"What?" I press.

"Will is working, but I also wanted to tell mom not to get all crazy and ask you about baby stuff and pregnancy."

"What?" my voice cracks.

"I know mom can get... excited about all things babies and grandchildren. So, I just didn't want her asking you a thousand and one questions, making this weekend awkward."

"Really?" Tears sting the back of my eyes and a ball forms in my throat, making it hard to swallow.

"Well now, this is super awkward..." Knox mumbles.

"You're a dumbass. Do you know that?" Beckett laughs.

"Thank you, Becks." I didn't want to tell him or anyone else that I was worried about seeing my mom this weekend. She's excited about our marriage and the possibility of us having kids, but I really don't need her bringing it up all weekend. I know she means well, but sometimes she doesn't know how to take a hint or read a room.

"Now, can you two assholes leave so I can get dressed?"

"My ass will thank me. Roll up that hose between your legs."

"Fucking stupid." Beckett laughs, throwing a pillow at him.

When we get out to the hall, Knox wraps his arm around my neck. "Well, that backfired."

"I guess he was just happy to see you." I laugh.

"Too soon."

"But is it?"

When we get downstairs, Emmett is in the kitchen with hoagie rolls sliced open on the counter with an array of meats, cheeses and other items, while mom cuddles Red up to her chest.

"Ev, isn't she just the cutest?"

"She is pretty cute."

"Donna, dear," Dad says.

"Dave," Mom whimpers out when red starts licking her cheek.

"Come on, sir-" Jax starts, but Dad cuts him off.

"Dave. Call me Dave." He chuckles, "And also don't finish that sentence. I don't need a dog in this house. I have Beckett already who eats me out of house and home."

"Did someone say my name?" Beckett asks, hopping down the stairs. When he sees the puppy in mom's hand, he gives a quick squeal. "I didn't know you were bringing them. I would have been up sooner."

"Seems like you were up soon enough," I mumble, covering my mouth.

"What was that, Everlee?" Mom asks, still laughing with red.

"Nothing."

"Are you being nice to your brother? He had a long night."

"Always."

"Never," Beckett says, walking towards the pen where Knox is.

"Oh. Hello there Beckett," Knox says in an awkwardly low tone.

"You know," Mom starts, "I just love seeing you all together. It just warms my heart at how well you all get along."

She's not wrong. I often wonder how this is real life. How they just blended in with my family so seamlessly. Almost like it's too good to be true.

"I'm so excited about tomorrow. Are you going to bring these little angels to the field?" Mom continues.

"I don't know."

"You better. Can't leave them at home all day. Bring their pen and let them get some fresh air. I'll help watch them," Mom says, pressing her nose to Red's.

"You will be running the games, Donna," Dad reminds.

"Well, you can watch them then."

"No." He laughs that kind of laugh where he knows he can say no all he wants because he'll be doing exactly what mom says.

"How did Emmett get wrangled into fixing lunch?" I walk over and stand beside him. He gives me a quick peck on the head and keeps working.

"He insisted," Mom defends. "I felt bad, then selfishly, I was like it's Emmett Monroe."

Emmett chuckles and lightly bumps his hip into mine. "Go sit. I got this."

"Are you sure?"

He cuts his eyes at me. "Go spend time with your family."

As I'm walking away, Jax is getting up from the table and walks into the kitchen to help Emmett. When he sees me watching him, he tosses me a quick wink.

Mom has now dragged dad into the pen with Beckett and the puppies, so I climb in too.

"Don't get any ideas, Donna." Dad laughs.

"Too late." She has her legs out in front of her with Red on her back laying over her legs as she rubs her stomach.

"Well, purple is Lizzy's, blue and yellow are Becketts and orange is Jax's."

"Jax doesn't have one," Jax calls from the kitchen.

"Oh, so you don't mind if I swap yellow for orange?" Beckett jabs, and Jax just cuts his eyes. "That's what I thought."

"So we could keep her? Would you be ok with that?"

I look at the guys and they don't say one way or another. I know we didn't want to give the pups to strangers and if they took Red, then blue and yellow would have another family member to grow up with. "If the guys don't mind, I don't mind."

"Men?" Mom's voice ticks up an octave, her hand freezing over Red's stomach.

They all say they don't mind and my eyes fall to my dad, who is staring at mom, mouth wide open.

"Yes?" She giggles with that innocent-not-so-innocent laugh I'm sure has won her many arguments throughout their marriage.

My dad sighs, but doesn't say anything.

"I'll take that as a yes."

After lunch, Lizzy and Tony come over for a visit. Mom invites them to stay for dinner then sends dad out for some more steaks and potatoes, and another batch of mushrooms. She's making her delicious mushrooms tonight, which is simply sliced up mushrooms in butter and soy sauce, but they are addicting. Emmett tells Jax to go with so Jax can pick up some stuff to make his new drink concoction. I love the old-fashioned, but this one takes the cake. It's dangerously good and masks the flavor of bourbon, so you don't know you're feeling it until you try standing up.

It's been three hours since dad and Jax left and I'm starting to worry. Neither of them are answering their phones, which Jax knows I hate. Beckett, Emmett and I walk onto the front porch to get in the car and search for them when we hear the gravel crunching from the entrance.

"They're home!" I yell over my shoulder.

Mom is joining us a second later on the front porch with a scowl on her face.

"I can see where you get *the* look," Knox says, shivering his shoulders.

As soon as dad walks to the back of the car, mom yells out, "Where have you been? You boys weren't picking up our calls."

"Calm down, Donna. We were close to home."

"Oh no he didn't," Beckett whispers.

"David Michael McKinley."

The guys all look at me, panicked like cats in a cage, ready to scatter.

With a calm demeanor and a smile on his face, he says, "Donna."

Jax joins him at the trunk.

"I got you a little gift," he continues, not bothered by her one bit.

He pulls a large box out of the trunk that Jax takes from him, then pulls out a bag of dog food and a bag that looks to be filled with dog accessories.

"Davie..." she says, sweetly, with a smile on her face.

"Nope. We don't do kinky pet names, mother," Beckett spits out.

"Oh, hush Beckett." She waves her head in the air dismissively and starts walking towards the car.

Jax calls the guys over to help unload the rest of the groceries while mom meets dad just below the stairs and wraps her arms around his neck.

"We can keep her?"

"You ask like I had a choice in the matter." He chuckles.

"You did. You could have said no."

"When we were out getting the odd list of ingredients for Emmett, we ended up beside a dog store. I had a pleasant conversation with Jax and so we decided to just go in and look at a few things and then ended up walking out with almost everything. I got the cheapest bowls and leash because I figured you would want to pick out your own."

"Davie poo."

"Oh lord. Don't you two start kissing. I can't handle it," Beckett interrupts.

"I don't say anything when you and Will kiss."

"Because we don't kiss in front of you, mother."

She starts to speak, then stops. "Fine. Well, I wouldn't say anything if you did."

"Ahh!" he screams, grabbing his hair.

Tonight is going to be a good night.

This weekend is going to be a good weekend.

JAX - EASTER EGG HUNTING

WALKING ONTO THE CHURCH field at the crack of dawn this morning feels weird. In some ways, it's like nothing's changed, while in reality it's so different. Ms. Mary won't be here this year, but we're having dinner with her tonight and spending more time with her tomorrow. Beckett and Will volunteered to come over to the house and watch the pups tonight, and then Will said he would watch them tomorrow since he's off, which is nice.

That guy from last year, Winston, is waving in my direction from across the field with a huge smile on his face. I look behind me, hoping to find someone else, but realize it's just me.

He's waving at me.

I don't hate him, but I don't like him either. His mood just grates on my nerves. He's like Knox, but more annoying and less funny. Like he's never had to deal with tough shit in his life and is just happy. Knox, on the other hand, has had to deal with a lot of tough shit and chooses to be happy despite it.

Oh God. Now he's running over.

"Wilson. How are you?"

He stutters for a second, then smiles. "So good to see you again. I didn't know you all would be back this year."

He doesn't even correct me when I say his name wrong.

"We're here with Everlee this year."

"Everlee?" His brow furrows as he looks around to find her. When the lines in his head soften, I turn to follow his gaze and see her walking down the hill with Callum and her mom. They seem to be in deep conversation about something while Callum just watches them with a smile on his face.

When I clear my throat, he looks back at me, a flush tinging his cheeks. "She looks happy."

Before I can respond, they're walking up to meet us.

"Winston." Everlee smiles. "How are you?"

"Doing good. Doing good. Winnie and I got engaged."

"Oh, that's so awesome. So happy for you." Everlee smiles.

"Your mom said you got married?"

"I did. Over Christmas."

"Which of these men is the lucky one?"

I hadn't noticed that Emmett and Knox had walked up with Beckett, Will, Tony, Lizzy, and the pups.

"All of them." She laughs, but doesn't elaborate.

"Winston!" Lizzy shouts. "What's been going on, man?"

He looks confused.

"You don't remember me from high school?"

Everlee's brows twist in confusion.

"From high school?"

"Yeah."

"You don't remember me? I'm hurt."

"I'm… sorry. I don't. But I feel like there's no way… I'd forget you."

She pats him on the shoulder. "I'm just teasing. I've never met you. Becks here told me who you were walking up."

A chuckle huffs from my chest. She's an idiot, but damn it, I like her.

"Are you running this shindig?" She loops her arm around his and guides him away.

It's hysterical how completely baffled he is.

Donna claps her hands together. "Don't you just love Lizzy? Such a light… that one. Take charge and get things done."

"She's something," I mumble.

Everlee rubs my back, but I lift her into my arms.

"Jax!" she squeals out with a smile spread across her face.

"What?"

Her arms and legs wrap around me.

"Get a room, you two." Beckett shoves my arm as he walks by to follow Lizzy and Winston.

"I love you," I whisper, then give her a quick kiss before standing her up.

Laughter echoes through the air as Knox and Lizzy dump bucketfuls of plastic eggs into the pen, causing the puppies to pounce and playfully scatter them around. I can't help but wonder if Lizzy's little show a second ago was Lizzy being Lizzy or if she was running interference for Ev.

I've noticed this several times, but never mentioned it. It's like she's always on, scanning situations and protecting Ev or distracting others with shiny toys, or in her case, utter ridiculousness. She's always so over the top that it's hard to imagine her as being that calculating, but she does it time and time again. Almost like she's always three steps ahead of everyone else. If it was anyone other than Lizzy, I'd actually be impressed. I chuckle to myself, garnering Ev's attention.

"What?" she asks, grabbing my hand and leading me over to the others.

"Nothing."

I'll never admit that I actually like or admire her wild-child best friend. At least out loud.

"These cuties are going to make it impossible to focus and hide the eggs this year?" Winnie says, walking up and slipping her arm around Winston's, leaving her ring on display.

That's precious. She's intimidated by our Ev.

She should be. Anyone would be lucky to have her.

"Winnie! Congrats on your engagement. Winston just told me!" Ev cheers, smiling.

"Oh my gosh. Thank you." She brings her left hand up to her mouth.

Lizzy coughs before her eyes lock on mine. We pass a glance to one another and before I realize it, I'm smiling at her and goddamn it, she sees it. Her eyes get wider and she shifts from side to side like a rocket ready to explode, but she doesn't say anything.

Fuck.

"What do you need us to do?" Lizzy asks, looking back at Winston. Her voice is the slightest bit shaky, like the happiness flowing through her is about to explode out in little beams and smack me right in the fucking face.

Ev must notice because she looks at me and smiles. All I can do is shake my head and roll my eyes before I slip my arm around her.

Winnie doesn't miss it and her eyes get wide with shock, but she doesn't speak.

That's right, Winnie. She doesn't need your Winston at all.

Beckett climbs into the pen with the pups and plays with them, throwing most of the plastic eggs out so we can hide them. He saves one of each color for the pups so they have something to do and says he will stay with them.

"He's just being lazy," Will says, picking up a bucket of eggs as he follows me to the left side of the field. We have the woods, while Ev, Lizzy, and Callum are on the right side of the field in the woods. Knox wanted to join them, but everyone shot that idea down. Putting those three together definitely spells trouble because they'll all think a stupid idea is a brilliant idea and get in trouble.

A noise pulls my attention and I find Knox riding Emmett's back as they head down the middle of the field, with Tony following beside them holding all three baskets and laughing.

Several hours later, the field is full of kids from all ages lined up, baskets in hand ready to find the eggs. The volunteers organize the kids into sections based on age, starting with the toddlers first. Beckett, while in the pen with the pups earlier, did his duty and threw eggs onto the field. That was his version of hiding the eggs for them.

As I scan through the crowd, a wave of joy washes over me when my eyes land on Mason. As our gazes lock, his eyes light up, and a faint smile dances across his face. He looks like he's in a much better spot this year than he was last year when we spoke.

He was having a hard time at his foster home because he was the oldest kid there, and one of the boys, who was the closest thing to a brother, had just been adopted. I was worried about him after Easter, so had Mrs. Mary do some digging around. She sent me the phone number for his house, so I reached out to him. A few weeks later, I sent him a phone so we could talk and text as much as he wanted and have kept in touch ever since. I told him I was coming into town this weekend and wanted to see him.

The whistle blows and the toddlers scurry, wobble, and fall, trying to pick up the eggs on the grass and the four to six-year-olds behind them whine that they're getting all the eggs. Another minute passes, and the next wave of kids goes until it gets to the teenagers who saunter without a care in the world onto the field. Most of them clearly don't really care, but they are out on the field because they have to be.

Mason walks over to me with an uneasy look on his face. "Hey," he says, simply offering nothing else.

"Hey."

I'd have to imagine it's weird talking to me face to face again after it's been a year. Sure, we've talked on the phone via video chat and text, but it still feels a little weird.

"You didn't hide the eggs, did you?" He holds up his empty basket.

"I did, and I made sure to hide them extra hard for you."

He laughs. "They never hide them hard. Plus, this is my tenth year doing it, so I know where all the good spots are." As the words of his statement hit him, his smile falls. Ten years. He's been in the foster system for ten years.

"Last year I had a lot going on, but this year… I hid them with you in mind."

"Yeah, right."

"I don't lie."

His eyes narrow as he watches me skeptically. "Fine. But I bet I can find them all."

"All the eggs? You've already lost that bet because you've been over here talking to me. The others are finding them."

"I'm talking about the tough ones you *said* you hid." He puts air quotes around tough.

"I'll give you a hint. They're on the left side of the field."

"Too easy. There aren't great spots over there. You got a handful at best with the fallen tree and maybe in the hole that's in the stump from that tree. Though I've never stuck my hand in there because Lewis got bit by a snake one year. No, thank you."

"I didn't hide it in the stump."

We start walking towards the woods on the left side of the field.

"So how's school going?"

"I don't want to go anymore." He sighs and kicks at a stick on the ground.

"You have to, though. You only have a couple of years left."

He steps into the cover of the woods and lifts a small bundle of sticks and pulls up an egg and holds it up with an I-told-you-so face on.

"Not mine."

"Sure." He laughs. "Let me guess. Any egg I find in this section you didn't hide, and the ones I don't find will be yours?"

"I won't lie to you. That one simply wasn't mine."

His eyes linger on me for another second before we continue walking, stepping further into the woods. He walks over to several other places and pulls up the eggs.

"See. This isn't my first rodeo."

"Ok. Let's save these for the others. Mine are a little further down, closer to the lake."

We step over branches and twigs for the next few minutes in silence. It's like I can feel the excited apprehension flowing off of him, seeking something new and different. Like it's a reminder that things can change. Maybe it's just finding Easter eggs for him, but at the same time it's the same every year. Same people hiding them in the same spots. That was before me. Before a change. He needs change. He needs to know that it won't always be like this.

"This is my section. Good luck." I pat him on the shoulder.

His eyes light up a little, bringing a smile to my face. He moves with purpose, looking in all the usual spots, the easy spots, but comes up empty.

"Ok. I'll give it to you. A little more difficult than usual. You didn't go for the simple spots."

"I told you. I'm changing it up. So. School."

Mason walks over to a tree and puts his hand on the trunk, and looks up. "It's boring."

"Are your grades good?"

"Straight A's. The classes are too easy."

"Have you talked about getting put in tougher classes?"

He grabs the low branch and lifts himself up, and grabs the egg on the back of the tree, before he jumps down.

"Fine. You got one. Don't get cocky."

We continue to move. "I don't know. I feel like they need to have a conversation with my family, but there's never any time. Some teachers are also concerned because it's my first year in high school, so they don't want to overwhelm me. There are a few other ones who give me extra work."

We move a little deeper into the woods, and I watch as he uses the stick he picked up a minute ago and flips over leaves, twigs, and bunches of sticks. He pauses at the fallen tree and looks over his shoulder at me with a smirk.

"I'll save you the time. I didn't put any here."

The brows on his face raise and we keep walking.

"Well, it's nice that you have teachers that want to challenge you."

"Yeah, but for what? Next year, when I get to tenth, I'm going to be in the same boat. Repeating the same stuff. Then what happens when I'm a senior?"

"Maybe by that time they'll have figured out another option for you. Let you start college classes or something."

He snarls his lip.

"No? What do you want to do?"

He shrugs. "Maybe join the military." Mason looks at me and his words soften to barely a whisper. "Like you."

My heart seizes in my chest for a second. "Really?"

He shrugs and continues walking. The moment is broken.

When he gets to a clump of leaves, he uses his stick to flick through them and pulls up an egg. "Really? This is just lazy."

A laugh erupts from my chest. "That wasn't me."

"Sure it wasn't."

I laugh again. "Mine are all above the knee."

"Because you're old and can't bend down?"

I blow out a breath and give him a playful shove. "Old or not, I can still take you down."

He laughs and we keep moving.

This kid. I like him. I see so much of myself in him. At least I had Callum, Emmett, and Knox, but man... this kid. I was drawn to him last year, and it's just like... I don't know. Something just fits with him. Like I was meant to find him and help guide him.

Minutes pass and the horn blows, warning us we have five minutes left. Mason has only found four of my eggs and has conceded that I'm a much better hider than others in the past.

Mason's eyes flick over my shoulder, then back to me and I get a strange prickle on the back of my neck. A small twig breaks and before I can turn around, a body is leaping onto my back, wrapping their arm around my neck. I don't have to look to know it's Knox's dumbass. He's the only one that could've gotten that close without me hearing him. And the twig at the end was because he knew Mason gave him away.

"Knox." I grab his arm and quickly spin out of his grasp, then sweep my leg, making him fall to the ground.

"Yo dude. Not cool. This is my nice shirt."

"The don't sneak up on people in the woods." I offer my hand and he gives a little hop before he dusts off his pants.

"Who do we have here?" Knox asks, looking at Mason.

"Knox, Mason. Mason, meet the thorn in my side."

Mason chuckles while Knox does a stupid bow.

"Emmett and Cal were looking for you."

"Here I am."

"Excellent. I'll go report 'here you are' and that should clear it up."

Mason chuckles again.

"Don't laugh at him. It just encourages him."

Knox bats his hand in the air. "It doesn't. I'm like this, regardless." He bows again. "Mason, pleasure." Knox flits off, moving through the woods without a sound. He was always so good at that.

"He's funny," Mason says.

I roll my eyes. "He's a pain."

"You like him."

"I bare him."

"Nah. You like him." He flicks his stick again. "I watched your face. You saw me look behind you and you knew he was coming up. You knew it was him."

"I did."

"How?"

"Because he's an idiot who always likes to play around, and because he was quiet. No one can get that close to me without me knowing. Well, no one here. Except him."

"Because of your time in the SEALs?"

"Yeah."

"I want to be like you. Like both of you."

"It's hard."

"So. I can do hard."

"You can't even find some Easter eggs." I laugh.

His gaze sets on my face as he watches me for a second like he's trying to figure out what to say, then a smile pulls across his lips and he starts walking. Within three minutes, he has found all of my eggs.

"You knew where they were all along?"

"Yeah."

"Why didn't you grab them before?"

"I enjoyed talking to you."

"Mason. We could have kept talking, regardless." I laugh. "Well, damn. I thought I'd done a good job."

"You did better than most. I'm just good at finding patterns and irregularities. Again, I've been doing this for a while."

When he says it this time, it doesn't hold the weight of sadness with it.

"Can I hang around you today? I see the others all the time." His voice is soft, like he's almost scared to ask.

"Absolutely."

EVERLEE - KNOX IN THE BOX

Beckett walks over to me with a shit-eating grin spread across his face, and my stomach turns with a combination of fear and excitement.

"What have you done?"

His brows furrow. "Why do you think I did something?"

With a pointed finger, I gesture towards his face, making a circle with my hand to emphasize my words. "Your face."

"Is beautiful? Handsome? I think you left out a descriptor or two."

"What did you do?"

"Nothing," he whines.

Tilting my chin down, my eyes lock on his.

"Oh fine. I may have grabbed an extra egg from the house this morning and brought it with me."

"Why?"

"I plan to throw it into the mix when we're doing our egg toss with the guys."

"You aren't going to cheat."

"No. Never. I just plan on throwing it at Knox in the middle to confuse him a bit."

"Beckett."

"Everlee."

"That's cheating. You can't do that. One, because I won't ever hear the end of it, and two, because you're better than that."

"I wasn't doing it to cheat. I just genuinely enjoy screwing with Knox. He's almost like a jack-in-the-box. You know what's going to happen when you keep poking him, but it still excites you every time." He laughs. "A Knox in the box!"

"It sounds like you're describing Jax."

"He's just scary. Like if the jack-in-the-box had a scary twin that no one knew about called Gack. He pops out with a knife in his hand." Beckett holds his hand up like he's gripping a knife and bobbles his body back and forth like a jack-in-the-box on a spring.

"What are you both talking about?" Jax asks, walking up with a boy beside him.

"Nothing," Becketts says too quickly.

Jax's brows peak, but he doesn't say anything.

"Who's this?" I ask, changing the subject for Beckett's sake.

"This is Mason."

"Oh! Mason!" I smile and hold my hand out to shake his. I thought hugging him may seem a little too forward or awkward since I've technically never met him.

"You're Everlee?"

"Yes."

"Wow."

"No funny ideas. She's already taken."

"It's a pleasure meeting you. I've heard so much about you." I smile.

Jax seems to have taken a special interest in Mason. After their conversation on the log last year, Jax felt a need to stay in touch. He hasn't said exactly what is driving it, but I haven't asked. It's not something that needs to be explained. I think it's sweet he's developing a relationship with this boy. I don't know what it's like to be raised in the foster system. The uncertainty about where you'll be, who will keep you, or if your parents will come back and get you. The hope they will, or maybe they won't.

We haven't talked much about Mason's situation, only that he's been in the system since he was five and has moved around to four different homes. Apparently, at first, it was because he was hard to manage, but as he's gotten older, the other moves were because the foster parents didn't want to do it anymore, or wanted younger kids, or who knows the reason.

Jax seems to think the house he's in now is where he'll finish out. From what Jax has said, Mason is a good kid. Smart. Though I'm not sure how much he knows about us. How do you tell a boy that? Do you even tell him? I guess it's something we should figure out if we're going to have kids or will it just be natural when it's our own?

Tightness clenches at my chest for a second as worry flutters through me like a dark butterfly spreading uncertainty.

No. This will be good. This is what we all want and it will be good.

"If you all don't mind, Mason is going to hang with us for the day," Jax continues, pulling me from my thoughts.

"Absolutely."

"I'm Beckett." He holds out his hand. "I'm Ev's cool, younger brother."

"Typically, if you have to say it, it's not true," Jax jokes.

Beckett grabs his chest. "That hurts."

"What's going on over here?" Emmett asks, walking over with Knox and Lizzy.

When I look over their shoulder, Tony, Will, and Callum are talking about something.

"Nothing much," Jax says.

Before he can finish the last syllable, Lizzy has her hand out. "Hi, I'm Lizzy."

"Hi Lizzy," Mason chuckles, and his eyes shift to Jax.

"This is the other thorn in my side," Jax adds, and Mason laughs.

"That is one of the sweetest things you've ever said to me." Lizzy rests her hand on his shoulder. "It's obviously symbolic of how you know I will never leave your side because I've embedded myself into everything that is part of you. And!" She points her finger in the air. "What has thorns? A rose. You are calling me a rose. So sweet," she chirps, then wipes away an invisible tear.

Mason laughs and Jax reprimands. "Don't. You'll only encourage her."

Every time I see a rose, all I can think about are the rose vibrators she purchased for me when I was in the hospital.

So many vibrators.

My mother calls out on the microphone that the egg toss is going to start in a few minutes, so we all walk over to that area of the field.

Knox stops suddenly and turns around, placing his hand on Mason's shoulder. "I did something to my arm earlier." He grabs it and rotates his shoulder, wincing in pain. "Would you mind taking my place with Jax for the egg toss?"

He's lying. He's been talking about retribution for losing last year for almost a month.

His eyebrows peak on his forehead as he waits for Mason to answer. "Please? It would take a lot of pressure off of me."

"Ok," Mason says softly, eyes darting to each of us for a second.

Knox perks up and claps, then immediately grabs his wrist.

Mason cuts his eyes at Jax, but doesn't say anything.

"I'm going to go check on the pups and cheer for you from the sidelines. Take them down!"

"Who are you cheering for, exactly?" I pop my hip out with a tone full of sass.

"You, of course, my darling."

He blows a kiss, then walks up the small hill to where the pups are playing in their pen. A minute later, Tony is walking down to meet Lizzy.

"Where's Knox going?"

"He hurt his arm, so he's going to sit with the pups and Mason here is going to fill in for him," Jax says.

Mason laughs. "We all know his arm isn't hurt, right? That he was pretending?"

The crowd laughs. Jax had mentioned this kid was sharp.

A few minutes later, we're taking our places. This year they picked a different part of the field which is longer, allowing for all the groups to go at one time.

Mom takes her spot on the microphone and goes through the rules, then hands out all the eggs. Same as last year, throw on the whistle and back up in five-foot increments.

Beckett and I move further down the field, putting several couples between us and the guys and Lizzy because we don't want any shenanigans. Not going to lie. I was a little nervous Beckett was going to leave me on my own this year and want to play with Will, but thankfully Will said he didn't want to participate. Plus, we have the family tradition to uphold and need to win back our trophy.

The horn blows and I toss the egg first. I made the change from last year so Beckett would be on the receiving end of the first long throw. Out of the twenty or so teams, two exit on the first round. By the time we get to twenty-five feet, there are ten teams left. An uncomfortable number because we didn't get much further last year. All the couples are still standing in their original positions, so we're fairly well spread out. There is one couple between us and Lizzy and Tony. Jax and Mason are beside them, and then Callum and Emmett are further down.

They also separated from the pack.

The whistle blows and I toss the egg. It's cutting through the air with a little too much speed. My hands curl by my lips and my right leg pulls up to my chest as I cringe. Beckett scoots back, following the arc and scoops it, and hops away from me, lifting his hands into the air. It's quite the spectacle.

My lungs burn, searching for a breath as I wait to see if it cracked.

He thrusts his fist into the air and goes into a star pose. The crowd erupts and even mom mentions the catch. Beckett gives a bow, and I can't help but roll my eyes.

Lizzy walks over and whispers, "Give 'em hell."

When I look at her, she has egg running down her neck and chest.

"Oh, sis."

"If only I were a freaking fairy like your brother..."

There are only four teams left. The guys, a couple I don't know, and us. It feels oddly reminiscent of last year. We take our steps back, increasing the distance to thirty-five feet. The wind stops blowing, and the crowd is silent. The only noise is the gentle lap of the water on the shore's edge just behind us.

My eyes lock on Beckett as my pulse thumps like a drum in my ears. I don't think I've ever wanted to catch an egg so badly in my life before. My gaze cuts down the line and I see Emmett and Jax both on the opposite side of me, preparing to toss the egg to Mason and Callum. Jax tosses me a quick wink that sends a heat through my core.

"Focus, sister," Beckett commands.

"Try to toss it straight this time."

"I have problems with straight," he says with a sassy head bobble.

The whistle blows, and the egg is up in the air. It feels like seconds pass as I watch it hang there, trying to measure the speed and the angle of descent. I take a few steps forward, bend the knees, readying myself, running through all the things one should do, not to end up with egg on them.

I hear an egg crack and the crowd moan, but I can't look. I need to stay focused. Three... two... one. The egg rockets into me and I cup my hands around it, swinging them backward, letting it lead me to the ground as I cradle it, praying it doesn't crack. I just need to hold on.

My elbow cries out in pain as it hits the hard ground first, followed by my hip, and then my head. Rolling over to my stomach, I open my hand and find the egg sitting there, uncracked.

Relief pours through me. I don't know how much life this egg has left and I'm just glad it's not me on the other side of the forty-foot throw.

When I hold it up, I look up and see Callum walking by with an egg on his face and I choke back a laugh. His eyes glimmer as he tosses me a wink. "Missed it by just this much." He holds his fingers up to show a small space between his thumb and index.

The other couple is also eliminated, so now it's just Mason and Jax, Beckett, and me.

My mom asks if we want to move closer together and Beckett and I yell out no at the same time. We're in a good spot. A lucky spot. Pretty sure I left elbow skin on the ground for that catch. I've marked it and we've become one. One with the earth. One with the egg.

When Mason and I look behind us to take another step back, we realize there's no marker.

Mom laughs. "Right. Well, we didn't think anyone would make it past this point. But I suppose I underestimated the competitive spirit of my children." She laughs again. "Let's do this." Her finger strokes her chin as she thinks up something on the fly.

This should be good.

"Let's move back to ten feet. You will all need to spin in a circle until I say stop, and then I will blow the whistle for you both to toss the egg."

We're fucked.

Jax chuckles and I shoot him a stink eye. He knows I don't do well spinning in circles.

How do we know this with such certainty you ask? On Valentines, the guys thought it would be fun to spin in circles on the swing until the straps were tight, then let me go.

They let me go, and (warning), I let my dinner go. I was like Elsa, but instead of shooting out ice, I was... well... I think you get the picture. Not my proudest or sexiest moment. It was a great way to top off the evening and what's best is the circle of mirrors caught it all. Ever puke while looking at yourself in the mirror?

A shiver moves up my spine just thinking about it.

"Let's go Ev!" Knox yells from the sidelines, clapping his hands. He's standing beside the others, laughing.

Fucker wants to see what will happen to me again.

"Be a ballerina Ev!" Beckett shouts. "Spot, or whatever it is they do."

"I'm not a ballerina, Beckett!"

"No shi...takes! No shitake mushrooms... were in my store... this week?"

"What?"

I can hear Lizzy call him an idiot off to the side.

He bats his hand. "Don't puke."

Blowing a few rapid breaths out of my mouth, I psych myself up.

You can do this.

"Spin!"

We all start spinning, moving at about the same pace. No one wants to spin faster than the others. I try to spot, though I don't really know how to. But I do what I can and I'm certain I look like an ostrich on a merry-go-round, whose necks stays a little too long in one spot while the rest of the body keeps moving.

I have confirmation a moment later when I hear Lizzy laughing. Hard. Like the kind of laugh you know, she is bent over and grabbing her stomach and there are tears in her eyes.

Twat face.

"Stop!" my mom yells.

We all stop and I wobble from side to side for a moment. I feel Jax's eyes on me and when I look up, his gaze is hard.

He's watching me like he's waiting to run to my rescue, which makes me love him even more.

"Ready! Toss!"

We throw the egg and it's a little wobbly on the exit, but Beckett dashes to the side to catch it.

Fiddlesticks and biscuits! Of course, Mason executed it perfectly.

"Well, let's back up to the next spot and repeat."

"No," I whimper out.

Lizzy's laughing only gets louder.

"Spot," Beckett encourages.

"For the love of God, will you stop telling me to spot!"

Jax laughs and I want to stomp across the field and punch him in the throat. And then fuck him, because... well, why not?

We spin, we stop, and I wait. I'm going to mess up. We're going to lose and I'm going to get covered in egg. We have tossed that egg around too many times for it to not have little cracks. Damn it!

"Toss!"

Shit! Shit! Shit! It's coming through the air, hurling at me. Great execution. It's getting closer. Shit, fuck, motherass! It's too fast. Too fast. Damn it! I freeze and cross my arms over my face and scream out.

Thwack! The egg magically misses all parts of my arms and smacks me right in the forehead. A sharp sting radiates over my face before the ooze of the egg does.

The crowd is silent.

What happened?

"What happened?" Beckett asks, looking stunned.

"Well, I guess that's a way to finish the game," Mom teases and laughs awkwardly, unsure of what to say.

"You ok?" Jax asks, walking over, grabbing my elbow, before he scoops a blob of egg off my face.

"I'm fine. Embarrassed but fine."

Beckett runs up to me. "What happened? You just stood there."

"I don't know. I... I guess I freaked out and... I don't know. I really didn't want egg on me."

"That turned out well, didn't it?"

"Let's give our new winners, Jax and Mason, a round of applause!" Mom cheers through the microphone.

A hand brushes over my low back, and a heat radiates up my spine.

Callum.

CALLUM - MINE

SHE'S FREAKING OUT. EVERLEE'S arms cross in front of her face as the egg continues to hurl through the air and smacks her right in the forehead. I can hear the crack from here and the oomph she makes.

Everyone freezes as silence falls on the crowd.

By the time I get over to her, Jax and Beckett are standing in front of her and remnants of the yolk are still on her face, even though Jax has scooped a majority off.

My hand brushes across her back, pulling her attention. "Let's go get you cleaned up."

She looks up at me with glassy eyes, which causes a twinge in my chest.

"What's wrong?" I ask as we walk up the hill towards the back of the church.

"I've got egg on my face and I didn't want egg on my face."

"Then you should have tried to catch the egg or, better yet, move to the side."

"I froze."

"Yeah, we all saw."

"Shut up." She smiles and smacks my chest.

On instinct, my hand moves up and traps hers against me. Her eyes shoot up to mine and her lips part.

"Everlee," I scold, knowing exactly what that looks means.

"It's your fault," she huffs. "Looking at me like you do. Trapping my hand. You know what that does to me."

A chuckle escapes as I let her lead through the door into the church. The air still smells of mothballs and wood. When I left a few minutes ago, I opened the doors to help air it out a bit, but I guess someone closed it. The light blue carpet has a nice bundle of leaves in the corner which must have blown in after I left.

"The bathrooms are to the left."

Everlee slides her hand out of my grip and runs it down my arm to my hand and clasps her fingers between them.

"Everlee."

Pushing the bathroom door open, she gazes up at me with an innocent expression. "What?"

I push the door open and slide my hand out of hers. "Hurry up."

"You aren't coming in with me?"

Taking a deep breath, I smile. "I can't."

"Please?" She slowly lifts the bottom of her dress and my cock twitches in my pants.

Just as I take a step forward, a group of young kids and their mom burst through the doors from outside and run down the hall towards us.

"I'll be waiting out here," I grunt out, pushing the door wider for the kids and mom to walk through.

Fuck me. That was close.

My back presses against the wall across the hall from the restroom. I wasn't fully hard, but half-mast for sure.

A minute later, Everlee walks out of the bathroom with a clean face and a slight blush. She pumps her eyebrows at me and grabs my hand without speaking.

Beckett is running up to us as soon as we step out.

"What's wrong?"

"Nothing." He frowns. "Just grabbing my keys. Mom needs me to go to the store to get some ice."

"We'll go," I spit out before he can finish.

"Really?"

"Yes?" Everlee looks confused.

"Yes." My tone is firm.

"Awesome. Thanks." Beckett walks away, then stops and looks over his shoulder at me. "You kinky fucker."

"Beckett!" Everlee whisper shouts.

"Sorry Lord!" Beckett looks up at the sky, holding his hand up in apology.

"Let's go." I grab Everlee's hand and she gives that cute little squeal she does.

My heart hammers in my chest and my stomach clenches. I need to feel my cock inside of her right now.

When we get to the car, there are people either coming or going. Too many.

Damn it!

We climb in and now my cock is pressing against my pants, ready to fuck her, and every time I turn around, there's someone there. If it wasn't at a church, I'd say fuck it and press her up against the wall, against the car, against anything and take her. Feel her tight pussy wrapped around me, feel her arousal dripping around me. Taste it on my lips.

This isn't helping.

My knuckles are white around the steering wheel as we pull onto the road.

I'm so focused on the yellow dotted lines on the road that I don't notice Everlee unzipping my pants.

"What are you doing?" I ask, when my pants spread open around my cock, giving it space.

"I felt bad for him. Trapped in your pants." She loosens her seatbelt and twists her body.

"Everlee. What are you doing?"

"Nothing." Her voice is soft as she leans down and licks the beaded arousal off the tip of my cock.

I feel like I'm about to explode and she's barely done anything.

Her hand wraps around my base, and she strokes up with a firm grasp like she's trying to milk me.

"Fuck, Everlee." My hands grip tighter around the steering wheel as my foot pulls off the accelerator.

"I haven't done anything yet." She giggles, then wraps her mouth around my cock and my hips buck off the seat, hungrily pressing deep down her throat as a wave of euphoria washes over me.

That was greedy and I need to show more restraint. I plant my ass firm in the seat and continue driving, counting the trees as I pass. Her mouth feels divine. Hot. Wet.

Her fingers scoop my balls, and she squeezes and the wheel jerks and her arms buckle and she chokes on my cock.

"Callum?"

Unable to take any more, I jerk the wheel again, this time on purpose, and pull off the narrow two-lane road onto a gravel drive.

"Where are we?"

"Fuck if I know."

Looking in the rearview mirror, I can still see the road, but I don't know how much longer I can wait.

When I get past another two trees, I slow to a stop. Ahead of us is an enormous field and just to the left in the distance is a white house with chipped paint. There's a hole in the roof and a chunk missing out of the front corner. I don't know how it's still standing. The flap of a butterfly's wing could probably knock it over.

"Looks abandoned." I unbuckle my seatbelt and tilt the seat back.

"Yay?"

"Shut the fuck up and climb on top of me."

Her eyes pulse wide with excitement. "Here?"

"Yes here. Now pull up your dress and ride me."

Her lips pull into a smile as she makes her way over the console and positions her body over my lap.

"There's not a lot of room. Should we move to the backseat?"

"I don't want to wait another second. Sit. Down."

"I'm not a dog."

A low chuckle escapes my lips as several thoughts and commands filter through my mind. Instead, I gently slide my hand around her waist, tracing the curves of her back, until my fingers find her ponytail, which I grasp and gently tug, tilting her head back. "Sit. Down. Now."

Her eyes flare again with excitement and her breath pulses. "Yes. Sir."

Without hesitation, she sinks down and my hand tugs once more, causing her to tumble back into the horn. Its blare scares us, and a field full of birds that go squawking and fluttering into the air.

"Sorry." Her eyes level on me before they roll into the back of her head.

With each gentle thrust, I maintain a slow and steady pace, grinding my hips into hers. Gentle, not because I want to, but because there's no goddamn space in this seat. Restraint would have been a wonderful thing to exercise, but I wanted her hot, wet pussy on me. I wanted to feel it wrapped tight around me and now I want to feel her walls quiver just before she comes all over me.

The more I think about her and *feel* her, my thrust become faster and more erratic. Her back hits the horn with every other thrust, so it sounds like a malfunctioning car alarm going off.

She leans forward and wraps her arms around my neck and rotates her hips, grinding back on me, and I swear she's going to make me fucking come before her. It's like this game she plays because she knows our rules. She's always been a rule breaker, but I don't like being one. Rules are in place for a reason. She's sort of fucked up most of mine, but damn it.

This.

One.

Geraniums. Lillies. Oak. Elm. Broken house. Hole in the house. Old-

Fuck me.

My balls are tightening.

"Everlee, you better fucking come right goddamn now," I seethe and her gaze slowly glides across my face and a wicked smile curves on her lips.

"Why?" Her voice is soft. "Are you about to shoot your hot-" She rubs her hands up my chest. "Come inside of me?" She moans out. "Oh, Callum daddy." She bounces faster.

If I didn't love her so much, I'd hate her.

Clamping down on my bottom lip, I close my eyes, trying with everything inside of me to hold it back. I slide my hand between us and find her clit and- she's drenched. My thumb rubs as she gives a little squeak.

"You won't win this Everlee."

"Judging by the teeth marks on your lip, I would venture to say I'm pretty close."

If it's a game she wants, it will be a game she gets.

Using my hand that's wrapped around her ponytail, I open it and guide her head to me, while I still work her clit. Her pulse is throbbing hard and fast in her neck, like it's calling out to me. Grabbing the top collar of her dress, I slip it off her shoulder and run my tongue across her collarbone and up her neck.

"Cal. No fair."

"I don't play fair. I play to win." With the end of my statement, I clamp down on her neck and suck. I was trying to be discreet, but baby girl wants it rough. She likes it rough. I can't give her exactly what she wants, but I *will* mark her. Her hands push against my chest, trembling with a feeble attempt to create distance, but I press my hands firmly on her back, anchoring her in place. My teeth sink into her soft flesh as I suck and lick, lick and suck.

Her arms collapse between us, and her groans turn to moans as her hips rock.

"Callum." She grinds her hips faster against my finger and onto my cock.

When I pull my lips away, there is a nice red spot on her neck.

Mine.

Gripping her ponytail again, I yank back and fuck her as hard and as fast as I can.

"Come for me, Everlee."

Please, God, let her come because I can't hold on any longer. Her walls start to quiver and that's my sign. My finger moves faster as do her hips as she lets the need for release consume her.

Guiding her head to my mouth, my lips take over hers, and I push my tongue in. Her mouth is hot and needy as she kisses me back. Hungry.

Using the hand that was on her clit, I wrap it around her lower back and press her to me and grind, savoring the sweet feeling of our connection.

Little whimpers vibrate from her throat as the tidal wave of ecstasy consumes her. She clamps around my length and a surge of pleasure pulses through me, culminating in my cock, and bursts out of me.

An involuntary groan escapes as our kiss deepens and slows.

A buzzing in the center console grabs our attention.

Knox.

EVERLEE - MEETING MAMA MARY

WE WALK UP THE three stairs to Mrs. Mary's front door. My heart hammers in my chest and my palms are sweaty. Callum and Emmett are standing in front, while Jax is behind me and Knox is standing beside me.

"Is it ok?" I thrust my neck in Knox's direction.

"It's fine. Just don't touch it or you'll wipe off the makeup."

"I don't know what you two were thinking," Jax leans down in and whispers with his hand resting on my hip near my ass.

When I turn, my lips are only millimeters from his. "Clearly we weren't..."

He chuckles and plants a quick kiss on my lips before he stands up straight and clasps his hands behind his back.

While we wait, it suddenly hits me. This is where they grew up. I'd been so concerned with covering my hickey from earlier that I hadn't even realized. I look around at the front yard through a new lens. The tall tree set off to the side with a tire swing, the deflated brown-once-white ball tucked against the side of the house.

The door creaks open and Mrs. Mary stands there behind a walker, wearing a beautiful sky-blue dress with a white flower broach with large white pearl earrings. The epitome of sophistication and class.

"Oh, boys." She smiles and throws her arms open wide, then backs out of the door bringing her walker with her. "Come in, come in."

"Good evening, Mrs. Mary. How are you?" Callum asks, walking in and giving her a quick hug as he passes.

"Doing better now. My health's been troublesome these last few months, but right now I feel like I'm sixty again!" Her chuckle is light and airy, like a spring day. "And you must be the lovely Everlee."

"Yes, ma'am. Your home is lovely."

She grabs my hands and gives a gentle squeeze. "Eh. It needs some maintenance and a few repairs."

"Why didn't you say? We could have taken care of it while we're here."

"No." She walks towards the kitchen. "Shut the door, Jaxxy."

With a smile on my face, I glance at him over my shoulder. He closes the door and glares at me with his finger in the air and mouths, '*Not a word*'.

So I mouth back, 'Ok Jaxxy'.

The intensity of his gaze sends an electric current coursing through my body. His glare turns into a smug grin because he can read my face- my body- like an open book.

Asshole.

"I've got the ham finishing up in the oven right now. Maybe another five minutes or so."

"It smells wonderful." My voice cracks with nerves and... heat.

"Darling. No need for nerves. I know about my boys... proclivities. Well, not all about it, but enough. Thought they could each settle down with a pleasant woman." She laughs,

"On their own, but these boys. They've always been connected at the hip." She grabs the oven mitt off the counter and hands it to Emmett. "Emmett doll, can you pull that out for me? I had to get Leroy's sister next door to help me earlier, but she's out at the hair salon now. My old wrists are just too weak."

"Yes, ma'am."

"Such a sweetheart still, I see." She pinches his cheeks, then looks at the rest of the guys.

Jax has made his way into the kitchen and is standing behind me. I haven't looked to see him, but I feel him. I always feel him. Feel *them*. It's like the very essence of my being knows theirs and vibrates when they're nearby.

"Knox, tell me what kind of trouble you've been in lately, because I know it has to be something." She tucks her walker close to the table and takes a seat in the chair that's already pulled out.

"Mama Mary." He clutches his chest in feigned shocked.

She tosses her head back and gives a laugh that sounds like, hoo hoo hoo.

"I've been a perfect angel."

Jax clears his throat.

"I see Jax is still giving you a hard time," she says, face beaming with a bright smile.

"All the time," Knox pouts. "I'm doing great, though. Club is doing amazing. Probably better than Callum's and Jax's."

I can't help but wonder if she knows about the clubs. Does she ask, or does she know better than to ask?

"You boys are much older now, but when I look at you, I still see the same handsome troublemakers that walked around these streets with your chests puffed out and head held high."

A natural silence falls over the kitchen for a minute, but is interrupted by the clanging of the stove's eyes when Emmett pulls the ham out.

"Let me see that." Mrs. Mary pushes her hand onto the table, helping her stand.

"You stay there, Mama Mary. I'll look at it." Emmett moves around the kitchen, opening drawers and pulling things out like he's not missed a single day here.

I can't help but wonder how much is the same. I'd bet everything. It feels as if time has been frozen, and the weight of that realization tightens my chest. She's alone here. I mean, sure, she has her church and probably people that visit, but she's here every day...

"How is your restaurant going?"

"Great! It's doing really well."

"Oh, that's good. I had no doubt it would do wonderful. Wish we had one here so I could try it. I'll never get up that way."

Emmett gives Callum an odd look, but doesn't say anything.

"How about you Callum? Jax? Your club doing ok? Better than Knox's and Everlee's?"

It's weird to hear her use my name so casually, but at the same time, it fills me with a warmth and comfort I didn't know I needed, or even wanted.

"The club is doing great. Lizzy has sort of taken over the digital piece of it, which has really helped to grow the business."

Jax interjects, "I mean, we were doing good before her..."

Mrs. Mary laughs. "That Lizzy. How is she doing?"

How does she know about Lizzy?

Knox speaks up. "She's great. She's getting married in a few months."

"I do love hearing your stories about her, Jax. I wish to meet her one day."

Jax talks to her about Lizzy?

"She seems like a wonderful girl. Full of life."

"Full of something," Jax mumbles.

Mrs. Mary looks at me and smiles. "Deary. You are beautiful. I'm glad my boys found you. Your parents are wonderful people and, from what I can tell, they raised an amazing daughter. These boys talk about you all the time. You have their heart, so don't break it." While her words carry a light and playful tone, her eyes betray a sense of unwavering focus and determination that rattles me for a second before she smiles again.

"I would never. These men are my everything."

"May I cut the ham?" Emmett asks, holding the knife in the air.

"Yes, but be careful. I don't want you chopping off a finger or something. That knife is sharp."

Emmett smiles and doesn't remind her he's a chef who uses knives every day. Instead, he allows her to be a mom and worry about him, and that causes my heart to melt.

Is there a kink with watching your grown ass adult men being mothered by a woman old enough to be their grandmother? Because damn.

The way they are with her. The way they care for her, talk to her, move around her. She is the woman who took them in when the world threw them away. She showed them unwavering love with firm guardrails, making them the men they are today.

Watching the way they interact is mesmerizing. It's almost like I can see back in time of how they all molded and fit into this home together with her. In some ways, it's like they never left. Emmett in the kitchen, being her right hand with dishes and drinks, fixing her tea exactly the way she wants it without even asking. Knox removing the decorative vintage Easter plates and teacups from the table and setting it for dinner. Jax washing used pots and pans at the sink while Callum helps her to the table.

These men. God, I love them big.

I don't speak much during dinner, letting them have this time with her and her with them. Who knows how many years she has left and I want them to get as much of each other as they can. Tonight isn't about me, it's about all of them.

After dinner, I force Jax to let me wash the dishes so he can join the others in the living room. After several minutes,

Emmett comes into the kitchen as I'm drying the last dish and wraps his arms around me from behind, and places his cheek beside mine.

"You aren't talking much. Are you bored?"

Turning my head just a little, I give him a kiss on his cheek. "I'm having a wonderful time. I simply love watching all of you together with her and I want her to have this time with you all and you all with her."

He gives me a squeeze, then turns me around and presses his hips into mine and grabs me under the chin and tilts it up. "I love you." He doesn't give me a chance to say anything before his lips press against mine and his tongue slides in.

My arms wrap around his neck as our kiss deepens, then he pushes me away, eyes dark like coal.

"We need to stop."

Smiling, I give him a quick peck, then push him further away.

"I'll help you put up the dishes."

"Emmett, go spend time with her. I'll handle this."

He looks down at the bulge in his pants. "I will help you put up dishes."

Ten minutes later, we're sitting in the living room with the others talking about the guys growing up and all the trouble they used to get into. Before realizing it, it's midnight. Callum and Jax help Mrs. Mary to her bedroom, while Knox, Emmett, and I clean up the miscellaneous cups and plates from a coconut cake she made for dessert. I've never been a fan of coconut cake in the past, but hers.... Wow! She insists the trick is to let it set for three days.

I'm really glad we could see her tonight and I look forward to spending more time with her tomorrow. I think we're taking her out for the day. We're going to take her to get her hair done, then take her to one of her favorite restaurants that she's very excited to take Emmett to, then finish the day at the center they opened in her name last Easter.

KNOX - BRO TIME

A HOLLOW SPACE EXISTS in my chest that Everlee usually fills. My fingers are almost raw from pressing the channel down button on the remote, but nothing grabs my attention.

Jax sits beside me on the couch, and I fall over and put my head in his lap. "Hold me. I miss her."

He shoves me off. "Get the fuck outta here. She's been gone for three hours."

"But it feels like forever."

"You're a fucking idiot."

My hands press into the seat to help me back up. I flick the television off and toss the remote onto the table.

Emmett walks into the room and quickly assesses the situation, then turns back into the kitchen.

"See. Even he's finding it hard to be here without her."

Jax just looks at me but doesn't speak.

Emmett calls from the kitchen. "I'm fixing us some drinks."

"Is it the one from Ev's parents' house with the ginger and apple cider?" I yell out.

"Yes."

"I don't know if I can," I moan, sadness ripping through me.

"I can't with you." Jax presses his palm on my face and gives me a light shove with a laugh.

Callum walks into the room. "What's going on?"

"Knox feels depressed because Everlee isn't here."

"She'll be home in a few nights," Callum says.

"It's toooo long," I moan. "Our house is just getting more and more empty. First the pups, and now Everlee."

"It's almost been three weeks. Ruby is beyond spoiled with Ev's parents, Lulu we see damn near every day, and Blaze and Sparky are living their best life at the firehouse with Beckett and Will. Plus, Ev said she'll send pictures of Ruby, Blaze and Sparky tomorrow," Callum says, sitting in a chair near the kitchen door.

Jax looks at Callum, then stands up. "I'm going to help Emmett. I can't with him."

Callum laughs and a minute later, Jax and Emmett are walking back into the room, each carrying a drink, with Woodford and Blanton following on their heels.

"Fresh mint and a peach garnish. Everlee would love this," I pout.

"Cal," Jax warns. "Get your boy."

Woodford and Blanton jump onto the couch and start licking my face.

"Down. Down, down, down." Callum claps his hands. "I've told you, I don't want them on the couch."

"Shut up and drink this." Emmett hands me a drink after I redirect the pups off the couch.

"How are you all not upset by her absence?"

"It's one night," Emmett says, brows raised on his forehead.

"She's at Lizzy's bridal shower."

"Exactly," Jax starts. "A bridal shower, not a bachelorette party."

"Oh. Right." I won't tell them I got confused, although they probably already assume.

"And even if it was the bachelorette party, it doesn't matter. She's ours and nothing will change that, even men waggling their dicks in her face. Plus, she's with her brother and her and Lizzy's mom."

"Right, but Betty went with them and that chick is wild."

"Wild?" Jax laughs.

"Fine. It's just that she's in her fertile window right now."

"What?" Emmett's head snaps in my direction.

Jax interjects, all kidding aside. "It's the window before her ovulation where she's most fertile."

"Exactly what he said," I say, thrusting my hands in his direction.

"How many days does this window last?" Emmett asks, setting his drink on the table and sitting on the floor so Woodford and Blanton can jump all over him. It's their early evening routine.

"Anywhere from five to seven days."

"But," Jax points out, holding his finger in the air. "If she just started it today, her most fertile days will be a few days from now."

"Right. Assuming that she's on a normal cycle," I counter, taking a sip of my drink. "Holy shit. This is good!"

Jax brings me back to the conversation. "Normal cycle. Is she on that? When was her last period?"

"Hold on!" I jump off the couch and race upstairs and grab the calendar that is tucked under my mattress. The irony that I'm hiding ovulation calendars and not porn under my mattress causes me to chuckle as I hop down the stairs.

Emmett is rolling around on the floor, growling at the pups when I come into the room.

Jax reaches for the calendar and studies it, counting and double checking my math, then flips back a few months. "Yea. I mean, you may be off a day, just because we don't have a ton of data to go off of. The first cycle was a shorter duration, but the last one held closer to the twenty-eight days."

"Agreed." I sit on the couch beside him and point. "So, if we look at the past few months, then I'm projecting her next period to start around May 7th. Giving it a twenty-seven-day cycle."

"Not May 4th? May the fourth be with us," Emmett says, lifting Woodford into the air.

"Anyway." I roll my eyes and continue. "I know there's still a lot of variables at play, but..."

"I guess we'll just have to fuck her Sunday, and the next day, and the next, and the next," Emmett teases, sitting up and taking another sip of his drink.

"Don't we do that already?" Callum asks.

"Yes, but for fun," Emmett counters.

"I feel like you two are making fun of us."

"We are." Emmett moves up to the couch to sit on the other side of Jax and puts his arm around his shoulder and leans forward to look at the calendar. "With all the writing, calculations, and red, yellow, and black circles, it looks like a thesis paper on the definitions and calculations of gravity or something."

"Gravity?" Jax laughs and looks at him.

"Something. Our girl is not a mathematical equation to be solved."

"This coming from the guy who wants to put a baby in her, maybe more than Knox." Jax tilts his head down, staring at Emmett.

"My method is less numbers, more fucking."

"That's a solid strategy," Callum adds.

"And one I can get behind," Emmett laughs. "See what I did there?"

"Dumbass," Jax mumbles affectionately.

Woodford and Blanton are toppling over one another, playing around one second, and the next, Woodford is bolting towards the door, sliding headfirst into the bells hanging on the knob.

"Knox's turn," Emmett and Jax both shout at the same time.

"I'll take them this time," Callum offers. "Never in a million years did I think we would all be sitting around a calendar talking about ovulations. I've turned the hot tub on and plan on sitting my happy ass in it when I get back."

"No! That's a wet heat and should be avoided!" I yell, nearly coming off the couch.

"Oh dear lord," Callum mumbles, slipping the harnesses onto Woodford and Blanton.

Jax sighs. "Lord help *me*. He's not wrong. I've been doing some reading as well. It could affect sperm count and motility."

"Motility?" Callum asks.

"Movement," I answer before Jax.

Callum opens the front door and pauses. "I never thought you two would agree on something, and if by the off chance you did, I never thought it would be sperm motility and ovulation calendars. It's weird watching you both finish each other sentences. It makes me feel uncomfortable."

EMMETT - SEXY PHONE CALLS

THE MUSIC ALMOST DROWNS out the sound of the bubbles from the hot tub.

"Water feels nice," Callum says, sipping on a freshly made bourbon drink.

"It does," Knox says, taking a sip of his drink. "We need to come up with a name for this." He holds his glass in the air.

"We do," Jax says, staring at the caramel-colored contents, nibbling on a fresh peach slice.

Callum continues with his previous train of thought, ignoring the conversation about the drink. "Wish more than just my calves were in it."

We're all sitting on the edge of the hot tub, not wanting to fry our ball sack. Knox made a point to mention that our balls are on the outside of our body because they can't get too hot. Which then, of course, sent us down a whole discussion of balls, wet heat, and reproduction.

Wet heat doesn't sound as kinky as one might think it is. So now we're all sitting on the edge of the hot tub, letting our feet and shins soak whilst we enjoy my new cocktail. Callum's not happy about it. He's not mad either. He just planned on getting in and soaking tonight until he learned it lowers his baby makers.

Knox continues to turn his glass in his hand. "This thing is dangerous. Like you don't even realize you're drinking bourbon because all the flavors marry so well together. Who ever thought lemon and bourbon together... and ginger?"

"What about Lemon Ginger Zinger?" Jax offers.

"Ehhh." The crowd moans.

"Autumn Elixir. It will cure what ails you," Knox suggests.

"Spicy Lemon Zinger," Jax offers.

"What is it with you and zingers?" Callum laughs, joining the conversation.

"I don't know. I just feel like it zings."

"La za za," Knox chimes.

"Zings, not sings dumbass."

"I was zinging," Knox laughs.

Jax grumbles.

"What do you think Ev is doing right now?" Knox asks, ignoring Jax.

"She's probably having fun with Lizzy, finalizing all the plans and decorations for tomorrow," Callum says, finishing his drink and setting it down.

"Did she send any pictures tonight?" I ask, setting my empty glass down, too.

"No," Knox frowns.

"She's supposed to go visit her parents and brother tomorrow morning," Jax informs.

"What time does the party start?" Knox asks.

"I think it's from two until four."

"Remind me why they had it down there again? It's the end of April, so it's not like it's warm," Callum swirls his foot in the water.

"It's warmer than here, but I think mostly because Lizzy and Ev's parents are there," Jax says.

"Right, but shipping all those gifts," he presses.

Knox laughs. "You're more concerned about Lizzy shipping her gifts back than the wet heat on your ball sack."

"Clearly, I'm taking the wet heat seriously since my ass is parked on the edge of the hot tub versus *in* the hot tub. I was really looking forward to a nice, relaxing soak tonight and then you and your wet heat bullshit."

"How many times can you say wet heat?" Jax asks, shifting his palms on the edge of the hot tub, causing his muscles to flex.

He catches my eye and a wet heat stirs in my stomach, so I quickly look away.

The song switches and we all just quietly listen to it. We've spent ninety-nine percent of the time Everlee hasn't been here talking about ovulation and bridal showers. She has us pussy whipped and I don't think I'd have it any other way.

Another twenty minutes pass and when a cool breeze blows across us all, we take that as our sign to go inside. We didn't get a name for the drink, but between all of them, a working name I will run by the guys tomorrow is Autumn Spice Elixir. It has that fall feel to it.

After a quick shower, I climb into bed and turn the lights off. I thought about sneaking into Jax's room, but didn't want to be too forward or too pushy. I feel like we're past a lot of that now, but still. Things are great with all of us and I don't want to ruin it.

Rolling onto my stomach and bunching my pillow under my head, I close my eyes and let the night carry me away.

"What do you what me to do?" a voice whispers, stirring me from my sleep. Jax? But who is he talking to? The hairs on the back of my neck prickle, but I don't move so I can try to figure out what's going on.

"Go over there. Let me see him," a female voice says.

My eyes shoot open as fury burns through my veins. What the fuck is going on? Jax is in my room with another woman?

"Hurry, before he wakes up," she says again.

"I am." Jax says. The bed shifts under his weight and a glow in my room casts shadows on the wall.

"I am, too," I hiss.

"Shit!" Jax and the woman both say at the same time.

"What the fuck are you doing, Jax?" I yell, rolling over to see Jax on his knees at the foot of my bed, completely nude and cock hard. I have to swallow the ball that immediately forms in my throat, so I can remember that I'm still mad at him.

"Stop. It was my idea," the woman's voice says, but I don't see anyone else in the room.

"Who is talking?"

"Me!" the voice squeaks, and Jax holds up his hand to show Everlee sitting on a bed... also naked.

Rage flashes to an intense heat and my cock shoots to attention.

Jax must notice, because the glow of the phone brushes across his face as I watch his eyes scan the sheet over my lap before he licks his lips.

"What are you two doing?" I prop my hands under my head, trying to look casual, because I'm anything but, on the inside.

"Well, I was missing you all, and Knox and Callum must be passed out, but Jax picked up."

"You were?" There's a hint of flirtation in my voice.

"I was."

"How much were you missing us?"

Jax climbs over top of me and drags the sheets down. The sheets brush across my skin and send shivers through my body.

"Turn the lights on. It's hard to see," she whines.

"Turn the lights on fifteen percent," I command, and the room is bathed in a soft, dim glow.

"Set the phone down. I want to watch." Her hands slide down her body.

"What does she want to watch?" I ask, heart hammering against my chest.

Jax leans forward and reaches across my body to situate the phone on the nightstand. His cock is rubbing against mine and I have to keep my hips planted on the bed, because right now every muscle is screaming for me to press into him and take what it wants.

He leans forward a little more and presses his pelvis into mine and a whimper escapes.

The only thing making me feel better about all of this is the fact he's torturing himself as much as he's torturing me. His arousal drips onto my stomach and… I blow out a steady breath and fist the sheets.

"Is this good?" Jax asks.

"Back up, let me see." He thrusts his hips once before he leans back.

"Asshole," I whisper.

His eyes meet mine and narrow to thin slits before his teeth scrape across his bottom lip. "I know."

"No. You need to angle the phone up a little more. It's cutting off the goods," she says, rubbing her hands up and down her body and between her legs, but not over her clit. She's purposefully avoiding that area.

"We can't have the goods cut off," Jax quips, before he leans over and brushes a few kisses across my chest before reaching over to the phone.

"Such an asshole," I whisper through set teeth as my eyes roll into the back of my head.

He thrusts his hips and his cock rubs against mine, one, two, three, times.

"Goddamn it, Jax," I grind out.

Ignoring me, he asks Everlee, "How's this?"

"Sit back."

He listens.

"Grab his cock."

He listens.

"Stroke it."

Goddamn motherass shitballs.

He listens.

"Yes, that is very good." Her hand strokes around her clit. "So very good. I'm so wet."

"Emmett is already dripping over my hand," Jax says, wrapping both of his hands around our lengths.

"Get the lube."

Unable to control my temper, I blow out a breath. It's in the nightstand drawer.

Jax releases our cocks and slides up my body, placing both hands beside my head as he thrusts his length across mine. The base of our cocks rub against one another as his eyes lock on mine.

"I don't know if we need it, baby. We're dripping with come."

"Kiss him," she moans.

He listens.

His lips are on mine without hesitation, his tongue pressing its way in.

"Emmett, grab your cocks," Everlee pants through heady breaths.

My chest and stomach tighten in a wave before my head pulses for a second. Wrapping my hand around our lengths, I squeeze as I stroke up. Our lips part open at the same time, still touching, as we each suck in a breath. He presses his forehead against mine and his eyes watch me as I continue to stroke us.

"You feel so good," he mumbles.

Everlee's moans are getting louder, so we both swivel our necks to watch her on the phone, legs spread at the camera as she slips her fingers inside of herself and her back arches off the bed.

"Squeeze your nipple," I tell her.

Her eyes pop open as she tilts her head in our direction and a smile spreads across her face when she sees us watching her. She pulls her fingers out of her glistening pussy and rubs her clit with one hand while the other slides up her body and pinches her nipple.

"Harder. I know you're being too easy," Jax says, slowly grinding his hips into me.

She nods and pinches harder, catching herself by surprise. A loud groan filters past her lips until she catches herself and clamps them closed. "Lizzy's in the next room over," she whispers through a chuckle.

"Please don't-" Jax starts to say, but cuts off when I grind my hips against him and begin biting and sucking on his neck.

"I want..." Her fingers are moving faster. "You to come..." Her hips are bucking. "When I do." Her hands are roving over her chest, around her nipples, up her neck.

Jax rides up my body and reaches for the lube in the drawer. He sits up on my hips, balls pressed to mine, and squirts lube in his hand before he strokes it over our cocks. Both of our hips clench and grind when his hands fall to the base.

"I want to be inside of you," Jax murmurs.

"Come." I wink.

He laughs, shaking his head.

A moment later, his lubed fingers are working my entrance and once again, I'm gripping the sheets, head turned to the side watching Everlee. She's slowed down and is watching us, teeth biting on her bottom lip while her fingers play between her legs.

"Are you edging yourself, love?"

"Not on purpose. I'm just waiting for you both." She smiles and blinks slowly.

Jax lifts my legs into the air and notches himself at my entrance. Our eyes meet and he pushes in slowly, getting just his head in before he pulls out. He pushes in again, this time getting further and pauses at the tight ring of muscle, then slides out.

"Jax." A low grumble rumbles through my chest.

"Jax," Everlee scolds.

He presses in again, holding nothing back and the sound that comes out of me is a cross between pain, pleasure and something else entirely. "Fuck, Jax." Goosebumps erupt across my entire body and my head tingles.

His breath shudders as my ass takes him fully. "Goddamn E."

"Fuck him," Everlee hums, finger moving faster.

His thrusts pick up faster and faster and then his hand wraps around my still-lubed cock and he strokes with each thrust.

"Jax."

"Yes!" Everlee moans.

"Ev?" Jax asks with just a word.

"Yes."

"E?"

"Almost."

Jax thrusts faster, his hand grips tighter, and slides quicker across my impossibly hard dick. I feel like it's going to explode and shatter like a glass dildo. Between him in my ass, stroking my cock, and Ev moaning and issuing commands in my ear. FUCK. ME.

"I can't wait," Everlee cries out as her orgasm crashes around her. Her legs open wide and her hips buck off the ground before her thighs snap shut around her hand.

"Oh. Fuck, fuck, fuck." Jax stills inside of me as he comes.

He pulls out a second later and slides down the bed, taking my cock in his hot, wet mouth. He sucks me in twice and I thrust, hitting the back of his throat and then I'm shooting down it.

"Jax!" I cry out, hands gripping the side of his head as I unload in his mouth. He swallows me down, then glides up my body and kisses me.

Everything and everyone is silent for a moment as we all catch our breath and let our bodies come down off the high.

"Thank you, boys." Everlee breaks the silence a few minutes later and we both turn our head to look at her. "I'm going to go now, but when I get home... we're doing this again, in person. Love yuns bunches." She winks and shuts the phone off.

"Yuns? I love her," I mumble.

"I do too. And you. Asshole," Jax says.

Caught off guard, I laugh. "What was the asshole for?"

"It just felt right." He gives me a quick kiss on the forehead. "Shower with me?"

"Always."

EVERLEE - GINGER BLAZE

LIZZY'S BRIDAL SHOWER WAS... how did Lizzy put it? Over the top. Wowzers banowzers wonderful. Which made me feel good. I feel like so much of this last year has been about me, so I was ecstatic we could spend the entire day focusing on her and her upcoming wedding and my promise to myself is to spend the next six weeks focusing on all things Lizzy.

Betty, Lizzy, and I rented out the house the guys stayed in last Easter which was weird being back in there without them. I think that's why I opted for the late-night video with Emmett and Jax.

Lizzy's mother flew in from wherever she's been living now and helped my mom decorate. The backyard of my parent's house was decorated with white tables and tablecloths, and bouquets and bouquets of flowers. Mom insisted I let them handle the house and decorations and my job was entertainment, since we didn't have a lot of gifts to open- most had been sent to her house before the party, so she didn't have to ship them home.

We did the traditional bridal shower thing, but I came up with a fun idea. Everyone wrote their advice for Lizzy and Tony on a sheet of paper and then we put it in a little wooden boat and pushed them out onto the lake behind my parent's house. It was so beautiful when all the boats were out on the little lake with the sun shining overhead and all the fresh buds of flowers on the trees. It looked like it came straight out of a movie or picture.

All was going well until I realized I didn't have a plan to get the boats out of the water. As the wind blew, it shifted some of them to the banks where we could lift them out, but it took us close to three hours… so… that was a fail. But in traditional Lizzy and Everlee fashion, no good deed and whatnot, and then when you add Betty to the mix…

Most people gave up, but of course we didn't and we had the most fun. Fortunately, this all happened at the end of the shower, so most said their goodbyes, grabbed a thank you gift, and left.

Mom tilts her chin down and points her finger at me. "If you all need a ride tonight, please call me. I don't want anyone driving after they've consumed beverages. Even if it's midnight. Or past. It will probably be past, won't it? Late?" She holds up her hand to stop herself from rambling. "You know what… it doesn't matter. Point is, call me."

"Thank you, mom."

"Thanks Mama McKinley," Lizzy says, giving her a hug.

"I'll watch over them. Are you sure you don't want to come with?" Betty asks, shifting her black and pink bedazzled fanny pack on her waist.

Lizzy and I saw it and gave each other a look, but didn't say anything. Betty is Betty.

"No. I'm going to stay here and catch up with my friend here. I haven't seen her in so long." Lizzy's mom walks into the room with her hair pulled back and some comfy pajamas on.

"Well, if you change your mind, let us know," Betty says.

"Ready, ladies?"

"Choo choo." Betty thrusts her fist in the air. "That's the party train, and she's a chugging." She walks towards the door, moving her arms and shoulders around like they are the wheels of a train.

Lizzy looks at me and her eyes get big with excitement.

Lord, I hope we don't get in trouble tonight. This isn't the bachelorette party...

We arrive at Will's and Beckett's house fifteen minutes later. We opted to leave our rental at their place and call a ride share. Beckett suggested we bring a change of clothes and toothbrush in case we don't make it home tonight, so...

"How was the shower?" Beckett asks when he throws the door open.

"Faboush!" Lizzy says, throwing her arms above her head and jutting her hip out.

"Sorry we couldn't make it, but we weren't invited." Beckett cuts his eyes at me.

"Oh stop. It was a bunch of prissy wedding gift stuff."

"I'm gay. We're gay." He points between him and Will before stepping out of the way so we can walk into their house. "We like prissy."

"Noted." I don't waste my time arguing with him because it won't get us anywhere.

"Ok, we don't like prissy," he admits when he sees this isn't going to be a thing. "So, I assume you didn't eat?"

"No. I figured we could go out to eat then head to where ever it is you want to take us."

Beckett's face pulls into a cheshire grin and my heart beats faster.

"I feel like I should call the guys now and ask for forgiveness."

"Nah, you're good. I've already talked to them."

"You did? What did you say?"

"That's for me to know and you to find out." He boops the end of my nose and my eyes land on Will, who has his arms clasped behind his body. With as big as they both are, I feel like they are our personal body guards tonight.

"Beckett!" I turn my attention to Will, but he just shakes his head and holds up his hands, exiting the conversation.

"Choo choo!" Betty says, slowly moving her arms again.

"Is that the party train? Hold up! Here I come!" Beckett waves his arms in the air and hooks his hands around Betty's waist. "Let's go!" He waves his hand over his head.

"He's all yours," I tease Will.

"Don't remind me." He laughs as we all head outside, then stops.

"Where's the ride share?" I ask, looking at our cars.

"I thought you called them." Beckett points.

"Why would I call them? I thought you called them when we were on our way over," I retort.

"I called them." Will holds up his phone. "They should pull in any second."

"Our hero," Betty coos. "And look at those arms. Hubba hubba."

Beckett throws his arm around her shoulders. "Betty. I feel like you and me are going to be great friends."

Two hours later, we have full bellies and are standing outside of two large black doors with bass thumping from the inside.

"Where are we?" I ask cautiously.

"Is this a sex club?" Lizzy rubs her hands together.

"Ew no. Not a sex club. You think I'd want to go with my sisters?" Beckett's nose scrunches.

"He called me his sister," Lizzy coos, nearly melting into a puddle on the floor.

"He always calls you his sister." I laugh.

"Yes, but we're in public."

"Probably shouldn't have let you take that third shot at dinner."

"Ehh. Who's counting?"

"Me. Me. I'm counting." I loop my arm in hers as Beckett knocks three times on the steel door. The echo rattles my bones. Very dramatic.

The rectangular peephole opens and a pair of eyes peek through, looking at each of us. Beckett and Will hold up their wrists as a black light flashes over it.

Where are we? I feel like it's some prohibition like place, but for naughty things.

The door unhooks from the inside and swings open.

Inside, the music is even louder and lights are flashing. It's some sort of nightclub.

"Where are we?" I ask, clinging onto Beckett's arm, more from excitement than fear.

"Forbidden."

"What is that?" Lizzy asks, clinging to Betty's arm.

We turn the corner and the room opens up to a large golden stage with disco balls and gold and silver streamers hanging down, with tables all around. We pause, taking everything in.

"Shut the front door! A drag club! Yes!!" Lizzy yells.

An announcer calls over the loudspeaker. "Welcome to the stage, our twins, Glitterati and Cliterati!" The music thumps as they strut onto the stage and get the crowd excited.

Lizzy looks at me wide-eyed and mouth open.

"Yeah!" Betty shouts, thrusting her fist into the air. She unzips her fanny pack and pulls out a stack of ones. "Let's get close!"

"We have a table reserved," Will says.

"At the front!" Beckett points to an empty table that is set off at the left center of the stage.

"Did you know we were coming here?" I look at Betty, and she's in her own world dancing to the music.

"No. I thought strip club, but this works too! I've never been to one, but it's been on my bucket list." She calls over her shoulder then screams out when one of the twins jumps into the air and lands in a full split on stage. "Woah! I don't know if I should be excited or massage my hoo-ha."

"Let's go to our table."

Just as we get to the table, they begin to sing *Diamonds Are A Girls Best Friend*. Betty and Lizzy, of course, don't sit; instead, they join several others in singing and energetically waving cash over their head, calling for the dancers to come over.

Beckett leans over to me and whispers, “We have a little surprise planned for Lizzy later.”

“What?”

“I’m not telling.”

“Then why in the hell did you even begin? You know it’s going to bother me.”

“I know.” He laughs and starts rocking in his seat, with his hand on Will’s leg.

“Ass,” I mumble.

He claws the air and hisses at me.

Two hours later, we’re four drinks in and all standing and dancing around the stage, living our best life.

A new queen walks out, and the crowd goes wild. She has olive skin and is wearing a red, glossy firefighter's uniform with a beautiful wig of long strawberry blonde hair that curls and hangs perfectly. “Please welcome Ginger Blaze to the stage.” There’s something about her that feels familiar, but I can’t place my finger on it.

Ginger Blaze walks over to us and speaks into the microphone. “Who do we have over here?”

“We love you, Ginger!” Beckett shouts, with a knowing smile on his face.

Ginger Blaze offers a wink and a smile and bends down on the edge of the stage and holds her hand out to Lizzy. “Lizzy Lulu. Is that you?”

Lizzy looks around, confusion coiled on her face.

“Go!” Beckett urges.

Ginger Blaze pulls Lizzy onto the stage while a fire pole lowers into the center and another performer brings out a chair.

“Now, a little fire house dalmatian told me it was your upcoming wedding, but this is *not* a bachelorette party.” She enunciates the last several words and the crowd cheers.

“What are they going to do?” I whisper to Beckett. I have to lean in close because Betty is damn near crawling up in a chair and screaming. With as much as she's been singing and screaming, it's a wonder she's not completely hoarse.

Beckett shushes me and squeezes Will's leg in excitement.

Ginger Blaze rubs her hand over Lizzy's shoulder, who is smiling and looking at me, trying to figure out exactly what's going on.

I nonchalantly shrug my shoulders and raise my eyebrows, causing her attention to shift to Beckett. He playfully waves at her and then blows a kiss.

"Do you mind getting a little wet? Of course you don't. I've heard your stud is the cat's meow."

"She's wet now!" Betty yells and screams, throwing a few dollars on the stage.

"I LOVE you!" Ginger Blaze shouts towards Betty, pointing her finger.

"I love you!!" Betty yells, waving her arms over her head and throwing a few more dollars.

The music starts and Ginger dances, clapping her hands in the air when the lights go off and a spotlight falls on the stage. *Hot in Herre*, by Nelly starts playing as Ginger moves around with her own version, which blends *to Girl on Fire* by Alicia Keys.

While the crowd claps and sings along, Ginger leans down and whispers something to Lizzy, who nods and smiles, then tosses me a quick glance filled with joy and excitement.

The song changes again to *Set Fire to the Rain* by Adele, and as Ginger walks across the stage, the crowd gets louder. Lights flicker off for a second, and the crowd gets even more wild and when the lights click back on, Ginger is in a skimpier firefighter's costume with a hose in her hand. The lights flash and cracks of lightning and thunder feel the room. *Rain on Me*, by Lady Gaga and Ariana Grande plays and at the 'Rain on me' part, water falls from the ceiling as Ginger moves her hose back and forth.

Bass is thumping, people are screaming and singing, the energy in the room cannot be touched. Beckett, Will, Betty and I have our arms linked around one another, singing and jumping in unison.

Everything shuts off and when the lights come back on, all the queens are on the back of the stage waving at the audience, who are still screaming while Ginger helps Lizzy off the stage.

"That was.... Amazing!!!" she screams, grabbing my arms, then turns to Beckett and punches him in the chest.

"Ow. What was that for?"

"I love you!" She gives him a wet hug and Beckett screams at first, then hugs her back.

With a sudden burst of brightness, the blaring house lights flash on, signaling everyone to leave. "You don't have to go home, but you can't stay here," the announcer calls over the loudspeaker.

As we make our way outside, Beckett is checking his phone. "Are you all wanting to go home or stay out a little later?"

Betty, Lizzy, and I look at one another, then shrug. "What did you have in mind?"

"We have a friend who has a late-night breakfast and coffee shop on the corner."

Lizzy and Betty both look at me and shrug again. Apparently, all the yelling and screaming during the show has caught up with them.

"Yes. I could go for some waffles and coffee," I say, deciding for the team. After that last number, there is no way I can go home and go to sleep.

"She has the best!" Beckett kisses the tips of her fingers.

"Doubt they're better than Emmett's." Lizzy jumps on Beckett's back. He wraps his arms around her legs to hold her up and they gallop down the street with her yelling and screaming.

Guess she didn't lose her voice. A smile spreads across my face.

As Will, Betty, and I follow them down the sidewalk, Betty loops her arm in mine. "Thank you for including me in your fun group and for inviting me this weekend."

"Absolutely! Thank you so much for coming. It looks like you're having fun."

"So much fun!"

We watch Beckett and Lizzy acting wild, and I'm filled with such happiness. I wish the guys could be here with us, but it would have been weird to have them at the bridal shower.

EVERLEE - GOOD MORNINGS

THE SOFT GLOW OF the under-counter lighting in the kitchen filters through the small hallway to the backdoor. I quietly push the door open so I can surprise the guys. The soft click of the latch behind me echoes through the house, making my muscles seize. Slipping out of my shoes, I leave them by the backdoor as I sneak through the kitchen and peek into the living room, where one lamp, on low, illuminates the room. My heart melts like a crayon that's been left out in the sun for too long.

They tried to wait up for me, but they're all asleep. Callum is sitting in the chair by the front door near the lamp with his crossword book that Beckett got him for Christmas sitting in his lap. Beckett got himself and Callum one so they can work on them together. Emmett and Jax's heads are touching on the back of the couch while Knox's head is laying on Jax's lap. It's clear that Jax was one of the first to go to sleep because there's no way he would let him use his lap as a pillow.

Woodford, Blanton, and Luna are in their pen sleeping. They woke up when I walked in, looked at me, then curled into one another and went back to sleep.

This wasn't the welcome home I was expecting, but I'm ok with it. After our flight got canceled, and being in an airport for most of the day, coming home, taking a shower and climbing into bed is exactly what I need.

I pull my phone out and take a quick picture before I walk over to Callum and give him a quick kiss on his forehead. His eyes slowly open and he smiles, grabbing my wrist and pulling me onto his lap before he closes his eyes again with a soft hum.

"We missed you," he whispers, nuzzling into my neck.

"I'm in desperate need of a shower."

He doesn't say anything and I wonder if he's fallen back asleep, but a minute later, he shifts to stand. We walk through the room and he pats Knox on the leg first to wake him up. If he didn't, I was going to. Having Jax wake up with Knox, using him for a pillow, probably wouldn't have been the best. Funny, but not fun.

The next morning, before I even open my eyes, my bed shakes. For less than half of a second, I think it's Lizzy, then remember I'm home.

Home.

My eyes shoot open and Jax and Emmett are lying on either side of me, completely naked.

Startled, I let out a laugh. "Well, good morning."

"Not yet, but it will be," Emmett says, rolling to his knees while Jax pulls down the sheet.

I'm giggling before the sheet gets to my legs in anticipation of their reaction. I didn't put any clothes on last night when I got out of the shower. One, because I was tired, and two because I really love sleeping in the nude with satin sheets, and three, because I was hoping one or all of them would surprise me because I really missed them.

"Everlee McKinley!" They both say in unison.

A heat races up my core and warms my cheeks. "What time is it?"

"Time for you to get a watch," Jax says, leaning in to plant kisses on my neck.

An involuntary moan robs me of my words as Emmett's tongue presses against my clit.

Jax moves down to my breast and sucks my nipple in his mouth and bites, causing me to scream out. The pain turns to pleasure like it always does with him because he reads my body and my expressions like they're his own.

"We really missed you," he says, swiping his tongue across my nipple.

"I missed you all. I wish you could have been there."

"You needed some you time with your friends and family, but next time only half a day, not two."

I can't help but laugh. "Next time it will be a week."

His hand clamps onto my chin and turns it in his direction. I'm trying to keep a straight face, a stern face, but Emmett is working my clit like a freaking magician and my eyes keep rolling into the back of my head as my mouth falls open.

"Jax, put your cock inside of her," Emmett commands, ignoring both of us.

"Yeah, Jax. Put your cock in me."

His eyes darken with an unreadable expression. Heat and something else. Damn, he is beautiful.

When Jax lifts me, Emmett cuts in. "Her back to your chest."

"What are you doing?"

"I'm going to play." Emmett smiles and my stomach clenches.

It takes a second for my pussy to stretch around Jax's girth and take him in, but Emmett is there, rubbing on my clit and helping. The way he watches Jax's cock slip inside of me nearly makes me come.

"Pull out some, Jax," Emmett commands softly, teeth scraping over his bottom lip.

Jax sinks his ass into the bed and pulls out only a little before he pushes back in. I'm still so tight, but the pressure feels amazing with Emmett teasing my clit.

After a few more minutes of Jax and Emmett playing with me, Emmett shifts in between our legs and his eyes meet mine. The raw fire and need in his look causes me to moan.

Fuck.

The things this man, these men, do to me without even touching me.

When Emmett lowers his head, I raise mine to watch him and goddamn. He starts at Jax's balls and runs his tongue up to his shaft to where it enters me, then finishes over my clit, where he sucks it in his mouth for a second.

"Hook her arms," Emmett says and Jax doesn't hesitate, and even chuckles a little.

"No," I whine out.

"That's not going to help you," Jax says.

When I keep wiggling, his legs pull up and wrap around my ankles.

"Fuck her," Emmett growls.

I don't know why he's giving the commands, but I'm here for it.

Jax's coordination astounds me as he not only holds me in place, but rocks his hips. It's like the sexy adult test of patting her head and rubbing your stomach. Only this one brings me joy… and pleasure. So much pleasure.

Emmett continues to lick and moan each time Jax pulls his cock out of my pussy, then sucks on my clit. It's all very slow and torturous. My neck hurts from trying to strain it to watch Emmett.

The pressure of Jax with Emmett's tongue playing with my clit causes tingles to erupt through my body. My body wants to take over and grind and buck, but I can barely move, which makes me want to move even more.

When I wiggling too much, Emmett sucks his teeth, tsking me.

He crawls up my body and runs his cock over Jax's, up to my clit, where he grinds his hips down.

"Did you miss us?"

"Very much," I whimper.

Jax's labored breathing in my ear continues to push my orgasm closer and closer. Knowing that he's getting off on feeling Emmett's cock rub against his while he's inside of me is so freaking hot.

"Do you like us like this?" Emmett asks, taking my breast in his mouth.

"I like you both any way."

"We know," Jax whispers before he sucks my ear into his mouth.

"Do you want us to both fuck you?" Emmett asks while he switches to the other breast.

"Yes, please."

Emmett slides his body up against mine, purposefully running and pressing his cock against my clit as he reaches over to grab the lube out of the nightstand. Feeling feisty, I run my tongue over his nipple ring that is hanging near my face.

He lets out a low breath. "Naughty girl."

"So," I say with an air of defiance.

Emmett rocks back onto his hind legs and begins prepping me, gliding his fingers along Jax's length to stretch me wider. He's playing, pressing his fingers in while his other rubs over my clit, bringing me to the edge. Judging by Jax's breaths, Emmett is bringing us both to the edge.

"E, you're supposed to be teasing her, not both of us."

"Oops." His tone is insincere, with a mischievous gleam in his eyes. He tosses the lube on the bed beside us and lines his cock against my entrance. "Pull out some Jax."

Jax presses his hips up just enough to slide out. Emmett works on sliding his shaft against Jax's as he guides them back in, using his fingers to make it easier. After a few small pulses, he crawls over me and slides all the way in and the pain and pleasure mix and I moan out, gripping the sheets in my hand because it's all I can grab since Jax still has my arms pinned.

"Goddamn E," Jax pants out.

Emmett presses his lips to mine and pulses his tongue in to match his thrusts and I fucking lose it. The slow build and pressure causes my orgasm to wash over me in slow motion.

"Fuck, Ev," both of the men groan in unison.

"It's your fault." I ride the wave, slowly moving my hips as much as I can.

"Your pussy has a chokehold on our cocks."

"Fuck me. Fuck me through it," I moan.

E presses his palms into the bed and grinds his hips, thrusting into me.

Jax groans out, clamping around me tighter. "Your piercings, damn." Jax's hips are thrusting on their own.

"Kiss," I command.

Emmett looks at me, and I slide my head out of the way.

He leans down and presses his lips against Jax's, right in my ear and the thrusts stop, but as their kiss deepens, consuming them, Jax's arms fall from mine and lock into Emmett's hair and their thrusts pick up.

"Yes. Yes." My hands grips Emmett's ass and pull him into me. I want more. I want it faster and fuck, I need it.

My body is buzzing like a live wire, ready to shock at the touch.

"Oh my God. Oh my God."

Their thrusts move faster and I can feel them rubbing against one another inside of me and I lose it.

"Oh my God," I cry out and squeeze Emmett's ass. "Come inside of me. Come. Oh, please." Tears are streaming down my cheeks as another orgasm slams into me. This one, ten times more intense, almost like an angry and ravaging storm that's pissed it didn't get this sort of reaction last time. The other was like a stream moving its way through a flowery meadow with the sun shining down. This one is like a fucking hurricane, dark and stormy and ready to wash out entire villages.

"Shit, Ev!" Jax and Emmett say in unison.

An uncontrollable scream bursts from my mouth as my stomach clenches, sending me up into Emmett's chest.

Both men gasp, and that's when I feel it. Their warm saltiness shooting inside of me, coating their cocks in our combined release as they continue to rub and grind. So slick. So wet.

When they both stop moving, Emmett collapses on me for only a second before he positions his arms, so he's not putting his full weight on me.

After they both catch their breath, Emmett slides out, then pushes me up Jax, so he slides out of me. He glides his fingers into me, so I sit up and watch him.

"What are you doing?"

He presses on my lower stomach and a smile spreads across his face.

"I'm pushing our come back inside of you." His fingers push in as deep as they will go and he wiggles them back and forth before dragging them out.

He does this a few times, playing with our come before he stands, grabbing my legs and lifting, so my ass is in the air. "We're getting you pregnant, love."

"You know that doesn't help, right?" Knox asks, grabbing everyone's attention.

"It doesn't hurt," Emmett says.

"I've been doing some reading."

"Of course you have." Jax smiles and his tone is light and accepting versus his usual jabby, playful tone.

Tilting my head up to look behind me, I find Jax and smile. He shrugs his shoulders and rolls his eyes.

"Did you and Knox make nice while I was gone?"

Emmett lowers me back to the bed so I roll over, so my chest is on Jax's.

"I'm always nice to him."

The entire room bursts into laughter.

"If I didn't like him, I'd ignore him."

"That is some grade school bullshit, brother," Knox chimes.

Jax ignores him and raises his eyebrows. "See."

"You love me!" Knox leaps across the room and onto the bed. "Also, Woodford, Blanton, and Luna are in your room."

"Who let them in there?" Jax asks, cocking his head to the side with a hint of annoyance, but not his usual amount.

"I have no idea." Knox grabs the lube off the bed and flips the cap open, squirting a small dot on the tip of his fingers and pinches them together, watching it ooze out. "They also have their leashes on and said they want you to walk them."

"They said that?"

"Yeah. It was the strangest thing. I was minding my business."

"In my room?"

"I was minding my business and all the sudden these sweet voices just echoed through the room and when I turned around, the dogs were standing there with their leashes on, saying Jax? Jax, where are you? I want you to walk us, dear sweet Jax. When they added the dear sweet, I knew I was hearing things."

"That was the moment you realized you were hearing things?" Jax huffs out a chuckle. "And again, what were you doing in my room?"

"Nothing. Why are you so defensive?" Knox is clearly toying with him, and surprisingly, Jax isn't taking the bait.

What happened while I was gone? Did they bond? They had a strong bond before, almost unbreakable, but there's definitely been a change in their dynamic.

"I'll go with you," Emmett offers, rolling off the bed.

"Yes. Excellent. I will watch over our girl here. Make sure no come escapes."

"Such the gentleman." Jax laughs.

"It's the least I can do. Team effort and all."

Jax shoves Knox's shoulder as he slides off the bed.

"I hate to see you leave, but I also don't love to watch you walk away as much as Emmett and Everlee do."

"You're a dumbass."

"Ass so tight you can bounce a quarter off of it."

"You're pushing it," Jax warns as he walks out of the room.

Knox's hand cups my breast. "Now. Where were we?" He pumps his eyebrows and smiles.

With a sly grin, I run my hand down his hips to his pants. "Do you have a mirror in your pocket? Because I can see myself in your pants."

Knox's hand freezes and his jaw drops, his eyes widening in shock as he slowly turns his head to lock eyes with me.

"If I wasn't already married to you, I would marry the fuck out of you right now." He hops over top of me and rips his shirt off.

CALLUM - THE SQUEAL

THE PEN IN MY hand taps on my crossword absentmindedly. I'm trying to remain calm. Trying to keep a straight face, but I can't concentrate. Just before I came down this morning, I heard Everlee squeal.

Squeal.

In her bathroom.

Squeal!!

And not like an orgasm squeal, but like an excited squeal.

It's been almost two weeks since Lizzy's bridal shower and since we had a fuck fest when she got back. We all had that entire day off and kept her on her back...or knees... or stomach. All. Day. Long.

We massaged her, fed her, fucked her, on repeat. She had breakfast, lunch, and dinner in bed. We didn't spend the entire day fucking her because her pussy wouldn't be able to handle it, but we did love and dote on her. We missed her when she was gone and just wanted to be near her. She told us about the drag show, even though Beckett had already told us he was taking her to one. We all wished him good luck. Taking Everlee, Betty, and Lizzy to a drag show is like giving toddlers ten shots of espresso, then setting them free in a toy store.

Emmett is at the stove working on his quiche and Knox is playing with the pups, while Jax is squeezing oranges to make fresh orange juice.

No one is talking because we've all read hundreds of articles at this point and know we're in the window of finding out if we're adding a little one to the bunch, but only I know about the squeal.

Turning my wrist over, I glance at my watch.

It's been fifteen minutes.

What is she doing?

Simple answer, killing me.

She's probably taking another test. That's what she's doing.

She wants to be certain.

DAMMMMMMN it.

A door closes upstairs, and the pen falls from my hand.

Never in a million years did I think I would be so excited and happy to be a dad. That was never an option for us, so I didn't allow myself to want, but now that I do... I want. I want very much. I want more than anything I have ever wanted in my entire life.

When her first step echoes through the stairway, everyone freezes. It's like we're all connected and they know. Even Woodford and Blanton freeze, which never happens.

She comes down on the last stair, and I watch her, looking for any sign.

"Good morning?" She smiles, letting her words linger in the air, watching us cautiously.

"Morning. I just put the quiche in the oven, so it should be ready in about twenty minutes."

"Thanks. I'm starving."

She plants a kiss on my forehead, then takes a seat at the end of the bar.

There's a palpable charge in the air, and I'm certain she can feel it too.

“How did everyone sleep?” A smile spreads across her lips, and my heart thrashes inside of my chest.

Jax looks at me, then at her.

“Great, Everlee. How did you sleep?” Jax asks, his words staccatoed.

“I slept great.”

“Great.” Jax’s tone is short.

Her fingers make circles on the counter as her smile continues to spread across her lips. “So… you may want to get all the sleep you can now.” She doesn’t look up.

My body tenses as I lean forward in my seat.

“Why is that?” I ask.

She looks up and her eyes are glassy.

“Yeah?” I ask.

“Yeah?” Emmett and Jax say in unison.

“Fucking yeah!?” Knox screams out, thrusting his fist in the air.

“Yeah.” She starts crying and laughing. “I’m pregnant.”

A loud crash pulls our attention. Knox is sliding across the floor on his stomach and two of the pen walls have snapped and clattered to the ground.

“Are you ok?” Ev asks, standing up with her hand still over her mouth.

Knox pops up and lifts her into his arms, spinning.

“We’re having a baby! We’re having a baby.” He stops moving as realizations sets in. “We’re having a baby.” He stands Ev back up. “There’s so much that needs to be done. We need to get the nursery ready, make a short list of names, find a car seat, stroller. Books! We need to read her or him books, but not your smutty ones.”

“What’s wrong with my smutty books?”

“Nothing. Nothing at all. Just need to keep it age appropriate.” His hands rake through his hair. “I need to make a list.” He runs to the office and starts pulling out drawers, calling out something about not finding paper, then runs back into the kitchen. “Digital. Digital list is good and I will share it with everyone so we can add stuff to it and mark it off when complete." He throws his hands into the air. "We're having a baby." He drops to his knees, lifts her shirt, and gives it a kiss. "I'll order some books, so I can start reading up on it now."

"Can you snap the pen walls back in place before you do that?" Jax asks, flicking water at him.

Knox doesn't even bat an eye as he walks over and puts it back together, like his mind is running a thousand miles a minute and he doesn't have time to taunt Jax like he usually would.

With Knox working on the pen, I walk over and wrap my arms around her, bringing her to my chest. We're having a baby. I'm going to be a dad.

Jax and Emmett walk up, so I step back and they both hug her. She wraps her arms around both their backs and squeezes. Knox walks up behind them and hugs, then looks at me, nodding his head, so I walk over again.

We're all hugging one another and just being in the moment. No one talking... just being.

The timer goes off on the oven some time later, breaking through the silence.

Emmett pulls the quiche out of the oven and sits it on the stove while Jax pours everyone a glass of orange juice.

"I don't want to tell anyone yet. It's still so early. I took three tests, and they all came back positive, but I just want a couple of weeks."

"You tell us, babe." I rub her shoulders.

"Ten dollars says Lizzy sniffs it out." Jax chuckles and slides the drinks across the bar.

"Probably. But her wedding is just over a month away. I want this time to be about her."

"She'll know something's up when you aren't drinking."

"That's why I have four delicious baby daddies that are going to keep me plied with non-alcoholic drinks. Plus, when I get happy, I naturally act like I'm drunk, so I've got nothing to worry about there."

It's really happening.

The news keeps hitting me in waves. Like I know what's happening and I'm excited, but then it's like I forget for a second, then remember again.

Emmett chimes in, "Yes, but we won't be at the bachelorette party." He walks to the pantry and brings back a cookbook, positioning it on the counter in his cookbook holder that Knox bought him for Christmas.

"What is that?" Ev laughs, ignoring his first comment.

"It's a pregnancy cookbook."

"A pregnancy cookbook?" She laughs, walking over to flip through it.

Emmett wraps his arms around her and sits her on the counter and brushes the hair out of her face. "Emmett Jr. is a wonderful name."

She laughs and leans forward, pressing her lips to his.

She is glowing. God, she is beautiful. The most beautiful thing I have ever seen.

"There's so much to do!" Knox exclaims, sitting on a barstool, foot bouncing rapidly.

Jax puts his hand on Knox's shoulder with a firm hold and looks at him. "Brother, I'm going to need you to calm down. You're getting antsy and it's putting that energy out in this room and making me antsy. I don't like it. We have nine months. We will get everything figured out."

"Ok. Ok." He's nodding while he speaks, but clearly hasn't calmed down.

Everlee walks over and wraps her arms around him and squeezes tight. After a few seconds, he wraps his arms around her and buries his face in her chest and starts crying. His back is shaking. Everlee's wide eyes shoot to mine and I shrug.

After a minute, Knox pulls back and wipes his eyes with the back of his hand. "I'm so happy, Ev. You've given me, us, something that I never thought we'd have. We've gone through some shit, you know that... but we have a chance... to do it right. To be better than all our parents. To be present and loving. For so long... I was terrified I wouldn't know how to be a father because I didn't have that growing up. Like I wouldn't know how to act, or what to do. But already... already there is this overwhelming desire inside of me to love and protect and be there for this baby." He places his hand on her stomach. "It's like a switch has been flipped, and I would give anything for this baby."

She runs her fingers through his hair and grabs at the root. "You're going to be a terrific father, and don't let anyone or anything make you believe differently."

Knox nods, then takes a seat at the bar.

Emmett waits a second before he slides the sliced pieces of quiche over the counter.

Silence fills the air again, before dings set off across all the phones in near unison. We all check our phones to see a small list of doctors, their addresses, phone numbers and reviews.

"What is this?" Everlee asks, after taking a sip of orange juice.

"It's a short list of OBGYNs in the area that are the best. I've already held interviews with each of them. If you would rather use your current one that's fine, or if you want to look at others, that's ok too. I can send you the full list of the other twenty I've interviewed, with notes on pros and cons."

"Thank you, Knox. This is great." Everlee's hand squeezes his.

"These are also ones that are more... open... to our situation. They will also do house calls if we want."

"This is great. Thank you so much."

"So this is where you've been going over the last two months. Interviewing OBGYNs?" Jax asks, stabbing the last bite of quiche on his plate.

"Yes. I needed to do something and thought it would help Ev out."

"Well, I feel like a jackass," I mumble and everyone looks at me.

"Why?" Everlee asks, walking around to get another slice of quiche.

"Because you have Emmett with his cookbook, Knox with all his research, Jax, I'm sure has done stuff behind the scenes. I mean, all I've done is fucked you."

"Fucked me good, you did, daddy." She winks, making me chuckle.

After several minutes, Emmett says, "I have to go into Bo's today to meet with Colby."

"How's he doing?"

"Good. He's great actually. He's been at Bo's since the beginning and loves the place almost as much as me."

"Doubt anyone could love it that much." Everlee smiles.

"Close." Emmett winks. "But he's the natural choice to take over as management. He and his girlfriend are expecting their first child in a couple of months, so I was a little concerned it would be too much, but he assures me he can handle it. Plus, it's a nice pay raise for him, so the money will help."

"Can you walk away from it?" Jax asks.

"Not that I didn't before, but now I have an even greater reason to. And I'm not walking away from it. I will always be around, but more of an ownership role and less hands on in the day to day. I will still curate the menus and the cocktails, but I won't have to be there daily, managing all the books and such." His eyes meet mine with a knowing glance.

After Easter, we talked about what it would be like, look like, if we moved. Moved away from the busy city and the clubs and Bo's and moved further south, closer to Ev's family and Mama Mary. Over Easter, Ev was so happy to be there with her family, and we had a wonderful time. It would be an enormous step. We have four businesses up here, but we all want to own them instead of manage them now. We want to be present for Ev and our child. Emmett and I haven't brought it up to Jax or Knox yet, because we're still trying to figure out what this all means, but… I don't know. As Ev's parents continue to get older, they won't be able to make as many trips up here, so we'll be making more down there. Plus, it's where we all grew up.

I give my head a slight nod, acknowledging I understand his unspoken message. Honestly, he was the one I was most concerned about not wanting to move.

"So… what are we going to do today?" Ev asks, then adds, "After we have lunch at Bo's."

"Maybe a pleasant walk with the pups. It's a beautiful day out," I offer.

"'Tis a beautiful day out," Knox chimes, walking to the sink to wash his dish.

"I'm going to head to Bo's in a little so I can work with Colby before you all get there, so we can leave after lunch."

"I can drop you off," Knox offers. "I need to run out for a bit this morning as well."

"Care to share?" Jax teases.

"Share, Ev? Always. Share where I'm going this morning? Nope."

"So elusive," Ev says, snaking her arms around his neck.

He twists and pulls her around to sit on his lap, then whispers something in her ear, making her laugh.

Knox pats her hip, signaling for her to stand, then darts up the stairs.

"Where is he going?" Jax asks.

She laughs. "He said… when Jax asks after I leave, tell him I'm going to take a shit. When he sighs and rolls his eyes and mumbles something about me being an idiot, then you can tell him we're out of dog food, so I'm running to the pet store to get more and that he shouldn't be so nosy."

Jax rolls his eyes with a grin tugging at his lips. "Ass wipe."

Ev throws her head back, laughing, like she's just heard the funniest joke. "He also said when you tell him all that and he calls me some name to say, love you too, pookie and I'm not really in the bathroom, I'm working on a new art piece."

"Art piece?" Emmett and I ask at the same time.

"That little shit!" Jax bolts from the counter and races up the stairs.

A loud crash echoes from upstairs, followed by cussing from Jax and laughter from Knox.

"You teamed up with Knox?" I ask, laughing.

"How can you say no to him?"

Emmett chimes in. "I think Jax secretly likes Knox's pictures. If not, he would remove the frame from his bedroom."

"Knox's dumbass would just hang another." I laugh.

Emmett dries his hands and gives Ev a kiss on the forehead before he walks upstairs. "I'm going to see if I need to intervene before I get ready to head out."

EVERLEE - MORNING REMEDIES

THE ACHE PULSING FROM my breasts wakes me up. As I roll onto my back, I glide my hand across the smooth satin sheets, feeling their coolness. The men are gone. Popping my head up, I look across the room and find the clock blaring a bright green 10:02.

Wow. I slept in this morning. I'm in week six of my pregnancy and have been exhausted… and nauseous. I have at least one meeting with the porcelain God every day, although this last week it's been twice a day. The guys have been great, though. Holding my hair back and plying me with water and warm towels.

We have an appointment next week with the doctor to get our first ultrasound and we're so excited. Knox put up a calendar in the kitchen, counting down the days. He's also marked when we should have the baby's room finished, car seat installed, and is making a list of everything we need. I don't know if I have ever seen him this excited.

We're thinking January thirteenth or fourteenth, which will make for an interesting New Year, but we'll find out next week. They had one day this week, but with Lizzy's wedding this weekend, it didn't really work out.

I've been running in between Lizzy and Emmett, helping them both plan last-minute details. The venue is about thirty minutes from here, but feels like hours. It's like someone plucked a French countryside and plopped it near a bustling city. It's absolutely gorgeous. Rolling hills with flowers and an old house with wraparound porch where she can get ready. They offered a location for the reception, but her hearts been set on Bo's. She had the entire restaurant rented out for all of Sunday. The DJ will be on the second level and dinner will be served on the main floor, then the tables will be moved to create space for dancing.

Lizzy and Emmett collaborated on a custom menu, and Emmett, of course, is creating a dish that he will name after her and permanently add to the menu as a wedding gift. I've taken both her menu for the wedding and the recipe card for her special dish and got them both matted and framed. I took my bridesmaid dress so they could match the color of the matte exactly. A deep purple with an elegant gold frame, to match her house décor.

It's crazy to think her day is almost here. It's this Sunday with her bachelorette on Saturday. Somehow over the last several weeks, I've been able to hide the pregnancy from her, which pissed Jax off, because he had a bet with Knox that she'd sniff it out on day one. Because of losing the bet, Jax must participate in a photo shoot with Knox. To make matters worse, Knox insists on displaying the pictures in Jax's massive rotating picture frame above his bed. I've not seen the pictures yet, but Knox has planned a different theme for each week that Lizzy hasn't found out, and occasionally they'll come traipsing through the house. I know one week was a safari theme because Jax and Knox almost got into it because Knox had matching leopard print banana hammocks and a large plush lion with some palm trees.

Even though Jax is angry each week, he still honors the bet, because his word is his bond. After the safari shoot, I talked to Knox and suggested something less... well, just less.

When I get to the kitchen, Callum has a fresh omelet and avocado toast waiting for me.

"How did you sleep last night?" Callum asks. "You were tossing and turning quite a bit."

"Did you rub my back? And did you make this?"

He laughs. "Yes. It seemed to calm you down. And yes, I can cook."

"I think I slept fine. Boobs are really sore, but I haven't thrown up today, which is progress."

He pours a glass of fresh orange juice and walks it around the island, sliding it in front of me before he gives me a kiss on the cheek as his hand slides to my stomach. "I love you."

"Are you talking to me or the baby?"

"Both of you." He boops the end of my nose.

"Where is everyone?"

"Jax and Knox took Woodford and Blanton to the vet for their checkups and Emmett ran to Bo's. He's so nervous about this weekend."

"All that stress can't be good for him."

"I don't think so, but I know he's trying to step back more and more. I think Lizzy's wedding is the last piece really that he needs to cross off."

"Do you think he will ever fully step away?"

"Like the day to day or all of it?"

"Day to day. Hands on."

"I do."

The way he says I do and the look on his face tells me he's had this conversation with Emmett, maybe even recently, because he said it with such confidence.

Callum takes a seat on the stool beside me and props his head in his hand and watches me eat.

"It's rude to stare at someone."

He chuckles. "Do you want me to stop?"

Cutting my eyes at him, I smile. "No."

"I didn't think so." He winks and my stomach tightens. "Are you ready for the bachelorette party?"

Swallowing down the last bite of omelet, I cut my eyes at him. "I don't know how I'm going to do it. I've been thinking about it all week. It would be so much easier if she knows, but I really don't want to take anything away from her day, her weekend."

"Her month."

I shrug. "I'd put her first for a year. She's always there for me and this last year, even more so. Lizzy can be a little much at times, but she's always been so supportive of me, so I don't want her to worry about one thing with this wedding. She's my rock and I love her so much. I will tell her when they get back from their honeymoon."

A wave of nausea passes over me and my stomach clenches. I've always heard of morning sickness, but I didn't think it would be this bad. My breasts are super sore and the nausea...

"I need to lie on the couch."

Callum takes my hand and helps me off the stool and as soon as I'm upright, I feel it.

"Nope. Nope. Nope." I bolt towards the downstairs bathroom. That was such a good omelet too.

Bursting through the door, I take the stance and wait. Callum is behind me a second later with his left hand on my lower back rubbing small circles, while his other hand is holding my hair back.

"Are you sure you want to be in here for this?" It's a stupid question, because he's been by my side almost every time. He's made this bathroom off limits for everyone but me and keeps it extra clean, just in case.

"I would be anywhere with you, love."

Looking at him, I smile. "Goooo-" Nope. Fuck. Shit.

Callum rubs soothing strokes up my back, while I puke up the not so beautiful looking omelet.

Ten minutes later, when my stomach feels settled and I've cleaned up and brushed my teeth, I walk into the living room and find Callum sitting on the couch with my cup of water.

"Here, I made you some ginger-lemon water and grabbed a banana for you."

"I don't know if I can eat. It's gotten a lot worse this last week."

"At least drink some water. I've heard ginger can help."

"You've heard?"

"Fine. I may have done some research to find what helps. I was hoping the omelet would, but I may have to go blander and just do hard-boiled eggs and avocado toast."

"I love you."

"I love you. Now come over here and lie with me on the couch." He holds his arm out, inviting me to come lay beside him.

He's wearing that dangerous combo of black joggers and a white fitted shirt that hugs him perfectly. This man is a sex God, and he's all mine.

My hand slips in his and he pulls me closer and I mold into him on the oversized couch. "Thank you."

He chuckles. "For?"

"Everything." A tear forms in the corner of my eye. I didn't plan on crying, but these hormones.

His hand softly glides around my cheek as his thumb brushes my tear away. "You have given me, us, everything."

His hand slides down to my stomach and lifts my shirt so he can palm it with his hand, his pinky brushing the top of my pants. Stupidly, I suck in a breath, because his hands on me still make me hot.

His chest vibrates with a soft chuckle. "I'm glad to see some things never change."

"Oh, stop." I blush, embarrassed by my reaction to him.

"You know," he whispers. "I'm sure I've read of some other things that help with morning sickness."

My pulse quickens. "Really? What's that?"

"Let me show you." Even though his words were a statement, the tone in his voice was asking for permission.

"Ok," I choke out. My heart races, heating my skin.

His hand slowly glides further down, dipping under the tops of my pants. He lets out another chuckle when he finds I'm bare. "No underwear."

"Why start now?"

He palms my pussy, driving me back into his cock. "Fuck, I love you so much."

"I can feel it. Your love... obviously." I chuckle.

He slides his hand out and sucks his finger in his mouth, then slips it back in, rubbing it over my clit. My hips buck softly at his touch, but his other arm that I'm lying on comes up and hugs me to him, making it hard to move.

"No moving," he says in his dom voice and the wave of pleasure that passes through me from head to toe... Jesus, take the wheel.

His hand glides back down, pausing a moment on my stomach like an apology for what he's about to do to mommy.

Mommy.

Before I can fully process the emotions, his fingers are sliding inside of me and a wave of pleasure courses through my veins. My body moves in response, but Callum hugs me closer to him as he growls softly into my ear.

"Sorry." Not sorry. His growl causes my pussy to throb.

"You will learn to follow the rules."

"You are delusional if you think I will learn now."

His teeth sink into my neck at the same time his pelvis thrusts, pressing his hard cock against my back. His finger pushes in further while his thumb rubs on my clit with tantalizing strokes.

"Callum," I whisper out.

"Everlee." The gravel is thick in his voice as his breaths are short and shallow.

"Put your cock in me, please."

I know he wants to, and God, I need him.

"Will you follow the rules?"

"No."

He chuckles. "Then no cock for you."

"You forget I have a wall full of vibrators and a house with three other men who would happily give me their cock."

"You're threatening me now?" I can hear the smile in his voice as his finger continues to glide in and out of me. He adds a third finger, which is the sign that he's about to fuck me. Preparation is key when he's about to push in hard and fast on the first thrust.

"Never." Ignoring his grip on me, I roll inside of his arms and press my hand to his face. "Just enlightening you. I don't need your cock."

His eyes darken and thin.

He knows I'm lying. I need his cock like I need air to breathe. This is just all part of our foreplay.

My hand slides over his pants and I feel his hard length pressing through the thin fabric of his pants. The smile on his face and the quick puff of air, tells me I just let out some sort of whimper or moan.

"You don't need my cock?" His brow peaks on his forehead.

My head shakes, because I can't form words. The amount of saliva pooling in my mouth could probably make the Hoover Dam jealous.

"So then I can just take it away?" He pushes my hand away.

"Cal-"

His hand awkwardly slides back into my pants. At this angle, he's having to twist his arm all around, but that doesn't stop him from knowing how to please me.

"You're so wet."

"It's not you. It's me."

He laughs. "Oh baby, I don't think that's the case."

I shrug as I reach back down, sliding my hand inside of his pants and wrapping my hand around his cock. Fuck me. It's warm and soft, but hard, and...

"So wet. I think I want a little snack."

"I think I want a little cock."

He freezes. "Did you just call my cock little?"

"What? Oh, God. No. I just. You were like a little snack, so I was like a little cock. Like, fuck. No, your cock is not small." I pause, catching my breath, when I see him smiling. "You're an asshole. I wasn't even paying attention."

"Because you wanted my cock? *Needed* my cock?"

"I repeat. You're an asshole." I smile.

In a second, he's over top of me and ripping my pants off and slinging them to the floor, quickly followed by his. His shirt is still on, which is a shame, but the curves and muscles in his hips and thighs are on full display with all of his ink.

He grabs his cock. "Since you don't need this, what if I just make you watch as I stroke it until I come all over you?"

"Callum."

"Everlee." He thrusts his hips, sending his hard length through the hole in his hand. A bead of arousal sits just at the tip.

He continues to pump his cock in front of me, his eyes closing in pleasure. "Callum," I pant.

My fingers move to my clit and rub, sensations and tingles building inside of me.

"Oh, no you don't. That is mine. Your orgasm is mine. Your come is mine. You are mine."

He drops his cock and slides down, settling between my hips. All playfulness aside, he licks and laps, swirling his tongue over my highly sensitive clit. Bundle of nerves crosses my mind, but I immediately cringe and push the thought away. No bundle of nerves or ball of pleasure. Oh my God. Or nub. Shitballs. Focus Everlee, because your fire rocket love sack is about to send you into orbit.

My fingers latch into his hair, grabbing near the root, as a moan escapes. Callum's hands slide up my hips and splay out over my stomach, pulling from me moan after moan. My thighs clamp to the side of his head like this season's most fashionable pair of earmuffs. My toes point, my muscles stiffen, and it hits me. The glorious fucker hits me, and I let out a scream. Is it silly to think this orgasm is more powerful than others I've had? Like somehow being pregnant makes them more intense?

My hips buck off the couch because he doesn't stop as I try to plant my palm on his forehead and push him away, but I can't. He acts like a rabid dog who has been starved.

"Callum. Callum. Cal. CAL!" I yell out, trying to grab his attention.

It's like a switch flips and he pops his head up, eyes leveled on me and he gives me an evil, sexy, fucking grin. In one motion, he pushes up and slides me down, thrusting into me. My hands shoot above my head and press into the arm of the couch to hold me in place. He drags his length out of me and slams it back in again, and I scream out.

"You feel so good. So hot. So wet."

His hips rock when he pushes inside of me again, and a ripple of pleasure pulses up my spine. Not wanting him to leave my pussy, I wrap my ankles around his waist and hook my feet together.

His smile will be the death of me.

"Ok. I'll stay." He tosses out a wink, with a wicked grin.

Nope. That. That wink and knowing smirk will be the death of me.

He rocks and rotates his hips, so I plant my feet on the couch and try to move with him. The steady rubbing and friction feel good. Too good. My hands clamp on his ass cheeks, holding him to me while I rock on him. Rather, try to rock on him.

"Well, well, well. What do we have here?" Knox's voice rings through the room.

When I look around Callum's shoulder, he's standing by the entryway into the living room with a large bag of dog food in his arms and another shopping bag on his wrist. It's filled with something, but what has me freezing is that it's a cloth bag that says dog dad on the side of it.

His eyes follow mine. "What? Each purchase helps support animals in need."

"So the dumbass bought us all one," Jax chimes from somewhere behind him.

"Don't let us stop you. I'd love to see how this finishes." Knox smiles and nods his head for us to continue.

Callum's forehead falls on mine and whispers, "I was so close."

"Don't stop." I rock my hips and stretch my neck up, finding my lips with his. The kiss starts off slowly, our tongues moving, exploring. Then, as if a blanket is thrown around us and we're thrust into our own private world, all the noises and thoughts of everyone else disappear. Our hips and tongues move in perfect synchronicity. His left hand slides up and grips my breast while he continues to rock. Something about the sensuality of it all sends my body soaring.

Pulling my lips from his, he presses his forehead against mine and we breathe each other in as our orgasms build. The ripple is slow, almost like it wants me to feel every single thing my body feels. The hairs on my neck stand on end, and a tingling sensation begins at the top of my spine and slowly travels down, causing my muscles to tighten. The feeling moves through my hips down to my feet where they point as the wave shoots back up and through my fingers, causing them to clamp onto Callum's shoulders, like they're urging me to hold on for dear life.

My orgasm hits, my back arches off the couch, and I know there's a sound coming out of my mouth, but I don't hear it. My eyes are focused on Callum, who is watching me. His jaw shifts, causing his chin to jut out, his eyes close and his mouth opens.

In a whoosh, noises come back, and his moans fill the air.

He stills inside of me while he catches his breath, then gives me a quick peck on the nose. "How's your nausea?"

Smiling, I return the kiss. "What nausea?"

Jax interrupts the moment of quiet bliss by yelling out from upstairs. "God damn it, Knox! Stay the fuck out of my room!"

A snicker in the room's corner has me tilting my head back to find Knox there, watching us with a grin on his face.

"What did you do?" I ask as Callum pushes off the couch to grab his pants.

Knox's brows pinch. "Nothing. Why do you automatically assume that?"

"Knoxxy baby." I walk over and cup his cheek with my hand.

"You know I can never say no to you, especially when you're standing in front of me naked and pregnant." He kisses my stomach.

"So?" I press, running my hands through his hair.

"I just thought he needed a new picture above his bed."

Callum chuckles as he walks into the kitchen.

"What is it?" I can't stop the smile on my face as idea after idea flickers through my head.

He looks at the pups and his smile gets bigger.

"Knox?" There is a jitter inside of me as the excitement builds.

"It may be me and the dogs."

"That doesn't seem so bad."

"Well, I may be in a thong... on all fours."

"You ass! Get it off!" Jax commands, barging into the room.

"It got you off?" Knox teases, then grabs my hips and positions me in between them.

"She won't be able to save you from my wrath."

"Fine." Knox pulls out his photo and swipes up.

"You can control it from your phone?" Jax is equal parts, surprised and pissed.

"Of course not." Knox holds the phone up. "I just wanted to get a picture of you." He presses the button and bolts out of the room, running up the stairs in the kitchen laughing like a hyena.

"Oh, you stop your smiling." Jax's tone softens.

When I turn around, he's right behind me, so I wrap my arms around him.

"How was your morning?" he asks, holding my pants up.

"Callum was helping me with morning sickness."

"Oh. Is that what he was doing?" He chuckles. "Well, let me know when you have late morning sickness, or afternoon sickness, or anytime sickness." He kisses my forehead and starts to walk away, but I quickly reach out for his arm.. "I'm not going to hurt Knox. Maybe scare him a bit." He winks and darts out of the room.

Callum walks back in with a glass of water. "Are you going to walk around pantless all day? I mean, I don't have a problem with it."

Laughing, I slip my pants on, then take the glass of water from Callum.

EVERLEE - BACHELORETTE PARTY

STANDING IN FRONT OF Lizzy's door, I take a deep breath and let a wave of calmness wash over me.

Nine more days.

Nine more days before I can tell my best friend, my sister from another mister, the best news and two days until her wedding.

Two long, booze filled days, where I'm going to have to lie more than I ever have to her. Tomorrow should be fine because I'll have my guys at the wedding, but tonight. Tonight is going to be damn near impossible. My only hope is to be the very best maid of honor and grab all the drinks tonight so I can quietly get my own.

My hand hovers in mid-air, frozen, as the door swings open before I can knock.

"Bitchhhhhh!" Lizzy is bouncing up and down, looking like she just stuck her finger in an electrical socket. "I'm so excited! What took you so long?" She's still bouncing from side to side. "Ev's here, Kiki!"

"Kiki?" My brow pinches in confusion. I've never heard of a Kiki before.

"Keeley. Kiki is Keeley's alternate personality." Lizzy turns her head and shouts over her shoulder. "The one who is going to let loose tonight and have fun! Maybe find her a new man!" A groan echoes from the kitchen.

"What happened to Mitch?" I whisper, leaning in.

Lizzy strikes her finger across her throat. "Last month."

My face pulls. I've met Keeley several times through Lizzy's parties and knew she was dating a guy named Mitch, who she thought was going to be her forever. They've been together for three years and were talking about moving in together, so the split is a little shocking.

"We've been drinking since two. Where have you been?"

Before I can answer, Keeley is walking up behind Lizzy with a purple feather boa wrapped around her neck.

"Love the skirt!" I say when she gets closer.

"You don't think it's too pink?" She hands us each a shot, then pats her skirt.

"Bubblegum pink suits you plus with the white top and purple boa, you look fire! And your legs!" I fan myself for good measure. "Legs for days."

She smiles, but it doesn't quite reach her eyes. It's probably a little hard being at a bachelorette party for your friend when you thought you were on the way to your own soon after to be back at square one. "Thanks," Keeley says, before turning back to the kitchen.

Lizzy holds her glass out in front of her and I tink the glass. "To an amazing night of debauchery!"

Heart pounding, I don't know what to do or say. I had a semi decent plan worked out for the bars, but I didn't consider the pre-party. She tosses her shot back, so I take the opportunity to toss mine back... and over my shoulder. I hope no one saw, or worse... I didn't check behind me first. Slowly turning around, I find the sidewalk behind me empty of people, but with a nice wet streak spattered across it. For good measure, I contort my face. "What was this?"

Lizzy hesitates for a second, then smiles. "Nothing but the best for you."

My stomach clenches. Why do I have this sick feeling she has her good alcohol down and is doing shots with it? When I walk into the kitchen, I see it on the counter. Her two-hundred-dollar bottle of tequila. It's supposed to be a sipping tequila, not a shot tequila. I'll buy her another bottle to make up for tossing it out.

"Let's do another shot!" she screams and several girls yell out, grabbing both ends of their boas and waving them in the air. Of course, they would want to do another shot. Shit is expensive.

My eyes flick to Keeley, who gives a slight head shake.

"Not now." I laugh, trying to ease into being the bad guy. "We have the entire night ahead of us and we don't want you puking your brains out before we leave the house!"

She loops her arm around me. "Such the mama." She pats my stomach and my breath halts. She tosses her head back and winks. "Soon enough."

Sooner than you think.

"Get this hooker a feather boa!"

"Are we ready to go?" I glance at my watch. We have reservations at six at a local cantina. We thought about doing a nice steakhouse, but she's going to be loud and excited and I didn't feel like getting kicked out or banned for defending her happiness.

"Waiting on-"

"Choo choo!" Betty's voice filters through the living room and she's holding a tray in the air as she dances her way through with Low right behind her, laughing.

"Betty! Low!" Lizzy screams. "Now the party has arrived." Lizzy looks over her shoulder at me and tosses a wink as she flits across the room. She is pure light and joy. I'm sure if you look hard enough, you'd see the glow emanating from around her.

"I've brought Jello shots!" Betty yells.

The girls scream as she sets the tray on the counter. This is going to be more difficult than I thought. If I just bolt for the door, would that be too obvious?

Betty's finger is flicking through the air as she counts the heads. "Oh shoot. Eight. I am one short."

"It's ok. I need to go check in with the driver, but I'll make it up later tonight." For good measure, I let out a celebratory woo as I walk out of the front door, thrusting my fist into the air.

"My angel," Lizzy and Betty both say at the same time, then burst out laughing.

Thirty minutes later, we're walking into the cantina. The music is thumping and lights are flashing. I've wanted to try this place out, but haven't made it here yet. There's a large U-shaped bar in the middle of the room with five bartenders, with high-top tables to the left and regular tables on the right. The walls on both sides have been retracted and open to patio seating as well, creating a nice cross breeze through the room.

"Right this way. We've reserved the patio on the bar side for your party," the hostess says, looking at each of us from head to toe. "Who is the lucky one?"

"This girl!" I fan my arms to Lizzy, whose hands shoot straight over her head as she pops out her hip.

The hostess laughs. "Congratulations. Where are you all headed after this?"

"Wherever the night takes us." I take the seat at the head of the table, letting Lizzy take the middle so the others can sit around her. I'll be next to her all day tomorrow and likely tonight, while I'm holding her hair out of her face while she pukes her brains out. Maybe we can do it together, because my nausea has really kicked up a notch.

Those who puke together, stay together...

"Round of shots!" Lizzy yells.

"You may want to slow down," Keeley says, eyeing me for back-up as Lizzy starts to protest.

"Boo."

"How about this?" I offer. "Let's get some chips and salsa, guac, queso… something on our stomach, and then I'll personally go get a round of shots for the table."

"Fine. I'm just so excited. Tomorrow is the big day. It's finally here. And I'm stressed. So stressed."

I push aways from the end of the table and walk to her, wrapping my arms around her neck. "We need you to be at the wedding and not in the hospital getting your stomach pumped."

"What would I do without you?" she kisses my cheek.

Keeley nods at me and I sit back down and order several of the appetizers and dips to spread along the center. We get waters for everyone and three pitchers of margaritas.

At least it's not shots.

And I told her to make them weak.

Is it a shitty thing? Maybe. But I'm helping make the night longer for my best friend. My hope is that they're already too buzzed to notice.

We gorge ourselves on a delightful mixture of nachos, tacos, burritos, and, likely, all the chips and salsa in the world. I literally don't think I can stuff one more chip in my mouth if my life depended on it.

But I feel good. Nausea has passed, and the baby seems to like it. My hand slides over my stomach for a second, as we stand outside waiting for the limo to pull around.

"Nice night," Keeley says, walking to stand beside me.

She's been quieter tonight, which I guess is to be expected. A person can go two ways I feel like when dealing with heartbreak. The quiet, self-reflecting way, or the balls to the wall, wild child.

"How are you doing?"

She looks at me as if she's reading my face, trying to decipher which question I'm really asking. Is she having fun tonight, or how she's doing after her breakup? Her shoulders slump. "I'm doing ok. It's been a month. This last week has probably been the best. We finally met and exchanged the box of things that were at each of our places."

I want to ask what happened, but don't. The last thing she needs tonight is to fall down that dark rabbit hole.

"That's tough."

She nods. "But in a way, it was a little cathartic. I think part of me kept holding onto the thought that maybe this wasn't over between us. When I saw him, and saw zero emotion in his eyes, zero look of interest, while tough, it was like ripping the band-aid off."

"Well, that's good. Wondering is sometimes the worst part."

"The only thing I may never know is why. I thought we were in a great spot. We were talking about buying a house together, marriage, kids, and then suddenly..."

"Whammo blammo." I smile when Keeley looks at me with her brows pinched.

Nodding my head to Betty, I smile. "She said it to me once."

"Betty seems fun."

"She's the best."

"Lizzy has talked a lot about her."

The limo is pulling around the corner, so we all step closer to the curb. "She is great. A little spitfire."

"I can tell. I feel like we're going to have a lot of fun tonight and she's going to be at the center." She pats the air with a worried brow. "I didn't mean-"

Chuckling, I grab her hands. "All good. You're probably right. She'll probably be right in the center with Lizzy. My job tonight is to make sure we don't end up in the hospital and that everyone stays safe."

"Do you know what Tony is doing?"

"I think he's going to some clubs."

"So no strippers? I would hate for him to make a terrible decision."

"I don't think so, plus I'm fairly confident he won't." One, because Tony is so in love with Lizzy, but also because my guys are there and they won't let him do anything stupid.

Jax has already made it clear to Tony that if he hurts Lizzy, Jax will hurt him.

"I don't think so either, but you never know when guys get around other guys." Her words trail off just as the limo driver comes to a stop in front of us. "Lizzy said your guys are with him."

My head snaps in her direction.

She laughs. "I hope it's fine she told me."

I nod, still unable to speak.

"Four. I can't even get one." She laughs awkwardly.

"It will happen when you aren't expecting it."

"Hope so." She climbs into the car and that's the end of our conversation. The music is blaring and champagne is being passed around.

Betty fills up the glasses, but Lizzy cuts her off when she gets to mine. My heart stops in my chest as I watch her.

"Only give Ev a splash. She doesn't like champagne and I don't want to waste it."

"You know me so well, boo."

Lizzy pumps her eyebrows and blows a kiss at me before thrusting her glass in the air.

"I just want to say…" She swallows and I can see her eyes starting to glisten, which will make mine, so I blink fast and look at her forehead. "Thank you so much for coming out with me tonight. This has been a long time coming, and I can't believe the day is finally here. I'm getting married tomorrow." She lets out a deep breath. "I'm getting married," she repeats. "We're going to have the most fun tonight as we say goodbye to the last day I'm a single woman, before that handsome man of mine puts a ring on it." She flashes her hand, twisting it back and forth, then jiggles her glass before bringing it to her lips.

Glancing at the splash of champagne in my glass, I hold it up and then drink it back. When I hand the glass back to Betty, Lizzy's eyes are watching me. Trying to break whatever the look is she's giving me, I blow her a quick kiss then tap on the window divider separating us from the driver.

JAX - BULLSHIT AND BULLIES

WE'RE THREE HOURS INTO this bachelor party, and I want to beat my head against a wall. We drove an hour to the marina where Tony's best man rented him a yacht for the night with a private chef and half-dressed women to deliver the food and whatever else anyone asks for. Two of the men have already disappeared several times. Tony, however, has been great. He's barely looked at the women, which is smart. If he did, I'd pluck his eyeballs out, put them on a skewer, toss them on the grill, then make him eat them.

Honestly, he seems a little... irritated. Most of his groomsman are single and the ones who have a ring on their finger seem like complete douchebags, but apparently, they went to school together. So, yay, frats and shit. They're treating this like a party night for them instead of celebrating Tony.

If we weren't parked in the middle of the ocean, I'd find some excuse and leave. Hell... I may still do it. The shore doesn't look that far away and I've swum longer.

"Don't do it." A hand slides onto my shoulder.

Knox.

"Do what?" I ask, turning to face him.

"Jump overboard. It's too far."

"No, it's not."

"You could do it if your life depended on it, but you're out of shape." He pats my belly and smiles. "We'd both hate if I had to save you."

"Shut the fuck up." I shove him in the shoulder and laugh.

Emmett walks over and places his hand on both of our shoulders. "I'm dying. What are we going to do about this? Tony looks miserable and his groomsmen are too worried about getting their dicks yanked than celebrating him."

"I say we throw the groomsmen overboard, move the yacht, then bet on which one gets back to the boat first," I propose, only half kidding.

Knox's eyes light up, then looks over his shoulder. "I call dibs are Mr. My-Biceps-Are-So-Sore-From-My-Two-Hour-Arm-Day guy."

"Why would you want him? He has to swim numb nuts."

"Because his arms aren't sore. He didn't work out for two hours today or yesterday. Hell, probably in at least a week."

Emmett looks over his shoulder. "Fine. I got Mr. I-Don't-Know-Which-Stock-I-Should-Buy."

Knox agrees. "Solid choice. He's got nice legs."

"You're an idiot," I mumble.

Callum walks over. "What are you three up to?"

"We're about to throw those douche canoes over the edge of the boat and then place bets on who makes it back first," Knox says, thumbing over his shoulder.

"Ooh." Callum rubs his hands together. "I've got Mr. High-low."

"Is that the same guy as I-Don't-Know-Which-Stock-I-Should-Buy?" Knox asks, brow furrowed, like it's the most serious conversation we've ever had.

We all look towards the group of men huddled on the other side of the boat.

"Blue shorts, nice legs?" Callum asks.

"Yep." Knox claps. "You can't have him, Emmett called him."

"Damn. Fine, I'll take Pink-Shirts-Are-For-Real-Men."

Knox puts his hand on Callum's shoulder. "Yeah, he's not making it back to the boat."

"Why do you say that?"

"I'm pretty sure he couldn't make it a lap in a kiddie pool."

"Damn." Callum frowns.

"Who do you pick, Jax?"

Knox seems way too excited, like maybe he's really planning on throwing them over the boat. I wouldn't put it past him. He's got a little bit of crazy in him and sometimes forgets to look at the line before he crosses it. Especially with pranks. He's the guy that always takes them a little too far and doesn't realize it until it's too late.

When we were heading out for training, the dumbass thought it would be funny to empty a bag of beef jerky in my suitcase before we got in the car. So my luggage sat in the blistering sun for hours, then got on a plane for another several hours, got lost for a day. When I opened my suitcase, I cleared out the bunks and thought a skunk had climbed in and died. Pissed was an understatement.

Another time, the dumbass took a banana that was rotting and hid it in the wall of my room. Little did he know that the hole he dropped the banana into was getting patched that day. It took us three weeks to figure out where the smell was coming from. He thought I'd found it and thrown it away the same day he placed it. Nope. That shit was almost liquid.

"I may throw I'm-A-Trained-SEAL-Who-Is-The-Biggest-Pain-In-Everyone's-Ass, in."

Knox turns to look at the other group. "Who, over there, is a SEAL?"

"No one. I'm talking about you, dumbass."

"I'm not over there."

"Jesus, fuck." I reach towards Knox and grab his shoulders and lift to pretend to throw him in, but in typical Knox fashion, he makes a scene.

"No, daddy. No! I'll let you put it anywhere you want," he yells out, then wraps his legs around my waist.

"You're a dumbass."

The other guys look with amused smiles on their face.

"I'm sitting you down," I bark out.

He waits a beat, then unhooks his legs.

When I look at Emmett, he has a shit-eating grin on his face and I just want to wipe it off. "Shut it," I warn.

"What? I didn't say anything." Emmett laughs, shrugging his shoulders.

"What do you think Ev is doing right now?" Knox asks.

"Probably making sure they all don't get arrested," I mumble. Those three spell nothing but trouble when they're together and then add in the other ladies I don't know...

"Everything ok over here?" Tony teases, walking over, hands spread out like he's on guard.

"All good. Jax thought it would be funny to throw me in. But if I'm going in, so is this guy." Knox pats my chest.

"Pretty sure if anything happened to any of you, Ev would kill me. She seems sweet on the outside, but I bet she has some kick ass on the inside."

"She's a black belt," Knox coos proudly.

"Yep. Exactly why I'll never cross her," Tony laughs.

"Did you all say you're thinking about going for a swim?" High-low asks, sticking his head into the conversation and the others follow.

I should remember their names, but I don't like them, so I don't care.

"No, Jax here thought it would be funny to throw me in."

"We'd come get you," High-low taps his friend's chest with the back of his hand.

"Kind. So very kind. But I'm like a fish in the water."

One guy in the back snickers and I can see where this is going, and it pisses me off. Not because of where it's going, but because they doubt Knox's badassness. Only I'm allowed to make fun of him. Not these dickwads.

Brilliant, witty, Knox must sense it in the air, because his back straightens. He's always been great at sniffing out bullshit and bullies and these guys reek of both. They were the jocks who walked around campus with a stick shoved up their ass, thinking they were the cat's meow with their hair parted to the side and the popped collar bullshit.

Knox continues to push a little further after seeing the reaction after his last comment made. "Pretty fast, actually."

High low laughs, "Bryce here was state champion, two years in a row."

Without batting a lash, Knox steps forward, sucks on his teeth and looks Bryce, also known as pink shirt, up and down like a headmistress would inspect a rambunctious student sure they've been up to no good, then simply says, "Nah. I don't see it."

Pink shirt obviously steps back offended.

So Knox, being Knox, doubles down. "I don't see it. You may have been state champ twice when you were like ten, but you probably can't swim all that good anymore."

Bryce's friends all laugh, while several looks of anger and surprise sweep across his face.

"Let's go!" Bryce says. Arrogant, macho asshole.

"In there now?" Knox is a master manipulator. I fucking love him. He hones in on people's buttons and taps them just enough to get a reaction from them, guiding them along the path Knox wanted them to go all along.

"Unless you're scared."

"Brother, I'm not scared."

"Then let's go," Bryce unbuttons this shirt. When Knox doesn't move, Bryce's temper flares. "Well. Aren't you going? Backing out? Scared?"

A little hothead. Knox is going to wipe him.

"I was going to stay dressed to give you a chance."

Bryce's friends ooh and ahh.

"No. When I wipe your ass, I don't need you coming up with excuses." He reaches his arm into the air then starts flapping them across this chest.

Knox turns to look at me. "He's going to wipe my ass." He turns back to Bryce. "That's kind of intimate. Are you going to watch me shit too?"

Emmett chimes in, "He's always been a bit literal."

"I'm not actually going to wipe his ass. What the fuck?" Bryce mews in disgust.

Knox's lips pinch. "Damn."

"Let's go then." Bryce flicks his wrist in the air as he stands in nothing but a pair of silk boxers with a neon-colored paisley design on them.

"Fine." Knox sighs and yanks off his shirt, causing buttons to go flying. "I really liked that shirt, too."

"You could have unbuttoned it." Bryce rolls his eyes.

"You seem to be in a hurry to get beat, so…"

"Fuck off."

I almost think I can see steam pumping out of Bryce's ears.

Knox's pants puddle at his feet as he steps out of them.

Arm's-So-Sore chokes. "Dude, he's a fucking SEAL."

Bryce looks at Knox, "What?"

"The tat." Arm's-So-Sore points to his chest, where Knox's tattoo is.

Bryce backhands the air and dismisses it.

Arm's-So-Sore asks, "Are you all?"

Callum answers first, then Emmett. "No, I'm a chef."

The fourth guy in the back who's been quiet most of the night gets excited. "Bro, I thought I recognized you from your pics in those magazines."

"What?" Bryce asks.

Apparently, Bryce forgot every other word in the dictionary since all he can keep saying is what.

"Cooking magazines," the guy in the back answers, stepping forward with a smile on his face.

Bryce's laugh is condescending, causing my fists to tighten at my sides, and a second later, I feel a hand on my shoulder. I know without looking it's Callum.

"Maybe you could have cooked for us tonight," Bryce comments, and Tony's eyes shoot at us with a worried glance.

"Come on Bryce," Tony urges.

Bryce throws his hands up in the air. "I'm all good, man." He takes the beer that's been dangling between his fingers and tilts it up. "Let's go, bro! My man is getting married tomorrow!"

"Maybe you shouldn't do this Bryce," Tony suggests.

"I'll be fine. State champion, right here." He thumbs at himself.

"Yea, like twenty years ago," Arm's-So-Sore says.

"Fifteen. And whose side are you on?"

"Yours, of course," he drones out like he's been asked this question a thousand times.

Knox hops over the railing with ease and jumps up and down a few times, shaking out his arms. "Where to?"

"That buoy and back," Bryce points out.

"That's far."

"Scared you can't do it?"

"Oh, I can do it, no problem. I'm scared you can't and then I'll have to haul your drunk ass back to the boat."

"Don't you worry about me." Bryce bends down and touches his toes. "Oh, yeah." He smells the air. "Did I mention I've been swimming again? Doing laps every morning at our country club's pool? Started last week."

"I don't think you mentioned that. You must *really* be in shape then."

Knox's words are delivered with just the right amount of fuck and off.

"On my mark," I say, since I'm the closest.

"Get 'em," Emmett encourages.

"Hoo-yah!" Knox chants back.

"Around the buoy and back. First to climb back up wins."

"Let's go." Bryce stretches his arms into the air.

"Three... two... one... Go!"

Both guys jump into the water, with Bryce getting a longer dive than Knox. They swim several strokes and are fairly close, but as they continue to swim, they fade away. It's dark out tonight, and the light from the crescent moon isn't enough to light that far out.

When I glance over my shoulder, I find Emmett being chatted up by the guy from earlier. When he sees me looking, he tosses me a wink.

The other guys come to the railing and start screaming and cheering for Bryce. The splashes from their hands cutting through the water start to fade and sound like nothing more than waves crashing off in the distance.

"Let's go Knox," I shout.

"Cheering for Knox?" Callum walks up beside me with a dopey grin on his face.

"Tell him, and I'll deny it."

Callum laughs, then grips the handrail, his voice dropping. "You think Ev is ok?"

"I think she's great, but probably not having as much fun because she's so worried about Lizzy finding out."

Silence stretches between us and out in the distance I see a head pop up near the buoy with a muffled shout following quickly behind. It disappears and about a minute later, another head pops. Knox must have been the first one around.

The guys beside me get louder in their cheering and clapping as slaps of the water get louder and louder. My eyes strain to see anyone or anything in the water, so I try to focus my hearing. Minutes pass and Knox should have been back my now, or at least visible.

Hands gripped tightly on the rail, I lean forward, staring into the darkness, trying to find Knox's stupid little head. But there's nothing. I don't even think they're swimming anymore.

The guys beside me are cheering and laughing, sipping on their beer without a care in the world.

"What's wrong?" Callum asks, picking up on my concern.

Emmett is over with Tony a second later.

"Quiet." I wave towards the guys, but they don't stop. Straining to hear, to see, to anything... heart pounding in my chest, I grab the one guy that is being the loudest by the throat and shove him backwards. "I said to shut the fuck up."

"What's wrong?" Tony asks, worried laced in his voice.

"They should have been-"

"Jax!" Knox cries out from an unknown distance away.

"Shit! Stay here!" I command before leaping over the railing and into the water blindly. It doesn't matter though. Knox needs me and Knox will get me.

The cool water bites against my warm skin, feeling like razors. Flashbacks of our cold-water training come crashing into me. Probably my least favorite of all the things we did.

"Knox!" I scream out, searching, but still not seeing.

Another second passes. "Jax."

Knox's voice comes from up ahead and to my right, so I make the adjustments and push forward.

Pausing, I listen for any sign, but all I hear is the water lapping against the edge of the buoy in the distance.

"Knox?" My pulse is pounding through my ears. If that little shit gets himself hurt or worse, I'll bring him back to life then kill him myself. He's Knox fucking Fisher. His life doesn't end doing a swim around a buoy off a yacht at a bachelor party.

"Here! Here!" Knox slaps the water to grab my attention.

Three strokes and I'm in front of him. "Are you ok? What's wrong?"

"I'm fine. It's Bryce. Grab him."

"I'm fine," Bryce grumbles through chattering teeth.

"He's weak. He won't be able to make it back."

"I can if you'll just let me go!"

"Fine!" Knox says, exasperated, throwing his hand in the air and letting go of Bryce's arm. "Let's go."

Knox starts kicking back towards the boat with ease. He was always better with the cold-water exercises than I was. He always used to tease me and say it should be the other way around since my heart is so cold… then when he wouldn't get a response, he'd pretend like he just had the greatest idea and say it's because he's so warm and full of energy, he's able to withstand the cold longer.

Bryce makes two strokes and dips under the water.

"I'm not dealing with your macho man bullshit. I'm helping you back to the boat if I have to knock you out and carry you. So just shut the fuck up and take the help or you're going to die or worse, get me hurt. I've got a lady and a baby waiting for me and I don't intend to miss a second of that life because you're a fucking idiot." I grab him under the arm, roll on my side and start kicking. Bryce kicks some, which helps. "Knox, get back to the boat and get some warming blankets ready."

"On it."

Knox kicks hard and fast.

"I could have made it," Bryce says through chattering teeth.

"You couldn't. You may be a national champion or whatever, but we've trained for this… for the cold. There was never a chance you'd win, not when the water is this cold."

"It's June."

"And this isn't the Florida Keys."

EVERLEE - CLUBBING

WITH A QUICK FLICK of my wrist, I check the time. It's almost midnight and I'm about ready to pass out, but I won't. Not tonight.

"Drinks!" Lizzy says, laughing and dancing in the middle of the crowd with her paper napkin headband crown thing that Betty made her. Since we didn't get a sash for Lizzy, Betty made her a napkin crown she could wear around. About an hour ago, Betty persuaded the DJ to let her on stage. Betty climbed up, seized the microphone, and announced to the entire club that it's Lizzy's last night of freedom before she ties the knot. The club cheered, and the DJ played a remix of Let's Get Married by Jagged Edge, which then sent the entire room into a frenzy.

"On it!" I walk over to the bar and wait patiently. At this point in the night, the bartender knows me because I've been ordering all the drinks for our party.

When a hand slides onto my shoulder, I stiffen and turn around, ready to knee whichever jackass thinks they can touch me, until I see it's Low.

"What are you doing?" she asks.

"Getting some drinks, you?"

"Are you getting ones with alcohol in them this time?" She cuts her eyes at me.

I've been caught.

"How far along are you?" She smiles.

"I don't know what you're talking about."

She laughs. "You forget a couple of things. I'm a bartender, so I know a weak drink when I taste it. Orange juice and grenadine? And the guys have been talking non-stop about putting a baby in you since December, and then all the sudden silence for the last several weeks."

"Don't say anything. I want tonight and tomorrow all about Lizzy. I will tell her after."

"You don't think she knows?"

"She hasn't said anything."

Low laughs. "That chick knows everything about you. She's been watching you like a hawk tonight."

"No."

Low cuts her eyes at me and twists her lips.

My eyes search the dance floor and find Lizzy in the middle of her friends, eyes on me with a worried brow.

"Shit."

Low laughs. "If I didn't know she was utterly in love with Tony, and you had your harem of men, I'd think you two were lovers. The way you're connected. It's kind of sweet and kind of creepy."

A chuckle escapes.

The bartender walks over. "What can I get you?"

Low orders, while my eyes watch Lizzy from across the room. She smiles and waves, then keeps dancing.

I've been worried this entire night about her finding out, only to find out she likely already knows, because really... why wouldn't she? She knows when I have sex. Surely she could sense when I'm with child.

Low taps my shoulder. "Carry your shot."

"What is it?"

"Lemon drop," she winks at me, then carries the tray of other shots through the club like a pro, with a tray balanced on her hand, way above her head.

When we get to the crowd, she brings the tray down and all the women grab a shot.

"To the last shot of the night before we take little miss home so she can get some rest before her big day!" Low's voice carries a unique blend of affection and authority.

Lizzy snarls playfully before cheersing the air with the shot glass, then tossing it back.

"Timer is set, Lizzy Loo. Twenty minutes," Low says.

"Come on, Mom." Lizzy's eyes sparkle. She's truly radiant.

"You made me be this person, Lizzy. You said I was the only one bitchy enough to get you to leave."

"That doesn't sound like something I would say." She laughs, reaching for my hand, so I give it to her and she pulls me in.

"It does," she whispers. "I totally said it."

"I know. I was there."

She throws her head back, laughing. "You were. This last shot was more potent than the others."

"Low got lemon drops."

"And you were getting?"

"Sex on the beach."

She nods and I think she's going to say something about the drinks or me being pregnant, but one of her favorite songs starts playing and she screams and jumps around. Although at this point in the night, they all seem to be her favorite.

"How are you doing?" A light singsong voice chirps from beside me.

Keeley.

"I'm good. How are you doing?"

"Fine. I was hoping to find a man here tonight to help take my mind off dickface."

"I had a dickface once. Went to a club with Lizzy and now I'm married to four guys. So be careful what you wish for."

Keeley laughs. “I keep hoping. I mean, not four, or even long term. But something to distract or take the pain away would be nice.”

“Who knows? Maybe you’ll find someone at the wedding tomorrow.”

“A girl can dream.”

Grabbing Keeley’s hand, I drag her over to the middle of the group and we dance. We dance hard for the next nineteen minutes. It takes Low three extra minutes to get Lizzy out of the club, which ended with Low throwing Lizzy over her shoulder and walking out. A few people were concerned at first until they saw Lizzy laughing.

On the way home, we stop a local late-night breakfast diner and grab all the eggs, bacon and pancakes we can stuff in our mouth.

When I tell you it’s the best bacon I’ve ever tasted… I nearly orgasmed.

CALLUM - QUICKIE

A COOL BREEZE GLIDES over my thigh as Ev slides the sheet out of the way and climbs into bed. The smell of lavender and honey dance around me as she tucks her little body up against me, throwing her leg over mine.

My hand glides up along her thigh until it's clamped around her bare ass. She lets out a little giggle and I'm done for. Everything about this woman has me falling.

"Everlee," I scold with a smile that won't stay off my lips when she's around.

"Callum." She sucks in a breath at the end, no doubt feeling my cock hardening under her leg.

"How was your night?"

"It was good. I just got out of the shower. Needed to wash the club off me."

"How was Lizzy?"

"She's good. I think she knows, but she didn't say anything. And Low knows."

"Low?"

"She called me out for giving the group orange juice and grenadine shots."

A chuckle slips past my lips as I pull her on top of me. Her nipples lightly graze across my hard chest as she props her chin up to look at me.

"She's also the one that told me Lizzy knows. I had a little bit of champagne."

Even through the dim light from the under bed lighting, I can see her pull her face.

"It was barely a sip."

"It'll be fine."

"I know, but..."

"It will be fine." My hand brushes the hair behind her ears before I cup her face and stare at her. "I love you, Ev."

"Is everything ok?"

"Yes." My cheeks hurt from how much I'm smiling. "I just missed you tonight. I know it's not very sexy to want to be around you all the time, but God I miss you when you're not around."

"I think it's very sexy." Her tone drops sensually low as her finger swirls on my chest.

"You do?" I ask, as my hands clamp onto the sides of her hips and shift her up a little so her pussy slides over my cock. A tingle shoots through my body and a switch flips, but I have to fight losing control.

She lets out a little hum with a playful grin tugging at her lips. She knows what she does to me and even after all this time, loves pushing my buttons. "How was your night?"

"It was good. Tony's friends are dicks. They rented a yacht with a private chef, which was nice, but also had half-dressed woman there to serve food. They seemed miserable, which pissed us off a little. Before we left, I passed them our business cards in case they wanted to do something different."

I know people on the outside may think there isn't a difference in what they were doing versus coming to work at Allure or Vixen, but even though Allure is a sex club, it's about empowering women to take control. If you want guys to look at you, it's because you want it and not because you're trying to make a quick buck.

"That's nice. We could always use more talent."

"If they call, we can have Low interview them and see what their interests are."

She gives a little wiggle when my finger glides up her spine to that spot between her shoulder blades that makes her squirm.

"Knox and Jax ended up in the water. One guy thought he could race and beat Knox in a swim. Water was freezing so the guy couldn't make it back so Jax had to help bring him back in."

"I bet he wasn't happy about that."

"It's Jax, so no. And to make it worse, he thought it was Knox in trouble, so of course, Knox is on cloud nine right now and giving Jax hell."

"I hate I missed it."

"The yacht was nice, though. Maybe we can do that for our vacation one year. Take a yacht to the Caribbean and sail around from port to port."

"That sounds nice, but this year we have the beach house again."

"That's why I said one year, not this year." I boop her on the end of her nose.

She plants her hands on my chest and pushes to sit up. She's a vision, legs spread around me, her perfect breasts hanging there begging for a hand to hold them, her nipples already hard and waiting to be pinched.

Her wet hair falls to the side as she watches me, watching her.

"You're beautiful."

"Will you still think that when I'm out to here with our kid?" She holds her hand out far in front of her.

"I will think you are beautiful every day for the rest of our lives."

Her hand clamps around my cock and slides up with a firm grip as her hips rock on the base. She's wet, so she slides along it easily.

"Do you like that?" she asks.

Tucking my hands behind my head, I watch as she rocks her hips on me and slides her hand up and down my length. "I always love watching you take what you want."

Her hand moves in sync with the rocking of her hips as she gets herself off on my cock.

"Callum," she cries out, but I don't move.

Her hips rock faster and faster, at pace with her hand. I'm going to come before I even get inside of her.

"Put it in me." She moans out.

In a second, I have us flipped and her on her back. I drop between her legs and run my tongue up her center and over her clit. She's drenched. As soon as I suck her clit into my mouth, her legs clamp around my head and she bucks her hips off the bed and rides my face, taking her orgasm. Her pussy is still pulsing when I slide my cock into her. She cries out, pressing her head into the bed. Her moans and the slick thwap of our skin meeting become our soundtrack as I pound into her over and over again, urging my own release along.

Tonight's not for taking time and drawing out the pleasure. Instead, it's about feeding our beasts and making them happy. We're both tired, but the beasts get what they want.

"Callum." The word puffs out in a weary exhale. A plea. A feeling.

"I'm coming, baby girl." And with that, my balls tighten and my stomach clenches. A wave of euphoria washes over me as my release explodes inside of her.

A second later, I collapse and fall to the side of her, our breaths shallow and erratic.

"Well, I didn't expect that," she chirps after a few minutes.

"Expect what?" I roll to my side, propping my head on my bent elbow.

"Sex."

"You came in here naked and crawled into bed."

"I was hot after my shower and never sleep with clothes on now... it's a waste of time."

There are no words, so I kiss the tip of her nose. "Go pee and then we can cuddle when you come back in."

"Yes, sir." She salutes me.

"Keep it up," I threaten playfully.

"Yes, sir," she says, lower and more seductive.

"Ev."

"Sorry daddy."

She squeals and takes off for the bathroom with her hand cradled between your legs, laughing the entire way there.

A few minutes later, we're both cleaned up and lying in bed with the fan on high and the sheets laying over our ankles.

"I love you," she says quickly and buries her face into the crook of my neck.

"I love you too, babe."

EVERLEE - BEST MASSAGE EVER

WHEN I GET DOWNSTAIRS the next morning, there's a glass of freshly squeezed orange juice and an omelet waiting for me at the bar. All the guys are in their usual spots, except for Emmett. He's not here.

"Good morning," Jax says, standing up and wrapping his arm around my waist, planting a quick kiss on my head.

Even though it was a statement, it sounded like a question.

"Morning. Where are you going? And where's Emmett?"

"Emmett's freaking out about today, so I'm going to check on him, then probably head out with him to Bo's and make sure everything is perfect."

"Ok. Give him my love."

"I will." He tosses me a wink.

"Did you have fun last night?" Knox asks.

"I did, and I heard you got a little wet?" I laugh.

"Did I?" He laughs. "I heard you were *also* wet."

My scowl turns to a grin when he looks at Callum, then sticks his finger through the hole he makes with his thumb and forefinger.

"Childish," Callum mumbles, going back to his crossword puzzle.

Knox laughs, then goes through all the events of last night. I don't stop him or tell him that Callum's already told me because he seems excited and I love the way he tells stories. The look in his eyes and the energy that pulses through him is infectious.

By the time he's done, he looks at my plate. "Are you still hungry? I can fix you some toast or another omelet."

"Toast sounds great."

"Avocado?" he asks, standing from his seat.

"No. Grape jelly." I smile. I just had this sudden craving for grape jelly toast. It reminds me of my childhood.

"Three slices of grape jelly toast coming up."

"I can maybe eat two, not three."

"One's for me." He winks.

My bridesmaid dress is hanging on a hook by the back-door. When Callum sees me looking, he answers my unasked question. "Brady picked it up for you this morning. What time do you need to head out?"

"Well, thank him. That was on my list this morning."

"I know." His smile causes my stomach to tighten.

"I'll finish up these delicious pieces of toast, then probably head over to her place. Limo is arriving just before lunch to take us out to eat, then we're going to get massages. Oh, shit." A sudden realization slams into me.

"What?"

"I was reading an article yesterday about dos and don'ts. I can't have massages until after the first trimester."

"Oh. And you can't tell Lizzy."

Even though he said it as a statement, because he knows there's no way in hell I'm going to tell Lizzy on the freaking day of her wedding, it still needs confirmation.

"No. I'm not telling her. Tomorrow, yes. Today, no. Damn it!" An exasperated sigh blows out.

"Ok. So maybe you can tell the masseuse in private after you go into the room."

"Just spend the hour talking?" I laugh at the ridiculousness of it.

Three and a half hours later...

"You'll definitely want suppositories and some pads," Lucinda says.

We've been talking for the last thirty minutes. She looked at me a little funny when she walked into the room and found me still dressed and sitting on the table. She was nice enough to elevate the head of the table so I could lie back on it. Then she gave me a warm towel for my face and played with my hair for a little while. It got repetitive, even though it was nice, so I told her she could stop. So now she's giving me a list of everything I'll need after pregnancy, but what everyone's going to be too shy to tell me. She also suggested I smear Vaseline on my stomach every night, then wrap it in plastic wrap to keep it all in.

"These are great," I say, typing the last thing onto the list on my phone I've started making. I have several. One to ask the doctor this week, one of things I know I want to get for the baby, and the last is things I'm going to need.

"Yeah." She shifts in her seat, switching the leg she's sitting on. "I wish someone would have given me a list like this when I was expecting."

"Well, it's very helpful."

"When's your due date again?"

"I'm thinking somewhere around January thirteenth."

"Oh man! Just missed having a New Year's baby."

"Oh yeah. That would have been pretty cool."

"All the news crews there and articles being written about you, dad, and baby."

"Oh." My voice trails off. Maybe not so cool. How would that work? Mom and daddies and baby. Hello world! I can see the headlines now. We'd be viral for so many reasons.

"You have really soft feet," a muffled voice echoes through the wall, and Lucinda and I both stare at one another.

"Did they just..."

Lucinda's hand covers her mouth, then whispers, "Yes. That's Leni's room. She had a rather..." she uses her arms to show large and bulky, "man with a bald head. He looked like Mr. Clean or something."

"Well, he has soft feet," I tease, chuckling again.

"You wouldn't expect it... a man that large."

We both giggle and pause, listening for anything else, but the voice softens.

"What if they heard us?" Lucinda wonders.

"Oh no. What if they *heard* us?" My cheeks flush red as a heat moves up my chest.

"Well, if he's having kids, he'll know what to get his woman." Lucinda giggles again.

A soft gong chimes from her phone, and she looks at me. "Oh, it's time. Come here," she says, standing from the seat and walking towards me. She runs her fingers through my hair, tossing it around a few times. "There. Now it looks like we've finished with the best head massage of your life."

"Thank you. I know this wasn't what you were really expecting."

"No honey, but it's ok. I've enjoyed my time with you."

She lowers the bed, then says, "Once you're dressed, you can step into the hall and I'll have some water waiting for you. Coconut or regular?"

"Coconut, please."

I roll to a sitting position and let my feet dangle for a moment, stretching my neck and arms. It may not have been a massage, but it was still very relaxing. Wanting to wipe a towel across my face, I grab the now cold towel that was under my neck and wipe my face quickly, pinch my cheeks, then grab my things and head into the hall.

It's empty except for Lucinda, who's standing there holding a bottle of coconut water. "How do you feel?"

She plays the part so well.

"Great. Thank you." My head tilts down, showing my sincere thanks for what she really did and *is* doing.

"You can head up front. I believe Lizzy has already paid for everything."

I slip her a twenty.

"Oh, I've already been tipped. It was part of the package."

"This is something from me, though. Best massage ever."

She giggles, then takes the money. "Thank you." She bows her head and leads me to the waiting room.

I find a seat and wait, rubbing my hands over my stomach. There's a baby inside of there. Our baby.

The door creaks open startling me and Lizzy walks out, eyes in a daze, hair a mess with a look like she's just had the best fuck of her life.

"Lizzy babe, are you ok?"

She walks over to me, arms hanging like limp noodles. "That was the best massage I've ever had," she moans.

I wrap my arm around her neck. "I'm glad you enjoyed it so much."

"How was yours?"

"Amazing."

We sit on the love seat for a minute while she lays her head on my shoulder.

"Ev," she starts, her voice low in that kind of tone, like she's about to ask something or say something that may be weird.

Hesitating a second before I answer, I glance at the top of her head. "Yeah?"

"So, I know-"

The door opens and Keeley and the other two women in her bridal party walk out.

"Later," she says, pushing off my lap and giving me a quick kiss on the cheek. "I love you."

With that, she pops over to the girls, throws her hands in the air and gives a squeal.

Ten minutes later, we're three doors down and at the salon to get our hair, makeup, and nails done.

Sitting in the chair in front of the mirror, I've looked at her a few times through the reflection and can't help but wonder what she was going to say.

She knows something... was she going to tell me she knew I was pregnant?

"What are we doing for you today?" the stylist asks, running his fingers through my hair. With a name like Sven, I feel like he's going to do an amazing job, whatever he does.

"Let's go for something different."

KNOX - DONNA'S STUD CALENDAR

WOODFORD AND BLANTON ARE sitting pretty with their tails wagging on the floor. "Don't you two look so handsome? Are you ready to see your sister today?"

"You put them in bowties?" Jax's voice booms from behind.

"We're going to a wedding. They need to dress up."

"They're dogs."

Gasping, I bend over and put my hands on the outside of their combined heads. "You don't listen to him. He's being a poopy pants."

"Bowties. Nice," Emmett says, walking into the room.

"Are we ready?" Callum asks, walking in behind Emmett. "Are we bringing them?"

"Lizzy sent a note and said Lulu is going to have a pen set up there so we can bring ours so they can play together," I say, grabbing their leashes from the peg. "Then I told her I would bring them back here to play on the way to Bo's."

"What, no dress for Luna?" Jax snarks.

"Jax, dear boy. I didn't want it to get wrinkled on the way over there. I will dress her in the car when we arrive."

"Fucking i-"

"Intellect," I cut him off. "I think that's what you were going to say. Remember, Emmett and you talked about this. Using our nice words today, not our grumbly words."

Emmett pats Jax on the back, who shrugs his shoulders.

"I have about this much patience for his bullshit, then no more." He holds his finger and his thumb in the air with the smallest amount of space between them.

"You always say that, but you love him riling you up just as much as he loves doing it. You are the peanut butter to his jelly." Emmett laughs.

Jax has spent most of the morning with Emmett at Bo's, making sure everything is set up. He said he was going to keep an eye on Emmett, but I think part of him, though he never will admit it, wanted to make sure it looked great for Lizzy. I've seen the way he treats her. It's with the same love and affection he has for me. The whole hates-that-he-loves-us sort of thing. It's sweet. My little softy.

When we get to the venue, there are valets waiting in the semi-circle drive. There's a red carpet that rolls from the curb along the sidewalk, up a few stairs and through a set of double doors to the other side of the building. Both sets of doors are open, revealing white chairs and a flowered arch on the other side of the thin, but wide building.

"Wow." The scene behind the arch is beautiful. Hints of mountain peaks are painted into the sky in the distance. Grabbing the camera from around my neck, I snap a quick photo. We're some of the first to arrive.

"Boys!" a woman's voice shouts and when I look up, Ev's parents are walking along the front of the building from the far right.

"What are you two doing out here?" I ask, snapping a quick picture of them.

"Sit," Jax commands and the pups sit immediately, even though their butts are swaying ever so slightly from side to side with bottled excitement.

"We thought we would take a little walk before this shindig starts. Just getting back. Oh... look at them." Donna's head tilts to the side as she walks up to us, giving each of us a hug and a kiss on the cheek before she squats before the pups. "Look at Luna in her dress and these boys. Which one is Woodford and which one is Blanton?"

The pups are about to lose it, but Jax has been working with them diligently over the last several months and made us also adhere to his training, which sucks. But I'll admit, they are very well behaved and have excellent recall.

"Left is Woodford. He has a little white tuft of hair on his forehead that's getting smaller the older he gets. My little boy is growing up."

"Oh, Knox!" Donna bats the air, giggling. "You are just too funny."

"He's something," Jax adds.

"Have you seen my Ev?" She laughs again. "I guess she's not mine anymore."

"No. She left first thing this morning and has been with Lizzy. It's been an entire afternoon of pampering and getting ready."

"I bet they're just having a blast. Becks said the bachelorette last night was a success. He said he and Will met them for breakfast at some ungodly hour."

"It was just after midnight, darling," Dave chimes.

"Seems late," she mumbles.

I loop my arm in hers, and we walk towards the building. "Ev didn't mention she saw the guys last night. Are they here yet?"

"Yes. We saw them before we left for our walk. Becks was, of course, walking around, critiquing all the things he loved and wanted to do for their wedding. Only a couple more months." Donna sniffles, then pats her nose with her free hand.

"Everything ok?"

"I just... this year... what a year." She laughs. "I know technically you all got married last year, but it feels like this year and now Lizzy and in a few months Beckett. Life is moving so fast."

She'll completely flip when she learns Ev is pregnant. It's one thing she's wanted since before we were married. But I can only imagine as soon as she finds out, she'll be asking when the second one is coming and then the third and fourth and so on.

"It has been, but it's all good things."

"Absolutely. I want a dance with each of you tonight. Need to work out these legs before they get too old." She pulls her arm from mine, pats my cheek, and walks over to a seat that has a man's jacket draped across the back of it.

"There's Lulu." I point to a pen that someone has set up in the back corner behind the last row of seats. She's barking and wagging her tail, and nearly jumping over the edge of the pen, but Beckett pops his head up and looks at us.

"Woodford! Blanton! My boys!" He shouts, hopping over the pen, and patting his legs.

"Am I chopped liver?" I ask, skipping towards him, knowing the pups aren't budging until they get the command from Jax.

"When it's between you and them..." He pauses, watching them sitting steadily beside Jax. "Oh, come on," he whines a little, flopping his hands to his side.

Just as I'm about to reach him, I hear Jax say, "Free." The dogs barrel past me, tails wagging as they skid to a stop at Beckett's feet.

Looking over my shoulder, I scowl at Jax, who has a sinister, yet playful, smile on his lips. "Ass," I mumble, which only causes him to throw his head back, laughing.

"They're so trained," Beckett says, lowering down to rub their ears and head.

"They have Jax."

"I should have brought Blaze and Sparky up here to see their family."

"Maybe we can get them together this summer at the beach or something."

"Lizzy said she got the same house we had last time."

"Yeah, Ev was talking about that. Six dogs in one house."

"Maybe I can swing by and get Ruby on my way up and get them all together."

"Can you imagine?"

"Heaven," we both say at the same time, then laugh.

Beckett stands up and brings me into a hug. "How've you been, brother?"

"Good. Great. I heard you crashed Lizzy's party last night instead of coming to hang out with us."

"I didn't know if you all were still on the yacht." He wiggles his fingers in the air and juts out his hip with sass. "Or, if you were home. Lizzy had been texting pics most of the night, so I knew I was safe there."

"Whatever," I huff.

"I'll hang out with you all night at this wedding until you're tired of me."

"My wish come true." I clasp my hands together and bat my eyelashes.

"Outstanding! Then I'm done here," Will laughs as he walks up.

"Oh stop. You know you would miss me?" Beckett coos, reaching out for Will's hand.

"Unlikely." His eyes twinkle with happiness before he looks at the pups. "Woodford and Blanton clean up nice. Love the bowties," Will says. "And Luna's just walking casually around in a dress, making sure everything's in order. Love it."

"Knox and I were saying we're going to get all the pups together at the beach next month."

"Oh lord. Does Jax know?" Will asks, pulling his face.

"Know what?" Jax asks, walking up.

"Nothing," Beckett and I shout at the same time.

"Yeah. Nothing sketch about that."

Needing to change the topic, I turn back to Will and Beckett. "Are you guys getting any ideas for your wedding?"

"Figured we would let Emmett handle it all." Beckett laughs.

"No. Please no. He's been a wreck for the last month," Jax says.

"He does parties all the time," Beckett presses.

"Yes. But family. He holds that as a very special job. Everything has to be perfect."

Beckett clutches his chest. "Be still my heart."

"I heard my name," Emmett says, walking up to us.

"All good things, all good things."

"Man, you boys clean up nice." Beckett fans himself when Callum walks over.

"Thank God I'm confident and secure in our relationship," Will teases.

"It's ok love bug. You know I only have eyes for you."

"Lucky me."

"Oooh," Donna squeals from behind. "All my men. Woo!" She fans herself. "Squeeze all in. Let me get a picture of you. So many boys. Who would have thought?" Her words taper off near the end like she's talking to herself, and I hear Beckett chuckling behind me. "All so big and handsome," she still mumbles to herself.

"Come on, Mama McKinley!" I urge her to join after she takes a few photos.

"Oh, I couldn't." She blushes a bit.

"Go honey. I'll get a picture of you. Get some different poses and we'll make you a hunky calendar."

"DAD!" Beckett yells. "I'm standing right here."

"Then you can stand right over there." He points to his side. "If you have a problem with that. Your mother is old. Give this to her."

"Bite your tongue, Dave. I've not got me any grandchildren yet, so I'm not too old." She turns and puts her hand on my chest and whispers, "I mean, I am getting older and older by the second, so let's make haste. Yes?"

"You got in Mama McKinley."

She turns towards the front. "Hurry up and take the picture, Dave. These men don't want to be standing out here smiling all afternoon."

"I'm trying, woman. You just stay still and smile."

"Oh hush, Dave." She puts her hand on her hip. "Tuck your chin Beckett."

"Mom," he huffs, and I burst out laughing.

"I love you all." My chest tightens, but only for a second as the feeling washes over me.

"Ok," Dave calls.

"Please send those to us, Donna," Callum asks.

She cups his cheek. "Yes, darling. Of course.

"Donna, dear. Do you want to grab our seats? There are a lot more people heading in."

"Yes. Although Lizzy put us with family. I think you're up there too. Bless her." Donna clasps her hands in front of her.

"It should start soon, barring anything crazy happening," Will says.

"It's Lizzy," Jax and Beckett say at the same time.

EVERLEE - BUSTED

"I CAN'T DO THIS!" Lizzy exclaims, and my heart drops.

"What?" I set my flowers down and rush over to her. "What's wrong?"

"I can't get this darn girdle thingy up my leg. My dress keeps getting in the way!"

"Ok. Well, let's use less dramatic exclamations on your wedding day."

"Huh?" She looks at me, face twisted in confusion. "Oh. Oh! Oh my God! Why would you even think that? I told you weeks after I started dating him, I was going to marry him. Now get on your knees, bitch, and stick your hand up my dress." She throws her head back in a loud cackle.

Someone clears their throat by the door and I turn to find Beckett. "I think I should leave you two alone. I knew this day was coming. Just thought it was going to be before you married a man," he laughs.

"No. You get your ass in here. Let's get an usie!"

Beckett plops on the bed and they put their heads together.

"Preferably not with my hand up your dress."

"No. That's what makes it great." Lizzy laughs again. I've seen her happy, but I don't know if I've ever seen her *this* happy.

She hops once to scoot closer to Beckett, which puts my hand uncomfortably close to her vagina. A garbled warning pours out of my mouth, but I'm so panicked it's just a mixture of sounds, like a baby learning they have a tongue for the first time.

Running my hand around her leg to confirm the bow is in the front, I slip my hand out. "Your *garter* belt is good to go."

"Oh, yeah. That's what it's called."

"Yes." I laugh and join her and Beckett on the bed for another, better, picture.

"Are you ready, sis?" Beckett asks, looking at Lizzy.

"I'm so ready, Becks. I love him big. Have you seen him yet?"

He nods, then fans himself and Lizzy squeals.

"I want to go marry that man, then fuck him and make a baby!"

"You could have stopped at man."

"Nah. That leaves out all the erotic details," Lizzy laughs again, giving Beckett a hug.

She pulls back, then grabs both of our hands. "You." She stops as tears fill her eyes. "Gahhh," she moans. "I told myself I wasn't going to get emotional."

"Have you met yourself? You let emotions run over you like a freight train." Beckett shrugs his shoulder into Lizzy's.

She smiles, then squeezes our hands again, and takes a deep breath. "You both have been there for me, helping me through so much. When we had to move to that new podunk town," she laughs. "That's what I called it at first. I was so mad we had to move and I *hated* it. But I walked into school that first day and I saw you. I saw *you* Ev, and I thought, wow, she does not know how to dress. But I knew. I knew we were going to be best friends, like I know I need oxygen to live. What I didn't know is that I wasn't only making a best friend, but that I was getting two. Sure, Becks was a little younger than us, but he was always there." She squeezes his hand. "I love you both so much. You both are my rock when I need a place to lean on. You've been there through all the ups and downs in my life and you've never faltered with your love in me once. For that, I'm so thankful. I just want to say that I love you all so much. You are so much more to me than friends or even family. You are a part of me, and I will love and cherish you forever."

Tears stream down my face. "Damn hormones," I mumble to myself as I pat my face.

I can literally feel the air shift. Like it's all been sucked out of the room.

No one is breathing.

I just freeze, hoping if I don't move, that will somehow cause time to rewind a little.

Lizzy bolts upright and stands in front of me with her hands on her hip.

"Everlee Elizabeth Fisher McCall Monroe McKinley!"

I don't want to look up, but she's like a freaking wrecking ball, so I know there's no use in prolonging the inevitable.

When I do, her eyes are wide and I can hear her feet click click clicking on the floor under her dress like a bottle rocket wobbling in its bottle before it shoots off, but you're not quite certain if the bottle is going to tip, so your heart beats a little faster.

"Say the words," she commands.

I shake my head.

"You say the words right now, hooker."

"I'm... pregnant."

Lizzy looses her mind screaming and throwing her arms in the air. "I'm going to be an auntie!" She lifts me into a hug.

"I really didn't want to tell you yet. This is your time, your special day. I totally didn't mean to say what I said just then... please... I'm sorry."

"Bitch please. I've known for a while."

"What?"

"I just needed you to say the words so I could talk about it."

"You knew?"

"You knew?" Beckett asks. "Also, congrats, sis."

"Yes. Girl. The glow you've had for the last several weeks. The fact you've been calling me less. Seriously, what the fuck? And I definitely knew after last night. First, you chuck my good tequila over your shoulder."

"Sorry." My nose scrunches. "I didn't think you saw. You didn't say anything."

"Girl. I had to let you live in your fantasy."

"That's why you stopped them with the champagne, too?"

"Well, partly, but also because you *don't* like champagne. It was also *good* champagne. I didn't want you trying to toss it over your shoulder in the car."

We both laugh.

"Oh, and my favorite. Those shots last night. Girl, I was trying to get drunk. Hard to do with orange juice."

"Damn. I really thought I was tricking you."

"Not at all. The first one got me. I thought I was just super drunk, but then realized what you were doing."

"Why didn't you say something?"

"Because I didn't need to get wasted, and I wanted you to feel included."

"Liz, last night, today is *your* day. The whole reason I didn't want to say anything was so we could bask in *your* day."

"Psshhh. Girl, like I just said. You are more to me than just a friend or even family. You are part of me. I mean, if you didn't want to be so selfish, we could have discussed this so we could be pregnant at the same time."

"Oh god no. That would be horrible." Beckett chimes.

"I love you." I hug her as tears flow down my cheek.

"I love you." She pushes me away. "Now we have to hurry. The quicker I get married, the quicker I can make hanky panky."

My chest warms with heaviness, and it feels like a weight has been lifted off my shoulders.

"So no one knows?" Beckett asks. "Like mom."

"Ha. No. She'll lose her mind. We're still early. Roughly six weeks. We have our first doctor's appointment this week."

Lizzy grabs my hands and squeals, face beaming.

"Can we please stop talking about this now? I really want to focus on you and your day."

"Oh fine. If you insist. Your make-up looks like shit, though. We need to get that fixed."

CALLUM - BREATHLESS

THE MUSIC STARTS, WHICH means our girl will be walking down the aisle soon.

Is this the kind of wedding she would have wanted? All the flowers and people? Is this what she dreamed of when she was a little girl growing up?

When I turn to look behind us, the bridesmaids start their walk down the aisle to a light and airy song. Very traditional.

"Where's Beckett?" Knox asks, looking at Will. "He was just going to check on the girls and he's still gone."

"I don't know."

"There's Ev," Jax whispers.

"Is he in the wedding? I can't imagine he'd miss it," Emmett says.

"News to me, if he is," Will whispers.

When I look at Ev's face, I can tell she's been crying. My heart lurches in my chest and I resist the urge to bolt out of my seat and run to her.

"She's been crying," Jax whispers over his shoulder.

"I see."

"Do you think everything is ok?" Knox asks. "With... you know." His brow twitches with concern.

"Yes," my tone betrays my confidence.

She finds me and gives me a smile and a wink, with a slight roll of her eyes, and shakes her head.

"She's fine." I blow out a breath of relief.

The men's shoulders collectively relax at the same time.

She starts her walk down the aisle, her fingers rubbing the silk wrapped stems of the flowers. When she gets to us, she gives us a quick glance and smiles.

She is mine. Ours, but mine. God, I love that woman.

She takes her spot at the front of the church and the music stops. People shift in their seats, looking from the back to the front as silence settles around.

"What's happening?" I ask.

"This can't be goo-" Before Will can finish getting the words out *Pour Some Sugar on Me* by Def Leppard blares.

Donna and Dave are in the row in front of us and Donna is smiling and clapping, completely lost in happiness, next to a woman who I would have to imagine is Lizzy's mom. She's beautiful, with a sort of regal sophistication. She's wearing a tight gold dress that shines against her deep brown skin. Her hair is short and tightly curled, with the tips dyed a deep gold color. She seems very much the opposite of Lizzy. Across the aisle, who I suspect is Tony's mom, is sitting there with a more reserved smile. When I see her eyes grow big with surprise, then settle, I follow her gaze.

"Oh, no," Will groans.

"Oh, yes!" Knox claps excitedly, twisting in his seat and propping his arm on the back of the chair, pulling out his camera.

Beckett is strutting... strutting towards the crowd with his hand in a rainbow unicorn fanny pack.

"I love this so much!" Knox says, bouncing in his seat.

He must know what's going on, because I have no clue.

"I didn't put two and two together on how or why his bowtie matched the girls' dresses perfectly," Will huffs with a question of disbelief etched into his face.

"He's all yours. Did you not know?"

"No." Will's face is glowing.

We all let out soft chuckles as Beckett does a pirouette and then tosses out a fistful of white rose petals.

"He's the flower man!" Knox exclaims before letting out a woo!

Beckett continues to dance and toss flowers down the aisle and into the crowd. When he gets to our row, he puts the flowers in the palm of his hand and blows them at us, spins and tosses another handful into the crowd on the other side.

Everyone is laughing at Beckett and clapping along with the music. When he gets to the end, he puts both hands in his fanny pack, pauses and on the last beat of the song, his hands shoot out and flower petals rain down on him and the crowd goes wild. The other bridesmaids shift back a step and allow him to stand behind Ev, who is wiping the tears from her eyes.

I sign, "Are you ok?"

"So good," she responds as best she can, with a bouquet in her hands. Then she signs something else that looks like "Lizzy knows." The look on her face confirms my thought, and I nod. It was only a matter of time. The question is how long she's known.

There is a pause in the music again, and *I Get To Love You* by Ruelle plays.

Something pulls inside of me and I can't help but look at Ev. Knox does the same thing and I have to assume Jax and Emmett do too, because her eyes get wide before she melts. She quickly nods her head towards Lizzy and then shifts her body, very clearly commanding us to stop looking at her and to focus on the bride.

After a reluctant moment, Knox turns his head towards the back. Her eyes flick back to mine for a brief second and pulse wide before she winks and looks back at her best friend. If we weren't married already, I would interrupt this wedding and marry the fuck out of her right now.

Everyone stands and my eyes glance at Tony, while everyone else looks at Lizzy. I will look at her, but watching his expression the first time he sees his bride...

When we got the pictures back from our wedding, that is the one that stood out to me among the others. The moment we first saw Ev. Everyone is so focused on the bride when she walks in that they miss the look of pure love and joy on the groom's face. Tony's eyes glaze immediately and he bites on his bottom lip and fidgets in his spot as he watches her. Clasping his hands in front of him, he gives them a light squeeze before his thumbs begin to rub the back of his hands.

Smiling, I turn just as Lizzy takes her first step down the aisle.

She is as radiant as the glowing sun.

EVERLEE - LIZZY'S WEDDING

BREATHE IN. BREATHE OUT.

Slow steady breaths, knees bent.

Don't pass out.

Lizzy's music starts and almost in perfect synchronicity, the crowd stands and looks towards the back, while my guys look at me. It takes my breath away, the breath I've been trying so hard to maintain, but their eyes... the way they're looking at me, makes my stomach tighten with butterflies. One would think they wouldn't affect me like this anymore, but they do.

Every. Damn. Day.

My eyes widen and a smile creeps onto my face. I give myself this moment, then shift my body towards Lizzy and nod at her. Jax rolls his eyes, and after a second, turns towards Lizzy.

There she is.

Stunning.

Breathtaking.

My very best friend in the entire world.

She's wearing an ivory form fitting mermaid style dress with a sweetheart neckline. The bottom of the dress is layers of light fabric, creating a soft ruffle look with a small sweep train behind her.

As my gaze sweeps across the audience to look at Tony, I catch another pair of eyes on me. Derek. He gives a quick smile, then looks away. I didn't even think he would be here. There's obviously no love lost between us, since we went on like half a date a year and a half ago. It's just a little awkward.

When my eyes land on Tony, he's tearing up and looking so in love. It's my favorite to watch the man's face when their bride walks down the aisle. All the eyes are on her, but looking at him is where the real magic is.

He loves her so big.

After a few seconds of just appreciating the love he has for my sister from another mister, I look back at her. Her fingers are fidgeting on the silk stems of her bouquet as her dad walks her down the aisle. His lips are moving ever so slightly, but I can't make out what he's saying.

She takes her time getting to me, but after her parents give her away, she steps in front of me. Handing my bouquet to Beckett, I quickly move the bottom of her dress around and give it a fluff. Lizzy, being Lizzy, tucks her cheeks in and lets out a woo, when I puff it out and the crowd laughs.

The crowd sits and the ceremony starts. The officiant they've chosen to marry them goes through her part relatively quickly, then turns it over to Lizzy and Tony to read the vows they've written. I asked Lizzy if she wanted to share her vows with me several times, but she didn't want to.

"Tony. My love. You were unexpected. I had always wanted to find my true companion, my soul mate, but after many failed attempts, I thought I was hopeless until we accidentally bumped into one another. And I swear, when we touched, I felt a literal spark travel through my body. I knew from the instant our eyes locked you were going to be special and after our first date, I knew you were going to be the one. I even ran home and called my bestie and gushed to her."

When he looks at me, I shrug and nod.

Lizzy takes a deep breath. "You complete me and not in the cheesy romantic bulls-" She pauses and looks at the crowd. "Schnizz. Sorry mom and dad."

The crowd laughs again.

"I had an entire speech planned, wrote it out and I've been practicing it several times a day for the last several weeks so I wouldn't forget any words, but now... I'm just too excited." Her hands dance in the air as she bobbles from side to side. She clears her throat, then turns back to Tony. "That's what you make me. Excited. Excited to do life. To try things. I love we get to explore all the different facets of our lives that make us who we are. I love we get to discover new things about ourselves with each other."

He tosses a wink at her, and she pauses, clearing her throat.

Unspoken Allure plug in the vows. Love it! Only those that know, know.

"Tony." She takes another deep breath. "I vow I will be by your side through the good times and the bad. I vow I will argue with you when you're wrong."

"When am I ever right?" he teases.

"Exactly! You can always count on me to be there, educating you on my way, the right way."

The crowd laughs again.

"I vow I will love you and that I will always pick you to be my partner if Everlee isn't there or available."

"Sounds about right. Chicks before di-"

Lizzy stomps her foot and nods her head towards the crowd.

"De-cidedly handsome men." He nods. "Sorry moms and dads."

"I promise I will never watch the next episode of any show without you, no matter how much I want to, or if it ever comes between choosing you or Lulu, I promise I will let you down gently."

Tony shrugs and smiles.

"I promise to have your back in public, even when you're wrong, and then correct you in private, and I promise I will never go over the budget on anything else again. This wedding should last me a lifetime. And I'll just make my budget higher."

"Seems about right."

Lizzy grabs his hands. "But above all of that, I promise I will love you with every breath in my body and fight for our marriage, even when it's tough. I will remember all the good times to help give reason to push through the bad times. I will always push you to be an even better man than you are today, even though that would be pretty hard, because you're already pretty amazing."

Tony's lips flatten into a smile as tears form on the rim of his eye.

"I had lots of other stuff planned, but I went off the rails near the beginning and could never find the track. So just know that my vows were going to be kick ass."

"Your vows were pretty kick ass and I don't know how I can top them."

"You can't, but you can try. Starting with how wonderful and amazing I am, will be a good start."

"Well, that goes without saying." He takes a deep breath and squeezes her hands. "Lizzy. Lizzy, Lizzy, Lizzy. You're a force to be reckoned with, a wild child, and the down-to-earth friend everyone needs. You say what's on your mind and show what's in your heart. Each day is a new adventure with you and gosh darn if I'm not the luckiest man. You've never met an obstacle you couldn't beat or a job that you couldn't handle. Just ask the fifty nail holes in the wall in our living room, but you found that stud."

The crowd laughs.

"I did, and he's standing right in front of me." She shimmies her shoulders.

"And I promise that is where I'll always be, and if I'm not in front of you, I will be behind you."

Beckett snickers behind me and it takes all I have to not shoot my hand backwards into him.

Tony's amused gaze flickers from Beckett back to Lizzy, "Where I will be cheering you on and supporting you on whatever wild idea you have. I promise to always tell you that you're the best driver on the road and always know where you're going, even if we are going in the opposite direction because it doesn't matter how we get to where we're going as long as I'm with you."

"Pookie. That's so sweet, but I would hope you would tell me I'm going the wrong way at some point."

Tony shrugs and smiles. "I promise to not steal the covers off the bed and never watch any other episodes of our shows without you. Likely because we will still be searching for a show to watch, which I also promise to sit patiently and wait for even after we flip through thirty different shows before we go back to the first one. I also vow to always share my food with you, even if you have your own, because I know mine's always better than yours."

"It is." Lizzy nods to the crowd.

"I promise that when I change the toilet paper, I will have the sheet start in the front, because we party in the front, not in the back. And last, I promise to always be your loving and faithful partner. And patient, extremely patient, partner. Because again, Lizzy Thompson, you are the love of my life, the peanut butter to my jelly, the sun to my shine. You are everything I could have ever hoped for in a partner and more. Your presence in my life brings me endless joy and laughter. You are loyal and caring, and you are my world. I love you, boo." Tony holds his hands up and looks at me. "Don't worry. I know boo boo is reserved for you."

I toss him a quick wink and wipe the tears from my eyes.

"Well," the officiant clasps her hands. "The love between you two is unmistakable. Do we have your rings?"

"Yes. One second," Lizzy turns towards the right and looks down the aisle. "Here, Lulu."

A second later, Lizzy squats down with her hand out as Lulu sprints down the aisle with a small bag hanging from her collar. She comes sliding to a stop in front of Lizzy and sits, tail swishing from side to side. "Good girl. Yes, you are."

Lizzy quickly unties the ribbon and catches the satchel in her hand while Beckett steps from around me and hooks a small rope leash to Lulu's collar and walks her off to the right. When I look to my side, I watch Beckett quickly lead Lulu back to the pen where Woodford and Blanton are waiting like the gentleman they are. The man standing by the pen must be the one that was holding onto Lulu.

By the time I look back at the wedding, Lizzy and Tony are exchanging rings.

"I now pronounce you husband and wife, partners for life. You may kiss the queen of your universe."

"I made her say the last part," Lizzy snickers towards the crowd.

"Shut up and give me a kiss, wife." Tony steps forward, wraps his hand around the back of her neck and pulls her towards him, tipping her back a bit.

The crowd loses it with whistles and hoots.

After a moment, he stands her back up, and she wobbles a bit in her spot. She takes a step towards the crowd and I quickly make work of fixing her dress, fluffing it behind her, then quickly back out of the picture.

I watch in silence as she smiles and waves at the crowd, pausing every few moments for a picture and Tony is there, smiling and letting her have this moment.

Once they're at the back of the makeshift aisle, I step forward to a waiting Derek. My eyes quickly glance at the men who are watching me, but are still sitting in their seat.

"You look nice," Derek says, holding his arm out for me.

"Thanks. You clean up nicely, too."

"You look good. Shit. I meant happy. Also, good, but that's not what I meant," he stutters over himself.

"It's ok. I knew what you meant."

"Are you dating the club owner?"

"Married, actually." I hold up my hand.

"Wow. Congrats."

I didn't know how to say I was married to all of them. I'm not trying to hide it, but I don't want it to be a thing tonight. That's one thing we need to figure out. I want us to be ourselves in social situations, but also don't want all the drama and looks.

"Thank you. Did you find anyone?"

We walk off to the side while the rest of the crowd disperses.

"I was dating a woman for a few months, but it didn't really work out."

"Oh, I'm sorry. Not trying to play matchmaker, but Keeley broke up with her boyfriend a few months ago."

He laughs, then stops when he looks behind me.

"Derek," Callum says coolly with a hint of a smile.

"Callum. Good to see you again. Congrats." Derek thrusts his hands towards me.

"I was just telling Derek about Keeley."

"I'll go find her. Nice catching up. Have fun tonight." Derek scurries off like a dog with its tail tucked between his legs.

"Did I say something?" Callum asks with a coy grin.

"I think it's just your general presence." Pressing my hand against his chest, I lean forward and plant a kiss on his lips.

"Let's go find a place to sit while we wait for the photographer," Callum says, sliding his hand down my back to just above my ass.

"Keep touching me like that, and we'll miss the photographer."

Callum laughs.

EVERLEE - LIZZY'S RECEPTION

SWEAT RUNS DOWN THE back of my neck and spine, causing a shiver as my nipples harden under my dress. We've been on the dance floor for three hours straight. The guys have continued to supply me with water. Callum and Jax have taken turns dancing with me during slow songs, while Knox and Emmett have been by my side the entire night. Knox because he just wants to dance and have a great time, and Emmett, because I won't let him leave. If he leaves, he'll go check on something and be the owner of this place instead of a guest at the wedding.

Colby is the running the show now and doing an amazing job. He has another month left before his baby arrives, so Emmett will step back in for a few weeks so Colby can bond, but until then, I'm trying to help Emmett stay in his new role. Colby's baby was the one thing Emmett was most concerned about, but had several conversations with Colby and his girlfriend. They were both excited about the opportunity. Plus, Colby loves this place almost as much as Emmett does.

Emmett kisses my temple and mumbles something about finding water. Knox grabs my hand and spins me towards him and positions his knee between my legs with his hands on my hips. He leans in and presses his lips just under my jaw and sings, "Ooh girl, you're so fine. You're so fine, you blow my mind. Ooh girl, I'm so lucky I get to call you mine." He rocks into me, moving and rubbing his leg in that sweet spot.

"Knox. Knox," I pant out, glancing around. "We're in the middle of the dancefloor."

"No one can see." He kisses my neck briefly, causing a ripple of pleasure to roll through my body.

"Knox." I nearly growl out as I fight with myself.

"We're just dancing, baby girl."

"You're trying to get me off."

"Is it working?"

"Almost." Why did I say that? I should have just said yes, but now he's going to see that as a challenge. A mission.

He presses his body closer to mine and grinds. "I want to feel my cock inside of you."

His whisper lights my body on fire, not only the words, but the very breath that travels across my skin. "Later. We're at Lizzy's wedding."

"Don't make me wait too long."

"As soon as we leave."

"Your dress is so low in the back. You know how we feel about these kinds of dresses. What it does to us. It's almost like you do this to us on purpose."

"Never."

He laughs. "Kiss me, now." He grabs under my chin and pulls my mouth to his. His tongue pulses in as his kiss makes me dizzy.

In my right ear, I hear a slurping and smacking sound. It takes my brain a minute, but I pull away from Knox and see Lizzy standing there.

"You hookers. No wonder she's pregnant. Fuck me. I almost got pregnant just watching the two of you. Making me horny on my wedding night in the middle of the dance floor. Shame on you two." She grabs my hand. "Now, if you don't mind. I've requested a special song for you and me, my love."

"I'm going to get some water," Knox says, tipping his invisible hat as he exits the dance floor.

"You do that," Lizzy calls, then turns and grabs me and gives me a hug. "I've hardly seen you all night, boo boo."

"I know. We see each other all the time. You can't be mad. I was giving others a chance to spend time with you."

"No. I guess I can't, but that doesn't mean I don't want to spend *any* time with you." She smiles and grabs both sides of my cheeks.

For a second, I think she's going to kiss me, but the beat drops and the crowd goes wild. Rihanna's S&M blares over the speaker and I stare at her for a second and she bursts out laughing.

"It was our jam in college and who would have known it's what we would love years later? Maybe it was our subconscious trying to tell us something."

"I can't believe you played this at your wedding?"

"Why? It's my wedding!" She shakes her hair in the air, then grabs my hands and starts swinging them from side to side. "*But chains and whips excite me!*" she screams at the top of her lungs.

"God help Tony tonight."

"Tonight? We've already consummated this bitch twice. I told him to put a baby in me! Stat!"

"Twice?"

"Why do you think we were late for pictures?" She spins me in a circle.

"Lizzy."

"Boo boo. Dance! Dance with me!" She leans over and shimmies her shoulders with a smile spread across her face.

Fuck it!

Let's dance to sex in the air because I don't care!

Twenty minutes later, the music stops. It's close to midnight, but I thought she had this place until two in the morning.

Lizzy has somehow made her way up to the DJ stand on the second level without me noticing. She grabs the mic and taps it a few times to get everyone's attention.

"All. I just want to thank you for coming here tonight and celebrating this moment with us. It means the world to us you're here. The party isn't over yet, but I know a lot of you turn into pumpkins at midnight, so I wanted to pop on here quickly and just say thank you from the bottom of my, our, hearts. We're going here until two and then taking the after party somewhere. Just not sure yet. We would love to have you at all the above, but understand if you can't or don't want to."

The doors from the kitchen swing open.

"But for anyone who wants... I thought we may need a refuel."

"What in the?" Keeley and Low both ask at the same time from behind me.

"It's a donut tower cake thing! Enjoy!" Lizzy squeals then claps, forgetting she has the microphone in her hands, so it sounds like a storm is rolling through. "My bad." She pulls her lips and gently sets the microphone down and steps away from it.

The DJ turns the music back on as Keeley, Low, and I stand in a half-circle.

"Is it bad I want to be first in line at the donut table?" Low asks.

"Oh!" Lizzy blurts on the microphone again. Guess she wasn't done. "If you need a kickass, awesome ride share, not tonight, obvi, but in the future, there is a five-dollar voucher in your thank you gifts to Betty's Bitchin' Rides. Woo Betty!"

"Woo!" A scream echoes across the room and the crowd turns to see Betty thrusting her hands in the air.

"I love that woman," Keeley says, nodding her head.

"I want to be like her when I grow up," Low says.

"Last night," Keeley starts. "I swear. I still can't believe she got up on the table and was dancing with that guy. She had her hands all over him. I could never."

"It's a gift to allow yourself to be that open and just have fun without a care in the world. Betty has surely mastered it," I say.

Low nudges Keeley's arm.

"What?"

Low nods her head to the side. "Looks like Romeo may want a second dance."

"Will you stop calling him Romeo?" Keeley laughs. "His name is Derek. We're just having fun tonight. He seems nice."

Low pulls her lips. "Eesh."

"What?" I ask.

"The dreaded nice," Low says.

"He is," Keeley defends.

"Do you want nice, or do you want someone to rock your world?"

Keeley blushes, "You stop Harlow."

"Oh, full name. Guess I'm in trouble." Low laughs. "You go dance with Mr. Nice. I will be at the bar. Holler if you need me."

We watch Keeley walk towards the edge of the dance floor. "You like her," I say, popping Low's arm.

"She's cute, but she's not into girls. I mean, one night with me and maybe she'd change her mind. Hell," she nods at me. "You give me one night and I bet you'd change your mind too and I know how much you love dick."

"Awfully confident." I laugh.

She shrugs. "I know how to please a woman and make them come over and over again."

"So why aren't you here with anyone?" I realize how that sounds given the conversation and after Low cuts her eyes at me. "Oh God, I didn't mean it that way."

"It's cool. I have a couple of women I'm seeing, but nothing serious. Inviting a date to a wedding is a big commitment, and I don't want them getting the wrong idea."

"Can't have that," I tease.

Low pushes me, laughing. "How are you holding up?" she asks, changing the topic.

"With?" I ask, eyeing her skeptically.

"You know... the B-A-B-Y."

"Ah. It's good. Morning sickness is a bitch, but I'm getting through it. The guys have been great."

"Yeah. They seem like they would be very hands on with you."

"What is that supposed to mean?"

"Those men adore you."

"They are pretty great."

"Who?" Jax asks, walking up, slipping his arm around me.

"These guys I'm kind of in to," I answer, looking up at him.

"Oh, really." A sly smile pulls across his lips.

"Yeah. I may go talk to them. See if they want to dance."

"I can't allow you to do that."

"Good luck trying to stop me."

"I will leave you two to whatever the fuck this is. It's like sexual tension meets... fuck. I don't know. I'm going to go find someone else to hang with that's less horny."

"Good luck," I call.

"I brought you a gift," Jax says, sliding around in front of me.

"You did? What is it?"

He pulls his arm from behind his back and, sitting in the palm of his hand, is a donut with bacon and syrup on it.

"Ohhh no."

"Yes. There were only two left, so I elbowed a great grandma out of the way and stole it for you."

"No you didn't."

"Which part?"

I look around the room for an injured woman, but only find people dancing, talking and having a great time.

"Thank you," I say just before I take a bite. It's some sort of cinnamon cake donut and the bacon and maple drizzle work wonderfully together.

"Whatcha doin' over here, sis?" Beckett asks, sliding up beside me with Will following close behind.

"Eating a donut. What are you doing?"

"Ooh, is that the bacon maple one? Let me get a bite." His neck lurches forward as he opens his mouth.

"No," I bark, twisting away and shoving the remaining bite of donut in my mouth.

Beckett's jaw drops at the same time he gasps. "The nerve. You better be glad you're with child."

"Really?" Jax asks, stepping forward and crossing his arms, looking every bit the protector.

"Ohh daddy. What's happening over here?" Knox asks, skipping to a stop, completely killing the moment. "How cute are these?" He holds up a little flower pot with seeds. "Let love grow. Don't worry, I got us six already and hid them in Emmett's office."

Jax rolls his eyes and steps back.

"Your boy was trying to flex on me," Beckett smiles.

"Jaxie-poo," Knox whispers, pressing the palm of his hand on Jax's chest.

Jax reaches up and bends Knox's wrist backward until Knox is dancing in a circle and crying for mercy.

"No Jaxie-poo bullshit."

"You don't complain when Ev says it."

"Gross," Beckett chirps.

"How are some of my favorite men doing?" Mom asks, walking up to us.

"Great, Mama McKinley," Knox coos. "Did you get your flower pot and seeds?"

"I did. I've already stolen two for Dave and me. Thought about hiding them, so no one takes them."

Knox looks at all of us, eyes wide.

"What's got you in such a good mood?" Mom asks, laughing.

"Love is in the air. What's not to be happy about?" Knox replies, spinning in a circle.

"What's happening over here, family?" Lizzy asks, walking up.

Jax blows out a puff of air but doesn't say anything. I reach for his hand, but he slips it out and presses it against my back, running his hand down my spine until he stops where my back meets the fabric just above my ass. The tips of his fingers dig in slightly as we all stand in a growing circle talking about any and everything.

Lizzy catches my eye from the other side of the circle and gives me a little wink.

A calm feeling washes over me as my eyes sweep around. Callum and Emmett have walked up to join us.

Family.

This is my family.

When I hear a small click, I look around and find the photographer on the stairs that lead to the second balcony. She just got this picture and I start crying. This will be my new favorite picture.

Pure happiness.

PART 2

EVERLEE - SURPRISE

MY HEART POUNDS IN my chest. We're waiting to have our second ultrasound for them to do all the measurements and to find out the sex of our baby. We had one around six weeks to confirm I was pregnant and because of that, we pushed the second one to nineteen weeks because Callum was traveling quite a bit. He wouldn't tell me where he was going, only that it's a surprise. It's been over a month now and he still hasn't told me. Part of me wants to ask him every day and the other part of me is telling me to leave it a surprise.

Frustrated, I squeeze his hand.

"Are you ok?" he asks.

My eyes cut to him. No, Callum. I'm not ok. You're keeping a secret from me and it's eating away at me. "Yes. I'm fine. Just excited."

Chicken shit, my subconscious laughs.

Emmett and Jax sit in the chairs along the back wall, while Callum and Knox stand on either side of the table I'm sitting on. Fortunately, there isn't much in the room, just some chairs, a trash can, a short bed and the ultrasound machine.

When we were here last time and Knox saw them insert the wand in my vagina, he got way too excited. Now, he likes to pretend he's an ultrasound tech when we include the vibrator in our sexcapades. He wants me to call him Dr. Love, which I can't. I simply can't, without busting out in laughter.

It's hard to believe that we're already near the halfway mark. This summer flew by even though we kept it fairly low key. We've all stepped away some more from our clubs and are trying to take more of an advisory, big picture, role. It's been working out really well. Emmett is still putting in quite a bit of time at Bo's, but he's done a good job stepping away as much as he has. It helped when we went on vacation.

Fourth of July was nice, not only because it was the beach, but it gave Emmett a break from Bo's, showing he could step away and it wouldn't all fall apart. We tacked on a few extra days to the end of our trip and rented the house near my parents and surprised them with the news. I felt a little bad waiting a month to tell them, but Lizzy's wedding wasn't the right time and I wanted it to be in person. It was also fun getting all the pups back together. It may have been a bit aggressive on our part because having six seven-month-old puppies and Luna and then nine adults in the house felt a little much, but they loved the beach. They spent almost as much time in the water as Knox did.

Beckett, being the darling pain in the ass brother he is, introduced mom to Instagram, and showed her how to create boards. So now I have hundreds of pictures to go through every day and if I don't like them in a certain amount of time, she calls or texts. She has boards for baby room inspo, items we'll need, names for if it's a boy or a girl. Sooo many picturessss.

Last week, we held a surprise baby shower for Colby and his girlfriend. They had the baby in July, but with everything going on, we weren't able to have one beforehand. We sent them a gigantic box of diapers and wipes, bought them a car seat from their registry, and lined up an entire week of meals for them when the baby was born, but still wanted to do something from Bo's. It was nice, but also made all of this more real.

There's a soft knock on the door and my heart stutters in my chest as my hand squeezes Callum's. This time out of reflex. His other hand cups over mine and his thumb rubs over the back of my hand affectionately.

"Are we ready to see our baby?" Doris, the ultrasound tech, asks.

She's just shy of seventy and I knew I was going to like her when she made a joke about her being sixty-nine and waiting all her life for this moment. One because, how could I not like someone who is sixty-nine, and two, when she saw my men, she fussed at us for nearly bringing her to her death early.

"We are," we say collectively.

"Let's see what we got here." She sits on the stool and jiggles the ball near the keyboard to turn the screen on. "How have you been feeling?"

"Great. Still a little nauseous every once in a while, but no more sickness. And the nausea may be more related to smells now. I seem to be super sensitive to them."

She rolls up my shirt and rolls the top of my shorts down, and tucks a small towel inside of them. "Let's see what we got here." She squirts the gel on the end of the wand and rubs it over my stomach. "Any guesses on what you're having?" Her brow furrows a second as she moves the wand around.

"Boy!" Knox exclaims, like he's been waiting his entire life for this one question.

"Girl," Emmett counters, coolly with all the confidence in the world.

I can't focus on anything else because I'm fixated on her face. Something's wrong. My heart beats faster and my hand squeezes Callum's. He looks from the guys to me.

"What's wrong?" he whispers.

I nod my head in Doris's direction.

The guys quieten down.

"Doris?" Callum asks.

She looks up, startled.

"Is everything ok?" Callum asks.

"I hear the heartbeat," I mumble, not quite sure what I'm saying or not saying.

She smiles. "What were your guesses?"

She's completely dismissed our question... but she's smiling.

My heart hammers in my chest. I can't even speak.

When no one speaks, she continues, "Oh, come on now. I don't have a lot of years left to wait." She offers another warm smile, which puts me at ease, but not as much as it should.

Knox and Emmett blurt out their guesses again.

"Tell me I'm right Mrs. D. You've always been my favorite," Knox coos.

"Honey. I'm the only one you've had."

"Don't tell him he's right. We'll never hear the end of it," Jax chimes in, eye flicking between Doris and me.

"Come on, Mrs. D." Knox clasps his hands together.

"I'm sorry, boys. You'll have to deal with Knox." She laughs.

"A boy!?" Knox exclaims, then looks at me. "We're having a boy!"

We're having a boy.

"Is he ok? Your face." Relief floods my system.

"Well," she pauses. "I don't know how to say this, but E-Man is also right."

"Come again?" Jax says, voice dropping.

She turns the monitor towards us. "You're having twins. I don't know how it was missed on the first ultrasound."

"Twins." My words catch in my throat.

"That would make sense why your nausea has been so bad."

"Twins," Jax says in disbelief.

"Twins!" Knox exclaims, happier than a clam in the ocean.

"That's why you made the face?" I ask, tears dancing on the edge of my rim.

"Yes, darling. I'm sorry. You would think this many years in the business I'd be able to keep my face together, but I was shocked. Rarely do I miss littles, but this one must have been hiding."

"Twins," I repeat, shock beginning to set in. "Twins."

"Twins," the room says at one time.

"Twins," I repeat, staring off.

"Are you ok?" Callum asks, checking in.

I nod without speaking.

"Are they identical? Can you tell?"

"They will not be identical. You had two eggs..." she pauses. "Oh my goodness."

"What?"

She pulls out her phone. "I've only read about this once. It's very rare."

"Good or bad, rare?" Jax asks.

"Neither. Just rare." She nods. "There's been less than twenty cases reported in the world."

"What?" I ask.

"Hot damn." Her face pulls. "Pardon my French," she says excitedly. "Heteropaternal superfecundation."

Knox dramatically clutches his chest and falls onto the bed, laying his head on my chest.

"What?" Doris and I ask, clearly confused.

"I thought you cast a spell and hexed me."

"Idiot." Jax leans forward and swats at Knox's leg.

She turns to me, face serious as can be. "You're in trouble with that one." She laughs and pats his leg lovingly. "You could have twins with two different fathers."

I look at my men. We've already discussed we wouldn't find out whose sperm created the baby unless it was medically necessary, but the chance that we could have two babies and two of them could be fathers.

"This is very fascinating. I'm going to read up on it and send you some info! In all my sixty-nine years, I swear. To see something like this. I'll be." She shakes her head and lets out a chirp of surprise. "Well, I need to finish taking measurements for the doctor. She's going to wonder what's taking so long."

"Lord." Jax groans.

"What?" we all ask.

"Lizzy. I can't be there when you tell her you're pregnant with twins. She's going to lose her mind."

"Thinking about Lizzy?" Knox teases. "The sooner you admit she's your best friend next to me, then you won't be so grumpy all the time."

"Never."

"Keep denying it." Knox sucks on his teeth.

"I must say," Doris starts. "You all are the first... group I've ever had. When Dr. Yiminitz told me... well, I didn't really know what to say or do. She's very open about her... preferences and mentioned she knew you all, though she wouldn't say from where or how, and I didn't ask. But anyway, you all left a lasting impression on me after your first visit. I just remember all the love and the way you all seem to just mesh together and work. It's amazing."

"Thanks. It's not easy, but someone had to marry them," I tease.

Jax rolls his eyes and grins and me. When I stick out my tongue, his eyes flare, causing a heat to rush through my body. Fuck.

I don't know if it's the babies, but my libido has been through the roof over the last week or so... which is saying a lot.

The fucker can see it too, because he chuckles, satisfied with himself. So I mouth, *ass* in his direction, which seems to stoke the flames between us.

Doris clears her throat, pulling my attention back to her. "Well, I've taken all the measurements I need. Heartbeats are strong and size looks good, but I will let Dr. Yiminitz go over all of that with you after she looks at the pictures and everything." She stands up. "If you want to use that towel and wipe off the jelly from your belly and just leave the cloth on the table, we'll go to your exam room where Doc will talk with you."

When we get to the hall, a hand grips around my wrists and tugs me backwards. Jax pulls me into his chest so my back is to his front. He wraps his arms around me and we keep walking down the hall. After a second, he leans his lips close to my ear and whispers, "You're going to be punished later for being a little brat in there, thinking you can call me an ass."

"Don't threaten me with a good time."

He chuckles and moves back to standing, but still keeps his arms wrapped around me as we walk into the room. He finds a chair and pulls me onto his lap.

"Well, honey. Doc can't do her exam with her on your lap."

"I know. She'll move to the table."

"These babies are going to be beautiful," Doris says, more to herself than to anyone in the room as she closes the door.

Our babies.

Two.

JAX - PEGS FOR DAYS

Two babies.

Twins.

When I pull to a stop in our driveway, I put my hand on Ev's leg. "You. Upstairs. Now."

She turns from looking outside and rests her eyes on my face before she lets out an indecisive hum. "I don't know. We have to pick up the guys soon."

Emmett got called into Bo's, Callum apparently forgot he had to check on something at the club, and Knox went to the bakery to place the order for our cakes for this weekend. We had already picked out the flavor, but the baker was waiting on what color to put in for the gender.

Ev's family is coming up this weekend and a few others are coming over for the gender reveal. We did it a little backward since we know now, but it will still be fun to surprise everyone with the twins.

Twins.

"Brady will handle it. He's already on his way to meet up with Knox and have lunch with him."

She opens the door casually. "I don't know."

The look in her eye tells me she's purposefully being a brat, and the flush in her cheeks and on her chest tells me she's getting moist just thinking about me. She loves when I'm dominant and take control, so that's what I'm going to do until I sink my cock inside of her pretty little pussy.

Pushing the door open, I slam it shut and stalk around to her side and pick her up. I move to sling her over my shoulder, but the thought of squishing her belly over my shoulder causes me to pause, so I just grab her around her knees and lift so her stomach is right by my face.

"Let's go. I'm not waiting."

She giggles, and that's all I need to hear.

When we get to my bedroom, I toss her gently onto the bed, then yank her pants off. She presses her palms into the bed and tries to push herself to the middle. "Nope." I wrap my hands around her ankles and yank her back down so her legs are bent over the edge. I push my pants down to the floor and tear my shirt off, tossing it on her face.

She snatches it off and laughs.

Dropping to my knees, I run my cheek up the inside of her leg, causing her to wiggle. "Don't move."

"Jax," she whimpers.

"Don't speak." I inhale the sweet scent of her pussy and feel her muscles clinch. Even after all this time, I know she still panics when we do this. She doesn't say it out loud anymore, but I can read it on her face, hear it in her breath, feel it in the way her muscles tighten. She doesn't know the power her smell has over us. How much we love it. It's addicting. Like a drug that was made specifically for us.

I lean in, so my mouth is hovering just on the outside of her pussy. When my eyes flick up, I see the tips of her breast heaving up and down, behind her growing belly, and just behind them is her face, neck craned up, watching me.

"Are you going to be a good girl for me?"

"No." She smiles, then falls back to the bed.

"Good." With that, I sink my tongue into her pussy and her legs clamp around my head. When she tries to thrust her hips in the air, I tighten my arms around her thighs and hold her down. She hates when we do this because she likes to move, but we love it. It's like a mini edging, because it takes her longer to reach her orgasm when she can't move her clit to just the right spot.

She strains against my arms to free her legs, but I press her hips further into the bed, trapping her as I lick up her center and suck her clit into my mouth. She tastes divine.

Her feet curl and press into my hips, giving her leverage to buck, so I shake my hips a little, freeing them from her, then press my tongue inside of her as deep as it can go. When I slide it out, I slip in two fingers and work her clit, her favorite combo. A few thrusts later, she's coming. I pull out my finger and press my tongue in and lick and suck.

"Jax," she cries out.

When she's done, I plant kisses up her body, around her stomach as both my hands grip it and give it a gentle squeeze, pulling it up towards her breast. She lets out another moan. "That feels so good."

I can't help but chuckle.

Kissing up further, my cock drags along the inside of her leg as I suck her left breast into my mouth, and then her right. I can feel her eyes on me, watching me. My lips kiss and suck along her collarbone, up her neck, to just below her cheek. When she presses her head back into the bed, her stomach rubs against my chest.

"Jax, fuck me."

"Not until you fuck me."

Her back falls back to the bed as I hover my face over hers, waiting for her answer. Her eyes rake across my face and a smile forms on her lips. "Really?"

I nod slowly.

Emmett is still too big for me to take and enjoy, but I love it when Everlee fucks me. Plus, it works out well for us. I can fuck Emmett while he fucks her.

Before rolling off the bed to get the strap on, I kiss the tip of her nose.

"It's been a few weeks and my belly has popped since the last time."

"We'll make it work, and also look at getting you a different style harness that can grow with you."

"Jaxie poo." She smiles tilting her head to the side.

"Ev," I warn. "You only call me that now because of what I said to Knox at Lizzy's wedding."

"I was calling you Jaxie poo before."

"Yes, a few times, but since then, it has picked up considerably."

She slips on the dildo and looks at me, a smile falling from her face. "Shut up, turn around and put your hands on the bed."

"One thing." I hold my finger up. "I think I just came seeing your pregnant belly with a strap on."

She breaks out of character for a second to smile, but it snaps back a second later. "Hands on the bed."

Never in a thousand years did I imagine this would be me, but fuck. I love it. I love her. I love Emmett. I love it all.

They are the only ones who can see me like this.

Only them.

A cool gel slides down my ass and over my hole as her fingers press inside and preps me. Slowly, methodically. I know she enjoys this. The power. This is a gift that she doesn't waste and it's one of the many things I love about her.

Just the thought of her pressing inside of me nearly has me coming. The bed is going to be soaked by the time we're done. It usually is, but fuck.

The tube of lube falls back to the bed at the same time I feel her there, pressed against me.

"Relax for me," she coaxes softly. Her hands run up my spine as she presses just the tip in.

A moan slips out from between my lips.

"Quiet, or I'll make you quiet."

She slides in and out, each time getting deeper and deeper, faster and faster.

Goddamn.

When she hits that spot, my cock jerks and my stomach clenches. “Ev,” I pant, fingers fisting the sheets.

She leans forward, her stomach on my lower back, and whispers, “Do you like the way I feel when I'm fucking you?” Her hand wraps around my cock.

It's fucking crying for her as she strokes it in long, slow pulls.

“Are you going to come all over your bed like a good boy?”

A groan rumbles through my chest as her words act like a hand around my neck. “Speak, boy.”

A tingle shoots down my spine, but I refuse to let myself come yet.

“Ev, you've got to stop fucking talking. I'm about to come.”

I can feel her smile as she kisses me on my side, before she runs her tongue over the tattoo that runs from my chest around my side to my back. She pulls back some, then bites.

My head bucks into the air and a growl rips from my throat. “God damn you, babe.”

Her giggles make me want to shove my cock inside of her and fuck her until she's hoarse from moaning my name.

Before I can move, she grips her hands onto my hips and pounds into me, hitting my prostate and making me see stars. I rock back into her taking, taking all she will give me.

Fuck, I need it. I need her.

“Jax. Jax,” she's crying with each thrust. Emmett added a couple of barbells into the inside of her harness so that with every thrust she gives us, the piercing rubs along her clit. “I need to you come,” she whimpers.

“No.”

“Fucking, Jax.”

“You know my rule.”

“Fuck you, and fuck your rule.”

“You are... fucking me. And no.” Tears stream down my face as I clench and hold my orgasm at bay. It's like a thread of string trying to hold back a damn. It's unraveling faster and faster.

The thwaps of her hips slap against my ass and echo through the room as her pants and moans act like dull scissors slicing over the string.

My hips thrust up and down, looking for anything solid to rub my dick against while my arms push backwards trying to claim her, but it's no use. She's in control. She's taking me.

Her hips rotate as she punches in, and I lose it. The control I was fighting to hold together breaks. A scream bursts from my lungs at the same time my hand wraps around my cock and I fucking lose it. I lose control. Just the grip of my hands sends me over the edge and I'm coming all over the bed.

"Jax!" Everlee presses in and doesn't move. "Fuck."

"Get on my face. Now."

When she pulls back, I take the moment, and turn around and rip the strap-on down her legs and with it a string of her come.

Before I can think, I'm sliding off the bed onto my ass with my back pressed against the edge of the bed as my hands wrap around her ass and pull her towards me. Her hands slide through my hair and grip the root.

"Jax. Oh my.... God."

I try to lift and pull us onto the bed, but I can't focus long enough. My ass is pressed off the floor while the back of my head rests on the edge of the bed while she's bent over grabbing the sheets.

As soon as I suck her clit into my mouth, her legs are buckling and she's moaning. She unleashes and squirts all over my face. I have to look away as her come runs down my chest and puddles around my cock.

After another second, I settle completely onto the floor and she slides down me until she's sitting on my lap.

Sweat mats her hair against her forehead, so I brush it behind her ears, then run my fingers under her chin. "I love you." I give her a kiss, meant to be quick, but she wraps her arms around my neck and locks my head into place and kisses me back. Her tongue swipes against mine as her body rocks against mine, before she pulls away.

"I love you, too."

EVERLEE - AND SO IT BEGINS

TWENTY MINUTES.

Twenty minutes until guests arrive and turn this peaceful day into love-filled chaos.

The creak of the rocking chair on the deck beside me and the sound of the wind whispering its song through the trees settles me, giving me false expectations of what the day has in store.

Wyatt offered his house when we told him we were having a gender reveal party and told us all the pups could come. It's only Woodford, Blanton, Lulu, and Luna this time because Beckett and mom and dad didn't want to bring their pups up for the weekend trip.

This will be the first time my family is meeting Knox's dad. Knox seems both nervous and excited. Things have been going well between the two of them. Wyatt calls without fail at least once a week. They even went camping together one night around the lake almost two months ago. It's when Knox told him we were having a baby. It was the same weekend Callum had to take off for his business trip.

"How are you doing, mama?" Wyatt asks stepping onto the porch. "Sorry. Is it ok if I call you that? If you'd rather, I can call you Everlee. I just..." He inhales a deep breath, then pats the railing before he turns to look at me. "I'm just so excited you're all here. It really means the world to me."

"Yes, that is fine and I'm happy we're here, too."

"I know this isn't your baby shower and what not, but I wanted to make you all something. It isn't much, but... I just."

"Wyatt, that is very thoughtful. You didn't need to do that."

"Well, I know, but... I just." Tears spill over the rim of his eyes. "I'm just so sorry for all the time I missed with Knox. I was stupid. And I know he doesn't have to let me back in his life and I just want to do everything right this time, you know? Show him I'm *in* this. That I'm not leaving."

"He knows that." I pat his shoulder. "He's been happier these last few months than I have ever seen him."

"Well, I think it's because of that little bundle of joy in your belly."

"No." I laugh. "I guess it's been more than a couple of months. This summer just flew by in the blink of an eye. What I really mean to say is this year. This year, he's been so happy. Now-" I hold up my hands. "I know that's not saying much since we've only been together for just over a year and a half, but the light in his eyes. It shines brighter and I think that has a lot to do with you. He talked about your camping trip every day for weeks after he got home."

Wyatt laughs. "That was just out here around the lake."

"It's not about where he was, but who he was with."

"Everlee. You really are just a peach. These boys lucked out when you walked into their bar."

"They did, didn't they?"

We both laugh just as a large expedition pulls down the driveway. Lizzy and Tony got a new car over the summer. Hers broke, so she went big. Said this was going to be her car for the next ten years, so it needed to be big enough to go through kids and sports. Which is crazy to think about, but I guess she's right.

She's going to lose her mind when we share the news. They all will.

As the car pulls to a stop, my nerves and excitement get the better of me. My heart races and my hands get clammy.

The doors open and I take a deep breath before I step off the front porch.

Mom is out of the passenger side door first, scurrying over to me, arms wide in the air. "Let me look at you."

Uncrossing my arms from my chest, I hold them wide open and spin in a circle.

"Oh Everlee. You are the cutest thing. Look at that belly. Remind me how many weeks?"

"Twenty weeks in a few days."

She clasps her hands and sets her chin on her knuckles.

"Get over here, preggers!" Beckett yells, stumbling out of the car. "Did you see that? Will shoved me out of the car!"

When I glance over Beckett's shoulder, Will is climbing out, shaking his head and rolling his eyes.

"Hello brother."

"Hello sister."

"Hello love," Will says, walking over to give me a hug.

"Hello, dahhhhling." A whiff of his cologne swirls around me, catching in my throat. I've noticed my sense of smell over the last month has gotten more sensitive.

"Is it too strong? Becks said you could smell everything now, and I almost didn't put it on, but just did a little dab before we got on the plane."

"No, it's fine. It smells good. It just caught me for a second." Looking over his shoulder, I wait for dad, but still don't see him. "Where's dad?"

"Oh, he's getting something out of the trunk."

"What?" My curiosity is peaked.

"A surprise." Beckett sticks out his tongue, so I swat at him.

"Children," Mom reprimands.

Gravel crunches behind me and my body tingles as my guys walk up.

"Dave. Hurry up," Mom bellows.

"Mama McKinley!" Knox yells, pushing past everyone else and giving her a hug.

"Knox." She grabs his cheeks. "How's my sweet boy?"

"Doing better now you're here."

"Oh. You." She swats her hand in the air. "Emmett, darling." She opens her arms again, giving Emmett a hug, then Callum and Jax.

"Afternoon, boys," Dad says, walking up with a large bag dangling from his fingertips.

"Mama McKinley, Dave, I want to introduce you to someone." Knox steps to the side and waves out his arm. "This is Wyatt. My dad."

"Wyatt. Pleasure to meet you. Knox has told us so much about you," Dad says, sticking out his hand to shake Wyatts.

"Same here. Knox and Everlee talk about you both as well."

"Nice to meet you, Wyatt," Mom says, smiling. "Beautiful home. And the lake." She points her finger in the air. "I love a lake front."

"Yes. Everlee said you and Dave also live on a lake."

Watching Mom, Dad, and Wyatt walk towards the lake talking about the water life brings a sort of peace within me. Maybe I was also nervous. My eyes flick to Knox, who is watching them with a smile on his face, when I hear a squeal, then feel arms wrap around me.

"Hey Lizzy," I say, reaching up to grab the arm around my neck and turning to face her.

"How is my little niece or nephew doing?"

"Great. Moving around."

"Probably trying to get away from that shrill and realizing they're stuck," Jax says, slipping his hand around my hip.

"Come here, you big lug!" Lizzy says, launching herself at Jax and wrapping her arms around his neck.

He gives her a hug with the arm that's not around my waist smiling, then asks, "Where's your better half?"

After she releases Jax, she fixes her shirt, pulling it down, and smiles at him. "I know you don't mean that, but Tony is on his way. Should be here any minute. We took two cars because of Lulu. Didn't think we could get all the people, luggage and puppers in the car. Plus, he had to get something." Lizzy squeals and claps her hands together.

"This can't be good."

"You're going to love it!" She pats Jax on the chest and he just looks down at her hand. "Ok, *you* probably won't admit you like it, but Knox and Emmett will love it. Callum will likely be in your boat. Ev's broody part of the collection."

"We're a collection?"

"So funny." She bats her hand, ignoring his question, and walks past him towards Knox.

Jax kisses the top of my head. "Are you ready for this? You know she's going to lose her mind."

"I am." My heart thumps fast in my chest. "I'm so happy."

"Me too." He gives my side a little squeeze, plants another kiss on my head, and walks towards the house. "I'm going to check on E and make sure he's not stressing out too much with the food."

"Remind me why we agreed to let him cater for his own party." I slip my hand in his and walk with him to the house.

EVERLEE - CONFETTI

My heart feels like it's going to pound a hole out of my chest and my stomach has twisted so much I feel like I'm about to puke. All our friends and family are standing around us with Low, Lizzy and Betty in the front row, hands clasped in a chain. I don't think Low was going to grab anyone's hand, but Lizzy made her because she's just too excited.

My fingers wrap around the string, holding the large black balloon in place with pink and blue ribbon tied to the bottom.

"I can't wait to see what we're having!" Mom squeals, grabbing Beckett and Will's hand. She smooshed herself between them, claiming she's so excited her old woman legs may give out and she may need them to hold her up.

Callum steps forward. "We just wanted to thank you all for being here today with us. If you would have told us several years ago, we'd be standing at Knox's father's lake house hosting a gender reveal party, we would have laughed at you. But this woman here. She is our life. She's changed our lives for the better and we can't wait to experience this next chapter."

"Here, here!" Mom says, thrusting her fist into the air before clapping.

My eyes dart between Lizzy and mom, my excitement nearly boiling over.

"Does anyone want to share their guesses?" Knox asks.

"Girl!" Lizzy yells.

"Girl!" Mom yells.

"Boy! I mean, look at those men. They're a lot of beef-cakes!" Betty shimmies her shoulders.

"Becks?" Knox asks.

"I have no idea."

"No fun!" Lizzy pulls her hand out of Lows and swats Beckett on the shoulder, then promptly sticks her hand back inside of Lows. Tony is standing behind her and wraps his arms around her waist and whispers something in her ear, causing her to grin.

"Are we going to do this?" Jax asks, playing the part of mildly irritated. He's not. This is all part of the plan, but he plays the part so well.

"Yes!" I squeal. Please let's do this, so everyone knows. I feel like a volcano ready to explode.

All the men grab the string of the balloon and we start counting down from ten. The crowd joins in around six.

When we get to three, Knox yells. "Wait. Wait. Wait. I forgot the scissors. I'll be right back." He runs into the house.

"Knox!" Jax yells and the crowd laughs.

"I had a pocket knife he could use," Low says.

Knox runs out a minute later, carrying another large black balloon and Lizzy, of course, is the first to see. "Noooo!" she screams and starts jumping up and down.

Mom chimes in next. "No. Seriously." Her hand clamps over her mouth. "Really? You aren't teasing me, are you? I know how you are, Ev."

Tears are trickling down my cheek as all the emotions from the day boil over.

"You're serious?" Beckett laughs and I simply nod.

"Oh my God!" Mom yells out, then grabs dad's arm. "Can you believe it? Two!"

"See. Good things come to those who wait." He laughs.

"You stop it! Oh, my gosh!" She squeals again.

"You didn't tell me!" Lizzy exclaims.

"I wanted to surprise you."

Her eyes narrow at me before she winks and grabs Betty's and Low's hands again. "Carry on," she huffs playfully.

"Ready?" I ask and the guys pull a knife out of their back pocket and I grip the scissors in my hand.

"Yes!" Mom and Lizzy both yell, then look at each other and laugh.

Knox, Emmett, and Callum have one balloon, while Jax and I have the other.

"One... two... three!"

We all stab the balloons and they let out a pop-pop, less than a second apart. Pink and blue confetti rain down on us and mom and Lizzy scream.

"One of each! Can you believe it?" Mom bursts out, then runs over to me and cups my cheeks. "Oh Everlee. I'm so excited." She pulls me into a hug, then pushes me away. "I can't believe you didn't tell us."

"We've only known for a couple of days. They missed one on the first ultrasound."

"Two. Twins." Mom sighs, then moves to each of the guys to give them a hug. "Congratulations. I'd say you'll have your hands full, but you got enough hands. I'm still planning on coming up here to stay for a week or two after they're born. Does this change your due date?"

"No, but it's likely I won't go to full term."

Beckett walks over and gives me a hug. "So, you're saying there's a chance we're going to have New Year's babies?"

"Oh." I hadn't thought about that. Shit. That would put them roughly two weeks early, which I feel is right in that sweet spot. Oh, the publicity.

As if sensing my worry, Jax rubs his hand up and down my back. "They will come when they come. No sense worrying about it right now." His head tilts down when he catches me looking at him.

"Well, shoot," Mom blurts.

"What's wrong?"

"I made you a baby blanket, but now I'm one short." Dad hands her the gift bag he's been carrying around, then she passes it to me.

Sitting it on the ground, I bend over and pull out the blanket. It's mint green and super soft, with polka dot panels and zig-zag patterns sewn throughout. "I love it, Mom, thank you. They can use this for their tummy time."

"How do you know about tummy time?"

"Knox reads to me and the babies every night about what to expect."

"Oh, that Knoxxy."

"That Knox is just an angel," Knox says in a high pitch, poking his head into the conversation, resting his chin on my shoulder.

Wyatt walks over a minute later. "Congratulations."

"Thank you," Knox and I say.

"Who wants some cake?" Emmett asks.

"Wait!" Lizzy blurts.

"What's wrong?" I ask.

"Tones and I got you a gift, too. Well, kind of. Not really."

"That's super clear." Jax chuckles.

"You shush." Lizzy bats her hand.

Tony hands her the bag, and she reaches in and pulls out two over-sized onesies that say big brother.

"What?" Callum asks, walking over.

"For Woodford and Blanton."

"You bought our dogs clothes?" Jax chimes.

"Don't pretend like they don't wear clothes. If you recall, they had bowties at my wedding."

"Bowtie is a lot different from a onesie."

"Well, they've worn other stuff."

"No, they haven't." Jax's tone lacks confidence. "Knox."

"What?" he asks over his shoulder from where he's talking to Beckett and Will.

"Have you been dressing up our dogs and taking pictures?"

Knox's eyes grow wide. "What? No. That's crazy. Why would you ask me something like that?"

"You little shit. If I find out, you've been posing them in my room!"

"Why would you say such a thing?" Knox turns back to Beckett and Will, who both start laughing.

"That little shit," Jax mumbles under his breath.

"Well, then." Lizzy claps. "Let's go get some cake. Woodford. Blanton. Come here, boys."

"Don't you do it." Jax's tone carries the weight of an idle threat, lacking any true conviction.

When we get inside, Wyatt is standing next to something that has a sheet draped over it with a bow.

"What is this?" Knox asks.

"It's my gift to you. Sorry, the wrapping isn't any better." He laughs awkwardly, looking around at the others.

"It's perfect."

He smiles. "Do you want to take the sheet off?"

I nod towards Knox, but he shakes his head. "You."

"Do it with me?"

"Anytime," he whispers, pumping his eyebrows.

A few people near us laugh when I playfully smack him in the chest.

"What? It's the truth."

"Knox!"

We each grab the sheet and count to three and pull.

There is a collective gasp from everyone as we all stare at the beautifully carved piece of furniture.

"It's a changing table." Wyatt runs over excitedly and pulls out a hidden shelf. "You can pull this out to put your diapers and wipes and stuff on and this here," he opens a door. "Is a built-in trash can. And then you have drawers and such down here. It will convert to a dresser as they get older, but now I guess I need to make another one." He laughs.

"This is beautiful Wyatt," I say, running my hand over the smooth wood finish. "The feel, the stain, the grain. It is breathtaking."

Tears trickle down my cheek as I continue to rub my hand over it. This just makes it feel even more real. Our babies will be here in the coming months.

Our babies.

KNOX - DENY 'TIL I DIE

It's so early, it's still dark outside, but it's my favorite time to run. Just before the sun crests over the horizon, when the world is still asleep. Everlee snuck into my bed last night and she's still asleep, so I have to use the light from my phone to finish tying my shoes. She looks so peaceful laying there.

When I woke up, my first instinct was to gently wake her up with my tongue between her legs, but I hesitated, knowing she's been sleep-deprived because of frequent trips to the restroom during the night. So, being the gentleman I am, I decided to wake up Jax and see if he wants to go for a run. On our way back, we can stop by the bakery and get Ev some of her favorite muffins.

Callum and Emmett are gone this weekend working on Ev's surprise. They won't tell me what it is because they think I'll tell Ev, which... I can't guarantee I won't. When she puckers out that bottom lip or touches herself or shoes, or her boobs. Really anything. I turn to mush in her hands.

The nightlight in the hall shines in a thin sliver under the door, so I shut my phone light off and tiptoe across the room. The door handle gives a little squeak when I twist it and the sheets on the bed ruffle.

Looking over my shoulder, Everlee has just rolled over, but not woken up.

When I get into the hall, I suck in a breath after I pull the door closed. I leave a small crack, nervous it will creak again.

Jax's door is cracked open, which is odd. Maybe he couldn't sleep either?

Pushing the door open, the light forms a growing wedge in his room and I find two sets of eyes looking back at me.

Damn! If there was more light, I'd take a picture. Blanton and Woodford are curled up on the end of his bed, watching me, tails slowly swiping back and forth over the comforter. A second later, I feel the boop from a wet nose on the back of my thigh.

When I turn around, Luna is sitting behind me. "Hey girl," I whisper, rubbing her head.

Woodford and Blanton hop off the bed and stretch before they walk over to greet me. "What are you two doing in here? You know if he catches you-"

"What in the hell are you doing in my room?" Jax asks in a tired voice.

"Technically, I'm not in your room. I'm just outside of your room."

"It's too early for this shit." Jax grabs a pillow and chucks it in my direction.

"I wanted to see if you wanted to go for a run, then surprise our girl with some muffins when she wakes up."

Jax grunts and rolls over, turning his back towards me.

I look down at the pups and whisper, "I'll take that as a no."

Just as I reach in his room to pull the door closed, Jax bellows out, "Wait! I'll come. Give me two minutes."

"I'll be downstairs."

That guy. I chuckle, hopping down the stairs into the kitchen. Even though the coffee pot is on a timer, I switch it on so the water can get hot for Ev, just in case she gets up before we get back. I hope not, but her schedule has been so weird lately. The books say it will get worse the further along she gets and I'll be right there with her, rubbing her feet, back, belly, or getting whatever she needs. I'm so excited and want to experience everything with her.

Jax still isn't down yet, so I open the pantry door and grab the marker on a string and mark out another day.

Technically, we have right at three months left, but the twins will probably come early according to all the books. Lizzy was asking yesterday, and the day before, and the day before, when we want to have our baby shower. With Beckett's wedding coming up in a couple of weeks, then Thanksgiving and Christmas right around the corner, we're running out of time.

We'll talk to Ev about getting a date on the calendar today. It will have to be a weekend at the beginning of November.

"You ready?" Jax calls out, walking into the kitchen. He's bent over and touching his toes when I close the pantry door.

"I figured no pups this morning. Just me and you?"

"Yeah, that works."

"Sorry puppers. We'll take you on a walk this afternoon."

Luna walks over into the pen and climbs onto one of the three cots. We used to keep them in the pen at night, but they can jump over it, so we leave it open and allow that to be their space.

"Let's go, bro!" I bounce, nudging Jax's arm with the back of my wrist.

He looks at me, but doesn't speak.

We lock the backdoor, then do a few stretches in the driveway.

"Ooh, feel the burn," I moan."You want to hit the bridge?" I ask, turning onto the road in front of our house.

"You want to run that far this morning?"

"Five miles there and five back."

Jax thinks about it for a second, then shrugs. "Ok."

Nodding, I run a little faster.

It's a small bridge that he and I run to sometimes. Like one of those two-lane bridges surrounded by trees you see in the movies. It's nice, because the stream running underneath it has a lot of rocks, so it always sounds like it's bubbling, which is really relaxing and if we can time it right, then we can see the sunrise.

I've come to this bridge a lot, especially at the beginning of the year when I was trying to figure out what to do about dad. It wasn't until the last few months on my morning runs with Jax that I brought him there. For so long, it was just my place, but I wanted to share it with him. I wouldn't call it *our* place, but I wanted him to know it's a nice place if ever he needed somewhere to just think.

Because it adjoins the woods, there are always animals and birds making noises, and because it's close to the water, there's a healthy amount of frog croaks as well. That was one of my favorite things to do with Jax when we were serving. When we had down time, we would both sit outside at night and just listen to the sounds around us and talk about our days with Mrs. Mary.

We get to the bridge a little over forty minutes later and run to the stone edge and press our hands against the cool stone to catch our breath.

After a few minutes, Jax looks at me. "Do you want to talk about it?"

"Talk about what?"

"Whatever is on your mind."

"I don't think anything is."

"You woke me up at the crack ass of dawn to run to your spot."

"I'm good."

He stares at me, doubt etched through the lines on his face.

Laughing, I nod. “I am. I mean, there isn't really anything. We just need to talk to Everlee today and get her to pick a date for the shower.”

“Lizzy has called me every day for the last week.”

“Yeah, me too, and also Ev.”

“I may change my number.”

“No you won't. We just need to get her a date before she picks one for us. And we also need to work on creating our registry.”

“We're not doing a registry.”

“We need to do a small one, at least. People are going to want to buy us something and I don't feel like getting a hundred blankets. Books say not to put those on the list because people will just buy those, anyway.”

“Is that what the books say?”

I stare at him, debating on calling him out, with his stupid little face. He doesn't know that I know he's also been reading books. When I snuck into his room a few weeks ago for one of my latest photo shoots, I found two hidden under his bed. But the problem is if I call him out on reading pregnancy books, then I would have to admit I was in his room when he wasn't there. So to save us all, I simply say, “Yes.”

He watches me, almost like the fucker was testing me to see if I would out myself, but ha ha ha. Jokes on you, buddy!

“I've been looking at strollers. Reading some reviews,” he offers.

“Me too!” I say excitedly. “We're going to need one lightweight.”

“And I'll want to be able to push and turn with one hand.”

“Yes! Also, one handed release.”

“And it needs to work with the car seats. We may need to get adapters or something.”

“And I've seen some that convert, like you can lay the backs down or set them up.”

“Like a bed in case they fall asleep. Love it!”

We both pause and just stare at one another. Who would have ever thought we would be so excited to talk about strollers?

"So today. You, me, Ev, and the baby store. Truth be told, I've been dying to get my hands on those little scanners to zap stuff around the store."

"I think I'll let Ev hold that."

"Come on, man!"

"Knox. I know how you are."

"Mannn. Spoiling all my fun."

"I was going to push you in the stroller to test it out."

"Shut the front door!" I yell, jumping up and down. "You were?"

"What the fuck? No, I was just kidding."

"That was cold and below the belt. Completely uncalled for. You know how I am."

An evil smile curls his lips. "I know. That's why I did it. Payback for your little bitch ass sneaking into my room and taking pictures with the pups."

An audible gasp leaves my lips, but I restrain my hands from clutching my chest.

He knows.

Deny 'til I die.

"I don't know what you're talking about."

He laughs, rolling his eyes. "Let's go get Ev her breakfast, then talk her into picking a date and building a registry today."

"I could kiss you!" I jump towards him to give him a hug, but he was expecting me and stiff arms me.

"Try that again and I will toss your ass into the water."

"You may take my jump from me, but you can't take my love for you!"

EVERLEE - SERIOUS BUSINESS

"KNOX! IF YOU CAN'T use that scanner responsibly, I'm going to take it away from you!" Jax scolds with a hint of amusement in his tone and a playful glimmer in his eyes.

We've been in the bottle section for thirty minutes now, and before that, we were in the crib section. Wyatt offered to build our beds so they match the changing tables, but he asked we take pictures of styles we like.

"There are so many options," Knox whines. "A few of the mom groups I'm on talk about these two." He holds up a tall bottle and short bottle and looks between them.

"Which do you like?" Jax asks, unamused.

"Well, it's hard to say. They both have different benefits in terms of gassiness and grip," Knox continues.

"I was asking Ev." Jax corrects.

"Oh, right."

"I was planning on nursing." I shrug, not offering anything else.

Both guys say, "It's nice to have a backup."

Knox nods towards Jax to finish. "In case we need to supplement or give you a break."

"Or your boobs."

Knox grabs Jax's bicep like he just had the best idea. "I've seen those bras that men can wear the simulate breast feeding."

"Shut the fuck up."

"Language!" I slap his arm. "We're in a baby store."

"Babies can't talk, plus I've been monitoring my surroundings. There isn't anyone near us."

Knox's eyebrows perk up. "You're really going to have to watch that mouth after we have the kids. They pick up on everything."

"You'll need to say less dumb sh-stuff."

Knox quirks his brows and his lips with a sassy look, then scans both the bottles and sets them back on the shelf. "It's best to try them and see which one our kids like best." He scans them both.

"Next section, carriers, sheets, then strollers!" Knox points into the air like a safari guide on a mission.

"Lord help me."

Hooking my arm into Jax's, I look up at him and smile. "You love this even if you're pretending you hate it."

"I love *you*." He boops the end of my nose.

Knox runs back over to us with a carrier hanging around his neck and one in each hand. "So I've narrowed it down to these three."

"How?" Jax asks, astonished.

"Well, by color, texture, clasps, total weight limit. These three have highest marks, but I will say, the one around my neck feels like it has more padding."

"No," Jax shakes his head, amused. "How did you narrow them down so quickly?"

"Oh. Right. Research online, obviously. While you've been researching strollers." Knox points at Jax. "Don't pretend you haven't been, because I saw your search history."

Jax starts to yell at Knox, but Knox continues and I slip my hand in Jax's and squeeze.

"I've been researching carriers. I was satisfied with your level of commitment in finding a stroller." Knox turns to me. "Do you want to try these on? See which you like better?"

"Nope. I've got four men. If we're out in public, my goal is to have you all carry them and save my back."

"So I can break it later?" Knox thrusts into his hand as a woman with a stroller walks by giving him a snooty glance.

He calls after her. "I was checking the flap and the swing." He thrusts his hips again, this time without the hand, while Jax and I laugh.

"Bro, you can't save that. Don't even try."

"Shut it and just try these on," Knox huffs, handing Jax a carrier. "We can carry Knox Jr. in this with some sunglasses on."

"While you wear your man purse?"

"Why do you have to pretend to be so macho? You're going to regret not having one of these fashionable and handy accessories when you're taking our kids for a walk."

"They're not dogs, Knox."

Knox jumps on Jax's side, giving him a koala hug. "I know that, Jaxie poo." Then jumps off just as fast.

"Remind me why I thought it was a good idea to come here with you."

Thirty minutes later, the guys are in the stroller section testing out all sorts of features on several strollers while I take a seat in the rocker section and stare at sheets on the wall. I told them I was testing out rockers, but truth is, I'm just tired and want to sit down. Plus, I know they're going to be in the stroller section for a while. On the way to the store, they were rattling off a list of must have features. They bicker quite a bit, but underneath it all, they have a connection unlike anything I've seen. The way they move, the way they think, everything, is in perfect synchronicity. I swear Knox knows what to say and do, to drive him up a wall because he knows him so well.

After an hour passes and I've almost fallen asleep twice, I decide it's time to head over to find the boys and see how much longer we're going to be. I quickly scan a set of olive-green sheets, some gray ones, and some woodland animal sheets. The foxes and deer are too cute. Also, little cloth play tents in the room with oversized stuffies just makes me melt.

On the way over to the guys, there's a tiny display full of soft fuzzy blankets and there's a light gray one with a cream-colored sherpa interior that feels like clouds. I add a few to the registry, smiling, knowing that I'm going directly against Knox's orders. He was very adamant about not registering for blankets, but it won't hurt if we have several of these.

The store is one enormous square with a track that goes around to each section. When I turn the last corner to get to the stroller section, I find a small group of women huddled around and laughing. As I get closer, I realize Jax is at the center of the women with several strollers lined up and Knox is walking up with a carrier strapped to his chest with a human child sitting in it.

"What's going on?" I ask, face twisted and confused.

"We've narrowed it down to these three," Jax says with an abnormally perky voice, as he studies one that looks more like a wagon than a stroller.

"Oh, hey babe!" Knox says, coming to a stop with a car seat in his hand.

I give my leg a small pinch, hard enough to feel it, but not enough to be noticeable. Nope, I'm not sleeping.

"Allison's been crying all day and Tabby here, needed a break and I needed to see what I thought about this carrier and I have to tell you. I really like it. Jax said he'll let me pick."

My eyes grow wider with every word he says until they are burning from the lack of moisture.

The woman, who I presume is Tabby, waves meekly. "Hi. Sorry I borrowed your friend. He just seemed really excited to help, and he had kind eyes."

Knox shimmies a shoulder and taps Jax.

"Yes, I heard her. She just clearly doesn't know you."

"You kid. He kids," Knox says quickly, looking at Tabby, then his voice gets higher and he bounces a little. "Isn't he so funny, Allison? Funny looking."

Allison balls her fist up with a smile and hops up and down in the carrier and kicks her legs.

"She thinks so." Knox smiles and Jax just cuts his eyes at him, but doesn't say anything.

"Did you find a rocker?" Jax asks, standing up from looking at the wheels of the stroller.

"I did, but I'll let you test them out." He probably knows I'm lying. I didn't try any, except the one I was sitting in, which wasn't bad. I mean, I sat in it for a while and almost fell asleep, so I guess there's something to be said about that.

Jax lets out a low hum, then turns to Knox, who is handing Allison back to her mom. "I like this one. Several of these women have the same one and agree."

The women chime in, nodding and calling out distinct features they like, mostly centered on the one hand release and weight.

Knox walks over, squats down, and studies the wheels-I don't understand their fascination with the wheels, then grabs the handle bar and bounces it a few times. "Nice suspension."

"Are you planning on taking them off-roading?" I laugh, reflexively grabbing my stomach while it jiggles, and suddenly feel like Santa.

Knox sees and his lips purse into a smile, before his eyes flick to our audience, so he doesn't speak. I can only smile, knowing that whatever he was going to say was going to be inappropriate and sexy. My stomach clenches at all the possibilities. I don't know if it's the hormones or what, but I have been H-O-R-N-Y the last couple of weeks like amped up levels, which is saying a lot.

Someone taps me on my shoulder, and when I look around, it's one of the women. She has a nervous smile twitching on her lips then whispers, "I think it's so great what you're doing for these men. Being a surrogate has to be so hard."

"Oh... I'm... not."

Her brows twists.

"Yeah, she's our wife," Knox calls over his shoulder like it's no big deal that I'm married to more than one guy. He lifts the stroller, sets it down, then pushes and pulls it, flips both canopies closed, then stands up and lifts the release handle and it collapses in half. "Yeah. I like this one too."

"Married to both." The woman's eyes grow large.

Another woman behind her mouths, 'Wow', more surprised than judgmental.

"You must have your hands full."

"You have no idea." Pretty sure their heads would explode if they knew there were four of them, so I just keep that to myself.

"Do you want to get it now or add it to the registry?" I turn around and ask.

Knox looks wide eyed and hopeful at Jax.

"Do you want to get it now?" Jax asks.

"Yes!" Knox explodes.

"I wasn't asking you," he chuckles. "Ev?"

Knox clasps his hands under his chin and sticks his bottom lip out. "Sure."

"Yes!" Knox thrusts his hands in the air and gives me a big hug.

"I'm going to fuck you from behind while we look at the stroller," he whispers.

An abnormally loud laugh bursts from my lips, then I realize I'm not sure if he's being serious or not, so then I laugh at that. And before I know it, I can't stop laughing and tears are streaming from my eyes.

"Oh, that happened to my girlfriend. We called it her prego giggles. She laughed all the time, and it was like once she started, it wouldn't stop for at least ten minutes. It was hilarious. People would just start making up things to say, calling out vegetable names or brands of cars and she would lose it."

"Carrot!" Knox shouts and I continue laughing and I have no idea why. I don't know if it's because the entire thing seems funny or because he looked so excited when he said it.

"Are you ready to go, giggles?" Jax walks over, slipping his hand around my waist, and presses his lips to my head.

"Yes. Can we do an early dinner? I'm starving."

"Of course. Where do you want to go?"

As I give a shy smile, my fingertips graze my lips, eliciting a playful eye roll from Jax. "Bo's for French onion soup?"

"Yes."

"Oh my gosh. I've been trying to get in there for months," Tabby says, shifting Allison in her arms.

Knox's ears perk up and he slides to stand in front of her. "Next time you call, tell them you're a friend of Knox Fisher and they'll get you a table."

"What? No. You're serious?"

"As I am about these strollers."

Jax puffs out a breath.

"We know the owner. He's a close friend."

"You're serious."

"Yes. I thought the stroller comment would clear that up." Knox laughs, intertwining his fingers in mine. "Don't forget Knox Fisher."

"I won't. Thank you so much. I seriously can't tell you how much this means. My day has just been one thing after another and Allison's teething, so she's been crying all day... and now..." she shakes her head. "Thank you."

"You're welcome. Bye Allison." Knox waves and Allison giggles.

"She seems to be laughing at you, so who's the funny looking one now," Jax mutters under his breath.

JAX - LONG LOST BUDDY

When we get to Bo's, we go upstairs to our table that we always have reserved and sit down.

"Just the three of you tonight?" the server asks, walking up with our waters.

"Yes. Do you want your usual for drinks and soup for you, Everlee?"

"Yes, please." She smiles.

"I'll be back. I'm going to wash my hands," Knox says, dipping away from the table.

Everlee opens the menu and reads each description like she doesn't already have it memorized. It's cute how her eyebrows move when she reads, like it's something she's never seen before and it's a mystery to be solved.

She must feel me looking because her gaze lifts to meet mine, and she smiles. "What?"

"Nothing. I just like watching you."

"I know." She pumps her eyebrows and smiles.

Her look causes my cock to twitch, making me shift in my seat. "Not what I meant."

"Shame. Maybe later?"

"Definitely." These last couple of weeks she's been hot for cock, which I mean... none of us are complaining. We haven't been doing as many group events, because it's getting more uncomfortable for her and her gag reflex has been extra sensitive.

"Ev?" a voice chirps, pulling our gaze.

"Keeley! Hey, what are you doing here?"

Keeley's cheeks blush as she looks over her shoulder. "So, I met a guy, kind of."

Ev looks around her, but doesn't see him.

"Oh," Keeley laughs. "He's in the bathroom. We just finished dinner, and I saw you up here, so I wanted to say hello and apologize for not being able to make it to the shower. Lizzy said it was so sweet and amazing... and twins!" She claps her hands quickly. "I was helping-"

"Look who I found in the bathroom!" Knox says, beaming. "Hudson Locke, himself."

My eyes nearly bulge out of my head. It's been years since I've seen him, but he looks the exact same. As they approach, I stand from the table and walk around it to give him a hug. "What are you doing state side, and here, no less?"

Locke laughs and looks affectionately at Keeley. "Well, it looks like I'm moving here."

"So, you and Keeley?" I ask, nodding my head towards the girls. He had talked about Keeley several times when we were overseas, but it was always more like kid sister vibes, not uproot your life and move here with her type vibes.

"Yeah." He shoves his hands into his pockets.

Knox looks over his shoulder at the girls, who are talking about the shower and the babies and everything else, then hooks his arm around Locke's shoulder. "So that's *the* Keeley?"

"Yeah."

"And her brother?"

"It was a little rocky at first, but I think we've worked it out."

"I never put two and two together," Knox says, shaking his head, still shocked.

"How could you? There are so many Keeley's."

"So you're done with the SEALs?" I ask, grabbing the top of the seat nearest to me.

"Yeah. For now. Thinking about getting into some contract work."

"Have you reached out to Dufrey?" Knox asks, rubbing his hands together. "He started his own company doing contract work for the government."

"Not yet. I lost his number, well everyone's pretty much. Same reason I didn't reach out to you jokers. Was at the beach over the summer and Key got mad at me and threw my phone into the ocean. I probably deserved it, but I lost all of my contacts."

"Love it! A little spitfire." Knox bounces, a smile still spread across his face. Locke and Knox became fast friends, even though we only were together for a few months before we left.

"I'll text it to you. Number still the same?" I offer, knowing that Knox is going to be too excited to remember.

"Yes, sir."

The server brings our drinks back.

"Oh man, I don't want to interrupt your dinner. We're just leaving and Key saw her friend. We're doing some house hunting this weekend, trying to find a place. Key's is too small."

"We have a place beside us we don't really use. It's mostly been a place for Ev's family when they come into town, but I don't think they will be here before Christmas, so it will give you a couple of months, and even then, if you haven't found a spot, her parents can stay with us."

"Oh man! You should totally stay there! You will love it. Plus, it's right next to us, so we can hang out and catch up. We have a hot tub and bar on our roof and we grill out! Oh, come on!" Knox is a step above dropping to his knees and begging.

Locke thinks about it for a second, then nods his head. "Yeah, that could work. That would give us eight or ten weeks at least to find a place. Just let me know how much rent is."

"No man. You save the money for the down payment on your house," Knox says, clapping his hand on Locke's shoulder.

"I can't just live in your house for free."

"We'll work something out then." I learned a long time ago that Locke is not one of the guys that will take handouts. He's worked all his life for what he gets and he has to earn it- same as us, so I can appreciate that. Just like we wouldn't accept the house, he won't either.

"Ok." He nods, satisfied. "You still talk to Brady?"

"Yeah. He lives in our basement. He drives us around when he's in town. We don't need him to, but he wants to. Same reason as the rest of us, I guess. We aren't good at taking things for free."

"That's the truth." His smile drops. "How's he doing?"

"You know. One day at a time."

We all nod, but don't say anything, and then a second later, Keeley is walking over, slipping her hand into Locke's. "Let's give them some space so they can eat their dinner, plus we have to go look at some places."

"They said we can stay in their extra house while we look, to take some of the pressure off and allow us to save for a down payment."

"We can't do that." She smiles.

"You-" Everlee swallows a spoonful of soup. "Sorry, it's just so good. Totally should! We don't really use it, plus you'll be close to Lizzy and me."

"It would be nice to have a little more time, so we're not stressing," Locke coaxes.

"Can we come by tomorrow and look at it?" she asks, tilting her head to the side and flipping her foot behind her.

"Of course! How about you come over in the afternoon? We'll show you the house, then invite Tony and Lizzy over and grill out some steaks. Emmett and Callum are getting back around lunch so it will be perfect," Everlee offers.

Keeley and Locke look at one another and smile. "Yes. That sounds like a date!" Keeley chirps.

"Let us know what we can bring."

"How about a dessert? Just nothing with fruit. Lizzy brings a fruit dish every time," I laugh.

"Don't pretend you don't love it. It's the first thing you go after when we eat." Knox playfully jabs me in the shoulder.

"Oh, they are so fun. I've had her fruit trays many times. Ok we'll bring a dessert!"

I create a group chat with Knox, Locke, and me, so Locke gets our numbers, then give him the address of our house. When they leave, Knox and I just look at one another for a second.

"He looks good," Knox says, taking a sip of his Old Fashioned and breaking the silence.

"Yeah. I never thought he would make it out of there alive. He was always the first one in and the last one out."

"Good dude though. You could always trust him to have your back, no matter the consequence."

We both nod in agreement.

Everlee lets out a moan, and we both snap our heads in her direction. She has the soup bowl tilted up to her lips, then looks sheepishly over the rim at us, as she slowly sets it on the table. "Sorry. It's just..."

"So good. We know." I lift her hand to my mouth and kiss her knuckles.

"I should probably get another bowl. They seem to each want a bowl for themselves," she says, pointing to her stomach.

"Yeah, that's probably best." I toss her a quick wink.

"Hey," she whispers as she leans forward. "Tonight, after we get home... I'll be the egg and you two be the chicken and we'll see who comes first?"

Knox gasps and shoves his fist in his mouth and bites. "I see what you did there. Check, please!" He throws his fingers in the air and pushes away from the table.

"Sit down," I bark, quietly.

"Did you need something?" the server asks.

"Oh no. I was just teasing." Knox looks at me and rolls his eyes and mumbles something under his breath.

Everlee orders her other soup, while Knox and I order three sandwiches. One for each of us and then a third to share with Ev, because she will inevitably take one of ours, even though she insists she doesn't want one. We order the wagyu, because we know it's her favorite.

EVERLEE - A VIBRATOR IS NOT A DOG TOY

THE BATHROOM IS WARM when I walk in and steam from the hot shower clouds the mirror. After dinner, we came home, and I needed to rest for a little. My back was hurting, and I ate a little too much food. Two bowls of soup, a full sandwich, then a few bites from both Knox's and Jax's. But I couldn't stop eating. It all tasted so good.

I told the guys the plans hadn't changed for the night, but just dragged out a little longer.

"I swear to God Knox, if that is you trying to play a joke..." Jax bellows from the shower.

Slipping out of my clothes, I don't speak, but tiptoe over to him. When I open the opaque shower door, he's facing the wall with his hands pressed against it while the water runs down his back.

His back straightens, but he doesn't turn around like he can sense it's me.

God, he's a sexy man. The way his muscles rip through his shoulders and down his back.

My hands rub down his spine, then around his waist to grab his hardening cock. A low groan vibrates through his chest and when he starts to turn around, I stop him, pressing him against the wall and he lets me.

"Everlee..." His tone is a quiet plea.

"I want you to fuck me."

"It's kind of hard if I'm not facing you." He chuckles under his breath.

"Not like this. But like this..." I rub my fingers further down his spine and between his hard and toned cheeks. He sucks in a breath and clamps them together.

"Relax," I whisper, kissing his back and pressing a lubed finger at his forbidden entrance.

"Ev..."

"Shhh," I whisper against his skin, sliding a finger out before pulsing it back in again.

His low and guttural moan bounces around the four walls of his shower as he gives himself over to me.

The way he is, everything about him, makes me dizzy with lust and love and need.

During the last few weeks, my strap-on has been a little tight around my growing belly, so I ordered a smaller hand-held dildo that I can use in place until after I have the kids.

Grabbing the tube of lube off the bathroom floor, I squirt a little over the tip and press it at his entrance, causing his hips to buck forward.

"What-"

"I bought us a little toy."

When he tries to look over his shoulder, I push his head back. "No peeking."

"You're killing me."

"Never. Now put your hands on the wall and bend over so you can take mama."

"Fuck me," he cries out, then leans over.

Carefully, I insert the blue dildo into his ass, moving it with a gentle rhythm, gradually increasing the depth, and applying more lubricant as needed. In only takes minutes until he's rocking back on it slowly, taking what he wants. What he needs.

"Give it to me, Jax." With my other hand, I reach around and grab his cock, letting it slide in and out while he rocks back on the dildo.

"Ev." He grunts out, still moving his hips. "You know… my rule."

"Fuck your rule tonight. Give this to me," I command, squeezing my hand tightly around his cock until he bucks.

"Damn you, woman! I will punish you for this." His tone is a silent cry.

"I love you too."

He rocks his hips harder and faster, impaling his ass onto the cock in my hand, and his cock into my hand. His cock is slick with water and soap as the hot water continues to pour down on us.

His back arches as his muscles clench. I know he's getting close to coming, but he's trying to hold himself back.

"Jax. You better fucking come!" I twist the cock slightly in his ass and he groans out, arching his back. Turning my hand silently, I grab around the base of his cock and rub the tips of my fingers over his balls.

"Ev… er… lee." Every muscle in his body clenches as his finger tips dig into the hard tile on the wall, water dripping down his back as his come shoots against the tile.

He throws my hand off his cock, rips the dildo out of his ass, tossing it carelessly to the ground, shuts the water off, then turns and lifts me. His fingers grip my ass while his face buries into my neck, lips pressed hot like fire to my skin. He quickly switches between kissing, sucking, and biting my skin, nearly sending me into an orgasm of my own.

"Damn you. Damn you, woman," he growls at me, sending a tingle through my body and making my nipples so hard they could cut glass.

He carries me out of the bathroom and lays me on the bed before he walks out of the room, leaving puddled footprints in his wake. The cool air blows across my skin, causing goose bumps to erupt on my arms and legs and a shiver to move down my spine.

A second later he's walking into the room with the rose vibrator in his hand that Lizzy accidentally got me a bouquet of when I was in the hospital. My head turns to the side as I watch him approach. He knows that thing and what it does to me.

"Given how you like to fall asleep after you orgasm, I'm going to tease you with this until Knox comes in here to finish you off."

"Jax."

He tosses the vibrator on the bed, then climbs over top of me and presses a finger to my lips. His semi-hard cock brushes against my wet pussy, making it throb for him.

"You don't get to talk right now, Everlee, dear. You're about to be punished."

"Jax."

Without speaking, he rolls me onto my side and spanks my ass with one hard, quick slap. Fire erupts across my skin, before he uses his right hand to rub over my ass and his left to rub against my clit.

"Jax," I stupidly cry out again.

He rolls me to the other side and slaps my other ass cheek while he presses the rose vibrator to my clit. My ass cheeks clench as a low moan escapes. So many sensations so quickly together.

"Everlee. You *will* be quiet."

I have to bite my lip to prevent myself from talking, because I want to fire back a sassy remark. Anything, but I hold it for now.

He rolls me to my back and runs his fingers up the inside of my legs, spreading them wider and wider. The pads of his fingers tickle the inside of my knee, causing me to squirm. With his eyes locked on mine, he slowly drops his head in between my legs and runs the scruff of his beard along the inside of my leg.

A moan escapes and I panic for a second, but he doesn't spank me. Part of me is relieved while the other part is a little sad. He slides up and gently swipes his tongue across my pussy, enough to tease me, but do nothing else.

My hands grip into his hair and hold him in place, and he chuckles under his breath. "What does mama want?"

"Mama wants you to stick your tongue in my pussy so I can ride your face."

He smiles. "You can ride my face, but I'm not going to let you come."

"Ass."

"I know."

He presses his tongue in and my back arches, sending my head into the bed and my hands over my breasts. His hands slide up my body and palm my stomach as he continues to eat me, tongue pulsing in and out before he swipes over my clit.

My orgasm is coming quickly, spurred on by all the foreplay in the shower with Jax earlier. Even though he wasn't touching me, seeing him feral like he was, causes me to go wild.

Knowing he will stop when he hears how close I'm getting, I bite my lips to hold back any noises, but my stomach contracts and with his hands on it, he pauses and looks up at me with a smile.

"Everlee, dear," he says in a low and oh-too-sexy voice.

Fearing the tremble in my voice will give me away, I simply hum a response.

His head tilts to the side. "Everlee." He sucks on his teeth with a tsk tsk tsk. "You were trying to hide your orgasm from me."

"No," I say in a rush, my voice filled with forced determination.

"Everlee," he says in a low voice.

Squinting my eyes, I try to keep my face as emotionless as possible.

"You need to set a good example for our kids," he says, sliding up my body, leaving my pussy throbbing and wet.

His lips brush over my belly, placing gentle kisses on it, while his hands move up to my breasts, gently pinching my nipples until I moan. They've gotten larger throughout the pregnancy, but most of the tenderness has subsided.

"I don't know where Knox is, but it looks like I'm going to have to fuck you." His hard cock presses at my entrance and I buck my hips into him.

"It's a tough job, but I'm glad you're up to the task. I mean, someone in this house has to." My lips quirk into a playful grin.

Shaking his head, he smiles and says, "Shut the fuck up." He leaves a trail of kisses up to my jawline.

"Make me," I whisper, body humming.

"Gladly." His lips crash to mine in a powerfully sweet and desperate kiss. As he enters me, a surge of pleasure courses through my body, escaping my lips in a moan. In that moment, with our bodies intertwined and lost in a state of pure ecstasy, our lips hover ever so close, breathing each other in. My fingers claw at his back as my hips thrust into him, needing more, but he stops.

"No, no, no, no," I cry out.

"Patience, my love." He leans back with his cock still inside of me and grabs the flower and places is over my clit. With the hum and suction going, he slides in and out slowly.

"Oh." A low groan rumbles from within. "Oh." My orgasm is so close. "OH!" I scream out as every nerve in my body sings in exultation. "Oh! Ohhh! I! Oh! Jax!" He tosses the rose onto the bed and fucks me hard and fast as tears stream down my cheeks. My body is still singing when he brings the rose back. "No, no, no, no." It latches on, sucking my swollen clit into its pedals of pleasure.

Jax continues to grind into me, stretching me.

"Jax. Take it off. I... can't."

He pauses for a second. "You say the word."

The word.

Cupid.

Do I want to say it?

My lips remain sealed as tears stream down my face. Seconds later, my chest is heaving off the bed as my second orgasm rips through me. I pull the pussy pleaser off and chuck it across the room, its hum vibrating against the floor.

"That wasn't nice," Jax teases.

"Fuck me, now." I grab both sides of his head and pull him into a kiss, then fall back onto the bed. His tongue pulses in before he pulls off our kiss and flips me over, then pulls me onto all fours.

Hands on my hips, with the head of his length notched at my entrance, he blows a warm wind across my back causing it to arch, then he slides in, unleashing his size and speed into me, over and over again until he's crying out my name.

He collapses to the bed and I roll over with my back pressed to his side.

"Knox is going to be sad he missed out," Jax mumbles, running his fingers through my hair.

"Where is he?"

"I don't know. I left him a note."

"A note?" I laugh and then silence settles around us as our bodies relax.

Silence.

Too quiet.

The vibrator.

"Jax?"

"Yeah?"

"Where's the vibrator?"

"Near the door where you threw it."

We both sit up in bed and find an empty floor, then hear a bark from downstairs.

"Shit!" Jax bolts out of bed and runs into the hall.

I roll out of bed, much slower than him, and race downstairs.

Jax is standing in the kitchen laughing, shutting the vibrator off.

"What happened?"

"Woodford thought it would be funny to take your vibrator, only problem is, his teeth must have hit the power button and turned up the speed. When I got down here, Woodford and Blanton were trying to attack it and bark at it, but they wouldn't get close to it."

"That's what you get for trying to take something that doesn't belong to you." I point at the pups and laugh when they both roll onto their backs and tilt their heads to the side, wagging their tails. "Awww."

"Oh, yeah. I can tell you're going to be the easy parent."

"Shut it."

EVERLEE - BECKETT'S WEDDING

"Oh my God. It's over. The wedding..." He turns toward me, his face a combination of sadness and disbelief.

"What do you mean, Beckett?" I ask.

"That was Emmett. He just called and said a sprinkler busted overnight at our venue and everything is ruined."

"No."

Beckett falls to his knees and buries his face in his hands.

Turning to Knox, I'm frozen for a moment.

"Who's ready to get married bitches!" Lizzy asks, bursting into the room, hands flared into the air. "Oh no. What happened?" Her eyes dart from Beckett to me.

Not wanting to say the words out loud again, I walk over to her. "Sprinkler burst at their venue last night, and flooded the place."

"Oh shiznit."

"Yeah." Flipping my phone over, I look at the time.

Ten after ten.

The wedding is supposed to be in just under seven hours.

"What are we going to do?" Lizzy asks, sitting down in the closest chair.

"I'm thinking." My hands rub over my ever-growing belly as I try to come up with an idea. It has taken Beckett his entire life to get to this point. Before Will, he was a playboy who stopped at comm in the word commitment.

When I look over my shoulder, Knox is on the ground with Beckett, trying to console him.

"I got an idea, but you need to come with me," I say.

Lizzy nods, equal parts excited and apprehensive.

"Knox. Get Beckett ready. We're still having this wedding. I'll text you and let you know where to bring him."

Grabbing Lizzy's hand, we turn towards the door. Mom and dad are walking in at the same time we're leaving, so I grab Mom's hand and pull her along with us.

"What's going on? What happened?"

"The venue is ruined and Beckett thinks his wedding is over."

"They could just go to the courthouse."

"Mom. We're giving Beckett the wedding he never knew he wanted."

"Well, don't you overdo it." She rubs my stomach.

"I won't. That's why I have Lizzy."

"I'll try... pulled a muscle in my back." She presses her hand to lower back and lets out a wince.

"I told you that the swing you installed in your house was going to hurt you."

"Well, it was better than the clap down pole Tony wanted."

"What?" Mom asks, confused.

"You know... clap twice and the pole descends from the ceiling."

"Tony wanted that?" Mom asks.

"Well, no. I lied. I did. Do. But Tony's still trying to figure out how to make it work."

"I can't with you." I laugh.

"Yeah."

"Mom." I look over my shoulder to see her falling behind, so I stop.

"How do you walk so fast being so pregnant? My goodness."

"Mom. Focus. Do you know the guys at Beckett's firehouse?"

"Yes. Why?"

"Do you have their numbers or addresses? Any way to get hold of them?"

"Well." She looks at the ceiling for a moment. "Yes. I have Goose's mom's number. Denise. So sweet."

"Mom." God bless this woman, but I need her to focus. And I'm hungry. It may be ten o'clock, but I freaking want Emmett's French onion soup.

"Yes. Yes. I'm calling now."

"Thank you. Ask her to have Goose call me."

Seven hours to pull off Beckett's wedding.

When I get in the car, Brady is sitting behind the wheel. He's back for a few weeks, before he goes back out to work with Michael on some job. He doesn't talk about it and I don't really ask.

The guys asked him to stay with me today, because they don't want me driving around. After today, Brady's going to head to the beach for a few weeks and relax.

He turns around and hands me a thermos.

"What's this?"

"Gift from the guys. I was just about to come inside and get you when you were walking out."

My heart swells with excitement.

When I twist the lid off, the hot smell of French onion soup swirls around me.

"That's not soup, is it?" Lizzy asks.

"The guys know me so well."

"Don't you need like bread and stuff with it?"

"I just like the broth. The bread gets too soggy and hits my gag reflex."

"You have one of those?" she asks coyly.

My eyes shoot open wide, then look at Brady in the front.

"Oh please. Let's not pretend Brady knows nothing. You have four guys and three holes."

"Fuck Lizzy. Shut up."

She cackles and leans her head back, closing her eyes. "You'll need to watch that dirty mouth of yours once you have your littles running around."

Ignoring her comment, I ask, "Didn't get a lot of sleep last night?"

"Just a wee bit tired."

Hmm. I've noticed she seems to be tired a lot more lately. Every time I bring it up, she dismisses me. Tony has been traveling more, so I hope everything is ok between them.

"Well, take a nap now, because we have a very busy day ahead of us."

She opens her one eye and looks at me before closing it as her hands brushes over her stomach and she settles into the chair.

Oh my God.

Lizzy's eyes shoot open. "What?"

"You're tired."

"Yes."

I poke her left boob, and she quickly jerks back, letting out a loud scream. "And your boobs are sore." My voice gets louder with each word that passes through my lips.

She looks at me, but doesn't speak.

"Lizzy..."

"Everlee..." Her eyes dance with a secret as a smile creeps across her lips.

"Lizzy..."

"Everlee..." she mocks.

"Liz-"

"Oh fine! Yes. I'm pregnant. Happy?"

I slap her on the arm. "Yes, I am happy! I'm going to be an auntie! But why didn't you tell me?"

"It's Beck's day."

"Hmmm. Like it was *your* day."

"I see the irony in the situation and was going to pretend I didn't find out until after, so you couldn't throw it back in my face."

Laughter consumes me. "I can't believe you would rob me of one second of this!"

"I know. I'm sorry."

"How far along are you?"

She pulls her bottom lip. "So..."

"Lizzy. How far along are you?" My hand presses into the seat.

"Don't be mad."

"Lizzy."

"I'm like four months."

"Four! Four freaking months, Lizzy! Were you ever going to tell me?" I rub my hand over her stomach and feel her little bump. "You have a little bump." My lip puckers out in equal parts excitement and anger. "You have a little bump!"

"I know, I know! I'm a shit friend for not telling you sooner, but there's been so much going on."

"I don't give a shit if the world is exploding and aliens are invading! You tell your best friend these things." I cross my arms and look out of the window, trying to process. A second later, I snap my head towards her. "Obviously, I'm super happy and excited for you, but I'm not happy with you." I lean over and kiss her belly, then look up and glare at her. "You have me conflicted, woman!" Anger winning for now, I look out of the window. Moments later, her hand slips into mine, and our fingers intertwine. We both give each other a gentle squeeze, but I don't turn to look at her.

7 HOURS LATER

Nerves threaten to tear my muscles apart as the jitters I've had for the last thirty minutes have caused my legs and arms to be a fidgeting mess.

"It's going to be fine. It looks absolutely amazing. Beckett and Will are going to love it," Lizzy says, grabbing my hand.

"You think so?"

"Honey. I know."

Once mom was able to speak to Goose and have him call me, the news of the five-alarm fire that was Beckett and Will's wedding spread like wildfire and everyone pitched in to help. Their crew from both firehouses sprang into action. I went to Beckett's firehouse and spoke with the chief and he agreed to clear one of the bays where the trucks park and allow us to set up there.

Fortunately, they were having a small wedding with mostly comprised the men and women at their firehouses, so they had the day off, anyway.

We grabbed the boxes of flowers from the venue, the chairs and anything else we could salvage and brought them to the firehouse. It's convenient that most of their friends drive trucks. What looked funny was the line of trucks lined one after the other, with an archway and loads of flowers and decorations looking like a convoy through town.

Jax took Will away for the day, while Knox had his hands full with a panicking Beckett. I almost had to block Knox's number for the day with the number of calls I've been getting.

But I didn't.

Emmett helped manage the food and refreshments, Callum directed once I told him my vision and mom made sure I was hydrated.

A hand slides around my waist and lips press to my neck. Leaning my head back, I savor the kiss, unsure who it is. When I feel a gentle nibble, that gives it away.

Jax.

He loves to bite.

"Will is here. Where do you want him?"

"Any word from Knox?"

"I've had lots of words from him today."

A smile parts my lips. "Recently."

"No. He's been a little too quiet. Which is always concerning."

When I turn around, I see a small crowd of people gathered outside of the firehouse doors.

"Let's get this show started." The sharp crack of my hand clap echoes through the large warehouse like building, causing me to jump when it bounces back to me. "I just wanted to thank you all for your helping this afternoon, getting this set up. I know you had all planned on attending this wedding, but maybe not being such an integral part. It goes without saying, but thank you so much. You have turned this firehouse into a gay man's dream." The crowd laughs.

"All because of you," a muffled female's voice echoes from beside me. When I turn, I find Lizzy with her hands cupped around her lips and tears streaming down her face.

"Because of everyone. I simply had the most to gain by not hearing Beckett moan for the next fifty years about his wedding." The babies have a foot lodged in my rib cage, so I press it down, then continue. "But in all seriousness, thank you! It looks truly amazing!"

Giving the band a quick nod, they start playing music while Goose and another guy lift the bay door. The groomsmen start to seat people while Lizzy grabs my hand.

"I know you're his best wo-man and what not, but your guys have given me instructions that you aren't to be walking back and forth too much."

Patting her hand, I give her a smile. "I'll be fine."

"But I won't be if I fail your men in best friend duty. So… they scare me slightly more than you."

"Seriously?"

"I mean, only by a little. Your pregnancy hormones have you…" she holds her hand in the air near her head.

"No, I meant you won't let me walk."

"Oh." She quickly tucks her hand behind her. "That's awkward. I was only kidding about your hormones. You've been perfectly normal."

Overcome with emotion, I reach across the space and pull her into a hug.

"Oh, ok. We're doing this. Cool, cool."

"I love you, Lizzy. So freaking much. You are the very best friend a girl could ever hope to have."

"Back at you."

Twenty minutes later, Beckett's jeep pulls up with Knox driving and Beckett blindfolded and his arms pinned behind him.

"Fuck me. What did he do?" Jax asks, standing beside me, jaw on the ground.

Knox gets out of the Jeep and runs around. "Well, don't just stand there. I'm passing the baton. He's been so unbearable. I didn't even have time to coif my hair."

Coif? I can't get the question out of my mouth because of my smile.

"Coif?" Jax mumbles beside me as we walk over to the Jeep.

"Are we here? Where are we? I hear violins," Beckett calls from the Jeep, swiveling his head from side to side.

"Knox?" I ask softly, staring at the scene in front of me.

"He was freaking out, and I thought you wanted it to be a surprise, but he was fighting me. So I had to bind his hands. Side note, he may have a kink. If it was Will," he hurried out the last part.

"Ew Knox!" I slap at his chest.

"Fucker, kept saying you've been Knoxxed, by Knots," Beckett calls, struggling with the binds. More for show than panic now.

"Idiot," Jax mumbles.

"Knots was his nickname."

"Yeah, I got that after the thirty-minute ride and explanation."

"Thirty minutes? Where were you?"

"Oh, I've been driving in circles," Knox smiles, proud of himself, then pats Beckett on the shoulder. "You may need to get gas now, though. This thing is a real gas guzzler."

"Gas guzzler? I can't." Jax bats his hand in the air and walks away.

"Don't leave me with him!" Beckett and Knox call out at the same time.

Jax stops and walks back. "Knox, go grab Lizzy."

"The Queen has arrived. Or is arriving." Lizzy laughs. "You know, since I'm still walking. I guess that was a little premature. Anywhoozle! Also, Emmett said he's ready."

"Liz?" Beckett turns his body.

"Who else has a voice-" Jax starts, but Lizzy interrupts him.

"Has a voice like an angel?" Lizzy finishes. "So sweet." She wraps her arms around Jax, who keeps his arms in the air, then gives a quick pat on top of her head. "Ev, your parents are waiting for you."

Glancing over my shoulder, I see them lined up at the mouth of the bay. "Keep his blindfold on until he's ready to walk down the aisle. I want to see his face."

Jax and Knox help him out of the car while Lizzy straightens her back and fixes her dress. He asked me to be his maiden of honor and asked Lizzy to walk him down the aisle. He asked her a few days ago, so she's not had a lot of time to process, which was his plan all along. We both knew if she knew beforehand, she'd be completely unbearable.

"Beckett, if I untie your hands, do you promise not to remove the blindfold?" Knox asks in a very parental tone.

Beckett sighs. "Am I getting married? Are we doing this?"

"Yes," Lizzy says. "And you're going to love it."

"Fine." He huffs and his shoulders drop. "Whatever you all did, I will love it. I would have married that man at the courthouse or in a field. Hell, even on the side of the street." He turns to where Knox had been standing. "Knox, I know I gave you a lot of shit today, so thank you for being there for me. I'm so grateful that Ev married you and I have you in my life."

Knox calls on the other side of him. "That was very sweet. Can you say that again, but facing me?"

"Who was I talking to?" Flabbergasted, Beckett turns to where Knox is standing now.

"No one."

"Why didn't you stop me?" he yells with a hint of humor mixed with frustration.

"It just sounded so nice."

"I was talking to air!" Beckett wipes his hands over his face and everyone lurches forward, screaming for him to stop.

"Let's do this!" I thrust my hands in the air, excitement vibrating through my body. I never thought I'd see the day Beckett would get married.

"Everything ok, darling?" Mom asks when I get to her and dad. "Why is he still blindfolded? He's not going down the aisle like that, is he?"

"Yes, everything is fine and no," I laugh. "He's not going down the aisle like that."

"Well, you youth... I don't know what's trending."

"Donna," Dad sighs.

"What?" she whispers to him. "They like to do things to be different and it's Beckett, so there's no tellin'."

Chuckling, I give the sign we're ready and the string quartet begins to play *How Deep Is Your Love* by Calvin Harris.

Looking over my shoulder, I find Beckett with his hands on Knox's shoulders, following him in a mini train. Knox sees me and nods for me to turn around, then blows me a quick kiss. Part of me expects to see Knox rolling his hands in a circle and kicking his feet from side to side, but daddy Jax is walking beside them, likely making sure Knox behaves. They get to a stop at the entrance, and the photographers are taking pictures, both from behind Beckett into the bay and from the front of the aisle, by Will.

Knox gently guides Beckett's hand onto Lizzy's arm, and Jax and he maneuver their way past us, down the aisle to take their seats alongside Emmett and Callum.

Callum catches my gaze and gives me a quick wink that makes my stomach twist.

Mom clears her throat beside me, so I lead her and dad down the aisle to their seat in the front, then take my spot to the left. Beckett and Will opted for a small wedding party and really made it their own, which is great. Will has two people standing with him, and Beckett has Lizzy and me. There were plenty of other guys from the firehouse, but Beckett felt if he picked one, others may get their feelings hurt, which would lead to a huge wedding party.

For comfort, I forwent the suit I had planned and opted for a high neck black chiffon babydoll dress. The weather has still been on the warmer side down here even though it's fall and the babies are like my personal inferno, so…

Lizzy waits a few beats before she whispers something to Beckett. His hands reach up to remove the blindfold, but he pauses. His chest puffs out and his shoulders rise. He pulls the blindfold off, but his eyes are still closed as he lets the cloth fall to the ground. When he opens his eyes, they grow wider and wider as his bottom lip trembles. His head falls to the side and tears stream down my cheeks. At the same time, his hand grips Lizzy's as he takes in the firehouse before him.

My heart melts even more when I look at Will with his bottom lip sucked in and his hands nervously fidgeting in front of him.

Lizzy must squeeze his arm or signal to move because he gives a quick nod and they walk down the aisle. Everyone stands to admire him in his tuxedo, indigo blue bowtie, and blue suede shoes.

They take their time getting down the short aisle, where Lizzy delivers him to Will, who gives her a little wink, before she takes her spot behind me.

"We are gathered here today…"

EVERLEE - WELL, SHIT...

ONE MONTH AND COUNTING.

The last week, I have felt... extra.

Extra bloated. Extra big. And if you ask the guys, they may say extra moody.

Lizzy is trying to go above and beyond in the friend department for keeping her pregnancy from me, by throwing me not one, not two, but three separate showers.

When we were visiting my parents for Thanksgiving, she threw us a small one there with my family and Mrs. Mary. A week later, she threw us a surprise one at Allure, which was... awkward at best. I'm not sure if it was planned, but got the feeling someone at the club mentioned something, so she and Low threw one together- the decorations were baby accessories from one of our role-playing rooms. It was nice, though. Everyone at the club pitched in and got the carrier Knox had picked out, two car seats, and a bunch of diapers.

Our main shower was just last week. Keeley and Locke lured us to their house with a lie about something being broken. We should have put two and two together when we were all walking over, but they were brilliant. They basically just asked Callum and Emmett, and of course, Knox and Jax had to see their buddy. And then, with all of them going, I had to go.

Again, very clever.

When we walked in, everyone was there to surprise us. Beckett, Will, and my parents were there, Low, Betty and Wyatt, too. Sophie and her family even made the trip over the pond. We got way more than we needed and Knox's dad delivered not only another dresser, but two handmade convertible cribs as well.

Yes. Obviously, I bawled like a baby.

While my family was in town, we did our Christmas as well. Mom went overboard and filled the kids' closets with more clothes than they will ever wear. So now I'm sitting in the middle of their floor sorting and hanging their clothes.

The room really came together nicely with each of the babies getting their own wall with the crib and dresser, which meet in a corner. Their spacious walk-in closet has separate walls for each of them to hang their clothes, with a shared shoe shelf tucked away in the back.

We have two rockers on the right wall with a share table in between so two of us can rock them, feed them, and put them to sleep and in the middle of the room is the oversize blanket mom had made.

A soft knock on the door pulls my attention. When I look up, Callum is standing there looking as hot as fire. He has a little more gray sprinkled into his hair, but his piercing blue eyes still hold those intoxicating flames in them.

"I was just coming to check on you. You've been up here for a while."

"Mom got us a lot of clothes."

"I offered to help." He walks into the room and settles on the floor behind me, encircling me with his legs and embracing me tightly.

"I know. I just... I know I've been unbearable the last few weeks. I'm not sleeping and I'm just hot and miserable. They're so big."

His hands snake down to under my belly and he lifts it up and I nearly fall back into him as my eyes roll into the back of my head. “Callum,” I moan out.

He chuckles in my ear, causing a shiver to run down my spine.

“That feels so good.”

“I know. Well, I don’t know, but I can imagine.”

He leans to the side for a second, rocking me with him, then lifts my shirt.

“Callum?”

“Shh.” He whispers and tingles prickle up my neck and over my scalp.

There’s a small click and then a second later, he’s rubbing lotion over my stomach, gently kneading it. Knox or Jax have been the ones to do it at night, while Emmett usually rubs my feet.

“Cal?” I ask softly.

“Hmm?”

“Where have you been lately?” The words get caught in my throat for a second as tears well in my eyes. I don’t know why I’m crying because I wasn’t expecting to.

“I’m working on something for us.”

"Okay," I say hastily, trying to hide the quiver in my voice. Fail.

He pulls me to the side and looks at me. “What’s wrong?” He wipes away the lone tear that’s trickling down my face.

“Nothing. I don’t know why I’m crying. I was just wondering where you’ve been. You’ve been traveling so much.”

“I know. I’m sorry.”

“And you won’t tell me.”

“I’ll tell you if you want me to. It’s a surprise that I was hoping would be finished by now, but I’ve hit a few snags.”

Taking in a deep breath, I blow it out slowly. I want to know, but also don’t want to ruin the surprise.

“No. I’ll wait. I was just scared that maybe… you…”

“Everlee?”

Tears stream down my face now. This is really not what I expected when I started talking to him.

"It's nothing. I really don't know why I'm crying. I'm sorry."

He laughs, sitting me upright again. "You have nothing to be sorry for, love. I love you and our growing family and if you thought I was going somewhere... I'm not. You have me for forever."

All I can do is nod.

He continues to rub my belly, lifting and providing a gentle pressure. The babies feel him, because a second later, there's a powerful punch or kick, I'm not sure what or who, right into his hand. I scream and Callum wrenches back his hand in shock before he puts it back down.

"I think you woke them."

We stare at my stomach and watch a body part push against my stomach as they roll over.

"Come here," Callum says, sliding backwards across the floor until his back is resting on baby boy's dresser.

He slips my shirt over my head and leans me back on him. My nipples have gotten bigger along with my boobs, and now rest on my stomach. When I try to cover them, he moves my hands to the side.

"What are you doing?" he scolds lightly.

"I..."

His hands guide up to my breast where he grips and massages them. It's been two weeks since I've let them touch me like this because while I know this is a beautiful process, I just feel... not.

"You are so sexy."

A mangled laugh erupts from between my lips that sounds like a cross between an elephant and a goose.

"Everlee." His tone is scolding as he pinches my nipple.

My head presses back onto his shoulder at the same time a moan escapes and a tingle shoots through my body to my clit.

"You are beautiful and so fucking sexy," he growls into my ear before he sucks it into his mouth.

"Callum. No..."

"If you want me to stop, you say our safe word. Until then-" One hand pinches my nipple while the other slides down my body and slips under my pants. "I'm going to keep playing until you come and then I'm going to fuck you until you come again."

"Cal-" Before I can get his full name out, his finger finds my clit, and it's singing hallelujah. My hand grips onto his muscled forearm as my head presses into his shoulder. God, how I've missed his hands- their hands- on me. "Oh, Callum." Either my clit missed him or it's super sensitive right now, because in less than a minute, my hips are bucking as my orgasm pulses through me in sweet sweet waves.

"Get on your knees," he commands, leaving no room for question and I obey.

He rips my pants down and hungrily smacks my ass before he notches his hard length at my entrance. He doesn't wait before he presses in and I moan out, screaming his name. Oh fuck me, that feels good.

He drags it out and slams in, delivering another rippling sensation through my body.

"Are you ok?"

"Yes. Yes. Don't stop. Please don't stop."

He unleashes, pounding his hard cock into my slick, wet pussy. The familiar thwap thwap thwap that I've missed so much fills the room.

Another orgasm builds quickly, the size of his cock filling every inch of me.

"You feel so wet and amazing," he growls, digging his fingers into my hips.

"So good. So, so, so, so, ahhhh." My second orgasm rips through me and my stomach tightens as ripples of pleasure flow across my skin like a warm breeze.

Callum cries out, then explodes inside of me. "Oh fuck, Everlee!"

"Sounds like I missed the party," Jax says, standing at the door, watching me as his bulge presses against the seam of his pants.

Giving him a half smile, my head falls back down as my orgasm still causes my stomach to tighten.

Callum pulls out and when I sit up, Jax tosses me the towel that's in his hands. "I was getting out of the shower when I heard this peculiar noise."

Placing the towel on the floor beneath me, I press my hands on my knees and feel another ripple in my stomach.

"That's odd."

"What's odd?" Callum and Jax ask in unison with an edge to their voices.

"My stomach..." My eyes grow wide. "Oh, shit."

"Oh, shit?" Jax steps forward.

"My stomach."

"Yes, you've said that. We need more," Callum urges, helping me to stand.

"I thought it was the orgasm, but-" My stomach tightens again and panic sets in. "I think I'm in labor."

A second later, there is a ruckus clamoring up the stairs as Knox, followed by Emmett, burst into the room. "You're in labor?" Knox shouts.

"You heard that from downstairs?"

"Of course not. I have the monitors set up and was testing them out when I heard you two."

"You listened to us?" Callum asks, and I can't get a read on his tone.

"Why are we still talking about this?" Jax asks, then turns to Emmett. "Get the car. Knox, get the go bags. Callum, get her pants."

"I need to pee."

"I don't think we have time for that," Jax says, grabbing my hand.

"Jax." I squeeze his hand. "I'm *going* to the bathroom. I'm full of come and don't need the doctor trying to sift through that. Plus, if I don't pee right now, I'm going to piss myself and not the figurative, but the *very* literal."

"Fine, hurry."

My head snaps in his direction as my eyes narrow to thin slits.

"Or take your time. Take all the time you need. Pee twice if you want." He holds his hands up in retreat.

When I get into the bathroom, I sit on the toilet and just pee. I don't think it's ever felt so good. My stomach tightens again and my pulse quickens. "Is it time to meet you, my loves?" I whisper, running my hand over my stomach. "It's a little early for you. You still have just over four weeks."

I have to wipe myself several times to get as much of our come out of the way as possible.

After I finish in the bathroom, Callum is waiting for me. "Let's go." He reaches for my hand.

"Where's Jax?"

"I think you scared him off." He laughs.

"He told a pregnant woman she can't pee."

"Unbelievable."

"You're mocking me."

"Never." He pulls my hand to his lips and plants a kiss on my knuckles.

When we get to the car, Knox is in the third row and Emmett and Jax are in the front. Callum helps me in, then runs around to the other side.

"How are you, mama?" Knox asks, leaning over the back seat.

"Who put baby in the back?" I ask, eyes wincing as another contraction hits me.

"Jax thought it would be best if I sit back here. Apparently, I'm too excited. So?" he presses, glancing at my stomach.

"I'm fine. They don't hurt, yet. Just feel like someone's squeezing my stomach, then releasing."

"That's good. I hope."

"How close are they coming together? They don't seem to last too long," Jax calls from the front with his phone in hand on the stopwatch app.

"Only a couple of seconds long, and several minutes in between."

"Tell me when you feel your next one."

"Yes, sir."

Emmett's eyes find mine in the rearview and I can tell by the creases in the corner of his eyes that he's smiling.

We're in the triage room at the hospital twenty-two minutes later.

There's a soft knock on the door, and then a nurse walks in. "I'm nurse Jackie. Doctor Yiminitz has been called and is waiting for my assessment." Her cheeks blush when she looks around the room at the guys. "Let's see what's going on here." She hooks a light pink band around my stomach and flicks the machine on to the right of me.

I've had a few ultrasounds over the last several weeks, and every time I see my loves, I breathe a little easier.

Right now is no different.

She runs the wand over my stomach and the thump thump thump of their rapid little heart beats is music to my ears and a second later, their little feet kicking and moving nearly brings a tear to my eye.

"There they are. Everything here looks and sounds great. Let's see how you're progressing."

She lifts the gown I had changed into when I first got into the room and squirts some lube on the tips of her fingers. I almost tell her that's unnecessary, but embarrassment robs me of my voice. It's probably not the first time this has happened.

She lets out a small huff and pulls her hand out, removing the glove and tossing it in the trash. "You aren't dilated at all, so I don't think you're in labor."

"Braxton Hicks?" Knox blurts out, stepping forward.

"Probably. But I want to keep her here for a few hours just to be sure. Sometimes sex can start the process."

A heat races up my chest to my cheeks.

The nurse pats my knee and offers a warm smile. "It's ok. It happens all the time. I'm going to step out, but will come back in a little while to check on you. The remote is right beside you if you want to watch television. If you need anything, you can step into the hall or press the call button."

When the door closes, we all look at one another and take a deep breath. Jax walks over to the machine beside me and looks at the paper that's inching its way out of the printer.

"Well, this is nerve wrecking," Emmett says, breaking the silence.

"But I just want to say that I'm proud of you all. It was good getting a test run in before the actual day."

My phone dings and I look down at it.

Lizzy: Well?

"Who told Lizzy? I swear if she can sense-"

"I texted her." Jax holds his hand up. "She's on dog duty, so I wanted to make sure she knew what was going on, just in case."

Pursing my lips together, I just grin.

"What?" he sighs.

"Nothing."

"Not nothing."

"You like her."

"I… I don't *not* like her."

Lizzy: Bitch, you better be pushin'!

Laughing, I look at the guys. "If I don't answer her, who do we think she'll call?"

Jax groans. "Just answer her, for all our sakes."

Everlee: Probably a false alarm. They are keeping me here for a few hours before they send me home.

It's close to midnight when the same nurse from earlier walks in. "I've been monitoring your vitals from the station, and there's currently no sign of contractions. Likely sex set it off, and, or, dehydration. Make sure you're getting plenty of fluids and try to take it easy these next few weeks."

"Bed rest?" Knox asks.

"Not yet. Let's just try to take it easy." She tilts her chin down and gives a playful, yet serious glare.

"You got it!" Knox nods, clasping his hands behind him like he's just received an order from his commanding officer.

"Is she free to go home?" Jax asks.

"Yes. Your doctor has reviewed the documents, and we're processing your paperwork now. Maybe another twenty minutes." She walks over and unhooks the strap from around my stomach and turns the machine off. "When is your next doctor's appointment?"

"Next week."

"Ok. She'll do an exam at that point and see if you've progressed at all."

"Thank you."

Just under an hour later, we're climbing into bed. I made the guys get me a chocolate milkshake on the way home.

What the babies want, the babies get.

CALLUM - OWW OWW

PULLING THE DOOR CLOSED with a gentle click, I stand outside of her room for a minute. It's been two weeks since our hospital visit and she's been in bed most of the time. Even though the nurse said she wasn't on bed rest, Knox has been super protective. Dinner is at six and at seven, we go for a walk around the house before one of us gives her a bath. After Emmett saw her trying to bend over to wash her legs, he made the executive decision that we give her baths now and take care of her.

Our first wedding anniversary was last week, so Knox and I decorated her bedroom, while Emmett fixed her favorites and Jax kept her busy. Not with sex, because Knox has the entire house freaked out about giving her an orgasm and inducing labor.

With New Year's Eve tomorrow night, I've been a little busier helping both of the clubs get ready. This has really been a test to see if we can step away from the businesses like we're wanting to after the babies are born and so far we've been very impressed across all of them. It may be hard, but when the babies get here, we won't want to do anything else.

I was hoping to have Ev's surprise complete by Christmas, but we ran into a few weather delays so it looks like it will be ready closer to Valentine's day, which will still make for a nice surprise. Knox has been going crazy trying to figure it out, but the guys and I decided he can't know because he'd ruin it.

After Ev's bath tonight, we decide to watch a movie. It's supposed to be Emmett's pick, but because Ev's been moaning a lot more today and carrying her stomach around, he gave his choice to her. Knox has set up some blankets and pillows on the floor in front of the couch, along with several bowls of popcorn and some bottles of water. Ev picked a new fake dating romcom, which actually looks pretty funny. She's all smiles and giggles the entire time she's watching these types of movies, which is nice to see.

Emmett, Ev, and I take the couch while Jax and Knox sit on the floor by her legs, each rubbing a foot.

"How are you feeling?" Knox asks. It's the question he asks at least twenty times a day, to the point Jax got signs on little paddles made so she can hold them up. Which, of course, turned into Knox, snatching one and chasing Jax around the house, yelling, 'Let me paddle that bottom, boy!'

"I'm good now that I'm sitting. There's just been so much pressure today. They've been moving quite a bit more as well." She laughs and lifts her shirt over her perfectly round belly. "See."

A lump protrudes from her stomach and moves from left to right at the same time another lump thrusts out.

She lets out a moan and leans to the side, pressing the one lump in with her hand. "Someone has a foot in my rib. I've loved being pregnant, but I can't wait for them to get here for so many reasons." She sighs and leans her head on the back of the couch as she draws in a deep breath.

The doorbell rings, which sets the dogs off, but before any of us can stand up, an all-too-familiar voice chimes in. "Hooo hooo."

Jax groans.

"Oh, stop!" Ev bats him on the shoulder. "I invited her over since she's been wanting to see this movie."

"I forgot she can't watch it at her house. Oh wait. She can."

"Boo boo bear!" Lizzy sings, walking around the corner, her belly now protruding, into the living room.

"Here Lizzy." I stand, offering her my seat.

"Too kind. Too kind." She plops on the couch beside Ev and leans over to give her belly a kiss. "Hello my babies. Auntie Liz is here."

Taking a spot on the floor on the other side of Lizzy, I grab a bowl of popcorn and hand it up to the girls. Ev rests it on top of her belly and laughs. "I'll be happy when I can breathe again, but this built-in tray is kind of nice." She picks up the remote and turns the movie on.

Halfway into the movie, I look behind me and find Ev has fallen asleep on Emmett's shoulder. Lizzy follows my eyes, then looks back at me, smiling. She leans forward and whispers, "How's she doing?"

"Ehh. She's not been complaining too much, just a lot of heavy breathing and sighing. I think she's ready. She said she felt a lot of pressure today, so I'm thinking she'll have them early."

Lizzy claps and gives a little squeal.

Jax and Emmett both laugh out loud, pulling our attention.

"I knew you were a romcom guy," Lizzy says leaning forward, patting Jax's shoulder.

"It's a funny movie," Jax defends.

"You tell her babe!" Emmett teases.

"Shut it." Jax squeezes his leg, and Emmett jumps a little, causing Ev's head to shift.

She lets out a small moan and then a louder one. A second later, her eyes are open and they lock into mine. "Oww!" She grabs her stomach.

"Oww?" Knox turns around to say, eyes wide with excitement. "Like oww oww?"

"No dipshit, like bow chicka bow wow." Jax smacks him in the back of his head.

"It was a valid clarification," Knox defends, eyes getting wider by the second.

Ev lets out a low guttural groan and looks at her stomach. "It's like oww oww."

"Oww oww!" Knox throws the remaining popcorn into the air as he bolts upright. "It's go time, boys. Oh my God. It's happening."

"I knew it! I knew when she texted me this morning saying she was feeling ick that things were going to happen!" Lizzy thrusts her fist into the air.

"Knox. Seriously?" Jax sighs, looking at the pile of popcorn on the floor.

"It was an accident."

"That's bullshit and you know it. In some fucked up reality of yours, you've always envisioned a moment where you could throw popcorn in surprise and you chose this time to do it."

"I. Well. You're not wrong."

"No shit." Jax smirks with a smug satisfaction.

Knox wraps his arms around Jax's and squeezes. "You know me so well, daddy. Daddy! We're going to be daddies!"

"Get out of here."

"Right! Babies time!"

Forty-three minutes later, we're at the hospital and Everlee has been admitted to a room where they have her hooked up to machines and are watching her vitals. They said she's in active labor, but hasn't dilated much yet. She's been trying to fall asleep for the last twenty minutes, but the contractions keep waking her up. Lizzy, of course, lost her mind when we texted because she is so excited we're having New Year's Eve babies. I've texted the clubs to let them know we won't be there tomorrow and Low replied immediately with exclamation points and celebratory horns.

Tomorrow is supposed to be a check-in with the general contractor for Ev's surprise, but I just emailed canceling that, too. I wish I could have Beckett and Will help with the surprise, but knowing Beckett, he would ruin it and I can't have that. Not after the months of keeping this thing a secret from her.

She's my world, and I'd do anything to make her happy.

My gaze falls on her. Our wife. It's amazing to see how far we've come in just under two years. She came into our lives like a wrecking ball and now our babies are doing the same. With her head turned to the side and her eyes closed, she rests her hands on the bottom of her stomach.

My love and her belly.

I pull in a deep breath and feel something tug at my heart.

We're going to be dads tomorrow.

EVERLEE - "IT'S NOT A DIL-DONT"

I PRESS MY HEAD into the pillow as another contraction hits me. It's been fourteen hours now and I've not had breakfast or lunch and I'm pissed. The contractions are coming closer together, but my water hasn't broken yet and they want to wait to give me an epidural because it will slow everything down.

So I'm breathing.

I've had four dicks in me at one time. How hard can this be?

Stupid Everlee. Stupid.

My stomach tightens, and it feels like I'm being ripped apart from the inside.

"Just breathe. Hee hee hoo hoo," Knox encourages, grabbing my hand.

"Fuck your hee's and hoo's! I need these babies out of me right now!" I growl out, squeezing his hand.

The nurse walks in, when I'm in the middle of my rant, and smiles at me.

"Sorry," I mumble, sitting up as much as I can to see her.

"Don't be sorry, honey. I've heard worse." She lifts the paper printing out of the machine and looks at it, then presses on my stomach, and finally peeks under the gown. "We're going to do another exam in just a little to see how far you've progressed."

Jax and Emmett just left to grab a bite to eat, even though they tried to lie and tell me they had to go check on something. They've been by my side the entire time and I know they're hungry, but they were refusing to eat since I couldn't. I appreciate their attempt at not rubbing it in my face, but I'm happy they left for a minute. I'm terrified of shitting the bed when I push these kids out, so all I've had is water and ice.

But it's the good ice. Which almost makes up for the pain and hunger I'm enduring right now. The whole focus-on-a-point and breathe shit isn't working for me.

At my last exam, the doctor said I've only progressed a little, which means several more hours.

Knox, of course, is in the corner, crash reading what to expect after the babies are born like he's prepping for a college final and Callum has been pacing the floor, taking phone calls and firing off texts and emails.

Leaning back, I close my eyes and try to relax and will these babies out in a safe, quick, and painless manner.

"Hoo hoo!" a voice chimes.

Before I even open my eyes, a smile pulls across my face.

Lizzy has been checking in on me most of the day, and when she found out my progress had all but stalled, she started sending me all sorts of ideas she found online to help move it along.

When I open my eyes, I find her holding a bouquet of roses–this time actual flowers- in front of her face. Even though I can only see her eyes, I can tell she has a shit-eating-grin on her face, which means she's up to something.

"Lizzy," Callum drones in a semi-amused tone.

"Boys. My darling." She flits over to my bedside and looks at me. "How are you doing?"

"Been better, but overall pretty good."

"I bought you a rose." She winks.

"Looks like several." I laugh.

"No. I *brought* you a *rose*."

"Lizzy."

She tilts the bouquet down and there, somewhat buried in the middle, is a red rose vibrator she had sent me a dozen of last year.

"I've been doing some reading and orgasms help… so. While it may be weird to have the guys… you know…" she makes a bed squeaking noise with her mouth. "I thought this little guy could help. I also brought him a friend to play with."

"Lizzy." I rub my hand over my face because I don't have any other words.

She looks behind her. "Callum. Watch the door."

He grumbles, but walks over and sticks his head out before he closes it.

"Excellent," Lizzy chirps before she pulls out the rose vibrator, which is attached to the base of a lavender colored dildo. "I know. It's super basic, but I didn't want to get anything too over the top."

The door opens and we all freeze as panic coils in my chest.

A second later, Jax and Emmett walk in, then pause and look at the vibrator and dildo in my hand.

"Is that a dildo?" Jax asks.

"Well, it's not a dil-don't." Lizzy snaps back with a smile.

"And a bouquet of roses this time." Emmett smiles, snaking his hand into Jax's.

"I've read that having orgasms help move things along and help with pain," Lizzy says, grabbing my hand and shaking the dildo in it.

"We also read that," Jax says, walking to stand beside Lizzy and rubbing my leg.

"So then, why haven't you been giving my girl orgasms? She literally *needs* them."

All the guys look at one another, but I jump in. "There's not really an easy way."

"Hence my gifts." She shrugs with a satisfied smile.

No one moves or says anything for a second, so Lizzy claps. "Let's go! I charged Rosie up for you all night."

"Liz," I sigh.

"Everlee," she retorts. "Like I think it would be a little much if I snatched." She laughs, shaking her head, then continues, "If I snatched that out of your hand, lifted your gown and did it for you."

"You think?" Jax remarks.

"Yes," Lizzy turns to him and says simply, completely missing his sarcasm. "But I would do it for you."

"Please don't. I love you and all and we have shared some close moments, but you... there... with that... that's like an entirely different thing."

"Well, it's not the ideal situation for me either, but friends don't let friends endure stalled pregnancies when they have a vibrator that can snatch their soul in under a minute."

"You should get that on a shirt," Jax chimes.

"Don't tempt me, papa bear." Lizzy claps his shoulder, smiling.

"You should try it," Knox says, walking over and rubbing my other leg.

"Excellent!" Lizzy claps. "I'm going to step out of the room for a bit. Do you want me to sneak you anything to munch on?"

"No."

"Right. The shits."

"Lizzy. Fuck." I press my head into the pillow and look at the ceiling for a minute as embarrassment washes over me.

"What? You shouldn't be ashamed of that. It's a natural thing. This is all so beautiful. Plus, I know about all the kinky stuff you all do. This is child's play."

"Go!" I yell with a smile cracking the corners of my face.

She kisses my forehead and whispers, "I love you", before she leaves.

"She needs her own soundtrack when she's around," Emmett laughs.

"Wrecking ball?" Jax adds.

Knox claps his hands, then rubs them together. "Shall we?" He grabs the rose vibrator from my hand.

I've been here for almost twenty-four hours. Having an orgasm or two isn't the worst idea. "Fine."

"Yes! I'll go wash them. To dildo or not to dildo?"

"My Shakespearean man."

"Well, I do have a way with words." He gives me a quick kiss on the forehead.

"No dildo for now. Ask me again in an hour." I laugh and pray I'm kidding.

JAX - NYE

I've never been a jealous man when it comes to Everlee and the guys, but Everlee and that vibrator... that may be a different story. She's on her second orgasm in less than five minutes and I'm so fucking hard. But this isn't about me right now, this is about our girl. Emmett is watching me from across the room with that fiery look in his eyes that makes me want to bend him over and claim him, but again. This. Isn't. About. Me.

Callum and Knox have been planted by Ev's side, and I don't know how they're keeping it together and keeping their hands off her.

A hand grips my shoulder, and when I look up, Emmett is there, looking down at me. "You ok over here?"

"Managing, you?"

"Same." His hand moves to the back of my neck and he squeezes. "Beckett's been texting, looking for updates and said he's trying to get flights for him, Will, and his parents, but said they're all sold out."

"Tell him to keep us posted and we can chip in on cost if they need help."

Emmett winks. He's already done that. "He said if they don't find something, they may just hop in a car and drive. It's just over twelve hours and they can split the driving."

Everlee's moans echo through the room, followed by a groan. She's pressing her back into the pillow as she grabs the edge of it and squeezes.

"Take it. Take it." She throws the rose at Knox, who fumbles it like a hot potato for a second before he grabs it. "Oh God," she cries out.

Bolting from the seat, I'm at her side with Emmett a second later. "What's wrong?"Con... trac... tion."

Callum kicks his shoes off, tears the pillows off the bed and climbs behind her and starts rubbing her back and hips.

"It felt... so good... then it hurt... so bad."

A laugh erupts from my mouth before Knox and Emmett both give me death stares. "What? Come on. That sounds like a song or something."

"Hand!" Ev commands, reaching out for me and Knox.

Her little fingers slide into our hands, and squeeze with a force that I never knew existed. Knox and I both lock eyes, each of us wanting to cry or scream out or something, but both of us holding it in for her.

Emmett is on the other side of me, rubbing a towel on her head, when two nurses run in, doing a stutter step, looking at us. There was a shift change a little less than an hour ago, so this is the first time they are seeing us, though I have to imagine a note has been left on the charts or chatter has filtered through the floor.

A second later, they snap out of it and move around the room, looking at the paper while the other walks over to stand beside Knox.

"Everlee, I'm nurse Bea. How are you doing?"

"Hurt...ing. Long... contraction."

"I'm going to do a quick exam to see how you're progressing."

Everlee nods and grips my hand tighter for another second before the pain eases.

Nurse Bea slips her gloved and lubricated fingers into Ev and feels around. "You're over halfway there. Were you wanting to have an epidural?"

"Yes! Yes please."

"Okay. We'll get a doctor in here to administer it for you."

"How much longer?"

"Hard to say. Still could be a couple of hours." She looks at her watch. "It's almost nine, now." She pulls her face. "It could be tonight or early tomorrow morning. I'm also going to send your doctor in to check on you and break your water. Hang in there, mama. Looks like you got an excellent support system here."

There's a knock on the door before it opens. "Are you decent hook- well, hello there," Lizzy stops when she sees the nurses in the room.

"Ma'am." The other nurse begins.

"No. It's fine. She can stay."

"We'll have to limit the number of people in the room during delivery," the nurse says with a slight scoff.

"Then we'll need to find a bigger room. If she wants all of us in the room, then we'll all be in the room," I say with an unamused scowl on my face. She's not going to tell us we can't be in the room during the birth of our babies. Especially, after we've already talked with our doctor and several others.

Nurse Bea shoots the other nurse a look, then jumps in. "This room is fine. We'll work out where everyone needs to be during delivery. We just need to make sure no one is in the way in case of an emergency." She removes her gloves and tosses them in the trash.

"Completely understand. You tell us where to be and we will. We're good at following directions."

Her cheeks blush, and she quickly mumbles out, "We'll be back in a bit to check on you."

Lizzy hisses at the other nurse who tried to kick her out when the door closes. "Can you believe them? Trying to kick me out of my boo's room."

"Don't worry. If she wants you here, you'll be here," I say, catching several looks of shock from others. "Stop," I warn, and the room erupts into laughter.

"What's in the bag?" Emmett asks, nodding at her.

"It's New Year's Eve. We've spent every New Year's together, except for maybe part of last year where I may have missed the ball drop, but I'm not missing another one. So I got us some decorations and sparkling grape to ring in the new year. Now don't mind me. I'm just going to decorate a little."

"Why do you have that look on your face?" Knox asks, matching her smile with his.

"I don't know what you're talking about." She laughs, then turns around and starts pulling black and gold paper decorations and signs out of her bag, setting them up on the window ledge. She grabs the remote and flicks on the television to NYE coverage. "This ok, mama?"

Everlee rolls her head to the side, with heavy eyelids. "Perfect."

Sometime later, there's a knock at the door and a male doctor with graying hair sticks his head in. "Good evening, I'm Dr. Markowitz, but you can call me Dr. Mark." He steps in, moving to the hand sanitizer mounted on the wall, and rubs his hands when he walks over to us. "I hear you want an epidural?"

"Yes, please."

Another nurse walks into the room a second later and again pauses before continuing. I guess it can be alarming seeing so many people in the room.

"Perfect. I'm going to have you sit up and hang your legs off the edge of the bed and lean over as far as you can." He looks at the rest of us, "I'm going to have all of you wait over on the other side in front of her."

"I'm going to step out," Lizzy says. "Give you all some space."

Emmett and Knox go with her. Part of me thinks I should go to, but I don't want to leave her side.

The nurse and doctor get to work moving in perfect synchronicity. I try not to look, because while I'm ok with needles, just the thought of that going into Ev's spine makes me queasy.

"You'll feel a little pinch and some pressure, but try to stay relaxed and just breathe for me."

"Okay."

Dr. Mark chuckles. "Ok. Here we go."

Sometime later, there's a knock on the door and Dr. Yiminitz pokes her head in. "How's my favorite group?" She pushes the rest of the door open, walks to the hand sanitizer mounted on the wall, and is rubbing her hands as she walks over to us. A minute later, Nurse Bea walks in.

"We're hanging in there."

"Well, everything seems to be progressing smoothly. I'm going to do a quick exam and then I'm going to break your water." When she pulls her hand out, she smiles. "Almost six. Looks like you may have some New Year's babies."

"Oh God," Everlee sighs.

"What?"

"Beckett. New Year's babies. Publicity."

Dr. Yiminitz laughs. "That may not happen. I wouldn't worry about it and worst case, if you have the first baby born, we just decline the news article."

A second later, there's a swoosh and a sigh from Everlee as liquid gushes out of her.

EVERLEE - TWO'S HAVE IT

The seconds click away while the minute hand moves slowly behind. It's been several hours and still nothing. Nurse Bea has been in to check on me several times, and last being close to thirty minutes ago. She said when she comes back, we'll be working on practice pushes since I'm getting closer.

11:03.

Less than an hour before the new year.

Callum hasn't left his spot behind me while Jax is passed out in the recliner beside my bed while Knox, Emmett, and Lizzy have all cuddled on the couch singing songs from the New York New Year's Eve party.

It's kind of crazy to think how much can change in a year. This time last year we were all standing in Allure having a blast and now we're all in a room waiting for me to push out two babies.

A soft knock on the door pulls my attention. Nurse Bea and Dr. Yiminitz stick their heads in. All the guys, including Jax, jump to their feet.

"How have the contractions been?" Doctor Yiminitz asks.

"Good."

"Pain?"

"Not terrible."

"Good. I'm going to do once last exam and then have you start practice pushing."

"Ok."

Dr. Y sticks her lubed fingers into me and starts smiling. "You're at ten. We can start pushing."

"Baby time?" Knox jumps in the air.

"Do you want me to head out?" Lizzy asks, pointing at the door.

"Boo boo. I want you right here with me, if you want to stay."

"Fine. I will, but I'm not holding your hand or looking down there. I'd like to look you in the face again, without seeing all that junk when I look at you."

Chuckling, I smile. "Fine."

Nurse Bea walks out and pushes two baby beds in, followed by another nurse who we haven't seen yet.

"Do you have names picked out for them yet?"

Lizzy side eyes me hard because she's asked every day for the last two months what their names are going to be and we haven't told her.

"We do."

"And they are?" Lizzy prompts, scooting closer to me.

"Still not telling you," Jax laughs. "But I'll tell you this. Lizzy is not one of the names."

"You kid."

"Do I look like the kind of guy who would kid around about something like that?"

"Your face is so hard to read."

"Get ready to push," Dr. Y says, bringing us all back.

Callum is still behind me, while Jax and Lizzy are on my right side and Knox and Emmett are on my left.

"Ok. Push."

This low guttural groan screams from my mouth as I bear down and try to push, hands squeezing Jax and Knox's.

"Good. Good. Do that again on your next contraction."

"Do you want a mirror, Ev? I heard that's great to help you visualize," Knox asks.

My eyes flicker to the doctor's and she nods.

"I guess. If that's not weird." I shrug, then feel another contraction coming along.

The nurse brings the mirror over at the same time I'm pushing with all my might.

"Good, good. You're going to feel some pressure down here. I'm rubbing along your opening to stretch it out to lessen the risk of you tearing."

"You're doing so good, babe," Callum whisper into my ear as he kisses the back of my neck.

Several pushes later, I stare at the clock, willing the second hand to slow down. 11:37pm.

Simultaneously, all of our phone's ding.

"Probably Beckett. I told him I would text," Emmett says.

"I got it." Lizzy grabs my phone off the bedside table and punches in my password.

"It's Beckett. I'll let him know what's going on."

"Let's push."

Sucking in a deep breath, I push with all my might.

"Good, good. Keep going, I see the head. Push Everlee. Come on."

Baring down and squeezing the guys' hands, I yell out as I push. Sweat drips down my chest, and my hair is matted on the back of my neck.

"Yes! Good job!" It feels like the strangest pressure just vanished in the blink of an eye. The nurse runs over with a blue sucker thing and seconds later, our first baby's screams fill the room and tears flow down my face. "You've got a little girl."

"There she is," the guys all say in unison.

My gaze moves to each of the guys watching them watch her. Dr. Yiminitz clamp the umbilical cord. "Who would like to do the honors?"

Everyone looks around without speaking until Jax steps forward, holding out his hand.

When Jax cuts the cord, Dr. Yiminitz passes her to me and I hold her against my bare chest as her cries quieten. Is it possible to love something so much so fast?

"Oh my gosh boo. She's so beautiful," Lizzy says with tears sliding down her cheek.

Nurse Bea walks over. "Let me take her from you so I can wash her up while you push for the second one."

Reluctantly, I hand her off, but Knox follows nurse Bea with his arms crossed, watching the nurse bathe her quickly and take her measurements for length and weight. The entire time she's working, Knox is keeping a watchful eye on her.

"What's her name?" Dr. Yimitiz asks.

"Anniston James McKinley."

"That's a beautiful name. Anniston James," she repeats it.

"Oh Evey boo. I love it. Are you going to call her AJ?"

"I don't know. Maybe Ann, Annie."

Another contraction refocuses my attention. I grab Emmett's hand, since Knox is still with Anniston.

Nurse Bea offers Anniston to Knox, but before he grabs her, he pulls his shirt over his head, then grabs the baby. "Skin to skin contact."

Nurse Bea blushes about a hundred shades of red and swallows before scurrying back over to stand behind the doctor.

My head falls to the side for a brief second, and my heart melts. Knox is cradling Anniston in his arms against his bare chest, bouncing gently. He catches me watching him and tosses me a quick wink.

A second later, a contraction pulls my attention back to the doctor.

"Ready Everlee? Let's meet this baby boy of yours."

Callum gives me a kiss on the crown of my head and I grab Jax and Emmett's hands. Jax cups his other hand over mine and gives it a gentle squeeze.

"Get ready to push," Dr. Yiminitz commands.

Building like a small wave inside of me, my stomach gets tighter.

"Good. Now, push."

Leaning forward, eyes focused on the mirror, I push with everything I have while letting out a deafening groan. When the contraction passes, I fall onto Callum while the guys wiggle their fingers inside of my palms.

"Sorry," I say sheepishly.

"Nothing to be sorry for, love," Emmett coos.

"I didn't need those two fingers, anyway." Jax smiles.

"Hey boo thang... not trying to rush or anything, but pretty boy on TV has started the countdown."

The timer in the bottom corner of the screen is counting down from ten...nine...

I'm going to have the first kid born in January.

Eight... seven...

Here comes another contraction.

"You got this. Push, Everlee," Dr. Yiminitz encourages.

Six... five... four...

My twins are going to split the year. Born in two different years and two different months with potentially to different fathers.

Three... two...

"Push!"

"Happy New Year!" Lizzy says quietly, more to herself than anyone else.

I scream out and feel the sweet release of pressure pass through me and seconds later, hear my baby boy crying.

Exhausted, I collapse backward onto Callum.

"Happy New Year," I whisper back.

"Well. You did it, mama," Dr. Yiminitz says, passing me my baby. I hadn't even seen Emmett cut the cord.

"Two babies. Born in two different months. Born in two different years. Do you have a name for baby boy?"

"Brooks Bennett McKinley."

"Brooks and Anniston. I love it, sis," Lizzy says, trailing her finger down Brook's back.

EVERLEE - HAPPILY EVER AFTER

THE LAST SEVERAL MONTHS have been a blur. Anniston and Brooks are all-consuming, and I don't think we'd have it any other way. The guys have taken to their role of dad seamlessly and anywhere they come up short, the pups step in. When we first brought the babies home, Woodford and Blanton didn't know what to do with them, but now they never leave their side. They each have picked their own baby- Woodford is always around Anniston, while Blanton is always around Brooks. Knox has trained the pups to get burp cloths, diapers, and wipes on command. Jax, of course, thought it was the stupidest thing until we all caught him sending Woodford away to get a diaper when Anniston had a blowout.

We moved the babies into their room when they turned two months and the pups either lie at their door or, if someone- Knox- forgets to close their bedroom door, they'll lie at the foot of their cribs. For the first several weeks, we let them sleep in the same crib together, but now that Anniston is rolling around more, we've separated them. This has been our largest struggle since the twins are nearly inseparable.

Beckett and Will have visited twice already and have such a hard time leaving. Uncle Becks always has a baby, if not two, in his arms the entire time he's here. And of course, he and Will brought each of them a firehouse onesie that he used his Cricut on.

Lizzy had baby boy Bronson on the sixteenth of March. I was right by her side through the entire birth, coaching her and encouraging her.

For twenty-six hours.

I think near the end she was trying to hold out to have a St. Patrick's day baby, but Dr. Yiminitz wouldn't let her. Said she had an hour left before they change tactics. Lizzy insisted it was Bronson's enormous head getting stuck in her tiny vagina canal. Her words, not mine.

She did me the solid of bringing an oversized dildo to grab instead of my hand because she didn't want to break it since I had two babies to feed. Nurses thought she was weird, but fortunately enough, Nurse Bea and Dr. Yiminitz led her delivery, and they remembered her from mine.

Timing worked out great for her delivery because Will and Beckett were already coming up for a visit for the St. Patrick's Day festivities, so they were able to see Bronson. It was at the hospital where Uncle Becks let us in on a secret. He and Will are trying to adopt and are a few weeks into the process. Lizzy still offered to be a surrogate, but they thought they would try this route for now.

Mom and Dad have, of course, been really excited and are talking about finding a place up here so they can spend more time with the babies. Callum said he'd talk to them about it at Easter and then help them find a place which is both parts exciting and nerve wrecking. While I'd love to have my parents here, it's also been nice visiting them on my schedule and then what happens when Will and Beckett have a kid. Are they going to think I stole mom and dad? It's a lot, but I'm trying not to focus on it too much right now.

When they were here after the babies were born, they ended up staying for a month. The guys didn't seem to mind it too much since it allowed us all more time to spend with one another and the babies. Mom was beside herself cooking in Chef Emmett's kitchen, a thing she only put on social media about a dozen times.

Now it's mid-April, and we just landed in South Carolina for the babies' first Easter. Becks already warned me that mom has gone overboard with the babies' Easter baskets, decorations, and outfits. She insisted that the seven of us cram into their house, since there's more room since Beckett moved out, but I'm not sure her math is mathin'. I told the guys I wanted to stay in the same house we stayed in last year, but they said it was unavailable and when I was talking to Beckett about it later, he said it had actually burned down two months after we left. Something about faulty wiring, which didn't shock me. It was an old house, but it was so cute.

Callum said he and the guys found another one they think I'll like better, and at this point I don't know if I care too much. I just need to get somewhere and pump, because I feel like my boobs are about to explode. Last time they felt this tight, they started spraying.

On their own.

Imagine two firehoses going off at the same time, only it's not water coming out. It's milk. Precious, precious, liquid gold. I'll tell you. Anyone who says don't cry over spilled milk has never pumped breast milk before. Here I am screaming and crying, trying to catch the liquid gold as I'm running around in a circle, because clearly the milk was shooting everywhere, and I had to catch it. Not me being the one it's shooting from running around like a crazed hormonal lady. The guys burst into the room thinking I'm getting mauled by a Siberian Tiger only to find me cupping what little milk I could save. Emmett ran to the kitchen and grabbed two clean bottles and we just stuck those over my nipples until enough pressure was released that they stopped. I asked the guys if they were up for a water gun fight after that, but the joke didn't land. And that's ok. I think I was just trying to save any sliver of dignity I had remaining.

Speaking of, I need to pump soon. "Hey guys. How much longer? Not trying to rush, but these nipple ladies are screaming for release."

Emmett turns around with a smirk on his face. "I can give you release."

"Cute. I'd take you up on the offer, but I'm pretty sure only Jax and Knox have experience being water-boarded. With each thrust in, you'll get a face full of milk."

"I could think of worse things." He gives me a wink, then turns to look at Callum, who finds me in the rearview mirror.

"Ten minutes."

"And why won't you tell me where we're going?"

"I did."

"You said to our rental house."

Callum nods, then looks down the road as he keeps driving.

My phone dings, pulling my attention before I can fire back a smart ass response.

"Mom asked if we got in ok and then asked when we're going over for dinner."

"Tell her in an hour," Callum dictates.

Ten minutes later, we're pulling down the road that leads to the house we stayed at last year.

"I thought you said we weren't staying here."

"Where?"

"The house we stayed in last time."

"We aren't."

"I know because it burned down. So where are we going?"

"To our house."

"What?" I'm so confused.

Knox cuts his eyes at me. "They're being super evasive with me, too."

"They?"

"Knox," Jax scolds.

"What is going on?" I ask when we turn onto the driveway of the house.

"Well, the other place *did* burn down," Callum starts and then pauses as a beautiful house comes into view standing where the old house stood.

"Cal."

Jax and Emmett say in unison, "So we bought the land and built a new one."

"You built a house for us to stay in?"

Mom's car and Beckett's Jeep are parked to the side.

"What's going on?"

Callum pulls the car to a stop beside the big oak tree with a tire swing attached, then turns to look at me. "This is our home. If you want to move here."

"What?" My eyes burn as tears form on the rim.

"Man! Why couldn't you tell me? I wanted to be part of the surprise," Knox pouts.

"You would have ruined it," Jax says simply.

"Lies."

"Wait. I still don't get it," I say, opening the door to look at the masterpiece.

It's a large white house with a wraparound front porch with several swings and rocking chairs surrounded by miles of fields.

Callum walks around the car and loops his hand around my waist. "This is our home. If you want to move here."

"Move?"

"You don't need to decide right now. Take a look inside."

Jax hands me the pump bag while Knox and Emmett get the babies out of the car.

As we walk up to the front porch mom, dad, Beckett, and Will step out and shout, "Surprise!"

"What are you all doing here?" I ask, still in complete shock.

"We wanted to be here for the big reveal. It's been so hard keepin' our mouth shut," Mom says.

"They knew?" Knox whines.

"Dude, you would totally ruin it! Hell, I almost did," Beckett adds, reaching for Anniston, while Will reaches for Brooks. "Though to be fair, I wasn't looped into the big secret at the time."

When I walk up the three stairs onto the front porch, I'm overwhelmed.

"Sis, you're going to love the inside."

I feel like I'm in a dream as I step through the oak-stained double doors. The entry way is huge- three stories with a spiral staircase starting on the left.

"We'll go up there later," Callum says, guiding me through the hall into the kitchen.

"Oh my God." I gasp. "It's huge."

"That's wh-" Knox starts, but Jax cuts him off with a look.

Three stainless steel stoves, an oversized white granite island with ten barstools around it. On the back wall is a large farmhouse kitchen sink overlooking the backyard, and two refrigerators on the wall to the left of the sink. To the right is a huge family room with a white shaggy carpet, and a fireplace with a wooden herringbone pattern running up the wall.

"This is..."

"Totes gorge," Beckett feels in the space I left.

"This is what you've been working on? The business trips you've been taking?"

"Yes."

The timer beeps. "Perfect timing." Mom clasps her hands together and does a quick twirl. "I've had the best time cooking in this kitchen."

"You... what?" My brain feels like it's going a thousand miles an hour.

"I made us some dinner. It needs to set out for about thirty minutes to let the flavors marry. Will that be enough time for you to pump?"

I stand there taking everything in for a second, but don't speak.

"Is she in shock?" Dad asks.

"Ev," Callum says, standing in front of me. "Go pump. We'll talk more in a little bit."

"You all built this... for us?"

"Yes." Callum chuckles. "If you want to move down here to be close to your family. We have a place and if you don't, then we can rent this one out."

"No!" I shout, catching everyone, including myself, off guard. "Sorry. No, I don't want to rent it out. This is... mine... ours. But the restaurant and clubs?"

"Bo's is always looking to expand. There's a plot of land I thought we could look at while we're here this week, that's on the water," Emmett says.

"And the clubs will still be ours, but we don't need to be around them. We want you, Anniston, Brooks. Our family. That's what's most important to us now." Callum grabs my hands and brings them to his lips and brushes a kiss across my knuckles. "You are ours, and we are us."

"But if Knox didn't know..."

"Love. I want anything you want. Cal's right. Home is where the heart is."

"Lizzy..."

Jax lets out a loud sigh. "So..." His hand swipes through his hair. "With Bronson here and Tony traveling off and on for the next year..." Jax's eyes dart back and forth.

"She can live here with us?" I shout, full of excitement.

"God no!" Jax retorts before he can catch himself. "We built her a house, too. Far away, but close enough." He points to the field.

"Shut the front door, Jaxie poo! Did you just say what I think you did?" Lizzy chirps and we all look around and find

Beckett holding his phone out. Lizzy looks exhausted but beautiful with a cloth over her shoulder, burping Bronson.

"Please tell me you have a top on," Jax groans.

"Can't do that, Jaxie poo." She swipes a hand in the air. "Back to the point at hand. Did you build us a multi-family compound? Do we have a little, rather large, garden in the middle and animals? Are we homesteading? Oh my God."

"Remind me why I thought this was a good idea?" Jax asks.

"You're the one who suggested it, brother," Callum laughs.

"Was I drunk at the time?"

Emmett claps Jax on the back. "We all know you love Lizzy just as much as we do, if not more."

"Love is a bit strong."

"Oh Jaxie poo! If Bronson burps in the next few seconds, then I know your love for me is true and deep." Lizzy pats Bronson's back quickly, and he burps, and before Lizzy can squeal, he vomits all over her. "This is why I walk around naked all the time."

"TMI Lizzy. TMI," Jax groans.

"We're going to be neighbors. Best day ever! Because judging by the size of that burp, it must mean you reallllly love me. Like so big!"

"Are we doing this?" I ask, tears trickling down my cheek.

"Up to you, love." Knox smiles.

"We're all in, if you're all in," Emmett adds.

"We go where you go," Jax says.

"Because this is what's most important," Callum finishes.

Knox claps his hands, and everyone looks at him. "We just did the thing."

"What thing?" Jax rolls his eyes.

"The thing... you know... where you all say cute little one liners and I always get left out." He points at himself while jumping up and down. "But not this time. I started it!"

Jax shakes his fist in the air and says in a mocking tone. "Yay."

I nod and without thinking too long about it, I smile and say, "Okay."

"Oh, yay!" Mom claps and starts crying.

"Does Tony know?" I ask.

Callum nods. "Yes. He helped build and decorate their house."

"You men have really thought of everything, haven't you?"

"We try." Jax walks over and wraps his arms around me. "We didn't want you to feel the pull of having everyone so far away. And this way, Lizzy is closer to her family and you. It just seems to work."

Stretching onto my tiptoes, I wrap my arms around his neck and give him a kiss. "I love you. I love all of you."

"Samesies." He pats my butt and I fall back to my feet.

"I'm going to go pump real quick, then we can eat, then go see Mrs. Mary Mae and introduce her to her... grandkids? Great grandkids?"

"She's on her way over." Jax smiles.

"Oh wow. How?"

"Mason." His head pulls to the side.

"Oh, that's great! I know you had plans to meet with him while we are here. Does he know, yet?"

"About the move? No. I wanted to wait until you knew."

"Oh. Duh. Ok. Let me go pump real quick before they get here!"

EVERLEE - THREE YEARS LATER...

NEW YEARS EVE

"Do you miss it?" Lizzy asks, picking at the fuzz on our large fluffy white carpet.

"Miss what?" I glance at her, then turn back to watch Lilibet chase Anniston, Brooks, and Bronson around. Lilibet just turned a year in July and has been a little fire cracker with her strawberry blonde curls and green eyes. She is completely opposite of Anniston's long brown hair and brown eyes, or Brooks' dirty blonde hair and blue eyes. It's so funny that each child is unique. Bronson's going to be a little heart throb when he's older, with his light brown skin and big green eyes and short, curly hair.

"Quiet?" Lizzy laughs, bringing me back to the moment.

"You were always my friend, so I never knew that word."

"Har har." She tosses a pillow at me.

The doorbell rings, and Knox runs down the stairs to get it. "Well, who do we have here?"

All the kids stop what they're doing and run to the door. "Knox!" I warn.

"Got them!" he says, just as Callum bounces downstairs to help run interference.

"Unkie Becks and Unkie Will," they all cry out in unison, reaching up for them.

"Gimme. Gimme," Knox demands, taking Sera from Will's arms. She's their two-year-old daughter and the light of their life. "She's gotten so big!"

"It's been two weeks, dip sh-nizzle," Jax groans when he sees the kids within earshot as he walks up the front porch stairs with a cooler and blanket in his arms.

"Shnizzle! Shnizzle!" Anniston yells out.

"You're a shnizzle!" Brooks retorts.

"Your face is a poopy shnizzle," Bronson chimes and the three of them laugh and run off.

"Down. Down," Sera coos, swatting at Knox's chest.

"Be good," Beckett reminds after her as she wobbles into Lilibet's arms for a hug. "I've brought a cockcuterie board. It's like a charcuterie board, but on a big wooden," he leans in and whispers, "Cock."

"Love it! Love it!" Lizzy screams, racing over and taking it from him. "Excellent assortment of cheeses, meats, and fruits."

"Mom and Dad aren't coming, are they?" Beckett panics.

"No, they're on a cruise in Alaska," I say before I realize the missed opportunity I had to scare him.

"How's Mason doing?" Beckett asks Jax.

Jax smiles. "He's doing great. Finishing up his last month of SQT."

"Squats?"

Jax tilts his chin down with an unamused grin. "SEAL Qualification Training. He's been doing really great."

"That's outstanding. When will he get to come home for a visit?"

"Not sure, hoping in about a month."

After we moved down here, Jax called a family meeting and asked if we had objections to him adopting Mason. We were all for it because we had seen the connection Jax and Mason had. It had been getting stronger over the year and a half, and they were already talking almost every day.

When I saw it at Easter the year before we moved down, I knew Mason was going to have some part in our life. While our family is non-traditional, there wasn't any pushback to having us adopt a sophomore in high school.

Soon after he moved in, he started working out and running with Jax and Knox every morning. He made it clear he planned on joining the SEALs after he graduated and was laser focused on that.

In his junior year, he hit a growth spurt and grew seven inches to a towering six-foot-five. So his senior year, he joined the men's volleyball team at school. He knew little about the sport, but knew team sports would help him get through BUD/S training. We knew he'd pass all the intelligence tests, because his mind is like a computer. In his Junior year, Jax spoke to the principal and worked it out so Mason could take advanced classes, which involved a few at the local college. He graduated top of his class and gave an amazing speech.

"We should totally throw him a party when he gets back."

"Maybe, but he's not the big party type."

"That's true. Maybe just a banner and some grilling out."

"Yes. That's more like it. Speaking of, Emmett and Tony are in the back on the grill," Jax says.

"Yeah, we saw them when we walked Sparky and Blaze back there."

"Oh geez. We have a full house. Seven dogs, nine adults, and five kids." I laugh.

Lizzy clears her throat. "And one on the way."

Beckett and I look at each other, and our jaw drops. "Did she just-" we both say in unison.

"I was going to tell you later tonight, but... well, you know I've never been good at keeping secrets.

"What's your due date?"

"July 31st."

"Seriously?" I nearly choke out.

"Yes. Why?"

"Because mine is due July 30th."

"You? What?" Lizzy grabs my wrists.

"Well, shit," Beckett groans.

"What? I mean, I know it's her fourth, but you should still be excited," Lizzy reprimands.

"Oh. I'm excited." Beckett starts, then pulls a paper out of his back pocket. "Our baby is due August 3rd."

"Shut the backdoor!" Lizzy shouts.

"Yeah. We went with our surrogate to the appointment last Thursday and found out."

All three of us scream and hug each other while jumping up and down.

"What's happening?" Emmett asks when he walks in with a platter of hotdogs and hamburgers.

"We're all pregnant!" Beckett squeals.

"Well, that's fucking awkward," Jax jokes.

"And we're all due within seven days of each other."

Jax grabs Will by the shoulders and says something, making Will laugh.

"I guess we need to get to work on our house." Beckett gives me a quick wink.

"Y'all are going to take the plot of land?"

"And live so close to you all? Of course!"

Lizzy and I each sold a piece of our land to Will and Beckett so they could build a house near us. When we say near, we aren't right beside each other, but close enough for a walk. Once Beckett and Will's house is complete, our houses will form a triangle around a large garden and farm area. We have all sorts of fruits and vegetables that Emmett and the littles have been tending to–and Knox when Jax thinks he isn't behaving. We don't have a ton of animals, just twenty chickens, a few ducks, some goats, and a few pigs. It's really the best place in the world.

Several hours pass and the kids are all sleeping in a fort that Knox built in Anniston's room, while the pups are all passed out on the screened-in porch, and Lizzy, Beckett and I are all surrounded by our men as the timer counts down.

Lizzy puts her hand on my knee and offers a smile as the count down hits ten. "This is it, Sis. This is the stuff dreams are made of."

"Yes, ma'am." I squeeze her hand, then bring it to my lips for a quick kiss. "I love you, sis."

"Love you."

Three... two... one!

Knox is across the floor first, guiding my head to the ground as he lays me out and presses his lips to mine. "I fucking love you so much. Happy New Year Baby!"

"I love you."

He slides his hand out and backs away at the same time Callum pushes him to the side and lends me his hand to help me to sitting. "Happy New Year, love."

"Happy New Year, babe."

Jax and Emmett plop on the carpet on either side of me. Jax presses his two fingers under my chin and guides my head towards him, giving me a kiss before Emmett moves my head back. "You taste so good."

"I love you both." I lean back and they each give me a wink before they lean in front of me and kiss.

"Twat teasers," I whisper, causing them to chuckle.

"Happy New Year," they say when they pull back.

Sitting on the couch, I watch everything around me move in slow motion. Will and Beckett are laughing about something, with their arms wrapped around one another, Lizzy is kissing a circle around Tony's face and Callum is walking over with a tray of sparkling juice. Knox is jumping onto Jax's side, giving him a koala hug, while Jax just rolls his eyes and Emmett laughs.

This is my life and my God is it a beautiful one.

To think, this all started with me walking into a bar one Valentine's.

Letting out a sigh, I rub my stomach. This is your family, little one, and I can't wait for you to meet them all.

I don't know what our future holds, but I know it will be amazing.

THE END.... FOR NOW.

Afterword

Well, there you have it. The end to our fivesome's story. Never fret though, because I love these characters as much as you do. We will see them make cameos in other books. I can't wait to share with you the other stories I have living in my mind that have been waiting for their chance to shine.

What I will be working on next are a few contemporary romances and paranormal romances like finishing Snow Hunted. I will republish as a complete book versus the cliff hanger that is currently out there. The world that we see in Snow Hunted is just the tip of the iceberg, so I will be excited to dig into that more. Parts of it were sprinkled into Deal with a Djinn so there will be a few tie-ins there.

As always, thank you so much for your love and support!

About the author

Hello lovelies! Follow me below for all the updates, behind the scenes and bonus content!

You can always email me at authorsnmoor [at] gmail.com or message me below. I do rely more on facebook, Insta and TT for most of my communication.

Websitewww.snmoor.com

Etsy Shop AuthorSNMoor

Tiktok@authorsnmoor

Instagramsn_moor

FacebookSN Moor Author – Author SN Moor Fan Group

GoodreadsS.N. Moor

Amazon

www.ingramcontent.com/pod-product-compliance
Lightning Source LLC
Chambersburg PA
CBHW021239190726
48289CB00005B/1402
* 9 7 8 1 9 5 7 2 4 5 1 8 8 *